PENGUIN BOOKS

## SOMEONE ELSE'S SKIN

Sarah Hilary lives in Bath with her husband and daughter, where she writes quirky copy for a well-loved travel publisher. She's also worked as a bookseller, and with the Royal Navy. An award-winning short-story writer, Sarah won the Cheshire Prize for Literature in 2012. *Someone Else's Skin* is her first novel.

# SOMEONE ELSE'S SKIN

## sarah hilary

PENGUIN BOOKS

PENGUIN BOOKS
Published by the Penguin Group
Penguin Group (USA) LLC
375 Hudson Street
New York, New York 10014

USA | Canada | UK | Ireland | Australia
New Zealand | India | South Africa | China
penguin.com
A Penguin Random House Company

First published in Great Britain by Headline Publishing Group 2014
Published in Penguin Books 2014

LIBRARY OF CONGRESS CATALOGING-IN-PUBLICATION DATA
Hilary, Sarah.
Someone else's skin : introducing Detective Inspector Marnie Rome / Sarah Hilary.
pages cm
ISBN 978-0-14-312618-8
1. Women detectives—England—London—Fiction.
2. Women's shelters—Fiction.   3. Victims of family violence—Fiction.
I. Title.
PR6108.I394S65 2014
823'.92—dc23      2014002352

Printed in the United States of America
1   3   5   7   9   10   8   6   4   2

Set in Meridien

To Anna, in defiance

*Five years ago*

They've cordoned off the house by the time she gets home. A uniformed stranger is unwinding police tape, methodically.

Marnie watches from the safety of the car, her fingers icy on the ignition key, the engine running as if she might make a quick getaway, drive past and keep driving . . .

She knows she won't get through the police cordon, but she also knows she has to. Whatever else is in the house – and she's scared, so scared her teeth ache – *answers* are in there. She needs to get inside.

She cuts the engine, burying the keys in her fist, their teeth biting the hollow pocket of her palm. She's shivering before she's out of the car.

An ambulance, there's an ambulance, but it's standing silent, no sirens or sweeping lights. The crew's in the house, no one's in a hurry to leave. That's not good. It means there isn't any hope, the worst possible thing has happened. Her face is wet and she looks for rain, but the sky's empty, grey, as if someone has dragged a tarpaulin across it. There's no rain, just the dull, raspy pressure that comes before a storm.

It's been raining all month. Like the rest of London, she's got used to it; there's an umbrella in her glove compartment, another in her desk back at the station, and in the bag at her shoulder. She's not going to get wet queuing for coffee or coming out of the tube station, or standing around at crime scenes. Be prepared isn't a motto, it's common sense. When you can pull it off. When it's not something so huge and horrible you're afraid to get close.

She looks for the PCSO.

There, wearing a fluorescent vest over his uniform by the side of Dad's car, the brown Vauxhall, his pride and joy. The car manages to shine even without the sun, like the windows to the house, dazzling her. As if everything behind the tape is made of glass, breakable. Even the hanging basket of petunias over the door. Breakable.

Marnie stands on the pavement, her teeth knocking together with cold, knowing she has to get into the house, knowing she can't.

She's fourteen again, home late, hoping to sneak in under her parents' radar. Her eyes are itchy with mascara, her tongue dry and patchy with tequila. It feels like a snake's crawled inside her left boot and strangled her toes to sleep. She's limping, heroic and guilt-stricken. She'll never make it in there alive . . .

She shakes herself back into the present. She's not fourteen. She's twenty-eight, petrified of what she's going to find on the other side of the police cordon. Silence, and that dark zoo stink that'll be in her clothes for hours and on her skin for longer.

She forces herself to think of something else. A different crime scene, one she's survived, worse than whatever's waiting in the house. Albie Crane . . .

She thinks of Albie Crane. A homeless old man, no next of kin. Burned alive in a doorway down by the docks, by kids high on pocket-money-priced pills. Back before the rain started, while it was still dry enough for an old coat and six flattened cardboard boxes to burn all night so that what's left is a sticky mess of flayed ribs, a blackly lacquered skull. Old Albie Crane with no one to cry for him, and she made herself repeat the lie, 'He was sleeping when it happened,' as if you could sleep through a thing like that. The worst she'd seen, or smelt, until the next thing: a couple in a house fire, melted together by the flames.

The PCSO is young enough to have acne, but it doesn't make any difference. He's in charge here. He could stop the Chief Constable crossing that line.

Something – a breeze, traffic – makes the police tape stiffen and turn. The sound it makes is *snick-snick-snick*.

The edge of her eye catches Mrs Poole, her parents' neighbour, huddled in the porch of number 12. Her face is spotty with shock and there's a foil blanket around her shoulders, but no one is with her. All the action is next door. No one else is hurt, or the cordon would be wider.

Normally, that would be a comfort, the fact that the damage is contained. Private.

Seeing Marnie, Mrs Poole moans, a hand coming up to hide her mouth.

Marnie ducks to pass under the tape.

'Miss. You can't go in there.' Up close, the acne is lurid, red and yellow. The PCSO squares up to her, authority lending him an inch in all directions.

She shows her badge, remembering too late that after the DS, it gives her surname. Rome, like the couple in the house. DS Marnie Rome. Greg and Lisa's little girl.

A big hand on her shoulder makes her jump.

Tim Welland, her boss.

Now she knows it's as bad as it gets.

'DS Rome,' he says quietly. 'Marnie.'

Using her first name. It's worse, much worse.

'Please.' She just wants to get inside the house. She's shaking with cold out here. 'Sir, please . . .'

He steers her with his hand on her shoulder, back towards the tape. She feels it tap the waist of her shirt. 'Sir . . .'

Welland has a scab above his left eyebrow, too high to be a shaving scar. It's crusty, ringed like a bull's eye. Red veins spoil the whites of his eyes. He looks ill. Old.

'Let me go in,' she says. 'Please. Let me go in to them.'

'Not yet. Not – yet.'

He holds her in place with his bear's paw, but he can't stop her seeing past his shoulder to where a SOCO is coming out, bloody knees to his white overalls and a polybag held in front of him, at arm's length.

A knife. Mum's bread knife, its steel teeth full of tattered red skin.

There's a low noise of protest, like an animal in chronic pain, before a dry barking sob. Marnie can't stand it, wants to block her ears, but it's her mouth she needs to block; the sound's coming out of her.

Welland lowers her to the kerb. She fights him. She's not this person. She won't *be* this person – the one who collapses and weeps at the roadside, who can't take the knock on the door, who falls and never gets back up again.

The *victim*. She won't be the victim.

'Take a minute, Detective.' Welland's hand is heavy on the back of her neck. She has no choice but to put her fore-head on her knees. 'Just . . . take a minute.'

# PART 1

**1**

*Now*

From the road, DI Marnie Rome's flat was stucco-fronted, very neat and narrow. Noah Jake imagined she'd furnished it plainly, with an eye for functional style. Wooden shutters at the windows, a stone-coloured vase filled with upright orange flowers. A hall-floor flat, two bedrooms, Noah guessed. He was curious to see inside, but not enough to make a nuisance of himself, resting his hands on the steering wheel instead and waiting, seeing the light lift from the stucco as the sun broke through London's cloud cover.

Some days it was easy to remember the city was built on plague pits. Nothing stood still, not even the road, throbbing with traffic from the main drag into the West End. He'd read somewhere – probably in one of Dan's exhibition guides – that Primrose Hill had narrowly missed being a mass graveyard; nineteenth-century plans were drawn up for a multi-storey pyramid taller than St Paul's, to house five million of the city's dead. This was back when the town planners were obsessed with Egyptology, hurling hieroglyphs at everything, on the advice of returning

3

tomb-raiders. Now it was the all-seeing London Eye that dominated the city's skyline, its spindle like a church spire, turning.

Noah checked his watch, and then the flat.

DI Rome's front door was dark blue, glossy. Like her eyes. The kind of door with deadlocks. In another minute, she'd be running late. He'd never known her to run late. Should he knock on the door? No, that'd be intrusive. He hadn't learned much about Marnie Rome in the five months he'd been working with her, but he'd learned that she was an intensely private person.

The blue door opened in any case, before her minute was up. She came down the steps to the car, wearing a dark trouser suit over a white shirt, a tooled leather bag at one shoulder. Everything about her was neat, from her short red curls to her low heels.

Noah checked the passenger seat of the car, even though he knew it was clean, dusting the sleeves of his suit in the hope it would pass muster. He reached across to push open the door for her. 'Morning.'

'Good morning.' She slipped into the car, dropping her bag on the floor. 'You were lucky with the parking.'

'I got here early, thought we'd better not be late.'

'You thought right.'

Noah started the engine, waiting for Marnie to put on her seat belt.

She saw him waiting and smiled, fastening the belt with extravagant care. 'Safety first, Detective.'

Safe was the last thing Noah Jake felt, half an hour later, looking at the photographs on OCU Commander Tim Welland's desk.

'Nasif Mirza.' Welland tossed down the photos, one after another, as if he was dealing a pack of cards. 'A person of interest in a serious assault. Involving a scimitar, in case that wasn't clear yet.' The photos made his desk look like the storyboard for a horror film. A glossy 18-certificate horror film with DVD-extra deleted scenes.

Marnie Rome picked up a photo and studied it before putting it back down. Noah kept his hands out of sight, under the lip of the desk.

Welland said, 'You're looking at what's left of Lee Hurran's right arm.'

What was left was yellow, knuckled by fat, frilled by torn flesh. The scimitar had severed Hurran's hand at the wrist. Not a clean amputation; it had taken two or three blows to get the hand off, the raw stump of wrist bone splintered by the impact.

Noah's palms prickled with sweat. It was stiflingly hot in this office; Tim Welland was in remission from skin cancer and kept the heating turned up all year round. Immune to the heat, Welland never broke a sweat. Nor did Marnie Rome. Noah glanced in her direction, seeing the crisp edge of her shirt, the cool skin of her neck. A bead of perspiration inched its way between his shoulder blades, itching.

'Hurran won't give evidence. Popular theory is that he's scared of losing his other hand, or possibly his balls.' Welland nodded at the photos. 'Nasif isn't fussy when it comes to butchery.'

'Hurran's still in hospital.' Marnie's eyes flicked across the litter of photos. 'They're monitoring for infection. There was a lot of dirt in the wound . . . Maybe he'll feel safer when he's back home.'

'Home being the shithole estate where they found him? I tend to doubt that.'

'We have the scimitar. With Mirza's prints on it. That's no good?'

'Not even close. The Crown Prosecution Service,' Welland

served each syllable as if it was an individually foul taste in his mouth, 'need more evidence before they'll make a move against Nasif. Apparently this . . . dog's dinner isn't enough.'

Marnie picked up the worst of the photos for a closer look. Noah wished he had her backbone for this part of the job. He was too easily disgusted, needed to toughen up, get used to seeing things like this. Things like . . .

Lee Hurran's hand, half eaten. By rats, or a feral cat. The hand wasn't found in the warehouse where the attack happened. Nasif Mirza, or someone, had tossed it over a wall, into a fly-tipped piece of scrubland.

'Ayana Mirza . . .' Marnie started to say.

'CPS wants a statement from her,' Welland said, 'about her brother's violent temperament. Better still, they'd like her to press charges for what was done to her.'

'We can arrest Nasif without her testimony.'

'For this?' Welland pointed at the photographs. 'Or the other thing?'

Noah didn't want to think about the other thing – what Nasif Mirza had done to his sister, in their family home. The pictures of Hurran's half-eaten hand were bad enough.

Neither he nor Marnie had met Ayana Mirza. They'd inherited the case from another department, a casualty of the recent public-sector cuts.

'CPS is cagey about the chances of bringing Nasif to trial,' Welland said. 'Other prints on the scimitar, the chance it was stolen, blah-blah. They think Ayana's evidence might swing it. She's a walking testament to Nasif's worst tendencies. No denying she'd look good in court.'

'And they don't see this as victim harassment?'

'They're cagey, Detective. You and I know what happens when the CPS gets cagey.'

'I know what happened to Ayana.' Marnie's eyes were dark. 'It wasn't just Nasif, either. It was three of them – her brothers.'

'The crap that happens in families . . .' Welland winced, as if he'd said something tactless, cutting his eyes away from Marnie.

She shrugged. 'It's a good living, if you're a psychiatrist.'

Noah felt he'd missed a beat, tuned out for a vital second. The heat was boiling his brain in his skull. How could Welland work like this?

'You'll want to tread carefully. She's terrified of her brothers tracing her. She's hiding . . .' Welland consulted a notepad.

'In a women's refuge in Finchley,' Marnie supplied. 'I spoke with Ed Belloc.'

'Finchley.' Welland nodded. 'What's Ed got to say about her?'

Ed Belloc worked in Victim Support. Noah hadn't met him, but from what Marnie said, he was a good man doing a difficult job. He'd helped the police to trace Ayana Mirza after she escaped her family.

'She won't risk upsetting the refuge,' Marnie said, 'or losing her place there. She doesn't have many options, can't afford rent. If she gets a job or starts claiming benefits, there's the danger her brothers can trace her through her National Insurance number. So . . . she's trying to stay missing.'

Welland nodded. He climbed to his feet. 'DS Jake, you'll want to check your emails. DI Rome, a word?'

Marnie waited while Noah left the office, knowing what was coming. She folded her hands in her lap as a contingency against fidgeting. The ends of her fingers were sticky from touching the photos; she wanted to wash. It didn't help that Tim Welland kept this place heated like a sauna. She'd bet Noah Jake was running a cold shower in the station's washroom.

When they were alone, Welland leaned back, steepling his thumbs under his chin. 'How're you doing?'

Under the hot light, the dome of his head was glassy and freckled. His face, with no eyelashes or brows, looked naked. Open. Good for drawing confidences, or confessions. He'd come close to losing an eye to the cancer. Even now, in remission for two years, the shadow of the disease tugged at the skin there, keeping the eye bleakly peeled so that those who didn't know about his operations – his battle – joked that Tim Welland slept with one eye open.

'I'm fine.' She smiled across the desk at him. The heat shone on the photos scattered between them. Teeth marks on Lee Hurran's dead hand. Had he asked to see it? she wondered. Hurran. Had he asked to see his hand, even though there was no hope of surgeons reattaching it? By the time they found it, it was long dead.

'I'm fine,' she repeated.

Welland searched her face for another answer. Some of this, she suspected, was box-ticking. Management 101: *Show concern for those under your command, especially at times of stress.* He wasn't enjoying it. 'I may do a terrific impersonation of an insensitive shit, but I know what day it is.'

'It's Friday,' she deflected, still smiling.

He nodded at the wall calendar. Pictures of bridges. Welland loved bridges. March's picture was the rolling bridge in Paddington Basin. It looked like a giant hamster wheel.

'Tomorrow . . . it'll be five years to the day. How're you coping?'

'By not counting,' Marnie said.

*Not counting, not remembering. Not sharing.*

'But you're still seeing him.'

'Yes.' She'd never made a secret of her visits, knowing Welland would find out anyway; murder detectives didn't go into secure units without lighting flags on the system. 'Tomorrow, in fact.'

'Tomorrow,' Welland repeated. 'On the anniversary.'

'It was booked ages ago. I'm not taking balloons.' The smile hurt her face but she stuck with it. 'If that's what you're thinking.'

'Of course I'm not thinking of bloody balloons. I'm thinking of what he did, five years ago . . .'

'A long time, five years.' She picked up a photo of Lee Hurran's hand, pretending to study it again. It meant she could lose the smile, for one thing. 'For him. Five years is a long time, for Stephen.'

'Not long enough,' Welland growled. He cleared his throat. 'Detective Inspector . . . Marnie.' He grimaced. First names weren't his thing. It'd been hard on him five years ago, outside her parents' house, calling her Marnie, holding her in his arms.

She decided to spare him any further discomfort. 'I've got a job to do.' She stood up. 'Clearing the way for the CPS, right?'

Welland looked relieved, hunching back in his chair, freeing his fingers to wash at his face, where the skin was taut from repeated surgery. 'Right.'

## 2

In Finchley, the clouds had beaten the sun into submission.

The women's refuge was brown concrete, built low to the ground, its flat roof swollen with too many coats of tar. Scaffolding cross-hatched the facade, red and white tape making barber's poles of the metal struts. A shallow wall of rain-welted polythene ran around the lip of the roof. With every window blacked out, it would've been easy to mistake the place for a condemned building, derelict.

'First impressions?' Marnie asked, as she cut the car's engine. 'I can't say I'm digging the prefab chic.'

'It's a serious contender for the most depressing place I've ever seen.' Noah peered through the windscreen. 'Maybe it's better inside . . .'

'That's what Ed says. About the average refuge, anyway.' Marnie climbed from the car. 'Not sure about this one.'

Noah followed her. Passing traffic shifted the polythene sheeting, the sound like sand under shoes. From the scaffolding, a seared metal smell. Holes pitted the path to the main entrance, where a dodgy tarmac job hadn't taken. The place was a dump.

'What're they doing to the roof?' Noah asked.

'No idea. Maybe it's leaking.' Marnie stood looking at the

blind windows of the refuge. 'Imagine living like this, without trace. I don't think I could do it. Could you?'

Noah said, 'If I was desperate, maybe. If there was no other choice.'

'Sure, if you were desperate.' She put a hand to the side of her neck. 'If this is where Ayana Mirza feels safe, we need to respect that. If we can persuade her to give evidence against her brothers, that's a bonus. But let's tread gently.'

Noah nodded. Above them, the clouds were gleaming, grey. 'It's going to rain,' he said. 'I hope they've got the roof properly sealed.'

'That's not rain.' Marnie glanced at the sky. 'It's a storm. Can't you smell it?'

Inside, the air felt stripped dry, charged with static. Now Noah could smell the storm. The silence in the refuge was artificial. Untrustworthy. Marnie tensed, turning back to consider the door as it swung shut behind them. 'What happened to the security?'

The Cyclops lens of a CCTV camera, mounted on the wall outside, gave back their faces in miniature. Marnie had her ID in her hand, but no one was asking to see it.

'The door was on the latch,' Noah said. 'Was it?'

'Yes.' Marnie stood taking stock of the silence.

'Maybe they've evacuated the building, while the scaffolding's put up.'

'Not according to Ed. Support staff work nine to five, Monday to Friday. There should be someone in charge. Come on.'

They started down an empty corridor that smelt of stale cigarettes, talcum powder and milk. At the far end: a fire exit, closed. The silence was thicker than ever.

Noah rubbed his fingers, chilled. It wasn't just the quiet; everything felt wrong about the refuge, as if they were walking into a trap or—

A scream tore up from their right.

Marnie Rome broke into a run.

Noah stayed at her heels, the back of his neck spooked into goose bumps.

# 3

As they reached the room, the screaming stopped. Abruptly, as if someone had thrown a switch. An obese girl in a black tracksuit stood with her hands over her mouth, in the middle of a huddle of silent women. The room had wide windows hidden by curtains, and murals on the walls: jungle animals in tall grass. Surreal.

A man was on the floor, a woman standing over him with a knife, bloody and wet.

DI Rome put out a hand to her. 'All right. It's all right now.'

The woman's eyes swung at her, wildly. The knife jumped in her fist.

Noah, who'd been reaching for his phone, stopped. Wanting his hands free in case she went for Marnie, or one of the others. His heart was pelting in his chest. On the floor, the man's feet kicked. Noah needed to get down there and help, but he was afraid to move while the woman looked like this: frantic, capable of anything. Static had stuck her long blonde hair to her face in spikes.

Marnie said, 'This is DS Noah Jake.' Her voice was rock-steady, calm. 'I'm DI Rome. We're here to help.' She nodded at Noah, her eyes not leaving the woman's fist.

The knife stopped jumping. The woman tensed with listening, as if her whole body was an ear, watching the calm expression on Marnie's face, hypnotised by it.

Noah had forgotten Marnie Rome could do this. Talk people down. He'd seen it at the station, but never in an armed situation. Keeping his eyes on the knife, he took out his phone and dialled 999. 'Ambulance, please.' He gave the address, aware of the breach of protocol; the refuge address was a closely guarded secret, for the sake of the women's safety.

It was a kitchen knife, an ordinary kitchen knife. In the woman's fist.

Someone had thrown a big bunch of yellow roses on the floor. The man's feet kept kicking, smearing petals into the carpet. He was wheezing, red spreading on his chest.

'DS Jake,' Marnie prompted.

Noah pocketed his phone and crouched, checking for a pulse in the man's neck, searching with his free hand for the source of the blood: a single stab wound at the base of the ribs on the right side. His fingers slipped in the mess of torn tissue and he pitched forward a fraction, sickened. 'Sorry, I'm sorry . . .' He put a fist to the floor to get his balance back, keeping his other hand tight over the wound.

'It's all right,' Marnie said. It took Noah a second to realise she was speaking to the blonde woman behind him. 'Put the knife down, or give it to me. I'll take care of this. Of you.'

The wounded man's face was square and pitted, pasty. The air staggered in his chest, pink froth bubbling from his lips. Noah glanced up, trying to get some measure of what had happened here. The woman's face was white, her eyes black. Her fist was red. She'd pushed the knife as far as it would go into the man's chest, deep enough to wet her fingers with his blood. An eight-inch blade. All the way in. That meant . . .

Noah felt the suck of the wound under his palm. Bright spittle frothed from the man's mouth. His lung was perforated.

*Shit.*

Noah needed to stop the lung collapsing. He had to stop it, right now.

He pressed his left palm to the sucking wound, sliding his free arm under the man's neck so he could prop him into a sitting position. It wasn't easy. The man was over six foot and heavily built, padded everywhere with fat and muscle.

Blood filled Noah's palm hotly. He had to stopper the stab wound, make it airtight.

He *knew* this . . .

Trauma training. In theory, he knew it. First time in practice.

'Here.' A slim dark girl knelt next to him, holding out a Pay As You Go phone card and a cotton scarf, orange and pink. 'Use these.'

A flood of relief pushed adrenalin into the right places. 'Thanks.' Noah could use the phone card, but not the scarf. 'Is there cling film? In the kitchen?'

She gave a sharp nod and straightened, disappearing from his line of vision. Noah took the man's weight, saying, 'Spit, if you can.' The less froth in his mouth, the better.

Behind them, DI Rome was holding the blonde woman. Noah couldn't see the knife now, but he could hear the woman sobbing, her teeth snapping with shock. One of the others said, 'How did he get in here?' It was a girl's voice, rising to a scream as she repeated it: 'How the fuck did he get in here?'

Marnie murmured something and the screaming stopped. The dark girl returned to Noah's side, with a roll of cling film. He covered the stab wound with the phone card in the hope it would stop more air escaping from the punctured lung, before reaching for the film, struggling with it until the girl knelt, the two of them passing the roll between them, the girl helping to support the injured man's weight. She was strong, despite her small frame. She tore the cling film

15

SARAH HILARY

with her teeth when Noah had enough to bind the man's chest three times, making the wound airtight.

'Thanks.' He looked at her for the first time, seeing a straight sheet of black hair, an oval face, almond eyes, the left one a milky ruin, burned at the lid and brow. 'Ayana?'

'Yes.' She was Nasif Mirza's sister, the woman they'd come to question. She was nineteen years old, but looked younger.

DI Rome crouched on her heels by their side. 'How's he doing?'

'His lung's collapsing. We've done what we can, but he needs to get to a hospital.'

Marnie shoved a stray curl from her eyes with the back of her hand. 'His name's Leo. Leo Proctor.' She nodded at Noah. 'Good job, Detective.'

'I had help.'

Marnie nodded at Ayana. 'Good job.'

Ayana wiped blood from her hand on to her skirt. 'I don't understand how he got in. It is safe. They always lock the doors. I've checked.' She stopped, aware that her voice was the loudest sound in the room; the wounded man had stopped kicking, his breath clicking wetly in his chest. 'They always lock the doors,' Ayana repeated.

Someone sobbed; the blonde woman with the bloodstained hand. An African girl with braided hair was holding her. Both women wore the same shapeless clothes: grey sweatpants and shirts.

'She's in shock.' Marnie looked down at the injured man. 'She's Hope Proctor. This is her husband. I'll make sure the ambulance knows where we are.'

# 4

*Fuck.* Two police cars. Three, if he counted the unmarked Mondeo.

Bitch had backup.

He sat very low in the car, pulling at the cap he'd bought at the tourist stall: *I ♥ London.* Its peak hid his eyes and mouth. He shouldn't be here. He shouldn't be in a car, let alone within a hundred yards of the women's refuge. The sudden wail of a siren had him fumbling at the car key, snagging its teeth in the ignition. Clumsy bastard.

*She* did that to you . . .

He dropped his hand into his lap, checking the mirrors. The rain kept coming, as if someone had unplugged the sky, sheets of the stuff, thick and chilly, making the car steam. He ran the wipers, clearing the inside of the windows with the cuff of his overalls, so he could keep watch.

Fucked if he was running.

It'd taken him weeks to track her down to this dump. The refuge stank, even from a distance. Damp. Yeasty. She'd smelt that way. It'd turned him on, once.

An ambulance shaved the pavement as it parked up, the

gutter throwing a wave of rain as the vehicle's back doors banged open.

*Shit.*

He slunk lower in the seat. Watching to see what came out of the refuge, whether it'd be a man or a woman, alive or dead.

Better not be her . . .

It'd better *fucking* not be her.

He wanted to do her with his bare hands. Just the two of them, the way it'd been before. Except this time, he wouldn't turn his back.

That'd been stupid.

He wouldn't make that mistake again.

# 5

The paramedics – one male, two female – arrived shiny with
wet. At some point in the last hour, the rain had started.
Monsoon-force now, slapping up from the roof of the
ambulance, stuttering in the potholed driveway.

'We've got him, thanks.' A paramedic nodded at Noah.

He moved out of the man's way before climbing to his
feet, stiff-kneed and shaking.

The paramedic glanced up. 'Okay?'

Noah nodded. 'Yes.'

'Leo, is it? All right, mate, we're going to make you more
comfortable.'

Noah stepped away, to give them room to work.

On the sofa, Leo's wife was sitting wrapped in a shock
blanket, her shoulders circled by her African friend's arm. A
female paramedic knelt next to them, winding a bandage
around Hope's right hand; she'd cut herself, on the knife.
Her friend was holding a wad of rusty cotton in her left fist.
Behind them, the jungle mural was an aggressive arc of
green, tall grass parting around a lion's pink muzzle.

Yellow light snapped across the ceiling, making the women
cringe: lightning.

DI Rome had been right about the storm. She was briefing the police team who'd arrived with the ambulance, speaking quietly, holding their attention. Noah watched, knowing what was going through her mind: the need not to compromise the evidence, to manage her witnesses; the fact that she'd have to reconstruct all this in court. Training drummed it into them: 'One chance to get it right, and in the right order.'

'Let's get you on the stretcher, Leo.'

Ayana and the others watched the paramedics with the false calm of those who'd witnessed trauma before, and often. Noah needed to wash the blood from his hands, make himself less frightening.

He left the dayroom and found the kitchen. Children's paintings were pinned to three of the walls, fastened to the fridge by magnets. Outside, the concrete yard was empty except for noisy sheets of rain. The ordinariness of it made Noah blink. Had he really just sealed a man's lung with a phone card? Yes, his palms were sticky with Leo Proctor's blood. Adrenalin made the ends of his fingers jump. His mouth tasted of copper coins, cheap.

A drawer hung open under the sink. He guessed it was where Ayana Mirza had found the cling film. He closed it, checking the other drawers for cutlery. Looking for knives like the one the forensic team had just bagged – the blade with Leo Proctor's lung tissue on it. Nothing sharper than a potato peeler in any of the kitchen drawers. Noah kept searching and found the knives, finally, on top of the fridge, in a blackened, greasy butcher's block. Out of the reach of children. Hope Proctor would've needed a chair to reach the block. Noah didn't touch it. He ran the hot tap, scrubbing at his palms with the pads of his thumbs, waiting for his pulse to slow.

Lightning cut across the yard, its bright reflection trapped for a second in the sink. He counted six before the thunder came. The storm was closing in.

'How're you doing?' Marnie Rome was in the doorway.

'I'm good.' He tore a sheet of paper towel. Dried his hands. 'You were right about the storm.' It sounded like someone was stir-frying the yard, rain spitting, sending up a smoky mess of steam.

Marnie came to the sink. 'We're going to be a while taking witness statements. Most of the women are calm, but I don't trust that to last.' She stripped off her jacket and rolled up her sleeves before soaping her hands as he had done. 'You impressed the paramedics with your first aid. Not bad for a copper was the consensus.'

'Trauma training,' Noah said. 'Did they say anything about his chances?'

'Just that you'd done good, but a punctured lung is a punctured lung.'

'Why did she do it, did she say?'

'She's not said anything.' Marnie's quick eyes flicked to the butcher's block on top of the fridge. She touched the left side of her neck, as if it hurt. 'Her friend with the braids, Simone, says the knife was Leo's, that he came here armed. If that's true, it was probably self-defence.'

'He came here with a knife?' Noah thought of Proctor's dead weight, his face turned inside out with pain. Hope was half her husband's size, weighing maybe eight stone. Leo was nearer seventeen. Noah's arm ached where he'd held Leo in a sitting position until the paramedics took over. 'How did she get it off him?'

'I don't know. It's something I need to find out. We're not short of witnesses, but it's too soon to start taking statements, that's what the paramedics think.'

More lightning lit the yard. Steel-coloured, like a snapped cable. Marnie rolled down her sleeves, leaving the cuffs loose.

'Let's make some tea . . .'

Noah searched for mugs in the cupboard above the stove.

Marnie filled the kettle and plugged it into the wall. 'The advice is not to move Hope until she's less stressed.' She glanced at the window, which was swarming with rain. 'Simone says she's scared of water. That Leo used to make her sit in the shower for hours on end, to get clean.' Her eyes blanked with censure. 'Just one of the reasons she was hiding here.'

Noah remembered the scream: 'How did he get in here?' and although they'd meant Leo Proctor, he knew the women might just as easily be afraid of *him*. A stranger, male. He wondered why Marnie hadn't come alone. 'How did Leo get in?'

'Something else I don't know. Jeanette, she's the screamer, is insisting the doors were locked, standard procedure. She's in charge of security, for what that's worth. From the smell of her, she was on a fag break. She's concerned to let us know she was taking care. A bit too concerned.'

'You think she's covering her back?'

'I'm entertaining that possibility.'

'Is she under arrest?'

'Hope? I should caution her before asking questions.' Marnie sounded reluctant. 'I'm thinking it can wait until she's less stressed. She isn't going anywhere.'

Noah thought of the way Hope shook as her husband lay with one lung collapsing, big fists empty at his sides. Leo wore a wedding band. Did Hope? Noah couldn't remember. He needed to pay better attention to details like that. 'What happened to her hand? I saw them bandaging it.'

'She was clumsy with the knife, but the paramedics say it's superficial, not much more than a scratch.' Marnie poured boiling water into the mugs. 'Jeanette says she didn't see anything more than we did. She was at her post, only arrived in the dayroom after Leo was laid out on the floor.' Her voice was tinder-dry, not believing this version of events. She picked a crushed yellow petal from the knee of her trousers. 'Roses. How romantic . . .'

'You think he meant to use the knife on her?'

'Why else would he bring it? I'm tempted to think the roses were for hiding the knife, until he got inside.'

Noah opened the fridge to get a carton of milk. 'What about our witnesses?'

'Simone. Ayana. Mab, who was hiding behind the sofa, but with a clear sightline. Two others I've yet to speak with . . . I'm discounting Jeanette, for now.'

Five witnesses. All women in hiding from abusive men. How'd it felt, seeing Leo Proctor walk in, wielding a knife? Watching Hope stab her husband, possibly fatally.

'Is there CCTV in the dayroom?'

'Only at the front entrance – if it's working. I've put a call through to the station about getting hold of the footage. No CCTV indoors. It's important for the women to know they're not under surveillance. It's one of the ways they feel safe . . .' Marnie picked up the tray. 'You're thinking how much easier it'd be if we had impartial evidence of what happened before we got here?'

'Infinitely.'

'Less legwork, more luck?' She looked mournful. 'No one loves us that much.'

**6**

Hope Proctor hadn't moved from the sofa, sitting under the mural of the lion's mouth with her friend Simone. Noah looked around, seeing the dayroom properly for the first time. A widescreen TV took up most of one wall, the plaster cracked around its steel brackets. Sofas and chairs faced the screen, as if the TV was a fireplace. Everything in the room looked cheap and disposable, with the surface shine of a catalogue purchase. The thin carpet carried a shallow stain, already turning black. Someone had cleared away the roses, but one or two petals remained, bruised by feet.

Hope and Simone weren't alone in the room. Three women sat on a second sofa. Two were young, dark-haired. The third was a much older woman in a floral dress, gloved hands cupped in her lap as if she was hiding something there, her mouth turned inwards, cheeks collapsed from lost teeth. Mab, Noah guessed. Jeanette, who should've been watching the door, was sitting apart from the others. Ayana Mirza was standing by the window, twisting the orange and pink scarf between her hands.

Thick curtains hid the view outside. The rain was a constant tattoo, drumming on the windows and walls. Hope flinched from the sound, as if the rain was hot and hitting her bare skin. Simone hugged her, the foil shock blanket rustling under her grip. She had Hope's blood on her hands, sheening her fingers.

'Tea.' Marnie Rome shared her smile around the room. It was a great smile, reassuring without being overfriendly. Noah was trying to learn a similar smile. 'I don't know who likes sugar. Could someone give me a hand? Simone?'

Simone got up from the sofa. She'd threaded the braids with lemon beads, glass. The beads tapped together as she moved, concentrating on the task DI Rome had given her. She was about Ayana's age, young enough to be pleased by Marnie's approval.

Hope Proctor reached for Noah's hand. 'You were with him. Was he scared? Was he angry? Oh God . . .' Her voice was fierce, low in her chest and deeper than he'd expected. Her face was blotchy with distress, her bandaged hand child-sized, fingertips icy with shock. 'I'm sorry, I'm sorry. Did he know – he was dying? Was he very angry?'

Noah sat in the space left by Simone. 'He was in shock,' he said softly. 'Like you.'

'The paramedics got here quickly,' Marnie added. 'That's a good thing. It means he has the best chance to pull through.'

Hope swivelled towards her, losing another layer of colour. 'Pull through . . . *Pull* . . . Oh God.' She put her hands to her face. The grey sweatshirt was much too big, its sleeves falling back to show bruises on her wrists and forearms. Noah had to look away.

Ayana was sipping tea, over by the window. She'd given him her phone card, knowing he could use it to stopper the sucking wound in Leo Proctor's chest. How had she known that, and what else did she know?

Noah couldn't forget the reason they'd come here, what Commander Welland was expecting from this visit: a statement attesting to Nasif Mirza's violent temperament.

Hope rocked on the sofa, holding her hair from her face. Noah could smell the blood on her hands. 'I'm sorry,' she said, in the same fierce voice as before. 'I'll be okay in a minute. You can charge me. You're waiting to do that. I understand.'

'There's no hurry,' Marnie said.

'Why were you here?' Each question was on an intake of breath, as if speaking was an effort, but one Hope was determined to make. 'Thank God you were, but why?'

'We came to see Ayana.'

Hope looked towards the window, then away, at the other women holding mugs of tea. 'I can't drink anything.' She dipped her head, her throat convulsing. 'Please. I'll be sick.' Her irises were slim rings around blown pupils. A frown emphasised the deep crease between her brows, suggesting this state of heightened anxiety was normal.

'You don't need to drink anything,' Marnie said.

Simone moved back to the sofa, opening the circle of her arms to hug Hope.

Noah crossed to where Ayana was standing. 'How are you?'

'I'm fine.' Her voice was very steady, her gaze unblinking. She had a south London accent, picked up at school, he guessed.

'That was quick thinking, before. With the phone card.'

'And the cling film.' She gave a slight smile. 'I saw it on television. A cop show. I watch a lot of television here. Soap operas. Phone-ins. Very bad for me. Everything here is a bad influence.' She widened the smile, showing even teeth. 'I like it very much. I read, too, and study. Criminal psychology.'

'A distance-learning course?'

She nodded. She couldn't leave the refuge, Noah knew that much. She looked at the sofa where the three women sat in silence, Mab and the two dark-haired girls. 'They offered me a place with other Asians. That is how they put it: *other Asians*. I knew someone in a place like that. The

26

women working there gossiped at the mosque.' She put her lips to the mug. 'I prefer it here.'

'Even now?'

'I don't know how he got in. It is *safe*. They are very strict. The doors stay locked unless we ask.' She frowned at the room. 'We like them locked.'

Like a prison. A prison with television and books, and the chance to study, make friends. Noah wondered about the phone card, whose number she called when she needed to talk. Perhaps the card was for the television phone-in shows.

Rain shook the window next to their heads. He could smell it, tinny and cold, through the heavy curtains. 'Let me get you a new top-up card, for your phone. You have a mobile?'

'Yes.' She touched a woven purse at her waist. 'Thank you. There wasn't much on the card. Less than five pounds.'

'I'll get you a new one,' Noah promised.

They couldn't quiz her about Nasif so soon after the stabbing. It would've been tough enough before, knowing what Nasif and the others did to her.

Ayana's brothers. In her own home. Two of them held her down while the third squirted heavy-duty bleach into her eyes. When they let her up, she managed to grope her way out of the house and into the street, screaming for help.

Surgeons saved her right eye. They couldn't save the left.

Blind in one eye, she could still see. The CPS believed her witness statement would help to put Nasif behind bars, but so far she'd kept quiet about what her brothers had done. According to the notes that Noah and Marnie had inherited, in the hospital after the bleach attack, no one visited Ayana. Until the third day, when a woman arrived, alone, clutching a hooded anorak. 'I have come to take my daughter home.'

It was Mrs Mirza. Ayana's mother.

Ayana didn't stop screaming until the woman went away.

# 7

'A knife?' OCU Commander Tim Welland echoed. 'At a women's refuge? I thought these places were meant to be secure?'

'We're working on that now.' Marnie moved aside to let the family liaison officer go past her, in the direction of the dayroom. 'We need to find out how Leo got in, and how he knew his wife was here. But first we need to make everyone feel safe again.'

'After a stabbing?' She could hear Welland grimacing at the other end of the phone: *good luck with that*. 'How's Ayana Mirza?'

'She helped Noah save Leo Proctor's life.'

'*If* they've saved it. From what you said . . .'

'Proctor was stable when the ambulance took him.'

'Do you think she meant to kill him?'

Marnie rubbed at the ache in her neck, petting the pain the way she'd learnt to, as it strayed around her body. 'It was self-defence, that's what our witnesses are saying.'

'Reliable, are they?' Scepticism soured Welland's voice. 'A knife in the lung sounds to me like attempted murder. I'm not saying she didn't have a good reason to do it; I don't suppose she was in that place from choice.'

'You haven't seen her, or heard her. She's scared he's going to live, but she's not making excuses. And yes, she's covered in bruises, of course she is.'

When she'd taken the knife away, Hope's hand had been shaking. Marnie had understood, for the first time, how frightening it was to use a knife as a weapon, deadly.

'I'm going to take her to the hospital,' she told Welland, 'and get her checked over.'

'How's DS Jake bearing up?'

'He's good. I've told him to get clean. He's got a change of clothes at the station . . .'

'A mess, is he?'

'Proctor leaked all over him, so yes.'

Welland heard the cool edge in her voice. 'Are you handling this all right?'

She looked the length of the corridor, to the locked fire exit. 'It's a domestic with a knife. Half this job's domestics with knives, but . . . Proctor's stable. I'll be surprised if he doesn't pull through. He's a big bloke, lots of padding.' Not a murder, in other words. 'To be honest, I'm more worried about Hope. I want to know what happened before she came here, to make her come here.' Answers. She wanted answers.

'Have your plans changed?' Welland asked abruptly.

'For tomorrow?' She shoved her hair from her face. 'No. Of course if Proctor dies . . . then I'll reschedule.'

'Stay in touch,' Welland said. 'I need to know you're on top of things.'

'Of course.' She pictured his open face, inviting confidences. Personally, she had no problem keeping secrets from Tim Welland. He knew too much about her already. She was glad of any secrets she could keep, insulation against his questions, his knowing.

*He knows how they died*, she'd often think, *how they looked when they were dead. How I looked, weeping in the street outside – but he doesn't know that I like salted chocolate or dumb TV spy shows where the heroine wears a different wig every week and kicks the crap out of everyone. He doesn't know* – if all else failed – *about the writing. The words on my skin.*

Secrets she'd kept from everyone. From Greg, her dad. From her mum, Lisa. From Lexie, the therapist they'd assigned her after the murders. Even from Ed Belloc, with whom she trusted most secrets, instinctively.

The clichés of her skin, teenage rebellion writ large. Embarrassingly so, now she was into her third decade, regretting the bilious girl she'd been, with her mascara-laden eyes and her biker boots, her studied solitude and near-autistic silences. She'd stopped being that girl when she was Ayana's age, nineteen; hormones shucking away like the bark on a plane tree losing London's poisons in the shedding of its scales. Fired with purpose, she'd considered a career with the air force. All that speed and power, the endless sky and adrenalin rush. She'd settled impatiently on the police. Never intending the choice to stick, seeing it as a way to rid her feet and fingers of their itch to get away, *escape . . .*

Afraid that if she took too long choosing a path, she'd become that girl again. The one who crept from her parents' house while Greg and Lisa Rome were sleeping and caught the first bus into town, to a place where she could pay a man with the cleanest hands she'd ever seen to inscribe her teenage skin with black, stinging secrets.

# 8

Not her in the ambulance. A stranger, big bloke with an oxygen bag over his face.

No one he knew.

He wiped the steam from the inside of the windscreen with the damp cuff of his overalls again. Under the peaked cap – I ♥ London – his mouth shifted to a smile.

Not her.

Then doors were opening and closing, police everywhere, and he had to start the car, pull away. He couldn't risk them catching him. He shouldn't be driving, too many points on his licence apart from anything else, but how was he supposed to get around?

The police'd love to pick him up. He knew that.

He parked two streets away, the engine running, wipers slicking rain so he could keep watch for them leaving, red tail lights telling him the coast was clear. He didn't need much. Just a chance. Maybe twenty minutes, maybe less.

Street lights were coming on, too early as usual. London trying too hard, thinking it could throw up a new building and no one would notice the shit on every street corner, the beggars and hen parties, puddles of puke, and whores everywhere.

31

He'd watched TV the other night, some crap with a bent politician who'd punched a bloke into a coma and couldn't stop crying about it, standing round in the rain, snot running down his face. The camera kept filming London from the air, trying to make it look like LA, with skyscrapers and fancy helipads, what a fucking joke. London never looked like that, not from down here, where life was lived.

He waited ten minutes, then drove around the block, back to within eyeshot of the refuge. Rain had made a river of the driveway, washing off the roof in a filthy waterfall.

The unmarked Mondeo was still there, and the two police cars, but they hadn't been for him, or her. It was just a coincidence.

People didn't believe in coincidences; they looked the other way. That was what he needed right now. Just ten minutes, or twenty, when everyone was looking the other way and he could do it . . .

Do her.

The refuge didn't look too safe, not much of a hiding place. Silly bitch, thinking he couldn't get to her in there. Failing all else, there was a fucking great hole in the roof.

He didn't need a lot of time. He'd have liked the luxury of taking his time, but those days were gone, he knew that; no more slow dances, seeing her squirm.

This time it'd be hard and fast – and over with. She wouldn't be running and hiding when he was done with her.

He reckoned he needed twenty minutes, tops.

# 9

*You fucking evil bitch your dead. You think your safe. Think again cunt.*

Blue biro had scratched the words on to a sheet of lined paper, torn roughly from a notepad. The ink had clotted in places, thinned in others. The author had gone back over some of the words, where his pen had failed.

Marnie Rome held the page to the hospital's overhead light, studying the clots and scratches, the scarred surface of the sheet.

You could tell a lot about a person from his handwriting. From what he wrote, the pen and paper he chose. You could tell the surface he wrote on, whether he was drunk or ill. It was all in the indents and impressions. Even if you didn't have the original, if all you had was the pad he used. Indents went deep, and you could create a vacuum on the blank page – run an electric bar over it, glass beads with carbon powder that stuck to the indents and revealed words like magic. Marnie had worked with a police documents examiner. She knew all about the tricks, the science involved.

*You think your safe. Think again cunt.* Not much magic needed here. No secret messages. Just three lines of hate-fuelled threat.

Marnie had found the letter in Hope Proctor's bag, unsigned.

She had no immediate way of knowing whether Leo Proctor had written it. She'd looked through his wallet, but the signature strips on his bank cards were worn to smudges; it was all chip-and-pin these days. She took out her phone and called Noah Jake. 'I need an example of Leo's handwriting.'

'Okay,' Noah said. 'What've you found?'

'Not much.' She turned the sheet of paper in her hand. 'Just a little light reading, courtesy of an illiterate . . . Where are you?'

'At the station, getting a change of clothes. How's Leo?'

'Alive, the last I heard. Try to get me a sample of his handwriting. Maybe there's something in Hope's things at the refuge. And see if you can speak with Ayana. You've got a connection with her.'

'A connection?' Noah echoed.

'She helped you keep Leo alive. You made a good team. Use that. See if you can't get what Welland wanted from this.'

'You think she'll talk to me, alone?'

'You're not alone. You have Family Liaison. And I've asked Ed Belloc to drop by later. Just . . . see how Ayana feels. I'm betting she'll talk to you. Sometimes it helps to be a stranger.'

'Okay,' Noah said. 'I'll do my best.'

'Good. I'll see you back there after I've spoken with the doctor, and Hope.' She rang off, checking her wristwatch.

In eight hours, it would be tomorrow. The fifth anniversary of their deaths. What'd she said to Welland?

*I'm not counting.*

Right, then.

She folded the threatening letter and put it in her pocket. She had to discount it, for now; dangerous to second-guess what Noah might come back with. The letter might not even

34

match Leo's handwriting, or he could've disguised his writing; the bad grammar could be deliberate misdirection. Hope was articulate, intelligent. How likely was Leo to be illiterate? He worked on a building site. Marnie didn't know much more than that. Not yet. She needed the doctor's exam to confirm how badly he'd abused his wife. She sympathised with Hope's effort to salvage some shred of dignity and privacy after the events of the morning, but she'd insisted on the exam. Hard evidence, Welland called it.

Hope Proctor had put a knife into her husband's lung. Marnie needed to know how, and why. At the refuge, Simone Bissell had said, 'She can't see straight. She puts things on the edge of tables and spills stuff all the time. He's hit her so much she can't see straight any more. She didn't know where she was sticking that knife.'

She stuck it in her husband's chest, deep enough to puncture his lung.

Leo was a big man. A big target.

Hope was scared, at the end of her rope. Marnie could believe that. The threatening letter was opaque in places, where Hope had handled it with sweating hands. It was possible she'd panicked, pushed the knife into Leo's chest in blind terror.

A kitchen knife. Black handle, sweeping steel blade. Thirty quid; maybe forty in a good shop. A proper piece of kitchen kit, endorsed by a celebrity chef, his signature printed in black on the silver blade, and again in silver on the sleek black handle.

Marnie had the knife in an evidence bag back at the station. It balanced beautifully in her hand. At least she imagined it did; she'd yet to work up the courage to touch it.

A hospital porter pushed an empty trolley through swing doors at the end of the corridor, the sound like a small explosion.

'She's ready for you.' The doctor, bespectacled, thirty-something, looked weary as he approached.

'What's the verdict?' Marnie asked.

'I've seen worse cases, but they tend to be working girls. Vaginal bruising consistent with object insertion.' He referred to his notes, reading in a routinely bland voice. 'Bite marks to her breasts and thighs. Fissures and scarring consistent with a prolonged history of anal sex. Surface bruising to her arms and legs. A belt most probably caused the bruises on her back. The sorts of injuries you might expect to see on someone indulging in sadomasochistic sex.'

This had happened in Hope's home. Behind closed doors.

Marnie's skin shivered; the sensation as familiar to her as yawning.

Home sweet home.

Did that exist for anyone, anywhere?

'The examination upset her,' the doctor was saying. 'I prescribed a sedative. You'll want to be gentle with her, although there's nothing wrong with her intellect.' He gave a shrewd, admiring smile. 'She's not in the mood to be patronised.'

'How's her husband, any change?'

'None at all.' He referred to a separate set of notes. 'I can tell you he has liver damage, long-term, not yet acute.'

'He's an alcoholic?'

'Almost certainly. His blood alcohol level indicates he'd been drinking heavily in the two hours before he was admitted.'

In other words, Leo Proctor went to the refuge armed and blind drunk.

'Apart from that? Minor injuries consistent with his work in construction, and his pastime of rugby. According to his hospital records, we've treated him for cracked ribs on a couple of occasions, contact-sport injuries. Eight months ago, we

36

treated him for two broken bones in his right hand. We call it a boxer's fracture.'

'Boxer's fracture?' Marnie repeated. 'Does that mean he broke his hand hitting someone?'

'Or some*thing*. A work-related injury, according to the records.'

'Can you give me dates and details?' She scanned the sheet of paper he handed her. Leo Proctor broke his hand eight months ago. Hitting something, or someone. Hope was living at home eight months ago. She pocketed the sheet, next to the threatening letter. 'How soon after he wakes up can we talk to him?'

'We've inserted a chest drain. Between that and the blood loss, he's best off unconscious. A punctured lung's a serious injury, especially when it involves a knife wound.'

'She panicked,' Marnie said. 'That's what the witnesses say.'

'Just bad luck she found his lung.' He looked again at Hope's medical notes. 'Or good luck . . . The cut to her hand, incidentally, is superficial. To answer your question, it's too soon to say when he'll come round.'

'But he will? Come round.'

'That's our expectation at this stage.'

Leo Proctor wasn't going to die. *Good.* Marnie wanted to question him, and she wasn't inclined to be gentle, the way she intended to be with his wife.

'Something else,' the doctor said. 'I've no idea if it's significant.' He nodded at his notes. 'They have matching tattoos.'

'They . . .'

'We nearly missed it on him, too much blood for one thing. Hers is, ah, just beneath her right breast.' This embarrassed him in a way the sexual abuse didn't. 'A heart with an arrow through it.' He grimaced. 'Hardly the most original sentiment.'

'Where's his?' Marnie's skin was burning under her ribs, and above her hips. 'You said you nearly missed it. Where's his tattoo?'

'The same place.' The doctor rubbed at his spectacles with a forefinger. 'It's why we nearly missed it. Because of the mess.'

He wiped his finger on his white coat. 'The tattoo is exactly where the knife went in. Bullseye, I suppose you'd say.'

# 10

'My name in Ethiopian is *beautiful flower*.' Ayana Mirza sat at the foot of her bed, in her narrow room at the refuge. 'In Kashmiri, Ayana means *day of judgement*.'

'Your brother . . .' Noah began.

'Nasif. It means *most just*.' Her smile twisted. 'Another of my brothers, Turhan, is *of mercy*.'

'Nasif . . . is a suspect in a serious assault.'

Ayana lifted her chin, showing the blind white of her ruined eye. 'Again?'

'This attack was with a scimitar. A man lost his hand.'

Ayana bit her lips together as if to stop herself from speaking. Silence stuffed the small bedroom. Noah looked around. No wardrobe, just a hanging rail for clothes, holding a couple of chain-store jumpers and a jersey skirt. Lined curtains covered the windows. The walls had been repainted so many times the gloss resembled pimpled skin. A shallow desk held a pile of library books and coursework from the remote-learning school. Nothing else in the room belonged to Ayana, not even the red dress she was wearing; she'd had no time to pack a bag when she left home.

'I promised you this.' Noah held out the phone top-up

card. He'd put ten pounds on it, thinking twenty would be too much, might seem insulting.

'Thank you.' She took the card, stroking it with her thumb.

'Your uncles have spoken up for Nasif. Everyone in your family has. They say he's very gentle. He has no history of violence.'

Ayana nodded, as if she accepted this. 'Of course.'

'You know that's not true.'

'I know you do not need my statement, to take action.' Ayana dipped her head at the sound of the television leaking from the dayroom. 'The police can act independently.'

Noah smiled at her. 'Is this from your distance-learning course?'

'It's true.' Ayana gestured precisely with her slim hands. 'The police are no longer reliant on a victim's statement and can act independently.'

'The victim isn't any help to us in this case.'

'Will they kill him, if he helps you? That is what my family will do, to me.' Ayana reached into the pocket of her red dress. She took out a cloth purse. 'Do you know what is in here?' She loosened the drawstring. 'Seed pods.' From the open neck of the purse: the spicy scent of garam masala. 'It's the smell of home.' Her smile made Noah's chest hurt. 'I keep this to remind myself. That it was never as simple as good and bad, safe and dangerous. Do you understand?'

Noah understood. Home, for Ayana, was a rich mix of love and loyalty, honour and obedience, reward and punishment. He understood this, but he still wanted her to speak up, speak out. She wouldn't be free until she did. He wondered which of the women at the refuge had purchased the seed pods for her, or whether she'd been carrying the purse when she ran from the house, after the bleach attack.

'I miss home,' she said simply. 'When I miss it too much, when I'm tempted to use this?' Holding up her cheap mobile phone with its chipped cover. 'I make myself remember the bad things as well as the good.' She dropped the phone back into the seed pods and fastened the neck of the purse. Through the wall behind her head, the television purred. She hooked her hair behind her ears and said matter-of-factly, 'Nasif has a sword. My uncle gave it to him when Nasif was six. It isn't a toy.'

'Did you see him use it?'

'Only as a game. To show off.' She folded her hands in her lap again. 'Sometimes he pretended he would use it if I wasn't behaving at school, but it was a game. He is a coward, like Turhan and Hatim. None dares do anything without the others.' She moved her gaze around the room. 'My mother kept me at home, learning to be a good wife, like her. To be unhappy, like her. My brothers took me to school when she allowed it. It was their duty to watch me there. If I talked to Western children, especially boys, they would report it. Sometimes they reported it even when I hadn't talked to anyone. I was bringing shame on the family. Who would want to marry a girl like that? And what else is there for me but marriage?' Her gaze returned to Noah. 'It isn't only girls. I know boys whose families have forced them into marriages they didn't want. Beaten them, for refusing to marry.'

'You could speak out against it. Against the sort of violence you suffered.'

'In a court?' Her smile was sad. 'And then what, return here? They would find me. They've told everyone they know. And they know many people. People who work in shops, or drive taxis. Even in hospitals. You don't know what it is to be always watched, by everyone, to be under constant surveillance.'

They were getting nowhere, turning in circles. Ayana was convinced of her powerlessness, seemed almost to relish it.

Noah had been wrong: he didn't understand her at all. He needed to check Hope's room, for letters from Leo. 'Can you tell me about what happened with Hope and Leo this morning?'

Ayana smoothed the skirt of her dress. 'What do you want to know?'

'Was it the first time you'd seen Leo?'

'Yes.'

'Everyone was in the dayroom,' Noah said. 'Is that usual?'

'Yes. After breakfast, we watch television. We take it in turns to make coffee or tea. It helps us to feel part of a family. We watch television together. Like normal people.'

Daytime television. Her definition of normal.

'Leo Proctor arrived just after nine o'clock,' Noah said. 'Is that right?'

'It was nine twenty. *Lorraine* was finishing.'

'You were all in the dayroom. Hope, Simone and the others.'

Ayana counted on her fingers. 'Hope, Simone, Mab, Shelley and Tessa, and me.'

'Where was Jeanette?'

Again, Ayana counted on her fingers. 'Smoking outside. Sneaking into our rooms. Eating the food in the fridge.'

'She was in the dayroom when we arrived.'

'She came in just before you did and started screaming as soon as she arrived. She was the only one of us making a noise.'

'Who saw Leo first?' Noah asked. 'Was it Hope?'

'Probably. The rest of us were watching television, but she isn't very interested in it. Not just *Lorraine*. Anything.' Ayana returned her hands to her lap. 'She's nervous, cannot settle to anything.'

'Early days for her, isn't it? I expect everyone takes a while to settle in.'

'She's been here three weeks. She was getting worse, not better.' It was clear from her tone that she disapproved of Hope's failure to settle at the refuge.

'Worse in what way?'

'Always moving around. Restless, as if she didn't want to be here.'

'How was she this morning?'

'As usual.' Ayana shrugged. 'No better, no worse.'

'Restless,' Noah said. 'Nervous.'

'Yes.'

'Where was she in the room when Leo arrived?'

Ayana thought for a second. 'By the window. She was always by the window. Not looking out, none of us does that, but she liked standing there. Perhaps the room felt stuffy to her.'

'How did she react to seeing Leo?' Noah asked.

'She turned very quickly. It made us all look to see what the trouble was. That's when we saw him.'

The door was behind the sofas, facing the television. The window had a clear sightline to the door. It made sense that Hope would see the door open before anyone else. 'All of you saw him at the same time?' Noah asked. 'When Hope turned?'

'Yes.'

'Did Hope say anything or make any noise?'

'She took a big breath.' Ayana imitated the sound, sucking air with a hiss between her teeth. 'She didn't speak.'

'Then what happened?'

'He stood in the doorway. She walked towards him.'

'She walked towards him. Are you sure it wasn't the other way around?'

'Look at the stain on the carpet,' Ayana said placidly. She was very sure of her recall. 'If he had gone to her, the stain would be by the window.'

'Did he say anything?' Noah asked.

'No. He held out the roses.'

'How did he hold them out, can you demonstrate?'

Ayana put her hands together, at arm's length from her chest.

'He used both hands?'

She nodded.

'Did Hope take the roses?'

A smile flitted across her mouth. 'No.'

'But she walked over to him. Got close.'

'If she'd had a gun,' Ayana shrugged, 'she could have stayed by the window. She had to get close. She had a knife.'

In the silence that followed this statement, Noah heard a jingle playing on the television, for cheap car insurance.

'What makes you think that *Hope* had the knife?'

'It is the only thing that makes sense. He would not bring a knife in here. Why would he? If he wanted to kill her, he would have done it at home. In here? In front of all these witnesses?' Ayana spread her hands. 'It makes no sense.'

'You think she meant to do it.' Noah felt chilled. 'It wasn't an accident.'

'He bled into your lap. Did it seem like an accident to you?'

'Simone says that Hope panicked.' He spaced out his words, speaking very softly. 'That she was scared, and she panicked.'

'She was scared,' Ayana agreed. 'But it wasn't panic. It wasn't an accident.' She knitted her fingers in her lap. 'Nothing is ever an accident, for us. No one ever *falls down the stairs* or *slips and hits her head*. We make excuses, to cover up, but these things are never accidents.'

'Where did Hope get the knife?' Noah asked.

'I suppose . . . from the kitchen. Or she brought it with her, from home.'

'Simone says it was self-defence, an accident. Why would she lie?'

44

'To protect Hope,' Ayana replied equitably. 'They have become close. She is the only one Hope speaks to, I think. And because Hope had a good reason to kill him.'

She touched the corner of her blind eye. 'A better reason than my brothers had for this. They said I looked at a boy, but I did not. I never looked at anyone but them. The joy they took in their duty. How happy they were, being my jailers. The way it made them feel so strong. Manly.' Her voice hardened, but she sounded bewildered, as if even now she could not believe what was done to her. 'That is why they did it. Because I looked at *them* the wrong way. No one else.'

She lifted her chin, challenging Noah with a stare. 'If I'd had a knife, I'd have done the same as Hope. Three times over. I would have found a way to make it stop. Just as she did. She had to make him stop. You cannot begin to guess what he had done to her, the ways he made her afraid. You should be glad of it. Of Hope. The police need all the help they can get with monsters like that.'

# 11

Hope Proctor was lying on a trolley parked against one of the hospital's grazed walls. A white waffle blanket covered her, from chest to feet. Under it, she wore a hospital gown, papery against her skin. Pink spots of shame showed under each eye, as if she'd pinched the skin; she knew what the doctor had reported, no secrets left to her.

Marnie drew up a chair next to the trolley. 'We don't have to speak yet. It can wait until you're stronger.'

'I want to do it now.' There was an undercurrent of fierceness in Hope's voice. 'It can't get any worse. Unless . . . How's Leo? They wouldn't tell me, except that he's still unconscious.'

'It's all there is to tell. He'll pull through, that's how it looks.'

Hope nodded. 'Good.' At the refuge, she'd looked terrorised at the prospect of her husband surviving the attack. Was it fear of reprisal? 'I don't want him to die. In case you thought . . .' Her face convulsed. 'I would *never* hurt him.'

'He hurt you. Didn't he?'

Hope's eyes slid away. 'That's . . . private.' Her voice dropped to a whisper. 'A marriage is *private*.'

Was that how Leo had convinced her to keep the abuse

to herself? What happened behind closed doors was nobody else's business. Marnie had heard the line often enough in domestic violence cases. 'The doctor told me about your injuries. I understand it's hard to talk about this, but you were living at the refuge. You must have wanted it to stop.'

'I wanted time.' Hope plucked at the blanket, her fingers colourless with cold. 'To think. Time for him to think, too. I thought . . . if we could just *think* about what we wanted . . .'

'What do you want, Hope?' She couldn't bring herself to say 'Mrs Proctor'.

'I *love* my husband,' Hope hissed fretfully. 'What's wrong with that, in this day and age? I loved him when I married him and I still love him. I took my vows in good faith.'

An old-fashioned sentiment. Hope was twenty-eight. Doll-like with her fair hair and heart-shaped face, little hands with pearly fingernails. She must have been a very pretty bride, in vintage lace, a veil, orange-blossom bouquet. When did she get the pierced-heart tattoo? Surely not before the wedding.

'You went to the refuge, three weeks ago. Why did you do that?'

'To think. I told you. To have time to think.'

'You've been married for nine years. When was the first time he hurt you?'

Hope pressed her lips together, looking away.

'Something happened three weeks ago,' Marnie said, 'to make you leave. What happened?'

'I panicked. Sometimes I get these . . . attacks. Panic. I don't know what to do.'

'Have you seen a doctor about them?'

Hope jerked her head in a nod. 'Leo took me, when it was really bad. He thought there should be pills, something to help me. To calm me down.'

Chemical cosh. Leo Proctor. What a man.

'Did the doctor give you anything?'

47

'Yes, but the pills made me sick. Dopey. I couldn't get up in the mornings. Leo needs his breakfast. He works in construction. He needs three square meals.' She recited the words as if they were a code by which she lived, her marriage vows in practice.

'So you stopped taking the pills. What happened then?'

'I was . . . all right as long as I was busy. Leo was on overtime, a big job that needed finishing fast. His hours were crazy. I couldn't keep up.' She held her hair back from her face before dragging it forward to hide her eyes. 'I kept getting things wrong. Burning food, buying the wrong things. I . . . broke a mirror. Seven years' bad luck. That's all I could think.' Her shoulders shook. Tears wet the neck of her gown. 'Seven years! Seven – *more years*.'

Marnie waited for her to calm down. 'So you went to the refuge. Did you tell him you were going there?'

Ed Belloc in Victim Support called it Rule One: if you're thinking of leaving your abuser, never tell him. Just go. Women who told their husbands they were leaving didn't always make it out alive.

'I didn't tell him,' Hope said, without conviction.

'But he found you, this morning. Did you call him, Hope? Is that how he found out you were at the refuge?'

Hope roped her hands in her hair. She'd fretted at the bandage on her right hand, fraying it. After a long moment, she breathed, 'Yes . . .'

'How did he react, when you told him?'

Marnie had to wait for an answer. Finally Hope said, 'He was worried about me. He wanted to know I was okay. He worries when I'm around other people. I'm not very good at reading people, not very smart. Sometimes that gets me into trouble.'

The doctor had admired Hope's intellect. Yet Leo had convinced her that she wasn't very smart. Classic isolating technique. Making everyone else into a threat. Leo as her hero, the one keeping her safe. 'Did he ask you to come home?'

Hope's face was crumpled like a newborn's, with the same unseeing eyes. 'No, he didn't. Not then. He asked if he could see me. When I said they didn't like visitors, he got . . . angry.' She wiped at her nose, mucus shining her hand. 'He wanted to see me. I'm his wife. Everyone at the refuge was a stranger. I might be in danger.'

'Did you feel in danger?'

Hope shook her head. 'I was safe. I *told* him I was safe. But he was worried for me.'

'Even though you said you were okay.'

'I told him I was making friends. Simone and Mab. Especially Simone.'

'How did he react to that? To you making friends?'

Hope reached for the blanket. 'I never had friends before.'

'Never?' Marnie helped her with the blanket. 'Or just not since you got married?'

'Since . . . school, I suppose. I'm not very good with people.' She twisted her hands in the waffled cotton. Thin strips of muscle marked what Marnie could see of the backs of her hands. The kind of muscle you got in a good gym lifting weights, or from hard manual labour. The cleaning staff at the police station had the same hands, just less well manicured; Leo liked his wife to look nice, in public. 'Leo told you that you weren't good with people.'

Hope stiffened. 'It's true. Leo doesn't lie. Not – not to me.'

'He lies to other people?'

'Only the usual things. Like when he's late for work, or rugby. Not what *you* mean.' She flushed, pulling at her hair again, searching for split ends. 'I know what you think, what you're trying to do, but I stabbed him. *Me.*' She thumped at her chest. It made a hollow sound. 'It was me.'

'It was you. I'm trying to find out why. You said you didn't want him to die.'

'I didn't. I don't.'

'But you stabbed him in the chest with a knife.'

'I panicked!' Hope's eyes swivelled away from Marnie.

'Why did you panic, Hope? What did you think was going to happen?'

She waited, but Hope stayed locked inside herself, one fist in her hair, the other balled against her chest. Marnie was acutely aware of the tattoo the doctor had described. Below Hope's right breast. A heart with an arrow shot through it. Her skin itched with empathy. 'Had he used a knife before? To threaten you? To hurt you?'

'No. *No.*'

'Where did the knife come from?'

'From – home. He brought it from home.'

An ordinary kitchen knife. The kind everyone has at home. Marnie told herself to concentrate on the woman on the trolley, not to let her mind stray in the direction of memories. 'The knife was yours. Yours and Leo's.'

'We bought it from Peter Jones, when – when we were first married.'

'How was Leo able to bring it into the refuge?'

'He – hid it in the roses.'

Somewhere in the hospital, an alarm shrilled.

'He hid the knife,' Marnie repeated, 'in the roses.'

'They're my favourite. Yellow roses.'

The roses were an empty gesture. Why couldn't Hope see that? Five years ago, on behalf of the Met, Tim Welland had sent a wreath. Lilies, a sickly topspin of decay, like a scented candle in a pathology lab. Marnie had hated lilies ever since.

A trolley bumped down the corridor outside the private room.

'Why did Leo bring the knife to the refuge, Hope?'

'For me,' Hope whispered. 'To make me feel safe.'

Marnie pinched the bridge of her nose. This conversation was . . . insane. 'Leo brought a knife to a women's refuge to make you feel safe.'

'Yes.'

'Did it make you feel safe?'

Hope didn't answer.

'Can you look at me, please? Hope.'

Hope lifted her head, a fugitive coldness in her stare. Resentment. Because Marnie was forcing her to confront the truth about the lies in her marriage?

'That's better. Thank you.' She gave her a supportive smile. 'Did Leo hand you the knife, is that how you got hold of it?'

'Yes. He said I didn't know these people. There were all sorts in there. Like a prison, he said. There's always violence in prisons.'

'He gave the knife to you, and you took it.'

'Yes.'

'Then what happened?'

'Then . . .' She wedged the flat of her hand under her nose. 'Then he held out the roses and – I was going to smell them. They looked so beautiful, perfect, only I scratched myself on a thorn . . .' She put out her left hand, searching its fingers, showing Marnie the scratch on the pad of her ring finger, looking bewildered. 'It didn't even hurt. I hardly felt it, just a scratch, but I panicked. I panicked.'

Her eyes flew wide. 'I stabbed my husband because of this!' Thrusting the scratched finger at Marnie. 'A pinprick! Nothing! Why? What sort of person does that? It was nothing – a scratch! How could I? *How?*'

Marnie took her hand. 'Hope . . . who can I call? Is there someone you'd like here with you? Family?'

They'd asked Marnie the same question, five years ago. She hadn't been able to think of anyone, not easily. Only

51

Ed Belloc, and it was his job. She was afraid he'd come as a professional, rather than a friend.

'I don't have any family.' Hope shrank, as if the outburst had stolen what was left of her strength. 'They died. Dad when I was little. My mum . . . last year. Cancer.'

'I'm sorry . . . How about friends?'

'Simone . . .'

'From the refuge?'

'Yes. If she'll come. I know she's scared.' Hope pulled her hand from Marnie's, to wipe at her nose again. 'I haven't any tissues; they were in my handbag . . .'

'Simone's scared . . . of leaving the refuge?'

Hope nodded. She turned her face away. 'I was the same. I thought I was safe there. I didn't think anything bad could happen as long as I was there. It was . . . my home. You're meant to be safe in your home.'

'Yes, you are.' Marnie got to her feet. 'I'll ask Simone if she'll come. And I'll bring your handbag.' She paused. 'There was a note, in your bag. Very nasty.'

'What?' Hope's voice was dull, desensitised. She rubbed at the skin under her right breast: the tattooed heart.

'A threatening letter,' Marnie said gently. 'In your handbag.'

'Oh.' She shook her head. 'That's not mine. I took it because it scared her so much. She was sure he didn't know where to find her . . . It's why I don't know if she'll come. She's so frightened . . .'

'The note was sent to Simone?'

Hope nodded. 'By Lowell.'

'Lowell who?' Marnie felt a new itch between her shoulder blades.

'I don't know. Just . . . Lowell. He did things to her . . .' Hope shuddered. 'At least Leo . . . He never hurt me, the way Lowell hurt her. He's a monster. Simone says he'll never give up, ever. Not until he's got her back.'

# 12

'What're you doing in here?' Hope's friend with the braids, Simone Bissell, stood in the doorway to Hope's room, challenging Noah with a stare.

'I wanted to take an overnight bag,' he invented, 'to the hospital.' He held up a plastic washbag. 'This is all I could find.'

Hope's room was pin-neat. What possessions she had, she'd tidied away into the wardrobe and the cupboard by the bed. Noah had searched for samples of Proctor's handwriting, but there was nothing of Leo's in the room. The washbag was the kind sold in airports, pre-packed with deodorant, a toothbrush, shower gel.

Simone's eyes were huge on his face. 'You shouldn't be in here.' Her accent was tricky to place. North London, but posh, not street. 'It's her room. Private.'

'It's all right.' He hunted for a phrase to reassure her. 'I'm a detective. I was here earlier, with DI Rome? And I've been talking with Ayana . . .'

'I know who you are.' She lifted her chin. 'You're a stranger. Hope doesn't know you. She's done nothing wrong.'

'She stabbed her husband.'

'You didn't see.' Her mouth wrenched. 'He's dangerous. Hope saved our lives. She saved all our lives.'

The bed had been made with military tightness. Noah had slipped his hand under the mattress on every side: nothing. The emptiness of the room mocked him.

'Why is she being kept in the hospital overnight?' Simone demanded.

'Just so we can be sure she's okay.'

'I want to see her.' Simone's eyes went around the room, measuring its emptiness, or checking to see what Noah had touched. 'She shouldn't be alone.'

'She's not alone. DI Rome's with her.'

'She should have a friend.' Simone's stare flitted to the window; for the first time, he read fear in her face. She was afraid of what lay outside the front door. He wondered what shape her fear took. A husband or father? Brothers, like Ayana?

'You'd do that for her?' he asked. 'Leave the refuge?'

Simone raised her chin at him. The defiance transformed her, gave rosy hearts to her mahogany cheeks. At some point, her nose had been broken, but she was still beautiful. 'She needs me.' She looked him over. 'You have someone, don't you, who would go back for you?' She nodded at the window, as if she was pointing out a wild animal enclosure, a place no sane person would stray. 'Back out there. You have someone.'

Yes, he had someone.

'DI Rome will be back soon. From the hospital. I'll ask her if you can visit Hope.'

'You will?'

'Yes.'

Simone nodded. 'She had to do it.' Her big eyes came back to his face. 'There wasn't any choice.'

'How did she get the knife?' He spoke as quietly as he could, knowing the ambulance crew had said it was too soon to start asking questions about the stabbing. 'Simone? How did she get the knife?'

'It was a test, to see if she dared . . .' Simone's voice dropped to a hot whisper. She rubbed her hands at her forearms, hidden by the sleeves of her sweatshirt. 'She told me things he'd done . . . Things you wouldn't want to believe. He must have thought he had broken her. That she wouldn't *dare* . . . He didn't think she'd dare . . . He thought he'd broken her in a thousand pieces, but sometimes . . . when you are broken . . .'

She drew her hands from her sleeves, knitting her fingers into a fist. 'You mend hard.'

# 13

The rain had stopped, street lights sitting in flooded puddles in the road. It was dark enough now to remove the cap – *I ♥ London* – as long as he kept low in the car seat.

He'd thought when it got dark that it'd be easy to see what was going on inside the refuge, but they'd pinned some thick stuff over the windows and all he could make out were shadows moving in the rooms at the front.

He couldn't stay much longer, not today. Things to do and he'd promised he wouldn't be late. This was his life now: always making promises, most of them to other people, but some to himself. Like this one, here and now.

Waiting for his chance, with her.

He chewed at his left index finger until he tasted blood. In the mean spill of light from the street, the hand was ugly, clawed like an old man's arthritic paw. He balled it to a fist, pictured smashing it into her . . .

It calmed him down.

The anger was like a new baby; sometimes you had to let it bawl itself out. When he was calmer, he put the finger back in his mouth and sucked at the blood.

He'd missed something, when he was avoiding the police

cars, waiting for the sirens to shut up. After the ambulance took the big bloke away. It flicked across his mind: *Who was that? What happened to him?* But he didn't really care. It didn't matter.

What mattered was the unmarked Mondeo.

When he'd driven back round to the front of the refuge, that was when he saw . . .

The Mondeo had moved. It was parked in a different spot, facing the other way. Same car; he'd checked the registration.

*What if they got to her before you could?*

While he was skulking around the corner, the Mondeo had gone and come back. What if he'd missed her, if the police got to her first? Just for a second, relief had squirmed in the pit of his belly, before he made himself remember what she'd done and why he couldn't let it alone; the promise he'd made to himself.

The police were still here, which meant *she* was still here. She wouldn't dare leave the refuge alone, he was sure of that. She knew he was coming.

He'd had fun writing the warning note.

*You fucking evil bitch your dead.*

Gripping the pen in his left hand – in what was left of his left hand – pretending to be some arsehole who couldn't spell, in case she decided to show the note to someone. He knew she'd know who'd written it.

He hoped she was afraid. He hoped she was shitting herself with fear.

She deserved it. For what she'd done.

She deserved everything he'd promised himself she'd get.

*You think your safe. Think again.*

# 14

From everything Marnie had said about Ed Belloc, Noah had pictured a big bear of a man, cuddly and capable. Asexual.

Ed, when he came, was five foot ten. Slim and soaked, rain running down his face, making a skullcap of his dark hair. He shook himself like a dog on the doorstep of the refuge, lifting a hand in greeting at the blurred lens of the CCTV.

Noah buzzed him into the building, fetching a towel from the nearest bathroom.

'Thanks.' Belloc scrubbed the towel at his head, offering his free hand. 'Ed. You must be DS Jake.' His hand was thin and chilled.

'Noah. Can I fix you a cup of tea?'

'Great. Thanks.' Ed mopped the back of his neck. 'Where's Rome?'

'She's just got back from the hospital. She's in the dayroom.'

*Rome?* The familiarity surprised him, but Ed had known Marnie for years, at least five years that Noah knew of. He was younger than Noah had expected. Thirty-ish, with the soft-focus look of a student midway through his finals.

Dressed like a student, in decimated cords and a blue shirt with a fraying collar which rain had soaked to navy. His hair was drying into bedhead brown curls and he had brown eyes, cute in a through-a-hedge-backwards way. Noah preferred something edgier, but he admired the way Belloc was working the look. Ed was the least threatening man he'd seen in a long time.

Marnie was waiting in the doorway to the dayroom, her face softening to a smile when she saw Ed. 'Thanks for coming. How was court?'

'Stuffy.' He finished drying himself with the towel. 'Good to get into the fresh air.'

She straightened his wet collar. 'Looks like you swam here . . .'

'So what's been going on?' Ed's eyes went over her shoulder, to the dayroom where the women were sitting. 'You said an incident. That can't be good.'

Marnie walked Ed and Noah towards the office. 'One of the women stuck a knife in her husband. We walked into the middle of it. It was lucky Noah was with me. He saved the husband's life.'

The office was a short, windowless room. Three of its four walls were partitions, drawing noise from elsewhere in the refuge. Little of the desk was visible under a litter of stained mugs, empty sweet wrappers and gossip magazines, celebrity cleavage shining from their covers.

'Who did the stabbing?' Ed asked.

Marnie moved a copy of *Heat* magazine out of the way, so that she could perch on the edge of the desk. 'Hope Proctor.'

'Not a name I know. How long's she been here?'

'Three weeks.'

'My last visit was a month ago.' Ed looked apologetic.

59

'I wanted to ask you about security here,' Marnie said. 'From the look of it, Hope's husband walked in, armed, no one to stop him.'

Ed was silent for a beat. Then he said, 'He brought a knife in here?'

'No one challenged him.'

'What time was this?'

'Ten, this morning. The door was on the latch. Is that usual, in places like this?'

'Nothing's usual, in places like this.' Ed towelled his neck again. 'I'd love to tell you trained professionals are in charge twenty-four-seven, but it's just not practical in most places. There *should* have been trained staff on duty. The door *should* have been secure. There are panic buttons and they should be working. We shouldn't have to rely on volunteers because resources are so stretched . . .' He scratched a hand through his hair. 'Where's Hope now?'

'In the hospital. Sedated.' Marnie glanced at Noah. 'DC Abby Pike's with her.'

'How bad is she?'

'She's bad.' Marnie touched the side of her neck. 'Shaken, ashamed. In denial. Nine years of abuse, a lot of it sexual. It was difficult, talking with her. She resented the questions . . .'

Noah reached a hand for the wall, feeling sick. This was the man whose life he'd helped to save? A rapist and a torturer?

'She's blaming herself,' Marnie said, 'even so. She says Leo had the knife for her protection, can you believe that?'

'That and a whole lot worse,' Ed said. 'About resenting the questions . . . It's nothing personal. Keeping secrets is empowering, even if you're the one getting hurt. Counterintuitive, I know, but I'll bet she felt stronger before she told you anything . . .' A frown pinched the bridge of his nose. 'Who else was here when it happened?'

'Simone Bissell. Mab Thule. Tessa Stebbins and Shelley Coates. Ayana. And the supervisor, Jeanette Conway.'

'Jesus,' he breathed, looking shaken. 'They all saw it? The stabbing? Mab and Simone and the others?'

'Yes.'

Ed had spent the day in court, Noah remembered. No wonder he looked whipped.

'Ayana helped Noah with the first aid,' Marnie said. 'She was a star. The others . . . seemed calm, at the time.'

'I can imagine. So . . . where're you up to with witness statements?'

'The witness statements can wait a while. We wanted to make this place feel safe again first, before we asked too many questions.'

Ed nodded, looking relieved. 'Thanks for that.'

'Tell me about the set-up here,' Marnie said. 'Resources are stretched?'

'Not just here.' Ed propped himself on the edge of the desk, crossing his feet at the ankle. He was wearing odd socks, one brown, the other blue. 'Right across the board. Funding cuts really hurt us. I hate to say it, but domestic violence victims are easy targets. They don't complain and they don't have the power to lobby. That makes them invisible.'

'You said you hadn't met Hope. She wasn't in our database either. I'm wondering how she got a place here.'

'She probably called the domestic violence helpline and got a referral that way. Is she local, do you know?'

'Very local. From Finchley. Is that usual?'

'Sometimes. Depends how anxious she was about her husband tracing her.' Ed scratched his knee. 'Did she say how that happened? The tracing, I mean.'

'She called him.'

'Ah.' He didn't look surprised, just sad. 'It happens.'

61

'The knife,' Marnie said. 'Simone and the others are calling it self-defence. I suppose that makes most sense to them.'

'Knives . . . are scary.'

Marnie glanced at the wall calendar, then away. Ed was watching her with a tender vigilance that made Noah wonder how close they really were. He played Belloc's statement back in his head, the careful space he had placed around the words: *Knives are scary.*

'Simone is more vocal than the others, convinced Leo got what he deserved, but it was self-defence. Panic.' Marnie said it as if she was testing the theory for soundness.

'Simone . . .' Ed hesitated. 'Has more reason than most to be scared of knives.'

Marnie quizzed him with a look, but he shook his head. 'It's not my story to tell, but . . . Go easy on her. Simone. She's not as strong as she looks.'

'She wants to see Hope,' Noah said. 'At the hospital.'

Ed looked surprised. 'Simone said that?'

'They're close,' Marnie said. 'She's been protective of Hope since we got here.'

'And she's ready to leave the refuge?' Ed thumbed a streak of rain from his cheek. 'D'you mind if I come with you?'

'To the hospital? I was going to ask if you'd stay here . . .'

'If that's where you need me, but I'd like to speak with Simone first, if that's okay.'

'Of course. Hope's sedated, in any case. I'm hoping they'll have a bed for her over the weekend. She's booked for a CT scan; from a couple of things Simone said, we should probably check for worse damage than they've found so far.'

Marnie straightened up, moving towards the door. 'I know it's getting late, and you're tired. I don't expect you to stay long.'

Ed said simply, 'I'll stay as long as I'm needed.'

'Thanks. Noah . . . you should go home. There's no need for all of us to be here.'

'Are you sure?'

'Go have a social life. I'll call you when there's news.' She glanced at her watch. 'I won't be around tomorrow, unless something happens at the hospital.'

'Okay.' Tomorrow was Saturday; Noah hadn't expected to see her. Unless, as she said, something happened at the hospital.

'Plans for the weekend?' Ed asked, after Noah had left the refuge.

Marnie went to the window, drawing back the corner of the heavy curtain. The sky had dried to scars and neon light; it never really got dark in London.

'I'm visiting Stephen.' She let the curtain fall back into place, turning to face Ed.

He ducked his head, fumbling for something in his pocket, conjuring the awkward ghost of his adolescence. 'How's that working out?'

'Not great, if I'm honest.' She kept her voice light. 'If it were up to him, he wouldn't see me. But his solicitor says it'll look good, going forward.'

'It's a long drive.' Ed's hair was in his eyes. 'If you want company . . .'

'You don't want to spend your weekend like that.'

'True. I could watch *Buffy* reruns and try to beat my personal best for cramming Kettle Chips.'

She smiled at him. 'All right, now I *have* to take you. Seven o'clock start, though.'

She thought this would put him off, but he nodded. 'I'll be ready.'

'About Simone . . . I know you said you couldn't tell me, but Lowell . . .' The threatening letter was folded in her pocket. 'Is he part of the story?'

He was surprised. 'She told you?'

63

'Hope told me. She said Lowell threatened Simone.'

Ed's eyes clouded. 'Recently?'

Marnie took the letter from her pocket and unfolded it, handing it across to Ed, who read the scrawled words in silence.

'No date.' He handed the letter back.

'No date,' she agreed. 'Does it sound like Lowell to you?'

'From what she told me? No. But I haven't seen his writing.'

'Where *is* Lowell?' she asked. 'In London?'

'Yes. The last I heard . . . Yes.'

'So if he's traced Simone to the refuge . . . Do we need to move her?'

'*If* he has.' Ed paused. 'She didn't tell me about the letter.'

'Should she have done? As a condition of her place in the refuge, or to keep you in the picture?'

'No. No, there's no requirement for that. Just . . . I thought she trusted me.' He smiled a bit. 'My ego. Sorry.'

He didn't have any ego. Or if he did, she'd seen no evidence of it. 'Speak with Simone. I'll make sure someone's here with the women over the weekend. At least we know the place is secure again.' Her Friday night all sorted out. No space for second thoughts about tomorrow's trip.

'I'll pick you up,' she told Ed. 'Tomorrow at seven.'

'I'll be ready.'

## 15

By 8 p.m., King's Cross was shaping up to sleazy, on the safe side of its rush hour for sex, drugs and dodgy music. Outside, the club was a blaze of blue neon. Inside, it was packed with people, none of whom was Dan Noys.

Dan had texted to say he was running late. Noah ordered a shot of vodka, to get a head start on the night. He needed to forget about his day. The refuge, all those lives twisted out of shape by hate and fear. The mirror behind the bar gave back a slice of his face, faceted by glass. He swallowed the vodka and turned to look around the club.

Music thumped from a sound system, inviting couples to dance. Two men were circling with the rhythm, hands on each other's hips. Away from the dance floor, other couples were drinking or chatting, groping or kissing. Noah started to relax; this was his version of daytime television: the definition of normal . . .

A warm hand touched his shoulder.

'You've pulled . . .' Dan kissed his neck.

Noah reached up, curling his palm to the shape of Dan's face, holding him to the kiss until he was done conveying relief, gratitude and raw need.

'Vodka?' Dan poked at Noah's empty glass. He was wearing his oldest jeans and a white T-shirt, with Red Chili climbing shoes. 'We're drinking tequila.'

They took the shots to a dark corner, where Dan leaned Noah up against a pillar and revived the kiss, urgently, as if his day had also been something he wanted to forget. He spent his week managing artists and their egos. Some nights he came home more knackered than Noah.

'Thank fuck,' Dan said hazily, 'for Friday.'

He came up for air eventually, going to fetch another round from the bar. After which, there was licking salt off each other's necks and sucking lime from each other's lips, until Noah's mouth started to buzz and sting.

'You guys want something stronger?'

Noah glanced up, seeing a stranger. Plaid shirt, eyebrow ring, right hand in the back pocket of his jeans.

Noah shook his head. 'Thanks.'

'You sure?' Plaid Shirt showed his palm, sweaty. Pills in a plastic bag.

Dan flashed a warning with his eyes. 'We're sure.'

Plaid strolled away.

'Good job your boss wasn't here to see that,' Dan said.

Noah rolled his neck, sticky from the lime.

'Reckon she's out on the razz?' Dan sucked the zest from his thumb. 'DI Rome.'

Noah didn't answer. He didn't know how Marnie spent her Friday nights, or her weekends. None of his business.

'Unless she's *happily married* . . .' Dan mused. 'Maybe she's got an ex. She looks the type. She's a ball-breaker, DI Rome.'

'I'm switching to Pepsi, you want one?' Noah moved away in the direction of the bar, not wanting a conversation – the usual conversation – about work.

Dan thought the police was a crazy career choice, for anyone. 'Debased' was the word he used. Also corrupt, ill-founded and run ineptly by people with rotten agendas. All this, and then Noah being half-Jamaican, to top it off. Had he made any friends during training? No, but he hadn't become a detective to make friends. He'd done it to make a difference. To people like Ayana Mirza, who'd fought to save Leo Proctor's life even though he was a stranger and possibly a wife-beater, someone who didn't deserve to be saved.

Across the room, Plaid Shirt was palming his pills off on another couple. Perhaps Noah should revise his definition of normal . . .

They'd made a difference, Noah and Ayana, to Leo Proctor's chances of survival. But what about the women in the refuge, what about Ayana herself?

Had Noah made a difference to how safe she was in that place, with its new stain on the carpet and the hole in its roof? How safe did she feel, right this minute? While Noah was ordering Pepsi in a bar full of people for whom 'stranger' meant guilt-free sex, no strings attached . . .

How safe was Ayana Mirza and the strangers she was living with, at that rain-ruined refuge in Finchley?

# 16

The rain had left breath marks on the inside of the refuge windows. Simone stretched her arm between the curtains to place her palm on the glass. It was cold and hard, slippery. She spread her fingers flat to the wet, thinking how her hand must look from the street outside. A hand with no body attached, the curtains hiding the rest of her from view.

Was the car still there, watching?

She had seen it when the police took Hope away: a parked car with its wipers working, jerking rain from the windscreen.

Someone was out there, watching. There was always someone. Simone was scared for Hope. It wasn't safe to leave here, not on your own. Not ever.

She drew her hand back through the curtains to study the spots of wet in her palm. She hadn't washed yet. Hope's blood had dried between her fingers. Unless it was Leo's. She lifted her hand and sniffed at it. The rain had a metal smell, like buckets, or bullets. She touched the tip of her tongue to the skin between her fingers – just a touch, a taste – and knew it was Hope's blood. It tasted too sweet to belong to a man. She turned away from the chill of the window, seeing the flat shape of the bed.

Hope's room was nearly empty. Simone had wanted to be the first in here after they'd taken Hope to the hospital. To protect Hope's space, her few possessions. Instead, the policeman had been first, searching with his eyes and his hands – for what? Another knife?

*How did she get the knife, Simone?*

She had told DS Jake that it was a test. That Leo didn't think Hope would *dare* . . .

Leo had broken Hope into a thousand pieces, Simone knew. Hope had told her, not everything, but enough. Even if she had said nothing, Simone would have known. She had known the roof was leaking before the cracks came, and long before the rain tore a hole up there.

Broken things were like bad mirrors; they gave out a peculiar light, like . . . catching sight of your face in a pail of milk spoiled by a thunderstorm.

Simone had known that Hope was in pieces before they ever said a word to one another. In the dark, in this room, she had given her hands for Hope to hold. In silence, sitting together, listening to the silence. Hers and Hope's.

Everyone else asked questions. Simone was sick of questions. With Hope, it was different. It was as if, a long time ago, she had dropped a pebble into a well and now – soon – she would hear it hit the water down there. Deep down, in the dark. But not yet. Not until the silence was done with them.

There was healing in the silence. To sit like that, with your hands in another's, not speaking but *knowing* . . . Simone could feel herself mending. And Hope, too.

She had told this to the policeman, DS Jake. Told him how Leo hurt Hope. How, when you were broken, you mended in a different way.

She folded her hand into a fist, slowly, hiding the wet from the window in the creases of her palm.

*You mend hard.*

# 17

*Five years ago*

The court is stiflingly hot. Every half-hour, a slice of cold makes it through the primitive air-conditioning unit to snap at her ankles, before the heat eats it up.

Stephen sits in the dock with his head bowed, a yoke of shadow on his shoulders. His defence team has coached him in how to sit. 'Keep your eyes down,' they've told him. 'Look sorry.' It's what Marnie would've told him, if she'd been responsible for his defence. She isn't, of course. She's here, in the words of the prosecutor, to see justice done. Whatever that means. She knew once, or thought she did.

They want her to give an impact statement, to stand up and tell this room of strangers how it feels, what he did. She's refused, because what could she say?

'The pain's in my head today, above my left ear. It's possible to put a knife there, if you hit hard enough. He put a knife into my mother's head there. I don't know why.'

If she took the stand that's all she'd say: 'I don't know why. I want to know why.'

They won't let her ask this question. Instead, they expect her to strip naked and show her hurt from every angle. To weep. To tell how much her life is changed, how little she has left. She isn't allowed to ask why.

Everything else – all the things allowed – it's just another way of him hurting her. She's damned if she'll let him beat that bruise, without answers.

Day after day they sit here. In the jungle heat of the court. Like a lizard and a locust, or a snake and a mongoose. She won't be cast as the victim, not even when they say it'll help with his prosecution. 'The jury needs to see what he's done,' they tell her. 'Show them what he's done.'

The jury have seen the photos, and the pathologist's face. Marnie thought the man would be better at hiding his emotions. She's seen the jury's eyes, their winces and grimaces. *You're not giving them me*, she thinks.

She won't talk about how much she loved them, what a hole he carved in her life. If she gave him that, he'd take it back to his cell to feast on, or fret over. He's had enough of their lives. She won't give him any more.

The sentence, when it comes, is not a shock, or a relief. She doesn't understand how it could be either of those things, although the court steps are always crowded with relatives – victims – who weep or rail, grateful or furious at the outcome. She can't see that there is any outcome. No 'finally'. Guilty doesn't mean a thing, when his head's bowed and no one's seen his eyes properly, to know if *he's* grateful, or furious.

When they take him away, that's different. Then, she wants to jump up from the rock where she's been watching and push through the steaming space that separates her and Stephen. To stop it happening: the taking away, the grilles and locks, all the barriers between her questions and his answers.

'What did they do?' she wants to know. 'Did they do something – *anything* – or was it all you? Was it all just *you*, Stephen? With your snake's eyes, your locust's stare – Was it all just you?'

her there.

# 18

*Now*

Sommerville Secure Unit sat on the border of Bristol and the Mendips. Its exercise yard was twenty square feet of tarmac where scabby tape picked out the corpse of a football pitch. Elsewhere it was steel and glass, reflective surfaces shivering in the weak sunshine.

Saturday morning, ten o'clock. Marnie had left Ed in the car park, stretching his legs after the long drive. He had a flask of coffee, and the weekend papers.

Marnie had telephoned the hospital at 7 a.m., for news of Leo and Hope. There was nothing to report. Leo was still unconscious. They'd scheduled a CT scan for Hope. DC Abby Pike was with her, keeping vigil.

'Just a minute.' Marnie's escort signalled her to a halt near the plate-glass entrance to Sommerville, bringing her up short before her reflection in the locked door. A strand of hair had worked loose from the knot at the nape of her neck. She shoved it back with two fingers. The glass served up her likeness without sympathy, showing every line and shadow. Coming here always made her feel ancient.

'Okay, come on.' Her escort dragged the door open and held it for the time it took Marnie to move inside the complex.

She was in a square room, its carpet a curdled sea of stains that sent up the smell of low tide, burning the back of her throat.

'Marnie Rome,' she said, in answer to the bored question put to her by the escort. 'I'm here to see Stephen Keele.'

# 19

Only one inmate in the visitors' room, sitting at a metal table under a ceiling strip of light. The light punched the colour out of everything.

Marnie sat in the chair on the other side of the table. Both chairs, like the table, were bolted to the floor; a contingency against furniture fights.

On the other side of the table . . .

Stephen Keele had a soap-and-water smell, with a hot metallic note underneath: prison cologne. From his pallor, it was tempting to think he'd spent the last five years in his room, without daylight, but he'd always been pale.

Marnie remembered meeting him for the first time, an oddly self-possessed eight-year-old, with an Old Testament angel's face. Black curls, blue eyes, a mouth that curved ripely over small, even teeth. Incarceration hadn't changed him, or not noticeably. He was nineteen, serving time for a double murder committed five years ago, when he was fourteen.

He sat upright in the chair, his shoulders bleached by the light. Marnie wondered what the grey tracksuit was hiding. Whether, like Hope Proctor, Stephen was disguising damage done to him. Or to others, by him. He kept his hands out of sight, under the lip of the table.

'I brought you a book.' She put it on the table. 'Short stories, I hope that's okay.'

He didn't touch the book. She waited for him to look at her, but he kept his eyes on the wall behind her head. 'Jeremy says you like reading.' She touched a finger to the book. 'These are some of my favourites.'

'Jeremy,' he echoed. His voice was the same. Precise, pitched low. Not the voice of a teenage kid. More like a thirty-year-old's. He still didn't look at her.

'Jeremy Strickland. Your lawyer.'

Stephen tilted his head to the left, as if he had difficulty hearing her.

He didn't have any difficulty that she was aware of.

He'd grown another inch. He'd been a skinny eight-year-old and would probably never be fat, unless he surrendered to the carb-rich diet here. As it stood, he was slim, angular at the hip and shoulders. Still with the angelic face, ripe lips.

She waited for him to take the book, or at least to acknowledge it. He did neither.

'How are you?' she asked, keeping the other questions at bay.

Somewhere in the secure unit someone was kicking a ball; an aimless repetitive sound like skin thumping on skin.

Marnie looked across the metal table at the boy who'd murdered her parents. 'I asked Jeremy if there was anything I could bring you. He said he didn't think so, that you seemed to have everything you needed.'

Slowly, very slowly, like a spider coming down from its web, Stephen's eyes found her. He withdrew his hands from under the lip of the table and reached into his pocket.

Each movement was calculated, calibrated. From the pocket he brought out a pair of spectacles, slipping them on.

Thin gold frames emphasised the fragile bridge of his nose. A smudge of white paint had dried at the corner of the right lens. He drew her book of stories towards him with the ball of his thumb, looking over the gold-rimmed lenses at the cover. Then back at her.

'I had the whole sky in my eyes,' he said, each word dropping like spiked honey from his tongue, 'and it was blue and gold.'

She couldn't breathe, all the heat shocked out of her. A world of loss in a single look and a handful of words he shouldn't have known, he *couldn't* have known, unless . . .

He'd seen her. Back then. Before he ripped her family apart.

He'd *seen* her. Naked.

77

# 20

Sunlight was a slap in the face.

Ed was standing by the side of the car, drinking coffee from his flask. Marnie went past him to the driver's side, climbing in and firing the engine. He jumped in the passenger side. 'Rome?'

She swung the car, its tyres spitting, headed for the exit. Sommerville was a lie. Everything about it – everyone in it – was a lie. She drove in furious silence, willing the adrenalin out of her fingertips, the steering wheel humming under her touch.

'Rome?' A fresh streak of coffee spoiled the sleeve of Ed's shirt.

She slowed and watched her speed, pushing the anger back into its box.

She refused to admit it was a mistake, visiting Stephen Keele. If it was, then she'd been making the same mistake for three years. Too late to stop now.

When they reached the motorway, she chose the slow lane, tucking in behind a horsebox. The car's vents drew in the autumn smell of the horses. She remembered a charm bracelet, a gift from her mother. One of the charms was a silver horseshoe. She'd kept it in a box in her bedroom. She had no idea where the bracelet was now, or the box.

'Stephen never changed my room,' she said. 'Not a thing, not in six years. I was there after the arrest. My posters were still on the walls, my stuff in the cupboards. Some of his clothes were in the wardrobe, but apart from that? It was exactly the same. That freaked me out.' She remembered the chill in her bones as she stood in the room that had been hers for eighteen years, expecting to find it changed beyond memory, beyond recognition. It was the room of a fourteen-year-old boy now. A fourteen-year-old murderer. Only it wasn't. It was her room, exactly the way she'd left it when she moved out to go to college. 'I thought they'd change it before he moved in. Not that it was ever pink or pretty. I was a tomboy. But I thought they'd clear it out, repaint. I remember Mum saying they were waiting for Stephen to choose the colours. I guess he never got around to it.'

'How was he?' Ed asked.

'The same.' She checked the car's mirrors. 'He was the same.'

Prison changed people. It was one of the tenets of her job. She had to believe that prison changed people. But not Stephen Keele.

'He had Dad's glasses.' She jerked the wheel in response to a car trying to cut in ahead of her. 'He must've had them all this time.'

'Are you sure?' Ed hesitated, picking his way through her mood. 'A lot of glasses look the same . . .'

'These were Dad's. White paint on the frame, from when he touched up the enamel in the bath.' She was strangling the steering wheel with her hands. 'Stephen . . . put them on. Looked at me, the way Dad used to look, when he had something tough to say.'

She didn't tell Ed what Stephen had said when he looked

at her through her father's glasses. Words that proved he'd seen her without clothes, without even knickers. He knew what she looked like. A secret she'd kept from everyone. She'd wanted to snatch the spectacles from his face and punch him to the floor. Scream and tear at him with her hands, wreck that angelic face, send him back to his cell – his *private room* – with blood in his eyes.

'He knew what he was doing,' she told Ed, 'just now, in there. And back then, too. When he was fourteen. He *knew*. Some kids are born . . . old.'

Ed touched a hand to her elbow, as if to take the charge from her; unstick her lock on the wheel. 'Service station up ahead. Let's stop and get some lunch. My treat.'

'A service-station lunch? That's no one's treat.' But she took the exit, leaving the horsebox to continue its journey without an escort.

Lunch was burgers of some description, with fries and orange juice that at least looked drinkable. Marnie broke the seal on the bottle. A rank of arcade games blinked and belched in the corner. At a table by the window, a family of four was pushing food into their mouths with mechanical concentration, as if the food was a precaution against talking to one another.

The low ceiling hummed with fluorescent light.

A memory came to her, stark and raw, of finding the book her father had been reading, on his chair in the empty house. She'd held it. Put her thumb in the place he'd reached until it grew warm with the beat of her blood.

Ed didn't ask if she wanted to talk. He encouraged her to eat. He was right; she needed the calories. She watched him shake extra salt over his fries. It was amazing he managed to stay so skinny, and that his skin wasn't the colour of an uncooked burger bun. She liked him, maybe more than a little. That didn't stop her wondering if she'd picked him for a friend because of his job. Victim support. She hated to think of herself that way, as a victim. She'd seen what Stephen had done, as much of it as they'd let her see. The stains on the tiles and the floor, and the walls. She'd not tried to hide from any of it, convincing herself that it would get easier. Easier to see him, to spend time with him. Easier to get at the truth of what he'd done. Instead, it was getting harder. Maybe she needed Ed, not just as a colleague or a friend. As a professional. 'I couldn't get out of there fast enough.'

'Sommerville?' Ed asked.

'The house. My parents' place. I couldn't wait to get away, to do better than they'd done. I wasn't just ambitious,' she toyed with the juice bottle, 'I was precocious, really believed I was worth more. When they told me about Stephen moving in . . . I felt sorry for him. Having to live in that dead-end village. That house.'

'Every eighteen-year-old feels that way when they leave home.'

She pushed her hair from her eyes. 'I don't know what I'm doing, Ed. What am I doing?'

'You're . . . going through a process. Trying to find a way through.'

'Am I? I used to think I was trying to come to terms with what he did, maybe enough to forgive him.' She shook her head. 'But that could be bullshit. Maybe all I really want is to see him in that place. To know he's stuck there. Being punished.'

'That doesn't sound like you, Rome.' Ed ate another chip. 'But okay, what if that *is* what you want? What's wrong with that?'

'I'll never get past this. If that's what I want . . . I may as well be in prison with him, in the next cell.'

Ed sucked salt from his fingers, concentrating on this task.

81

It helped, the way he continued as if nothing out of the ordinary was happening. It grounded her.

'You should charge for this,' she said.

He eyed her plate, pretending she meant the food. 'My treat, remember?'

'I meant the therapy. Unpaid overtime.'

'Hey.' He smiled at her. 'We do what we can, okay?'

She finished her juice, fitting the cap back on the empty bottle. 'Tell me about the women at the refuge. Tell me about . . . Mab. When did you first meet her?'

'Right back when I was a rookie. She was in the first refuge they sent me to.' Ed crooked his mouth into a smile. 'She made me a cup of tea, in her best china, and talked for hours about the Blitz, the people she met in London when she was living rough . . . Eventually she told me about the man she married. An American evangelist. GI Joe with God-knobs on.' He lost the smile. 'He beat her, as penance for his sins. They had a son, a chip off the block. When he was thirteen, he started hitting her too. She came to believe she deserved it, or . . . Not that she *deserved* it, but that it was inevitable. She told me once that she could hear herself ticking inside. Danger: UXB. The violence is in her, that's what she believes. There's no escape from it.'

He rubbed the sad expression from his mouth. 'She tried to do everything expected of her. Marriage, religion, raising a family. It all led to the same place: violence. There were lots of things she wouldn't tell me. Mab needs . . . she needs her secrets. Some corner of her life that's just hers. Does that make sense?'

'Yes.' It made perfect sense, and not just for Mab.

'She showed me a few of the things she saved from the bombing raids. Just little things like expired coupons, broken bits of jewellery. Nothing valuable, except to her.'

Marnie watched his face as he spoke, the fond light in his

eyes, the tender shape of his mouth. 'What about Simone? Did you talk to her about the threatening letter?'

'Not about that, no. She was upset about Hope. I'm glad she's made a friend . . . I've learnt to be patient with them. Mab and the others. They return to abusive husbands, or withdraw complaints. Refuse to press charges. They fail, in other words. You can't lose your temper with them. Everyone else does that.'

'The cycle of abuse. Isn't that what they teach? Abuse, forgiveness, more abuse . . .'

'That can be how it goes, yes.'

It was how it was going with Stephen Keele. All right, he wasn't beating her up, but Marnie felt bruised every time she left the secure unit, emotionally sore; he rubbed her nose repeatedly in what he'd done, and she kept going back for more. Not forgiving him, not that, but returning. Why? Why was it so hard to leave him there to rot?

'I made a promise,' she told Ed, 'to look out for him.'

'A promise . . . to your parents?'

She nodded. 'We talked about their age, and his. Mum couldn't face the thought of him not having anyone if they got sick, or when they were too old to look after him.'

'They wouldn't have expected you to honour that, under the circumstances.'

'Probably not. But who knows? If there's one thing he's taught me, it's that I didn't really know them. I'd no idea that they needed to foster someone, in order to feel worthwhile.' It was the hardest thing to forgive: the fact that he'd made strangers of her parents. All her happy memories destroyed, because who were they? The couple who'd taken in a damaged boy, lavished love on him? She didn't know them. He'd wiped out her entire childhood. She turned the empty juice bottle on the greasy table. 'You know, I was a great judge of character, as a kid.'

'You still are,' Ed said.

'At work maybe, on a good day. Back then, though . . . I was suspicious of people, always knew when I was being taken for a ride, or patronised.' She rubbed, without thinking, at her ribs. 'But him . . . I just didn't see it coming. Not even an argument, let alone . . . that.' It made her furious, even now. Her blindness.

'No one did,' Ed said. 'No one could've done.'

'What you said about losing my patience, with Mab and the others . . . Did you think I'd do that?'

Ed moved his hand in protest, then stilled it. 'Maybe.' He drew a careful breath. 'They're not . . . your kind of victims. They didn't fight back. They're keeping their heads down, staying in the shadows.'

'Not my kind of victims?' That stung. He was too close to naming her worst fear: the stigma of victimhood. 'You think I'm not in the shadows?' She dropped her voice to a whisper, shaking. 'I've spent the last five years living under a shadow so long it's . . . I *know* all about shadows. About keeping my head down and hiding.'

Ed waited, without flinching, until she was done. Then he said, very quietly, 'You took back control. You toughened up, and you stopped being a victim. That's what I meant.' The colour had gone from his face.

'Maybe,' she conceded. 'On the surface.' *Not under the skin, though. You could've X-rayed me and seen the shadows inside.* 'I coped, at the time. Even after seeing the house, identifying the bodies . . . I got on with it. Made DI by the time I was thirty-three.'

She'd worked late, and hard. The longest hours, toughest cases she could get. A world of reassurance in those folders; she didn't even mind the paper cuts.

*At least I've got my work. A job to do.* That'd been her mantra. It had suited Tim Welland. And it had suited her, or so she'd thought. Distance. Numbness. Other people's problems. 'I was a career bitch. A ball-breaker. Well, you don't need me to tell you that. I was Welland's golden girl. His dragon-slayer.'

'It's amazing what we can cope with, when we have to.'

'Catches up with us, though. With a vengeance.'

'Nearly always,' Ed agreed. He moved his tray a fraction to the right, as if he was clearing the space between them, making room for her confession.

'If I told you I was terrified . . .' She stopped, waiting for a man in a car-creased business suit to walk past their table. 'Back then, I mean. Every day. *Terrified.*'

'I'd believe you.'

'Could you see it? I thought my disguise was pretty good.'

'It was.' Ed traced a pattern on the table with the pad of his thumb. 'But . . . I knew you before.'

*Before.*

She hardly ever thought about her life before Stephen Keele. She'd spent the best part of the last five years refusing to look in that direction. Moving forward, as if the route behind was cut off by heavy rockfall. Just a long, tortuous tunnel ahead, and her on her stomach, or that was how it felt, crawling on her stomach with a flashlight clenched between her teeth.

'I made it, though.' She spun the empty juice bottle on the table. 'I did make it.'

'You did.' Ed, tuned to the irony, didn't miss a beat.

It was the first time she'd done this, talked with Ed about how she really felt. 'I have his notebooks, from school. I suppose you'd call them a diary. I thought they'd have clues of some kind – answers. I asked Kate Larbie to take a look. I met her on a self-defence course, but she's a documents examiner. I thought there'd be something. If I could just decipher it . . .'

85

'Could you?' Ed asked. 'Could Kate?'

'Nope.' Behind her, a coach party jockeyed for position in the queue for coffee.

Ed hesitated. 'You know you can talk to me, any time.'

She lifted the corners of her mouth, economic with the smile. 'I missed my window for counselling. Actually, not true. I got counselling, twice a week for six months.' Six wasted months; she didn't start getting better until the self-defence course. Someone should tell the Met's psychologists to fund kick-boxing classes.

'I didn't mean you could talk to me as a counsellor,' Ed said. 'As a friend. I hope.'

Marnie stole one of his chips. 'You're the only one I've talked to about this. My boss thinks I'm sticking my hand in a fire just by visiting Stephen.'

Ed lightened his tone, to match her new mood. 'Interesting metaphor. I'm guessing Welland's the type that complains about family Christmases.'

'He likes bridges and vintage cars. He's an Alvis man.'

'Huh.' Ed looked bemused. 'I don't get cars. Never learnt to drive.'

'There's time. You're what – thirty-four?'

'Is that a good guess, or have you been checking up on me?' His eyes gleamed. 'I'm a Sagittarius, if you're interested in that kind of thing. Ayana says it means I'm an extrovert. As evidenced by my tendency to spend the weekend eating Kettle Chips and watching *Buffy* reruns.'

'You're here now.'

'Yep.'

'Damn, Belloc. You're good at this.'

'At what?'

'Holding hands without creeping people out.' Marnie looked him over. 'Must be the bedhead.' She reached to pick a piece of lettuce from his fringe. 'Or the takeaway chic.'

Ed ducked his head over his plate. Was he *blushing*? 'Any time,' he said.

*Strangers on a Train* was the book her father never finished.

Upstairs, in their bedroom, she'd found a scarf her mother had been knitting, in shades of green, half-done. Feather-soft wool. Sea green and moss, and ivy.

Marnie didn't know whether the scarf was meant for her, or Stephen. She only knew that her foster-brother, the boy her parents had loved after she'd left home, took a bread knife from a butcher's block in the kitchen five years ago and stabbed Greg and Lisa Rome twelve times, before sitting on the bottom step of the stairs soaked to the skin in their blood, waiting for the police to arrive.

# 21

'You all right?' Tessa Stebbins wore her hair in a tight ponytail at the back of her head, her arms wrapped round her chest.

Ayana said, 'I need the lavatory.'

Tessa looked past her, at the open door of the refuge bathroom. 'It's not bloody blocked again, is it?' She made a snorting noise like Shelley Coates; she was always copying the other girl. 'You should use the other one. It was working five minutes ago.'

Ayana didn't know how to explain, so she nodded, and watched Tessa walk away.

Neither lavatory was blocked. Both bathrooms had just been cleaned, and the kitchen too. The bathrooms, the whole refuge, reeked of bleach.

Ayana couldn't get away from the smell.

The memory burned her face and hands, and her throat. It was like fire but worse, white-hot, eating into her skin.

She couldn't go outside – she *couldn't* – but she wished she could, even if it meant hunkering down in a gutter or behind a bush, like an animal.

Instead, she went to the utility room at the far end of the corridor, the only room they never cleaned. She closed its door behind her, heaving up the heavy lid of the chest freezer so she could cool her face on its fumes.

Her bladder ached so badly she was afraid she would wet herself. She had done that before, more than once. Always when her mother was there to make her kneel and scrub at the stains on the floor.

She wondered which of her brothers had been made to scrub the bathroom floor after the bleach attack. Hatim, most probably. Poor petrified Hatim.

The freezer lid was heavy. She propped it with her shoulder, taking its weight. The smell was slightly less strong in here.

There had been too many strangers yesterday. Hope Proctor's husband, the police, paramedics. All the women were upset, even Shelley Coates. Ayana had seen Simone at the window, watching the street. She never did that – none of them did – but she'd seen something out there. Ayana recognised the fear in the other girl's face. It didn't feel safe here any longer, and now this – this *smell*.

She moaned in pain, looking around her for something to use. A bucket or a bottle. It was humiliating, but she couldn't hold on any longer. By morning, the smell of the cleaning fluids would have faded and she would be able to use the bathrooms again.

She wanted to go back to her room, her books.

What would DS Jake think if he could see her like this, weeping for the want of a bucket, after she'd helped him to save that man's life? Or DI Rome with her smooth skin and her clear eyes, seeing everything? Had DI Rome ever looked afraid, really, truly afraid, the way Simone Bissell did when she watched the street? Did DI Rome even know how it felt to be that scared? Of cars and cats, and dry leaves coming down from the trees and – and taps dripping into sinks and postmen delivering junk mail and the smell of someone else's borrowed clothes or—

A car backfired in the street and she jumped, the lid of the freezer shutting with a thud, her fingers scrabbling at its rubber seal. Her heart staggered and stuttered in her chest, like a rat caught in the cage of her ribs.

She leaned into the hard lip of the freezer, trying to get her breath back, lungs labouring like Leo Proctor's.

The tops of her thighs burned, as if someone had taken a belt to her there.

She looked down, at the stone floor of the utility room. A dark shadow spread under her feet from the wetness running down her legs. She sobbed, seeing her mother's face, her mouth stretched with shouting. This rage she has, which sometimes sounds like fear. It cracks her voice and the palms of her hands, cracks her knees when she bends to work. Ayana must kneel next to her and scrub and scrub and never raise her eyes or voice. It is the only way she can be close to her mother and so she kneels, again and again, watching their hands move together across the floor, scrubbing at the dirt that is never gone for long. If she slows, her mother raps her knuckles in warning. Later, in front of her sons, she strikes Ayana for failing to finish in time. The next day they are down again, side by side, scrubbing at the floor.

The morning she lost her eye, Ayana and her mother cleaned the bathroom floor. Her brothers' hairs were every-where, black commas and question marks on the white tiles. Her mother breathes heavily as she works; there is still so much to do. Ayana, thinking of a book she is reading, does not move fast enough. Her mother shakes a fist in her face and warns her what will happen if she does not pay attention to her family, her duty.

'You want a real mess to clear up in here? Huh? You want to *be* that mess?'

Her mother is not in the house when it happens. But

Ayana knows: she gave her permission, to Nasif and Turhan, and poor scared Hatim. It was done with her mother's permission.

She can never go home.

## 22

It was chilly by the time Marnie reached home. She'd dropped Ed at his place, turning down his offer of coffee, kissing the corner of his mouth. 'Thanks, for today.'

Her flat had the sterile chill of a meat locker. Her back ached after the long drive. She stretched it, wincing. The spine stores the memory of pain. She'd read that somewhere. They'd found the protein responsible for managing the body's response to central neuropathic pain syndrome. Whatever that meant. She was grateful for anywhere the pain strayed that wasn't a reminder of the bloodless wounds on their bodies.

Her mother had wanted Stephen to choose the colours for his room. Marnie's old room. He hadn't. He'd left the room alone, as if he'd expected Marnie to come back.

No, as if he knew he wouldn't be staying.

Memories bluntly crowded her chest.

*Marn, we've got some exciting news.*

They'd been so happy to have a child in the house again. Marnie hadn't been a child since she was eleven, and not much of one then, independent even at that age, happiest in her own company. Solitary, the way she'd thought Stephen was when they first met.

*Marn, this is Stephen.*

She'd held out her hand for his, because it seemed to be what he wanted, what he was. His hand had been cold, and soft. His eyes were cold too, but there'd been nothing soft about his stare, like the diamond head of a drill.

*He's such a little boy, Marn, and he's had such a hell of a life. We'd like to make it up to him, just a little.*

*Great, that's great.*

Had she been jealous? She was twenty-two when Stephen moved into her parents' house. She'd been living in London for three years, priding herself on having made a clean break. Not like her friends or flatmates, who went home every reading week and for the holidays, coming back with gifts of food, meals for the freezer, home-made cake, like children from a party. Not Marnie Rome. She was done with all that. Put childish things away. A card at Christmas, a present of books, proof of her taste and intelligence. On her way to being a detective, single-minded, not missing a trick. Free from all the mess and fuss of family life, from the ties that bind.

Until the phone call in the middle of the morning. The afternoon at the house, stretching into evening, night. She'd begun to think – for the second time in her life – that she'd never get out. Away.

Remembering that night was like turning the pages in a flicker book, its details blurred and jerky. She remembered the smell, and the way her shoes stuck to the floor in the kitchen . . .

Heat shivered behind her eyes. She lifted her arm, sniffing at her sleeve.

The smell of the secure unit was in her clothes and hair. She'd be carrying it on her skin for days, like prison ink. No escape.

Her phone buzzed at her hip. She pulled it from her pocket and peered at the display.

A text, from Ed: *Here if you need me.*

She bent her forehead, pressing it to the phone's small screen. She'd made a promise to herself five years ago that she wouldn't reach for Ed until she was sure it wasn't panic or despair making her reach. More than once she'd come close to inviting him in, for more than coffee. He liked her; she knew that. It wasn't ego on her part, and anyway it was mutual. She was attracted to him. Right now, if she made a move, it would be a smash-and-grab one-night stand. It wasn't worth ruining their friendship, to satisfy her skin's aching for someone else's touch.

She stood and straightened all the cushions on the sofa, shaking and knocking the shape of her body from each square in turn, before putting it all back in place. By the time she was done, she was out of breath. When she switched off the lights, shadows stole back the living space. She moved through the flat soundlessly, undressing and standing for a long minute in front of the wardrobe mirror.

No mythical creatures. No pierced hearts, or entwined roses, or barbed wire. Just words. Because words hurt. Specifically, they hurt when inked across your ribcage and at the sharp points of your eighteen-year-hips.

*Shall I kill myself, or make a cup of coffee?* Two lines, parallel, across the last two ribs on the right side.

On the other side of her ribcage: *An invincible summer.*

*Places of exile . . .* across her left hip.

And curved around the bony jut of her right hip, *I had the whole sky in my eyes, and it was blue and gold.*

Pretentious, post-teen genuflection. The invincible summer when she read too much Albert Camus, and decided to make a statement on her skin. That should've been the end of it. But after Stephen Keele stabbed her parents to death, she found herself craving the peculiar, indulgent torture of the tattoo parlour. Like being punctured by a pencil lead, over and over again. The tattooist keeps wiping away ink and blood with a sterile cloth, which hurts even worse than the needle itself, as if he's scrubbing a freshly skinned knee then skinning it again, scrubbing it, skinning it, over and over. Each stage of the process has its distinct pain. The needle. The scrubbing. The day when the bandages come off, and the ink begins drying under the skin and it starts to feel like slapped sunburn. She had to treat her skin like a baby's: washing it and keeping it moisturised. Keeping clothes away from it. Not scratching, that was the hardest part of all. Scratch and you end up pulling the ink right out of the skin, so the whole thing'll have been for nothing. Religiously, she scooped soft water over the tattoos, day and night, patting them dry with more tenderness than she'd shown her body before or since, lavishing lotion, blowing cool air like kisses.

Of course, it was about punishment. She'd never bothered denying that. Except for that first time. At eighteen, it'd been about rebellion, a shocking secret she was keeping from Greg and Lisa Rome, the hidden skin she brought to the family dinner table, under layers of dark clothes. She liked the ritual of it. The lesson in accepting – relishing – small amounts of pain. An exercise in self-control. More than that, it was her insurance against intimacy. No casual sex, unless she wanted to explain the tattoos. She tried to imagine Ed's reaction to the neat lines of ink that ran coyly across her hips, emphasising their narrowness, her lack of curves. She couldn't come close to imagining his reaction, drawing a blank that matched the pale spaces between the lines of text.

How did Hope Proctor feel, facing her skin each morning? The tattoo which matched Leo's, embellished by the bruises he'd branded on her with his fists.

Marnie turned from the mirror and switched off the light, finding the bed, its pillows unnervingly soft under her head. She didn't set the alarm clock, not wanting the sudden noise snapping at her in the morning. Instead she told herself, 'You need to wake early. Six o'clock.' Her subconscious, more reliable than any alarm, took custody of the instruction.

*I had the whole sky in my eyes, and it was blue and gold.*

She'd been twenty-six. He was twelve. Stephen Keele. Watching her undress, in that house, on a rare visit home to her parents and their new foster son. Two years before the murders.

She shivered at the thought of Stephen's eyes reading her skin. She was afraid to dream, in case he was waiting for her. She could feel his stare, crouching in the corner of the room. Watching.

Her phone woke her from semi-sleep, red whorls in the blackness, at 5.25 a.m.

'You asked for news of Leo Proctor's progress.' It was the doctor from the North Middlesex. 'He's conscious. By the time you're at work, he should be fit to answer questions about what happened.'

'How's Hope?'

'Comfortable. We haven't told her the news about her husband. Hard to say how she'll take it. I thought you might like to be the one to break the news.'

## 23

Row after row of windows, scalded by pollution, stared out from the brick facade of the North Middlesex hospital.

Noah Jake climbed from the Mondeo with Ed Belloc and Simone Bissell while Marnie Rome drove away from the main entrance, in search of parking. A thin rain was spitting, cold and spiky. Simone didn't have a coat, just a shoulder bag, soft cloth printed with sunflowers. Ed took her inside. Noah followed.

A sleek desk formed the front line for the hospital's Information Centre. Severe strip-lighting, the visual equivalent of nails across a blackboard, cross-hatched the ceiling. Simone pushed her hands into the sleeves of her jumper. 'I need the bathroom.'

The woman at the desk pointed her to the left.

Ed Belloc touched a hand to Noah's elbow. 'You okay?'

Noah glanced at him in surprise. 'I'm fine.' He realised he was squaring his shoulders, and that his nose was pinched shut. He relaxed. Smiled. 'I was thinking about Ayana. This business with her brothers . . .'

'You're asking her to give up her hiding place,' Ed said. 'The first place she's felt safe. That's not going to be easy for her.'

'I understand that, but I want them punished for what they did. Nasif and the others.'

'It's a natural reaction.' Ed hadn't stopped watching the bathroom door, on the lookout for Simone's return.

'I could go and see if she's okay,' Noah offered.

Ed's eyes travelled past him, to the main entrance. 'Rome's here,' he said with relief. He smiled at Noah. 'Best if she does it.'

Marnie returned from the lavatory with Simone. The four of them went on foot to the third-floor ward, where beds were separated by limp curtains on metal rails. In the bed next to Hope's, a huge woman with a sunken face was moaning over a crossword. An oxygen mask made her eyes misty. Her breathing was scruffy, difficult.

DC Abby Pike was seated at a discreet distance from Hope's bed. She stood up when she saw DI Rome, coming across to meet them.

'How's she been?' Marnie asked in a low voice.

'Quiet. Sleeping, mostly. Worried about how Leo's doing.'

'Why don't you take a break? We're going to be here a while.'

'Thanks, boss.' Abby gave Noah and Ed a big smile, a softer version for Simone, before leaving the ward.

Simone sat on the chair next to Hope's bed. A blue Aertex blanket covered Hope's legs. They'd propped her upright with pillows. The effect was of a rag doll artfully arranged.

Ed and Marnie stood at the foot of the bed, not moving any closer. Simone drew Hope's hand from under the sheet and held it. The two women spoke in whispers, just loud enough for Noah and the others to hear.

'I've missed you,' Simone said. 'I've been so worried about you.'

'I'm all right.' Hope's hand was loose and unresponsive in Simone's grip.

'Detective Inspector?' A doctor beckoned from two beds down.

Marnie left Ed's side and walked over to where the man was waiting. The doctor told her something, too quietly for Noah to catch the words over the hospital radio that was streaming music into the ward. From her bed, Hope Proctor watched them with an intensity that made Simone turn her head to see what was going on.

Marnie's mouth had pressed shut. Noah knew that look, it meant trouble. The doctor turned and walked back down the ward, without looking at any of the patients. Marnie nodded at Noah to come with her. Ed didn't need a prompt to stay with Simone and Hope. Noah and Marnie followed the doctor out of the ward.

In the corridor, Noah said, 'Hope seems a little better.' It wasn't strictly true, but he wanted to get Marnie talking.

She shot him a look. 'She's a mess.' She didn't stop moving, following the doctor up a flight of stairs.

Noah had to lengthen his stride to keep up. 'Are we going to charge him?'

'We need her to give evidence. You heard what Ed said about these women. The longer the abuse lasts, the less chance of the victim pressing charges. You can get used to anything, apparently.'

'But if *she's* facing charges over the stabbing . . .? What will it be, attempted murder? Manslaughter? She could go to prison, for years. Won't her solicitor persuade her to give evidence against Leo, as part of her defence?'

'He'll try. We'll all try. You saw how quick she was to take the blame, back at the refuge. Entrenched victim mentality.'

The doctor had gone ahead, but he came to a halt now, waiting for them.

Marnie told Noah, 'Leo's awake. Let's see what he's got to say.'

## 24

She was here, in the hospital. He'd seen her, he'd fucking *seen* her.

Sweat crawled all over his body like a rash. He sat doubled up at the wheel of the car, *I ♥ London* cap pulled low, heart punching in his chest.

This was it. This—

From the back seat, the sound started up, as if it'd been waiting for him to get this near, as if it *knew*.

A thready whine, like a fly on loudspeaker, sounding like you could mute it with a swat of your hand, but you couldn't. You could only make it worse.

He swung round in the seat anyway, furious because *she was here*.

This was his chance, maybe the only one he'd get.

The whine climbed higher, scraping at the inside of his skull.

'Shut up,' he threatened. 'Shut up or she won't be the only one getting what she deserves.'

## 25

Leo Proctor looked less sick than his wife did, despite the trauma of surgery to repair a hole in his lung. The blood transfusion had left him flushed, pink-cheeked. He was bigger than Noah remembered, with the look of a one-time sportsman run to seed. A pad of fat sat under his chin, jowls waiting in the wings of his face. Watery eyes, pale brown, fixed painfully on Noah and Marnie.

Marnie showed her badge, standing by the side of his bed.

Leo shut his eyes, then opened them again. 'Where's Hope?' he whispered.

'She's safe,' Marnie said. 'She's with a doctor.'

The cool tone she used underlined the implication: *We know what you did.*

Leo wet his lips with the tip of his tongue. 'Is she . . . okay?'

'She's exactly as you left her.'

Noah took a step back, as discreetly as he could, in order to get a better perspective on Marnie and the man in the bed. 'She didn't mean to do it,' Leo whispered.

'*She* didn't mean to do it?'

'The knife . . .' Leo wet his lips again.

'Hope didn't mean to stab you. Is that what you're saying?'

101

It took Proctor a moment to process the acid in her voice. His eyes slid away, staying down. He closed his hands into fists. His head bent forward, his mouth drooping at the corners. A caricature of shame. He knew that they knew.

Marnie said briskly, 'There's some confusion over the knife.' Leo didn't look at her. 'Did you take the knife into the refuge?'

Noah hid his surprise by pretending an interest in the chart at the foot of the bed. If Proctor made a confession under these circumstances, the CPS would almost certainly discount it. He was in pain, on medication, in a hospital bed. It was a measure of Marnie's bad mood: asking questions that might muddy a conviction. Until they could prove otherwise, Leo Proctor was the victim here.

'Yes . . .'

'Yes, you took the knife into the refuge. Why did you do that?'

Leo's chin was on his chest. He mumbled something that sounded like, 'For her.'

Marnie folded her arms, turning her head away from the bed. She caught Noah's eye, and flinched a little. Then she looked back at Leo Proctor. 'Why was Hope in the refuge?' She used her blandest voice.

'I . . . don't know.'

'You don't know. Why do most women go to refuges, do you know that?'

Proctor drew a shattered breath. 'To . . . escape.' He raised his head. His eyes were wet. 'To get away.'

'What was Hope escaping from?' He was silent. 'Was it you, Mr Proctor? Was she escaping from you?'

Leo didn't answer. Tears crawled down his flushed cheeks. Marnie took a sheet of paper from her pocket and smoothed it flat, holding it where Leo could see it. 'Did you write this letter to your wife, Mr Proctor?'

'No.' A whisper, thick with tears. 'No.'

'This isn't your handwriting?' She put the letter away, staring down at the man in the bed. 'You hurt her, didn't you? You beat her, and you raped her. You had her branded, for pity's sake; I've heard about the matching tattoos . . . It got so bad she finally worked up the nerve to leave. Did you try to find her? She wasn't very far away. Then she called, to let you know that she was safe. That's when you knew for certain where she was. How did it feel, knowing she got away? That she was with other abused women, swapping stories about abuse. About you. You didn't like that, did you?'

Her voice remained bland despite the agitation of the man in the bed. The blandness made it worse, as if she was reading a witness statement or a charge sheet. 'You took a knife, and you bought roses. Because that's how it goes with men like you. Roses in one hand, a knife in the other, or were the roses an afterthought? An extravagance. She wouldn't be expecting roses, not from you. Not your style. Nothing says "I love you" like a broken rib.' She stopped, at last.

Leo was weeping openly, his chest heaving, face collapsed under the flood of tears.

Noah couldn't look at him. He couldn't look at Marnie, either. He was sorry for the man in the bed, and ashamed of Marnie's tactics. After all that she'd taught him about the CPS, about evidence-gathering.

He made himself think of Hope, lying like a broken doll downstairs. Maybe he should be pleased to see Leo Proctor reduced to tears, but . . .

He'd helped save Leo's life. Fuck it, he'd *fought* to save the man's life.

This wasn't right. He made himself stay where he was, at the foot of Leo's bed, but he didn't want to be here, in any part of the hospital. He didn't want to be the person backing up Marnie Rome's strategy for putting this right.

# 26

Marnie caught up with Noah Jake in the corridor. He was studying the view from the window. Rain pocked the glass by his head. He looked up when she approached, his face thinned by censure.

'He's admitted taking the knife to the refuge,' she said. 'That gives us intent.'

Noah put his hands in his pockets. A muscle played in his cheek. 'Nothing he tells us right now is safe. For one thing, he's doped to the eyeballs.'

'He took the knife to the refuge,' she repeated. 'Why do you think he did that?'

'I don't know. That's the point, isn't it? We don't know. Not yet. And why ask him about the letter, when Hope told you it was written to Simone?'

'Because I don't know if that's the truth or if Hope's covering for him. The letter plus the knife makes a damning case – and I *know* she's protecting him. Because she's traumatised. Terrorised. You didn't speak with the doctor who examined her. Her injuries tell us she was abused for years. Raped, for years.'

Noah's eyes darkened reflexively. 'They don't tell us *who* was abusing and raping her.'

She wanted to shock him over to her side. 'Eight months ago, when Hope was living at home, Leo broke his hand. A boxer's injury, the doctors call it. You know what that is?' She closed her fist, showing it to him. 'You get it from punching someone.'

'He works in construction. He could've broken his hand at work. Or playing rugby.'

'And his wife's injuries are just a coincidence? Come on, it was him. He's a bully and a coward. We both know it.'

'That's not enough, though, is it? You're always telling me we need hard evidence, to build a proper case. What you just did in there—'

She cut him short. 'You didn't like it. Good for you. Feel free to file a complaint against me.'

Noah raised a quick smile, the way a child raises a hand to fend off a slap.

Marnie turned away before he could reply, heading back down the stairs to the ward where Ed was waiting. She was in the wrong, and she knew it, but she had no intention of stopping, or retracting the words she'd spoken to Leo Proctor to reduce him to tears. Her one regret was that she had to tell Hope that the man who'd made her life a living hell was alive and kicking.

Someone had closed the curtains around Hope's bed. There was no sign of Ed.

Marnie came to a standstill. 'Hope?' No response. 'Simone?' Nothing.

She drew the curtain and looked inside the cubicle.

The chair where Simone had been sitting was empty.

So was the bed.

# 27

'Hope Proctor,' Marnie said to the woman in the next bed, 'did you see her leave?'

The woman tapped at the oxygen mask over her mouth, and shook her head.

Where was Ed? Marnie pulled out her phone as Ed and Noah came through the swing doors. Ed was carrying a hospital gown and robe. 'I've alerted hospital security.' He was grey with worry. 'But it looks like they've gone.'

'Both of them?'

'Together. Hope wanted the bathroom. Simone said she'd take her. They looked safe. Hope was in her robe.' Ed shook his head, putting the robe and gown on the bed. 'Simone must've had a set of clothes in her bag. I'm sorry—'

Marnie cut him short, looking at Noah. 'Speak to security. Tell them we need CCTV from the exits and entrances. And find Abby Pike.'

Noah nodded, and went.

Ed shook his head. 'I should've stayed with them . . . Jesus, Rome, I'm so sorry.'

'Don't be. I should've checked Simone's bag. And I shouldn't have told Abby Pike to take a break.' Her palms

106

pricked with sweat. Her armpits too. 'I'm in charge here, not you.' She crouched to check the cabinet next to Hope's bed, needing to hide her face from Ed, just for a minute, until she had it together.

'How's Leo?' Ed asked.

'Awake. That's what the doctor wanted to tell me.'

'Do you think Hope guessed as much?'

'Yes, I do.' The cabinet was empty. She straightened and turned to face him. 'But it doesn't explain why Simone brought clothes. *Before* she knew he was awake. She was planning this escape. She must've been.'

Ed pushed his hands into his hair. 'Damn,' he said. Then again, with more feeling, '*Damn*.'

'Don't,' she snapped. 'I need your help here. Do the freaking-out on your own time.'

His look of injury made her flinch, just as Noah's disapproval had, in Leo Proctor's room upstairs. She softened her voice: 'I need your help. You need to tell me about Simone, the sort of person she is, where she might go.'

Ed nodded. 'I'll give you whatever I can, but I can't believe she's done this. She's the last person I'd have expected to do something crazy.'

'Crazy would've been leaving on an impulse, with Hope in her hospital gown.' Marnie pointed at the discarded gown and robe on the bed. 'This was planned.'

'Taking a sick woman out of hospital . . .' Ed shook his head. 'I thought Simone had more sense. She can be forceful, I knew that, but I never thought she'd take a risk with someone else's health.'

'Perhaps she thought she was doing the best thing for her friend.'

'I should've stayed outside the bathroom door.' Ed was still beating himself up. 'But I didn't want them to feel under armed guard.'

Simone had counted on Ed's chivalry and that angered Marnie, but she was the one who'd sent Abby Pike off duty. Abby would've gone into the bathroom with the women. Hope would've returned to bed. What had Simone said, to make Hope run? If Hope had confided in her, told Simone that she saw a chance to stop Leo's abuse and took it . . .

What then?

'How's Hope going to manage physically?' Ed asked. 'You said the medical exam made grim reading.'

'No recent injuries, or nothing debilitating. The CT scan was clear. I'm more concerned about her mental state. Which bathroom did they use? Where did Hope get changed?'

'The bathroom you fetched Simone from, when we first arrived.'

'She was checking it out,' Marnie realised. 'I found her testing the locks on the doors, thought it was a privacy thing. *Stupid.*'

She'd been stupid since Saturday. The visit to Sommerville had left her fretful, squeamish. She'd exorcised some of it upstairs, giving Leo Proctor a taste of his own medicine, but she was in danger of making more mistakes, worse ones. She was hitting out at random – to see what lit up and what broke.

Ed was staying close. As if she might need him to catch her, in the event she tripped over her own feet. His vigilance made her want to shove him away. 'You're going to tell me everything you know about Simone Bissell. Forget about confidentiality, and the need to allow these women their secrets. I'd say Simone knew exactly how to exploit your respect for her privacy, wouldn't you?'

## 28

'Anything?'

Abby Pike was out of breath, her face flushed from running. 'Nothing.'

'Let's try the bus stop. Maybe someone saw them get on a bus.' Noah wasn't hopeful. He kept remembering what Marnie had said about the way these women lived without leaving a trace. It was as if Hope and Simone had vanished into the hospital's sterile air. He remembered the intense way Hope had studied the doctor's face when he was telling Marnie that Leo was awake. Could Hope lip-read? Perhaps she didn't need to. She'd known the chances were in favour of her husband's recovery. She'd known what that might mean.

No one at the bus stop had seen an African woman with braided hair, or a blonde woman answering to Hope's description.

'We'd better check back in with the boss.' Abby glanced at Noah. 'Who're you calling?'

'Ron Carling, back at the station. He's checking the CCTV from the refuge.' Noah nodded at the street cameras. 'He can check this lot, too.'

\*  \*  \*

When they returned to the ward, DI Rome was talking to a man in a cheap suit with a guarded expression. From the hospital's administrative team, Noah guessed.

'She wasn't under arrest,' Abby whispered to Noah. 'What does that mean?'

'The hospital hadn't discharged her. They'll implement their missing persons procedure. Effectively, she's gone AWOL.'

'I don't get it,' Abby said. 'Why would Simone persuade her to run? She wasn't in any fit state, for one thing.'

'Her husband's just woken up.'

'Shit. Do you think she knew that?'

'She knew there was a good chance of it.'

Abby pulled her jacket on, buttoning its front. 'She didn't look well enough to walk out of here, let alone run. Wish I hadn't taken that break. If I'd stayed here . . .'

'The DI told you to take a break. Ed Belloc was with them.'

'Poor bloke,' Abby whispered. 'Looks like she gave him a right bollocking.'

Noah glanced at Ed. Abby was right; Marnie had chewed chunks out of him. It made Noah reluctant to share the news that no one had seen Simone or Hope leave the hospital. Unless the street CCTV yielded a clue, they were screwed.

'AWOL means we can bring her back, right?' Abby dusted lint from the front of her jacket. 'Even though she wasn't under arrest?'

'If we can find her.'

Marnie saw the pair of them and jerked her head for Noah. He walked over, with Abby following. The man in the cheap suit turned to look. They all did. Only Ed Belloc had any hope in his eyes. Noah shook his head. 'The hospital's CCTV shows them leaving by the front entrance at 11.37 a.m., towards Bull Lane. There's a bus stop on Bridport Road, but no one remembers seeing them boarding a bus.'

'That's London for you. Everyone minding his own

business.' The hospital administrator sounded resigned, uninterested in the women's fate. He'd tackled worse, in all likelihood. At least Hope Proctor wasn't recovering from surgery, or psychotic.

Noah said, 'I've asked the station to start looking at street CCTV.'

'Well, good luck.' The hospital bureaucrat waited a moment, then took his leave.

Marnie said, 'I'm treating this as abduction.'

'On what basis?' Ed Belloc looked like someone had wrung him out. 'Simone's not an abductor.'

'I don't know what she is or isn't. That's what you're going to tell us. Abduction will get us more manpower than missing persons. We don't know that Hope went willingly. Abby, you've spent more time with her than any of us. What do you think?'

'She stayed in her bed, sleeping mostly. I tried talking to her, but she wasn't keen. Didn't want to listen to music, or read. I offered to get her a magazine or a newspaper, but she said no thanks, she wasn't interested.'

'How was she with the staff?'

'Very quiet and polite, did as she was told, said thanks a lot.' Abby lowered her voice. 'Some of the women make a fuss about food, or bed changes. Not Hope. I'd be surprised if she enjoyed the meals, but she ate everything. Kept saying she didn't want to be a trouble to anyone.' It was easy to imagine, from the description she gave, that Hope Proctor would've gone with Simone Bissell just because Simone told her to.

Marnie nodded at Abby. 'Call it in, and get things started. We'd better check the refuge in case they went back there, but it's a long shot.' She looked at Ed. 'Does Simone Bissell go by any other names?'

It was a routine question; Noah doubted whether Marnie

expected any answer other than no, but Ed Belloc said, 'Nasiche Auma.'

They all looked at him. Noah heard Marnie suppressing a sigh.

Ed spelt the name out for Abby Pike, who wrote it down. 'She was adopted by a British couple, who renamed her. She's a British citizen. As far as I know, she only uses Simone Bissell.'

Ed was reluctant even now to break confidence with the woman he'd been trying to help. 'She was born in Uganda. Nasiche Auma is her birth name.'

# 29

'Nasiche Auma was born in the Apac district of northern Uganda in 1988. She doesn't know exactly when, or exactly where. She believes the couple who adopted her altered her birth certificate. They were aid workers. Charles and Pauline Bissell.'

Ed put his hands on the cafeteria table. 'This is the story as she told it to me. I believed it at the time. I still do, but I've not had it independently verified.' He looked at Marnie. 'In case that's important.'

She nodded. 'Go on.'

Noah made notes as Ed continued with the story. He felt sorry for Ed. Marnie's mood hadn't improved, or not conspicuously.

'Her village was a recruiting ground for the Lord's Resistance Army, who took all Simone's brothers before she was six years old. At the time of her birth, the LRA had taken around three thousand children. They trained the boys to fight. The girls they sold to arms dealers as sex slaves, or kept them for themselves.' Ed paused. 'This part is certainly true. There's plenty of independent evidence about the LRA and its crimes against children in northern Uganda, the Congo and elsewhere. Although it's reported to be getting better, in recent months.' He drew a breath. 'Pauline and Charles Bissell, a British couple, took Nasiche from her village to the Apac hospital, on the pretext that her eyesight was suffering because of poor nutrition. Really, they wanted to save her from the LRA's recruiters. They flew her home to London, where they adopted her. She hasn't been home, or seen her birth family since.'

'How did she end up in the refuge?' Marnie asked.

'I'm getting to that. You need to know her story to understand how she ended up in the refuge.' Ed straightened his spine in the chair. 'She was ten when she came to London. The Bissells had money. They sent her to private school, paid for extra tuition to help her learn English quickly, took her to ballet classes at the weekends.' He glanced at the window, a stitch of concentration between his eyes. 'Nasiche means *born in the locust season*. She knew it was her name, although the Bissells never used it. They were worried the school wouldn't be able to pronounce it properly, that it'd get in the way of her making friends. She was always Simone, in England.' He waited while an elderly couple went slowly past the table, to find a seat beside the cafeteria window.

Marnie had elected to remain in the hospital, chiefly to be close to Leo Proctor in order to get permission to search the Proctors' house. A call to Jeanette Conway had confirmed that Hope and Simone hadn't returned to the refuge. No one knew where to look for them. Marnie thought the Proctors' house was a long shot, but she wanted to rule it out. Getting a warrant would take too long. Quicker to shame Leo into giving his permission, but they needed the cooperation of the medical staff, who weren't too pleased with the state of their patient after the first round of police questions.

'The Bissells wanted Simone to study medicine,' Ed continued. 'They dreamt of her returning to Uganda as a grown woman, a qualified doctor. They spent a lot of time educating her about the brutality of the LRA, the desperate state of affairs in Uganda. I think they spent a lot *less* time making Simone feel loved, or independent. She told me they were controlling, took all her decisions for her. I think she blamed them for what happened when she left them – they never encouraged her to develop her own judgement, or to make choices. It left her wide open to what happened next.

'She dropped out of school when she was seventeen, started hanging around with a street gang, self-harming . . . She told me it was a way of connecting to the life she would've lived if she'd stayed in the village, in Uganda. The Bissells hit the roof. They fought with her. Simone accused them of being tyrants, said the LRA may as well have recruited her. I think if they'd said they loved her, or if they'd talked to her about how lonely she felt, things might've worked out differently. As it was, they fought. She packed a bag and left.'

Ed broke off to drink from a bottle of mineral water. It was hot in the cafeteria, the air parched by central heating. 'She lived rough for a while. Her survival instincts were rusty, after nine years of being mollycoddled, but she soon sharpened up. She didn't get into any trouble, knew how to avoid danger. Instinctively, or so she thought. The way she described it to me . . . like a war zone under her skin . . . and *shame*. She talked about shame, before anything else happened. Survivor guilt. She'd escaped, that was how she saw it. The rest of her village, the kids she'd played with, they'd be soldiers now. She tried to feel like a soldier, to convince herself she could survive on the streets. Maybe she would've done, if she'd stayed on the streets.' Ed turned the bottle of water between his hands. 'She fell in with a boy.' He stopped, looking at the notebook in which Noah was recording the conversation.

'His name?' Marnie prompted. 'I'll worry about protocol once we've found her.'

'Lowell Paton,' Ed said. 'He'd run away from home, he said, because his parents were drinking, fighting all the time. Simone realised plenty of kids had it worse than she did, but she couldn't face going home. "I was too proud", that was how she put it. She and Lowell became friends. They looked out for each other, took it in turns to try to find work, because a couple always looks dodgy. Sometimes it's better to be single.'

Ed's face shadowed. 'One day Lowell came back with a big grin on his face, saying he'd found a security job in a block of flats. New-build, "proper posh". He said they could doss down in one of the empty flats. Simone didn't ask how a homeless teenager got a job involving keys, security. She went with him, moved into a studio in the basement, just a small place but with hot water, heating. It looked like heaven. They slept on the floor, on a mattress Lowell found in the lock-up next door. Simone went to investigate, came back with sticks of furniture, plates and cups, a kettle and toaster. At the end of the first week, she had the flat looking like a proper place. She had some of the savings she'd taken when she left the Bissells, and she bought food, cooked a chicken. Lowell said it was the best meal he'd eaten in ages. Simone joked that if he wanted to thank her, he could do the washing-up.'

Ed rolled his neck as if it hurt. 'That's when he hit her the first time. Not a little slap, no build-up. He punched her, broke her nose. Then he made her go to the kitchen and wash the dishes with blood running down her face.'

He was silent for a long minute. Neither Noah nor Marnie spoke. Eventually, Ed said, 'It went on like that for over a year. She couldn't get away. He had the keys to the apartment, kept her locked up. She finally figured out that he wasn't a homeless kid. He wasn't even a kid. He was twenty-one. His dad owned the company responsible for selling the flats in the new-build. Sales weren't going well. It was company policy not to show the studio flat, because it was so small. Lowell had a set of keys, could come and go as he pleased. There were no neighbours to hear Simone if she screamed. She didn't dare to, most of the time. He'd hit her without provocation – kept hitting her – and she began to believe he'd kill her. The longer he kept her in the flat, the more certain she became that he'd do it, because what other way out did he have?'

'No one checked the flat in over a year?' Noah was incredulous.

'That's what she said. She'd sometimes hear voices, or hammering. She found out later that the building regulators delayed the licences needed for the sale of residential premises. The materials hadn't passed a safety inspection. Effectively, she was living in a condemned building.'

'He was abusing her,' Marnie said, 'the whole time?'

'He told her he loved her, bought her presents – jewellery and her favourite flowers – enough to make her doubt what was really happening. When he wasn't doing that, he was beating her. Classic abuse.'

'How did she get away?'

'She stopped eating and lost a lot of weight, persuaded him she needed a doctor. She was afraid he'd panic and leave her there to die, but she didn't know what else to try. She'd tried pleading, promising not to press charges, giving him what he wanted – "Sex, he always wanted sex" – but nothing worked. He didn't get her a doctor, but he did get more relaxed about turning his back on her. He'd been very careful up to that point, never giving her the chance to run, or to attack him. When she'd lost a couple of stone, he still wanted sex, but he stopped hitting her. He started to say she

117

disgusted him. He didn't know why he bothered with her. She was bony, her breath stank . . .'

Ed drew a short breath. 'He'd liked raping her during her period, but her periods stopped because of the weight loss. This made him angry at first, then annoyed. He stopped caring whether she wept when he raped her. One night he drank himself to sleep and she was able to take the keys and leave.'

'Why didn't she go to the police?' Marnie asked.

'She did. They said she was too confused to give a proper account of what'd happened. She was hallucinating. They took her to hospital. She had a body-mass index of fifteen. The hospital diagnosed severe malnutrition and admitted her as an emergency. When the police went back to question her, she refused to talk to them. They decided she was too traumatised to cooperate. That's when they called me. She wouldn't speak to me either, not for a long time. I found her a place in the refuge. Eventually she started to feel safe, but it took a long time.'

Marnie waited in silence when Ed stopped speaking. Out of respect, Noah guessed, for the horror he had unfolded. 'You said she had a particular reason to fear knives,' she said then. 'Did Lowell cut her? If he had a blood kink . . .'

'No, it's about the only thing he didn't do.' Ed gathered a fresh breath. The telling of Simone's story was hurting him; deep lines scored either side of his mouth. 'When she was eight, she was circumcised. By her mother and another woman.'

Noah could hear an empty, outraged ringing in his head.

'What happened to Lowell?' Marnie asked in an unforgiving tone. 'Was he arrested?'

'And later released, without charge. The studio flat was empty, no trace that anyone had lived there. I'm guessing Lowell's father helped to tidy up.' Ed wrung a smile from his mouth. 'Assuming, of course, that Simone's story was true.'

'What reason would she have for lying?'

'None that I can see. A refuge is a last resort. No one would choose to go there unless they were desperate.'

'She didn't want to go home?'

'To the Bissells? She didn't think of it as home.'

'They didn't try and find her, when she first ran away?'

'I think they must've done. Simone said they were afraid of the adoption being challenged, because it wasn't legal. I looked into it, and as far as the law's concerned, she's a British citizen and their daughter. They notified the police when she left home. She was in the missing persons database for a year. The Bissells tried to visit her in the hospital, but she wouldn't see them. She didn't want them knowing the address of the refuge.'

'Had they abused her?' Marnie asked.

'She wouldn't say. I doubt there was physical abuse, but she was a traumatised ten-year-old when they took her from Uganda. From what she said, they started the school and ballet classes almost the second she arrived in London. They never spoke about her village, unless it was to say how she might return there when she was a doctor. They never spoke about the circumcision, although Mrs Bissell knew what Simone's mother had done. They seemed to think it was politically incorrect to judge the customs of another country, even when those customs involved mutilating young girls.' Ed moved his mouth tenderly, as if it hurt him. 'Simone said she felt gagged, forbidden from being Nasiche, after ten years of being her. The Bissells didn't seek help for her, to recover from the trauma of leaving her village, or for what happened when she was eight. That qualifies as neglect, in my book.'

'Do you think the Bissells abducted her?' Noah asked. 'Or were the birth parents complicit?'

119

'Hard to say. Simone doesn't know. I'm not sure which would be worse.'

'She didn't feel that the Bissells were rescuing her?' Marnie said. 'After what happened with her birth mother?'

'If she did, she never expressed it that way to me.' Ed ghosted a smile. 'You think that's what was in her mind today. That she was rescuing Hope.'

'Perhaps. What do you think?'

'She's been in the refuge for more than three years. Hope's the first person she's been close to and it happened in – what? Three weeks? You said Hope had only been there three weeks. That's what I can't believe.'

'There's been nothing like this before? In the three years you've known her.'

Ed shook his head emphatically. 'Nothing. She's been reliable, helpful, loyal . . . And now I sound patronising, as well as gullible.' It was going to take a long time for him to get over the shock of Simone repaying his trust with deceit.

'We need to talk to Ayana and the others,' Noah said, 'about how close they really were. Hope and Simone.'

'And if they were planning to run.' Marnie got to her feet, touching a hand briefly to Ed's shoulder. 'You'd better get back to work. Can we give you a lift?'

'I'd rather come with you to the refuge,' Ed said. 'Let me help you talk with the women. I can do that.'

'Okay.' Marnie nodded. 'Let's meet there. Noah, we should swing by the station. There's something we need to do.'

# 30

That fucking sound, a thready mewling from the back seat.

'Shut up,' he snarled under his breath, then rapped the words aloud: 'Shut up!'

The mewling rose in pitch, clawing at the exposed nape of his neck. He tried counting to ten, getting as far as seven before the noise started up again.

It was the soundtrack to his day: a constant nails-on-a-blackboard reminder of how she – they, the lot of them – had him by the balls.

He punched a fist at the dashboard. 'Shut up! Shut the fuck up!'

He punched until the plastic groaned and the skin split at his knuckles, blood springing up in a beaded line.

'You little shits!' He wrenched around, showing his spoiled fist, bunched and bleeding. 'Look what you did!'

The twins, strapped into matching child seats, stared back at him with round eyes and mouths, surprised into silence for a second until – in stereo – they began again, the same soundtrack as before, pulling air into their small lungs, expelling it in bellows.

Their fault he'd lost the women. Lost *her*. He'd been right on her tail, not believing his luck when he saw her come out of the hospital, with her little friend.

The friend was a problem, but not a major one. He wasn't scared of that. They moved too fast, though, knew how to lose themselves in the crowd. Bitches. Then the twins had started up . . .

He'd lost her. Because of the fucking twins. He could smell their sour-milk breath. Freya's stink, second-hand, the ruined breasts she wouldn't let him touch, always sore after the twins' feasting. 'Shut up, you greedy little bastards.'

He'd watched them in the hospital, struggling to survive. Born too soon. In Perspex cradles, his heart bursting, willing them to fill their lungs, to live . . .

*Loving* them past the point of bearing. Such a long time ago. A lifetime. He didn't recognise these two squat monsters behind him, strapped into trendy car seats that cost more than he earned easily in a week – and he *had* earned money easily. Everything had been easy, once. Until the twins.

'They'll change your life.' All his mates had said that.

He hadn't known it was a warning.

If it weren't for the twins, he'd never have gone to that nightclub six months ago, after a bit of peace and quiet. A change of scene, something to remind him how life had been, before. That fucking dump with its mirror-balled ceiling and its concrete walls, the promise of cheap cocktails and free sex, guilt-free. One Night Stan's: that was where he met her. The bitch that took his life and turned it inside out.

He balled his fist and licked at the split knuckles, feeling a sluggish tug in his crotch at the familiar taste.

'Shut up,' he muttered again, under his breath, but this time he wasn't sure whether the threat was for the twins, or himself.

# 31

*Six months ago*

Under the spinning strobe light in the club is where he first sees her. The light is punchy, blue. Strips the colour from her skin. She could be any age. Anyone.

It isn't his idea. He doesn't make the first move. True, he's in a bruising mood, slammed out of the house an hour earlier, sick to the pit with Freya and the twins. No one tells you the half of it, the new-father thing, afraid it'll put paid to the human race, probably. The sleepless nights, sure, everyone has a sob story about that. But no one tells you about the fear, the gutting knife that gets you under the balls whenever they start up. No one tells you about that sound, like tearing tissue paper, when babies turn over in their cots and you hold your breath, begging for the screaming not to start, because if it does, it'll never stop, it'll last all night and longer.

Six weeks in and it's his turn to feed them, to get up and fumble in the fridge for the bottle she expressed before she went to bed. Last night he worked a double shift, was dog-tired. Groaned when they started up – groaned and turned away to bury his head in her breasts. Except that's not allowed, he's not allowed to be tired, or to groan when she's been with them *all bloody day*. She shoved him off, too sore to be touched. The nails on her toes, uncut in eight months, scratched like razors at his shin.

Tonight's different. Tonight, he's escaped for an hour, because if he stayed he'd break something and they can't afford to replace anything; they're saving up for a double buggy. Double everything.

Under the strobe light in the club, her skin shows welted and purple. Just a glimpse, when she leans towards him and the neck of her T-shirt gapes open, showing thin stripes on the colourless skin across the top of her ribs.

On either side of them, couples kiss and grope, noisily. The whole place stinks of pheromones; a man not much younger than him has both hands up the bandage skirt of a girl who can't be more than eighteen. It's obscene. Desperate.

It turns him on.

Not the groping. The disgust and shame: things he associates with sex, now. Since the twins, okay, he can't get it up at home. First, Freya's too sore – stitches, bleeding, the works – then, when she was ready, they're both too bloody tired, and those tits – Christ. Leaking when the twins cry, stinking of milk, the same putrid-sweet smell as their puke. He can't do it. Can't get it up. Be a man.

Under the strobe lights, *her* tits are small and hard. More like muscle than fat.

She smells of clean sweat and money. Coins.

It's not until hours later, in the hotel room, that he discovers the coppery smell is blood.

# 32

*Five years ago*

The therapist, Lexie, sits perched on a footstool, hugging her knees. Her hair is corn-coloured and cut in spikes around her small ears. She wears a green tunic with cropped leggings, flat leather sandals that show off painted toenails. She looks like a pixie, perched here. Nothing about her is real, but Marnie's on her guard. She knows the tricks, how these professionals will wear you down with their chirpiness. She isn't going to fall for Lexie the Pixie.

'Where is the pain today?' Lexie asks, cocking her head at Marnie.

It's their twelfth session. Twelve weeks and three days since the murders. They established at the eighth session that the pain – a physical thing – is sly and mobile, like a door-to-door salesman who finds you no matter how far or how often you move.

Today, the pain is in Marnie's neck. On the right side. A trapped nerve, jumpy.

'In my neck.'

*A pain in the neck.* She hopes Lexie doesn't take it personally.

125

Marnie stopped taking this personally – Lexie and her forest of pot plants, the grubby scent of patchouli – at their fourth session. It's just paperwork, form-filling, something she must do to keep her job, stay with the Met. The proof of her sanity, apparently, lies in how often she can tell this stranger how badly she's hurting. She resisted, at first, but she's learnt to abase herself at Lexie's sandalled feet, to offer up the sacrifice of her soreness.

'In your neck,' Lexie says, nodding sagely. Her earrings, miniature bluebirds, quiver and dip. 'Can you describe the *sort* of pain it is today?'

'Stabbing,' Marnie says, almost without thinking. Almost.

Lexie makes a note in a spiral pad. Has she worked it out? Does she know what Marnie's known for weeks? That the pain moving around her body is – always – in one of two dozen places. In her head or neck or chest, or in her shoulders. Never any lower.

You could map the places where the pain has crept, and if you did, you'd have a map that matched the pathologist's reports on Greg and Lisa Rome. The stab wounds, fatal and otherwise. Twelve wounds apiece, shared out by the kitchen knife.

Marnie didn't realise it, at first. The pain felt indiscriminate and she blamed it on stress, on sleeping awkwardly or sitting hunched over her laptop, searching for Stephen's name. She got into the habit of touching her hand to wherever the pain went, and finally the penny dropped.

It's their pain she's feeling.

Precise, nagging.

In her head or chest, or in a dozen places in between.

All the places he put the knife.

# 33

*Now*

Marnie Rome sat in the small room at the rear of the police station. Alone, except for the thick polybag on the table in front of her. Behind her, a grimy stack of metal shelves housed what had been the contents of someone's desk: a mug and an ancient bottle of contact lens cleaner; hand gel. A street map of Hendon.

'Just you and me,' Marnie said under her breath, to the polybag. She'd locked the door to the room. Strictly speaking, this was against the rules, but she didn't want Tim Welland stumbling in to find her addressing rhetorical statements to an evidence bag. Shortest route to a psych assessment she could think of, and she didn't have time for soul-searching, not with Hope gone and a hole through Leo Proctor's lung. She'd put it off long enough. Should've done this days ago, while the blood was still fresh.

The knife had sweated, leaving a red rash of condensation inside the evidence bag.

She poked at it with the end of one finger, like a kid testing a hollow wasps' nest.

'You don't scare me . . .'

Not the first knife she'd sat with. Not the last, either.

Just a knife. Another knife. She put her fingertips on the clean side of the stained polythene, to get used to the feel of it.

'Fingertips are so important,' a forensics expert had taught her, not long after she joined the Met. Like an extension of your five senses, you can touch something with your fingertips, even through latex, and *know* it's vital. He'd told her how he'd spent one Sunday night searching for a knife thrown at high tide into the Thames. At low tide, when he was in the river, the search was hazardous with mud. Filthy, sucking mud, debilitating to wade through, impossible to see through. Relying on the blind ends of his fingers to find the weapon – and he did find it.

Through the polythene, Marnie felt the blade of the knife Hope Proctor had used to perforate her husband's lung. Just another knife.

She shut her eyes, in self-defence. Smelling the bright zest of oranges – her father making Christmas punch. Another memory, green, of her mother making salad . . .

Half an avocado nestling in her hand, olive meat around a chestnut pit. Thwacking a knife, the pit stopping the blade lengthways across the fruit. A twist of her wrist and the pit was out, dislodged from the blade when the knife tapped the lip of the bin. She'd watched her mum pitting avocados that way for years; always a second's disquiet when it seemed she was about to lose her fingers to the knife.

Orange and avocado. The colours of kitchen knives. Even now, Marnie smelt citrus, not blood. Memory was a brilliant liar.

She forced herself to concentrate on the knife in the polybag. The knife Hope Proctor had turned on her husband. Why? How?

Hope was five foot five, an inch below Marnie's height. Nearly a foot shorter than her husband, and she weighed half as much as Leo did. She stuck this knife between his ribs, chipping one of them – it had shown on the X-ray. The impact must've jarred Hope's wrist. Then the softer resistance of the blade entering flesh, sinking in deep enough to stain her fingers, and the handle of the knife.

Marnie smoothed the polythene with her fingers. When the knife's blade skims across the bone's surface, it leaves little indentations, even if the knife is brand new. These are often clues.

The knife her parents used to slice oranges and pit avocados . . .

Later, the same knife was full of clues, rank with evidence. They wouldn't let Marnie near enough to read the clues. Kept her in the cold, the way she'd kept the memories. Only the memories wouldn't stay down, worrying at her like an excited puppy shut out for too long.

*Death casts the longest shadow.* Who said that? Someone who didn't know about death, not intimately. Shadows were cool places, hiding places. Death was direct sunlight, no shade. A place to burn. She shoved the polybag to arm's length and stood, so suddenly her head spun. Pulling her phone from her pocket, she rang Noah Jake.

'Come to the old interview room a minute, would you?'

'I'll be right there.' He rang off.

She unlocked the door, pulling it open. Noah wouldn't waste any time, even if he hadn't heard the urgency in her voice.

Sure enough, he was in the room before she'd counted to thirty. 'What's up?'

'Stand under the light.'

He moved to the far side of the table, doing as she said. He lacked Leo Proctor's bulk – there was no fat on him anywhere

– but he wasn't far off the same height. She picked up the bagged blade, turning it so that the handle was snug in her palm. The polythene had a particular smell, like dirty skin. She stepped around the table, close to where Noah was waiting. 'Keep still,' she warned.

Noah didn't move. She bent her elbow at a right angle and thrust at his torso, stopping short when the bagged end of the blade touched his shirtfront. Too low.

Too low to hit a lung.

'Move back a pace.'

Noah did as she said, keeping quiet. She liked that about him. She tucked her elbow tight to her waist. Thrust.

This time the tip met the curve of his rib. Still too low for his lung.

Noah asked a question with his eyes. She shook her head. 'Keep still.'

She tried the blow from eight different angles. With the knife horizontal. Vertical. With it pointing upwards, and downwards. Had Leo been dead, this would have been an easy task for a pathologist, instead of a tricky one for her.

Eventually, she hit a spot between Noah's fifth and sixth ribs. She froze, her arm outstretched, wrist flat. Noah stayed in place, waiting for her to take the stiff end of the polybag off his shirtfront. 'That wasn't easy,' she said, laying the knife back down on the table.

'No?' His eyes gleamed. 'I'd say you were a natural.' He lost the smile in the same second. 'Sorry. What d'you mean, not easy?'

'Easy would've been stabbing you in the stomach. A worse way to die – slower. More time for someone to try and save your life.' She walked away from the knife. 'Not that anyone in Finchley was likely to do that. They were all too scared or too busy thinking you deserved what you got . . .'

Noah picked up the bagged knife. 'I'm Leo?'

'You're Leo. You brought a knife into a women's refuge. Why did you do that?'

He held the bag in both hands, careful not to close his fist around the handle. Held like that, it looked like a peace offering. 'I wanted to scare you. Her, I mean. Hope.'

'You could do that without a knife. You're a big bloke, with big fists. You don't need a knife to scare people.'

'Then . . . I was going to hurt you.' Noah eyed the knife with dismay. 'Kill you?'

'So why aren't I dead? Big bloke like you. Little thing like me. Why are *you* the one in hospital, fighting for your life?'

He took a long moment. Then, 'I gave you the knife.' He held it out towards her. 'I . . . must've given you the knife.'

'And then what?' Marnie said. 'Stood still while I stuck it in your lung?'

'I made a mistake.' He frowned, his face thin. 'I was testing you, and it backfired.' He looked down at the knife in his hand, then placed it back on the table. 'You took me by surprise. I didn't think in a million years you'd fight back. I was reminding you who's boss, teaching you a lesson for running away.'

'You didn't think I'd do it.'

'I didn't think you'd dare.'

'So I panicked. Is that what you think?'

Noah touched a hand to his shirtfront. 'Panic would've got me stabbed in the stomach. You . . . you must have meant to kill me.'

He dropped his hand to his side. 'Ayana was right. You meant to kill me.'

'Ayana?'

'I wrote it up, put it on your desk. She said it was deliberate: Hope had no other way to make the abuse stop. A different kind of self-defence, I suppose you'd call it.'

'But not panic.' Marnie came back to the table, pushing

131

a finger at the polybag. 'The knife didn't find his lung by accident.'

'If it was deliberate . . .'

'Then Hope had every reason to run.'

Noah said, 'She killed him to stop the abuse. That's a good defence, and we had the medical evidence of what he'd done to her. She didn't need to run.'

'Not if she was thinking clearly. And if her closest friend had a good reason to trust the police. If we knew the first thing about her closest friend.'

'Surely . . . if it was deliberate, someone would've said something. *Seen* something. All those witnesses . . .'

'All those abused women. Probably still covered in whatever bruises they had when they escaped from their husband, or son, or brothers. Not one of them was likely to see Leo as anything other than a threat . . .'

Marnie reached for her jacket. 'Time to get back to the refuge. Find out what they really saw.' She glanced at Noah. 'Don't take this the wrong way, but I want to do the interviews with Ed. He knows these women, and they trust him.'

'Understood,' Noah said. He picked up the knife. 'I'll take this back to Evidence, and see you over there.'

# 34

Mab Thule sat upright in a straight-backed chair, both feet planted on the floor of her room at the refuge, red cotton gloves on her hands. The chair was wipe-clean plastic, wheezing whenever she moved. She held a fork in one hand, its tines bent out of shape. She'd torn the seam of the chair's cushion and was poking a gloved finger into the hole. The cushion was lumpy, as if she'd squirreled things into the torn seam. She was like a magpie on a nest of dubious treasure, her head cocked at an angle. The left glove, loose on her hand, looked empty. She leaned forward, pinning Marnie with an intent stare. Her lips worked and Marnie moved closer, to hear what she had to say.

'You would feel your heart fall over.' Mab sat back, exhausted.

Marnie looked helplessly at Ed. He reached for Mab's hands, taking the fork and putting it aside, gripping her fingers in his. A smile stitched itself to Mab's sunken mouth. 'Teddy . . .'

'Yes.' He smiled back at her. 'We need your help. We need to work out what happened here on Friday. With Hope and her husband, and with Simone. Hope was friends with Simone, that's right, isn't it?'

'You would,' Mab said sadly. 'You would feel your heart fall over.'

Ed put her hands back in her lap. 'Can I get you anything, lovely?'

She shook her head. Held out her gloved hand, palm up. Ed returned the fork. He nodded at Marnie and they carried the chairs out into the corridor.

When they were a safe distance from Mab's room, Marnie asked, 'Is she well enough to be here?'

'She's not well enough to be anywhere else. Social services assess her on a regular basis. They made a push a while back to have her moved to residential care, but they backed off after looking at the finances. It's cheaper to keep her here, at least until she needs nursing care.'

'She doesn't need that now?'

'She needs help getting dressed and washed,' Ed said, 'but the others look after her. They take it in turns. It works well enough.'

Marnie glanced up the corridor, in the direction of the dayroom. 'What's wrong with her hands? Or does she wear gloves for the cold?'

'She lost two fingers to frostbite, when she was ten.' Ed's face was drawn with anxiety for Hope and Simone. 'So who's next on your list?'

'Not Ayana, she's studying. I said we'd respect that, unless it was absolutely necessary to disturb her. So . . . how about Shelley Coates?'

Shelley Coates was the youngest of the five women who'd witnessed Leo Proctor's stabbing. Twenty-three, heavily made-up, eyes small and brown. She wore a silver ring through her right nostril. Her downturned mouth made Marnie think of a puppet's jointed jaw.

Mab Thule's room was shabby, but it had charm. Shelley's room had all the charm of a motorway Travelodge. Cheap furniture, its laminate veneer curling at the edges. A slackly made bed with a discoloured headboard. Ceramic hair straighteners on the bedside table; Marnie could smell burnt hair and see a strand or two melted to the straighteners.

Shelley sat cross-legged at the foot of her bed, tossing a hank of dark hair over her shoulder. Her tracksuit was black velour with rhinestone trim. She wore stacked trainers, white, with a gold chain at one ankle. Her vest was cut low across her chest, D-cup, most of it angled at Ed. He was either pretending not to notice, or not noticing.

'Hi, Shelley. Thanks for this.' Marnie didn't offer her hand. None of these women liked to be touched. 'We won't keep you longer than we need to.'

Shelley looked from Marnie's flat pumps to her flat chest, pigeonholing her with the stare: dyke copper. 'Okay.' She chewed the word around her mouth as if it was a wad of gum.

'We need to go over a few details from your statement, about Friday.'

Marnie and Ed had agreed they wouldn't ask questions that would make the women anxious about Simone and Hope, remembering the panic from Friday; they were keeping their disappearance to themselves, for now. 'You were in the dayroom when Leo arrived.'

'Yeah. A bunch of us was watching *Lorraine*. We switched off when he came.' She turned the nose ring. The skin around it had crusted, healing from an infection, or a punch.

'How did he get in here, do you know?'

'Walked past that dozy cow Jeanette.' Shelley screwed her mouth into a scowl. 'She's always on a fag break. That or stuffing her face.'

Ed said, 'Easy, Shell. She's a volunteer. You know what that means.'

'Yeah, lick her arse or you'll chuck me out on mine.' She turned the scowl into a grin, leaning a little more of her chest in Ed's direction. 'Mab's been at my stuff again, so you know.'

'What was it this time?'

'Couple of rings. Nothing special or I'd have made a fuss. Got them back, anyway. But you said to tell you, if it happened again.'

'All right.' Ed nodded. 'I'm sorry to hear it. I'll talk to her again.'

'Had he been inside the refuge before?' Marnie asked Shelley. 'Leo Proctor.'

Shelley shook her head. 'Nah.'

'Had you seen him hanging around, outside maybe?'

'He done that, someone would've warned her. Called you,' nodding at Ed, 'or the cops,' boxing Marnie with another stare.

'Did he say anything, when he came into the dayroom?'

'No.'

'How did Hope react?'

'She jumped into his arms, silly cow.' Shelley looked around the room, as if trying to pinpoint her objection. 'It was the roses. She's the kind falls for shit like that.' She plucked at the thin chain around her ankle. 'Least I give him some back. My Clark.'

Marnie glanced at Ed. 'Clark is Shelley's boyfriend,' he said.

'What did you give him back?' Marnie asked Shelley.

'Grief. Aggro.' She sniffed. 'Least I didn't lie down and take it.'

'You think Hope did that, with Leo?'

'I know she did. I seen her bruises in the bathroom. She don't lock the door. He don't let her lock it at home, that's what she said. I seen the state of her.'

136

'Did anyone else see her bruises? Simone, for instance?'

'Dunno. Just know what I saw.' She folded her arms, held herself tightly. 'I'd have stuck the frigging knife in him myself.'

'You think it was . . . revenge?'

Shelley shook her head. 'Not her. She's the sort sticks around no matter what. She panicked. Simone saw that all right. And the rest of us.' She sucked at her bottom lip, taking off its topcoat of pink gloss. 'You got her on suicide watch, right? She's that type. You know?'

'You think Hope might attempt suicide?'

'Depends.' Her small eyes scanned Marnie's face. 'Is he dead yet?'

'He's conscious. It looks like he's going to make a full recovery.'

'Shit.' Shelley hugged herself, blanking her eyes. Then she said, 'Typical,' grinding out the word through her teeth.

'What's typical?'

'Bastards like that get to live. She'll go to prison and he'll walk. Fucking typical.'

'You don't think Hope should go to prison.'

'You're shitting me.' Shelley unfolded her arms, taking hold of her ankles. She challenged Marnie with a stare. 'It's not like she had a choice. He'd have done her, if she hadn't got to the knife first.'

'How did she get to the knife, in your opinion? He's a big man.'

'He's a brick shithouse.'

'Exactly. So how did Hope get hold of the knife?'

Shelley shrugged. 'She must've taken him by surprise. He got used to her being his bitch, doing as she was told, didn't expect her to fight back.' She drew a big breath, keeping it in her cheeks before letting it go. 'Being here,' she looked at Ed, almost shyly, 'it makes you see you're worth more

137

than whatever crap they've made you think about yourself. It gives you back your nerve.'

Ed smiled at her. 'You've never had a problem with nerve.'

'Yeah,' Shelley agreed. 'But women like Hope . . .' She shrugged again. 'You should've seen the state of her. That's all. You seen that and you'd know why she done it. She'd no choice. Just trying to stay alive.'

Tessa Stebbins was half the size of Shelley Coates, but just as hard-boiled. 'Bastard got what was coming to him, didn't he?'

No hair straighteners or nail varnish in this room. Her bed was tidy, its covers pulled tight. Tessa shoved at the pillows as if the neatness annoyed her.

'You'd been here a couple of weeks before Hope arrived.' Marnie referred to her notes. 'What did you make of her, when she first showed up?'

Tessa's dark hair was tortured into a ponytail so tight it gave her a brow lift. She kept her arms folded across her chest, the corner of her eye on Ed. 'She was a mess.'

'In what way?'

'Every way. Bruises. Crying. Jumping through the roof every time someone switched channels on the telly. Crying. The usual things.' She lifted the barricade of her arms to rub her nose on her velour sleeve. Dressed like Shelley, but Tessa's tracksuit was bubble-gum pink with rhinestones. The tracksuit was too large for her. Marnie wondered if it was on loan from her new friend. 'Shell saw the state of her, in the shower room. She covered up, during the day, but Shell saw.'

'Did she talk about her husband at all? To Simone, for instance?'

'Yes. Yeah.' Tessa blinked. Her eyes were like a cat's, yellow-green. 'Not just to Simone, either. When she was crying, feeling bad about leaving him. Worried about who was cooking his meals. I mean, for fuck's sake . . .' She bit her lip at the curse word, as if it was a new piercing she wasn't used to yet. She was doing a good impersonation of a hard case, but Marnie thought she saw a frightened kid underneath.

Tessa's boyfriend, Billy, had shared her among his friends, forcing her into sex to pay his debts. In the refuge, Tessa was aping Shelley Coates's mannerisms, consciously or unconsciously. Looking to align herself with the alpha female. It was a con trick; Marnie saw it all the time in prisoners. She wondered whether Shelley was taking advantage of the fact, whether in fact Tessa had swapped one bully for another.

'Simone says she saw Leo with the knife.'

'Yes. I mean yeah. I saw him too.'

'You saw Leo with the knife.'

'Yeah.'

'But he was the one who got stabbed.'

Tessa grinned, revealing capped teeth. 'Yeah.'

'How did it happen, do you think?'

Tessa pointed her shoulders at the ceiling. 'Guess she'd had enough. I mean, a knife, that's serious shit. That's not messing about.' She put her thumb to her mouth, ran her teeth along its nail. 'My Billy . . . he never done knives. He was scary enough without them, but yeah. Knives are scary shit.'

'Why do you think Leo brought the knife here?'

'Obvious.' Tessa rolled her eyes. 'He was going to finish her. So she'd no choice, had she? It was him, or her. Self-defence. End of.'

Tessa had nothing to add to what they'd heard from Shelley Coates. Marnie let her return to the dayroom. In the corridor, she rolled her neck tiredly. 'We'd better catch Jeanette next. She goes off shift at four.'

Ed must've heard the reluctance in her voice, because he said, 'Volunteers are a mixed bunch. I'd like to think most people wouldn't take a job like this for the money, which apart from anything else isn't great, but not everyone has a vocational muscle.'

Jeanette Conway didn't look like she had muscles of any description. She filled the white tracksuit she was wearing so thoroughly it was hard to see how she'd left room for underwear. Her features clustered sulkily at the centre of her face, corralled by pallid, marbled flesh. Marnie remembered the scream that came out of her on Friday. The woman's mouth looked too small to make such a loud noise.

Marnie said, 'We'd like to go over what happened here on Friday.'

Jeanette squared her shoulders, shooting a look at Ed. 'All right.'

'The door was unlocked. Is it usually unlocked?'

'No, and it wasn't on Friday. We keep it locked.'

'It was open when I got here,' Marnie said levelly. 'There was no one on the desk.'

'I was in the dayroom.' Jeanette looked to Ed. 'Trying to sort out what that bastard was up to. I was looking out for them, just like you tell me to.'

Ed didn't speak. His body language was passive, but he wasn't giving her anything she could interpret as an alibi.

'How did Leo Proctor get into the refuge?' Marnie asked.

Jeanette shifted in the chair. She'd masked the stink of cigarettes with Juicy Fruit gum and air freshener. 'Hope let him in,' she said sullenly.

'Hope let him in.'

'She must've. The door,' she screwed her mouth to a rosebud, 'was locked.'

'Why would Hope have let him in? She came here to get away from him.'

'You know what they're like,' this directed at Ed. 'They can't help themselves. The thieving and phone calls are nothing. There's much worse goes on. She's not the only one. I seen Shelley Coates's bloke hanging around and all.'

'You're saying Leo Proctor had been here before,' Marnie said. 'Hanging around.'

'I seen Shelley's bloke.' Jeanette made a noise of disgust. 'And that's not all I seen.'

Marnie waited for her to elaborate.

Jeanette smiled primly. 'They can't help themselves,' she said again.

Ed scratched at his head, drawing her attention back to him. 'What happened in the dayroom, between Hope and Leo?'

'He tried to give her them roses. She wouldn't go near him at first. Then she did.' Jeanette picked at a cuticle. 'He didn't look like he was going to cause trouble. No more than the rest of them, anyway. He was quiet.'

'Didn't anyone ask him to leave? Simone, for instance?'

'No.' Jeanette rolled her eyes. 'Why would she?'

'She and Hope are friends.'

'Is that what they are?' Jeanette smirked.

'You don't think they're friends? Or you think they're more than friends?'

Jeanette just shrugged.

'Didn't Hope ask Leo to leave?' Marnie asked.

'No.'

'Did they speak to one another at all?'

'No. Leastways, I didn't hear anything. I thought she was going to kiss him. She got up close. Like she wanted to smell the roses. Then he went down.' Jeanette folded her arms and looked around the room, reciting the next words in a bored, nasal tone. 'I didn't see the knife until after. If I'd seen the knife, I'd have rung the police, whatever. It didn't

141

look like it was going to kick off, but I guess he wanted to take her home, or he was mad at her for being here.' She shrugged with scorn. 'He's big, didn't need the knife, could've carried her out. She probably weighs about six stone.'

'She stabbed him.'

'Yeah.' Jeanette returned her stare to Marnie's face. 'How'd she do that? I mean, they'd all like to do it, to whoever put them in here. She didn't look the type, though, not really.' She shook her head. 'I guess that's why she freaked out afterwards.'

## 35

'Is anyone else having a gorilla-in-our-midst moment?'

Jeanette had clocked off. Marnie was in the office, with Ed and Noah. Her thumbs were pricking. There was no news of Hope or Simone. No sightings. Hours of CCTV footage to check, with permissions taking longer than usual to work through the system.

'Simons and Levin,' Noah said, in answer to her question. 'Harvard psychologists. Is that what you mean?'

Marnie saw Ed's quick glance at Noah and smiled. 'First-class degree in psychology.'

Ed sketched a salute.

'So Simons and Levin get these volunteers to watch a basketball game on tape,' she said. 'They're meant to count ball passes. Midway through the game, a two-metre-tall pantomime gorilla walks across the pitch and waves at the camera. In every test, less than half the volunteers see the gorilla. Is that right?'

Noah nodded. 'Some of them thought Simons and Levin switched the tapes. They couldn't believe they'd missed the monkey. But they did.'

'Fifty per cent in every test just . . . didn't see him.'

'Her. It was a woman in the gorilla suit,' Noah said. 'You think the women here missed something they should've seen?' He paused. 'Something like Hope *meaning* to stab Leo?'

'No way of knowing, but I'm wondering.'

'Back up,' Ed said. 'Hope *meant* to stab Leo?'

'It's a theory we're working on. Not the only one, but if she meant to kill him and if Simone *knew* that . . . It's a motive for them to run, as soon as they knew he was awake.'

'She told Leo she was living in the refuge,' Noah said. 'Why do that? If she's running now . . . I don't understand.'

'The pull of home,' Ed murmured. 'I'm amazed Ayana's held out this long without calling her family. Most women make the call within days of coming here.'

'We still don't know whether she'll give evidence against Nasif,' Noah reminded them.

'That can wait,' Marnie told him. 'It'll have to wait. We've got two missing women, one of whom might've tried to kill her husband.'

The television's soundtrack was ceaseless. Didn't the women ever switch if off?

'What was that about Mab and Shelley's rings?' she asked Ed.

'Mab's a bit of a magpie. I put it down to the scavenging during the Blitz . . . She's in the habit of picking up anything the others leave lying around. I've asked them to be careful, but . . .' He shook his head. 'We usually find the stuff in the chair cushion – you saw her. It's harmless. The others understand. They're pretty patient with her, in fact.'

'Right.' Marnie stretched, rubbing at her neck. 'I'll be straight with you, Ed. These are the worst witnesses I've ever met, and that's saying something. None of them knows the value of honesty. They've learnt the hard way to deal in other currency. Lies, or platitudes, whatever we want to hear. No such thing as the plain truth. They've probably learnt to lie to everyone, friends and family. Doctors. The police. Themselves. They don't even know they're doing it, I bet. It's a survival instinct. A reflex.'

Ed said, 'I can't argue with any of that.'

'I thought the problem we'd have would be keeping them from talking about the stabbing before we took their state-ments. We kept them apart, we were careful to do that. They hadn't spoken among themselves before we took statements. Even so,' she spread her hands, 'different versions of the same thing. At least . . . Shelley thinks Leo got complacent. That he never imagined Hope would fight back.'

Noah nodded. 'Simone said something similar, that he gave Hope the knife to taunt her for being passive. A way of marking his territory.'

'Tessa thought it was simple self-defence,' Ed said.

'Yes. And Jeanette couldn't come up with a reason why or how Hope got hold of the knife.' Marnie frowned at an ink stain on the pad of her finger. 'Ayana believed she meant to do it. Her only guaranteed way out, but even so . . . However you cut it, we've got five versions of the same thing. Self-defence gone wrong. I suppose they share the same triggers. They didn't need to talk in order to exchange versions of what they saw. Too much shared experience did that for them.'

'Yes, it did,' Ed said.

'So that means – what? That they'd all like to stick a knife in their abusers?' Marnie shook her head. 'I don't believe that. It's possible to survive trauma without resorting to violence.'

'We're not saying they'd *do* it,' Noah countered, awkwardly. 'Just that self-defence would be the obvious inference they'd draw in that kind of situation, given their own experiences.'

'Self-defence is one thing. Violence is different . . .' Marnie stopped. She bit the inside of her cheek, checking her phone for messages from the station. 'It worries me that they want to please us. We're authority figures. We scare them. Even I was scaring them, and God knows I'm a pussycat.'

Ed said, 'Ayana wasn't scared. You said she thought Hope meant to kill Leo.'

'That's what she told Noah. Ed . . . you know Ayana better than we do. Should we be giving more weight to her evidence than anyone else's?'

'Perhaps. She doesn't miss much.' Ed linked his hands behind his neck. 'She's hyper-alert when it comes to women, scared of her mother, almost more than she is of her brothers. That might mean she steers clear of other women, from instinct rather than anything else . . . You're right about currency, about the way these women deal in honesty, or don't deal. Violence isn't just something they've grown up with; it's a way of communicating. Fear's the same, and anger. Even for Ayana. Her mother grew up with rules, violence. She passed it along, her legacy to her daughter.'

Marnie listened for sounds of the women in the dayroom, but the television was like blotting paper, soaking up all noise except its own. 'No one had anything new to say about Simone. You saw her and Hope together at the hospital – that wasn't pretence, was it? She really cares for Hope.'

Ed nodded. 'I'm sure she does, but knowing Leo's awake, and if it wasn't simple self-defence? If Hope *did* mean to kill him and if she admitted as much to Simone . . . I can see Simone wanting to run. It would be instinctive, whether or not she planned it. Her experience of the police wasn't a happy one.'

'So where would she go? If she's trying to hide Hope?'

'I don't know. I wish I did. The only places she knows in London are the Bissells' house and the flat where Lowell kept her. She wouldn't go back to either of those.'

'All right. Let's try something else.' Marnie nodded at Ed.

146

'You should get back to work. This next bit's for us to sort out.'

'Are you sure?'

'I'm sure.'

'Okay. If Simone gets in touch, I'll call you right away.'

'Same here. Thanks.'

When Ed had gone, Noah asked, 'Where now?'

'The Proctors' house.'

'I thought we needed Leo's permission.'

'We only need his keys.' She held up a bunch on a fraying key ring. 'The hospital hadn't discharged her. We have reasonable grounds for concern over her safety. Let's see what's at the house.'

Houses said a lot about the people who lived in them. The Proctors' was a new-build, masquerading as old. Reclaimed red bricks, Victorian possibly, over a modern shell of breeze blocks. Hollow walls, Noah guessed.

This was where they lived, Hope and Leo Proctor, where she ran from.

The house was like all the others in the street, except in one respect. All the windows at the front had slatted wooden shutters. All the shutters were tightly closed. The shutters stole six inches of living space, an extravagance in a house of this size. How much had it cost? And what were the Proctors hiding, or hiding from?

'They're never out of the house at weekends. *She* doesn't say hello, keeps her head down most of the time. He's at work all hours. Mind you, lots of families are like that nowadays. I'm not saying there's any funny business.' The Proctors' neighbour, Felix Gill, swilled his stomach back into the waist of his trousers, indulgently. 'They're a nice enough couple . . .' He finished admiring Marnie's ID and handed it back. 'No one's at home, if you ask me. I haven't seen *her* in a few days.' He folded his arms, resting them on top of his gut. 'She the one you're looking for?'

'We've come to get a few things.' Marnie deployed her smile, disarming Gill.

'I don't have a key,' he said. 'Sorry. I offered, but they didn't fancy swapping keys.'

'That's all right.' Marnie held up the bunch she'd taken from Leo at the hospital. 'We've got everything we need.'

Inside, the house felt empty. It smelt empty, too. With the recent chill of a place unlived in for a short while. They checked the rooms perfunctorily, before returning to the living space on the ground floor.

The sitting room had the dodgy chic of a showroom: everything arranged to evoke the idea of gracious living rather than its reality. A small sofa with matching armchairs, a low table in pale wood, like the bookcase. Woodchipped walls and ceiling, sisal flooring, rough underfoot but it probably did a brilliant job of hiding dirt and wear. Otherwise, the colour scheme was white, off-white and guano. A television, smaller than the average in a modern household, was screwed to the wall opposite the sofa. DVDs in the bookcase, in place of books. The shuttered windows hid the view of the street; impossible to know if Felix Gill was still out there, watching the house. No plants or flowers. No photographs or pictures.

The room at the back of the house was dressed for dining. There was no other way to describe it. The table had a runner of grey linen with lavender trim, matching placemats and plates, smaller ones stacked inside larger. Fake diamonds the size of a child's fist were scattered artfully up the runner. One wall was papered with a pattern of purple flowers, aiming for regal but falling short. The back of each chair sported a satin bow, the same colour as the table runner. The room wasn't camp, exactly, but Noah had been in nightclubs with more restrained decor. He found it hard to believe the Proctors ever used the room, for eating or anything else.

They went upstairs, to the bedrooms. In the front room, a double bed stood under twin prints of fruit on the wall. White bed linen with a silvery throw folded back at the foot. The bed didn't look slept in, its pillows smugly plump. The shuttered windows leaked light in weak stripes on to the *faux* wood floor. A mean-fisted chandelier hung from the ceiling, its glass pendants snatching their reflections as they stood at the side of the bed.

'Take off your shoes.'

Noah glanced at Marnie. She was looking at the smug pillows. 'I want you on the bed.'

'You want . . .?'

'You're six foot. That's about Leo's height. This bed looks small . . . Better take your shoes off before you test it.'

Noah toed off his shoes and lay down with his head on the pillow nearest the door. The bed was at least ten inches too short, his feet dangling past the silver throw. He eyed the chandelier. 'Maybe Leo sleeps in the other room?'

'Comfy? The bed.'

Noah shifted, testing both sides of the mattress. 'It doesn't feel slept on.'

The second bedroom was the same: an undersized bed in a neutrally decorated room. Marnie ran her finger along the shutter's wooden slats, inspecting for dust. She didn't ask Noah to lie on the bed; it was obviously the same model as the first one.

'Show-house furniture,' she said. 'They make it small, so the rooms look larger.'

The bathroom was spotless, all surfaces gleaming. No hair in the plugholes. Black and white towels, fluffy enough to be new, folded in stacks on a pair of white wicker laundry baskets. Showroom toiletries, in ceramic dispensers. Marnie opened the wall-mounted cabinet, exposing an impressive collection of pill bottles and plasters, antiseptic creams, Vaseline. She checked the labels on the prescription bottles. 'Hope's antidepressants . . . She stopped taking them because they made her clumsy. She broke a mirror.' She ran a finger around the cabinet's mirrored doors. 'Not this one.'

Noah inspected the date on the pill bottle, and its contents. 'It doesn't look like she took many.'

'No. I don't suppose Leo liked the clumsiness.'

They went downstairs to the sitting room. Marnie sat on the sofa, inviting Noah to join her. The sofa was big enough for two, assuming intimacy was on the agenda. They disengaged their elbows and stood, looking around the room a second time.

'Do they really live here?' Noah wondered. 'Or is the whole thing just for show?'

'A marriage is private.' Marnie walked to the bookcase. 'That was Hope's line when we spoke at the hospital.' She opened DVD cases, looking inside each one before sliding it back on to the shelf.

'Private would be . . . dirty towels in the bath,' Noah said, 'a porn stash under the bed. There's nothing here that needs to be behind closed doors.'

'So where do they keep their secrets? They did a good job of covering up the abuse, until now. What was the neighbour's line? A nice enough couple . . . And Leo was holding down a job. Hope wasn't saying anything, to anyone, about what was going on here, before the stabbing. I thought we'd find . . . something.'

She looked around the room, shaking her head. 'Behind closed doors . . . These secrets are buried deeper than that.' She looked at the wooden shutters. 'Someone's cleaned here recently, but not in the last couple of days.'

'Hope's been in the refuge longer than that. So unless Leo does the cleaning . . .'

'He gets someone in. Or he *got* someone in. To clean up before he went to the refuge, to deal with Hope.'

'So maybe someone else knows what he was hiding.'

'Maybe.' Marnie walked to the rooms at the back of the house. Noah followed. The kitchen was fitted, and showroom-clean. Slick surfaces, granite. No cups on the draining board. Polished fruit in a bowl on the table. No magnets on the fridge door. No evidence of living. The space smelt of carpenter's glue, like a stage set.

A knife rack stood by the window above the sink. Noah wondered if the knives were real; everything in the kitchen had the air of a prop, unused. But they were real, he knew that. One was missing from the rack. The knife Hope Proctor had used to stab her husband. 'What happened to Simone,' he started to say, 'in Uganda . . .'

'It happens here.' Marnie opened the fridge.

Noah saw cans of beer and a couple of bottles of wine, not much food. 'Here?'

'In the UK. In London.' The fridge gave out a pulse of cold. 'In the last four years, we've had – God knows – well over a hundred calls from girls and women at risk from FGM. Female Genital Mutilation. Last estimate said over a hundred thousand operations had been carried out in the UK.'

'But . . . it's illegal.'

'Illegal to operate. Illegal to arrange to operate.' Marnie shut the fridge. 'A hundred thousand operations. Zero convictions. You can imagine how Ed feels about that.'

They shared a bleak look; sometimes this job felt like throwing rice at a house fire. Marnie's voice had softened when she mentioned Ed. It made Noah wonder if they were sleeping together. He'd been wondering it on and off since Friday. Ed wasn't just cute; he was smart and serious, and warm and funny. Noah knew what Dan would say: 'Stop pairing. Not everyone needs a soulmate. Casual sex works for the vast majority of the population.' When Noah challenged him on this statistic, Dan prevaricated.

'Come on,' Marnie said.

They went into the hall. The cupboard under the stairs had a latch on it, locking from the outside. She slid the latch and opened the door.

It was just a cupboard under the stairs, the place people stored their vacuum cleaner, not much room for more than that. Raw stone floor and walls. A smell of damp. And worse.

Noah set his teeth.

Marnie wrapped her arms around her chest. 'Can you smell it?'

He could: the ammonia stink of a scared animal.

'Classic abuser's technique,' Marnie murmured. 'Isolate your victim, narrow their field of reference. *She doesn't say hello, keeps her head down . . .*' She looked again at the cramped space. 'He kept her in here.'

They could both see it. The squeezed shape of Hope Proctor huddled under the stairs, her body folded to fit inside. Door locked from the outside, nothing but her panicked breath for company, and the bruises he'd planted on her.

'We need to ask Leo some more questions,' Marnie said inflexibly. She made no reference to her earlier interrogation, or Noah's criticism of it.

Seeing the hole under the stairs – smelling it – Noah was forced to side with her. He might not like Marnie's methods, but he couldn't ignore the implications of the cramped space he was seeing. 'How'd you think he'll react to the news that she's gone?'

'Last time, he took a knife to her hiding place. That gives us a fair idea . . .' Her phone buzzed. She checked the display and turned away before taking the call. 'Marnie Rome.' She listened in silence, her shoulders up, tension in the nape of her neck.

'Where is he now?' Her voice was clipped. 'Is he still in hospital?'

Noah shut the cupboard door, sliding the latch as quietly as he could.

'Understood. I'll be there as soon as I can. Thanks.' She shut the phone in her fist and shoved it into her pocket.

'Leo?' Noah feared the worst. That Hope's husband had heard of her escape and somehow gone after her, or made an escape of his own.

'Not Leo.' Marnie swung round to face him. She was pale, blue shadows under her eyes. 'I need the car. You'll have to take the tube back. Check in with Abby. See how she's getting on. Call me if there's any news. I'll be gone the rest of the day.'

'Is everything okay?'

She didn't answer, going across the hall to the front door.

Felix Gill was watching the Proctors' house from his window. He saw Marnie walk to the car, get in and drive off. Noah made sure the front door was secure before pausing on the pavement to check his pockets for his Oyster card. His phone buzzed against his hip and he pulled it out, checked the display: Ron Carling, from the station.

'I've got something,' Carling said, 'from the CCTV. A Prius. It was outside the hospital this morning, about the time you said, but get this. The *same* car was outside the refuge in Finchley the day Leo Proctor got stabbed.'

'The same car. You're sure?'

'It was at the refuge. In the same street, then parked up two roads away, round about the time they took Proctor in. CCTV's like a fucking rash round that part of town.'

'You have a registration?'

'Yep, running it now. Prick in a Prius,' Carling said, contempt and triumph slugging it out in his tone. 'He's been watching the women.'

# 37

*Six months ago*

Under the tight clothes from the nightclub, she's a mess. The coppery smell is blood, recent, on the tops of her thighs. It's shocking, brutal, but it turns him on. He knows it shouldn't, he knows that. Except all the lines are blurred, and if he's taken this step . . .

It *helps*. It helps that it's more than just a quick shag. He doesn't have a name for what it is, but it's something more than shameful, or dirty. It's . . .

Evil. Out of his control. Not something he can ever confess to Freya, in a pang of guilt or panic. He can't ever confess to this. That makes him feel safe. Hidden.

In the hotel room, on the cheap slippery surface of the bed, she straddles him. Knees knotting in his armpits, pain pinning him in place.

'Shit . . .' he hisses. 'Don't . . .'

She leans low over his chest, those tight tits pressed tighter, nipples like hot nail-heads. Her thumbs find the tendons in his neck, easily. This isn't her first time at this game. That's all it takes – knees, thumbs, her splayed heat in a straight line up his stomach – for his balls to shrivel, trying to crawl back up into his body.

'You're hurting . . .'

'You're kidding.' These are the first words she's spoken. Her voice is sing-song, sweet. Her teeth grin against the side of his neck. 'I haven't even started yet.'

Freya and the twins are sleeping when he gets home.

He creeps into the bathroom and washes the smell away, shamed and grateful in equal measure, like a dog allowed to drink after a long car journey. The house is so quiet; he can't believe it. He sits on the side of the bath and listens to the quiet. Not just in the house. In him. It's as if she reached in and switched off the noise, the bellowing.

He already knows he'll go back.

# 38

*Now*

Thunder from a flight path hit the secure unit's steep roof before rolling to the ground, where it gathered pitch, a snowball of sound. Marnie hunched her shoulders, keeping close to the wall, feeling as if she was under the stairs in the Proctors' house.

Sommerville Secure Unit had never called before. She'd given her number for emergencies, but contact, when there was any, came through Jeremy Strickland, Stephen's solicitor. Not this time. This time Sommerville's Head of Secure Services had called her. As soon as she'd seen the caller display on her phone, she'd known this was seriously bad news.

Paul Bruton greeted her on the other side of the door. 'Thanks for coming so quickly. Let's go to my office. I'll get you some coffee.'

'How is he?' Marnie asked.

'Back in his room.' Bruton checked his watch. He kept to the left-hand wall of the corridor, as if this was a rule he had to follow. 'The hospital discharged him earlier.'

'Why didn't you call me when it happened?'

'He didn't want us to. We had to respect that.'

'Why?' His sanctimonious tone exasperated her. 'He's an inmate, not a guest.'

Bruton gave an ingratiating smile. 'You're here as a relative, not a detective inspector. Inmates have the right to refuse visitors.'

She nearly snapped back: *I'm not a relative. He has no relatives, and neither do I. He killed them.*

Instead, she said, 'But he wants to see me now. What changed his mind?'

'I'm not sure. He isn't communicative at the best of times.' Bruton held open the door to his office. 'Shall we?'

She took a seat, turned down the offer of tea or coffee, asking for a glass of water.

Bruton delegated this chore to someone on the end of a phone, plucking at the knees of his trousers as he sat behind his desk. His face was as bland as a balloon, nearly featureless at first glance. Over the suit trousers he wore a green Plain Lazy sweatshirt. He was a man in two parts: the top half chosen to appeal to the kids incarcerated here, the bottom half representative of his usual wardrobe. He had too much hair, starting too far back on his head. At intervals when he spoke, he gathered the hair in his hands and flung it back from his face, imagining, no doubt, that he looked like Hugh Grant. Smiling family photos littered the surface of his desk.

A girl in black leggings and a white hoodie brought the glass of water. She avoided Bruton and Marnie, concentrating on her task with the air of someone trying to earn privileges. She'd chewed her nails to the quick, the cuticles ragged and bloody.

'Thanks, Lynne, that's great.' After she'd gone, Bruton said, 'I'd better tell you what happened. I'm afraid it's not a nice story.'

'I guessed as much from the fact that he spent the night

in hospital.' Marnie drank a mouthful of tepid water. 'But they discharged him, so I'm assuming it's not as bad as it might've been.'

'He'd been in the hospital since Saturday. It was . . . a very nasty assault.' He took his hair in his hands, grimacing. 'I'm sorry, I should have been clearer on the phone.'

'Yes, you should.' She set the glass down, the ends of her fingers slippy with sweat. 'So how bad was it?'

Stephen's room was at the end of a corridor that stretched the length of the secure unit's main building. The red eye of a security camera watched Marnie as she walked. Weird acoustics; too many echoes in here, three for every footfall. When she cleared her throat, the ceiling took the sound and threw it back to her as growling.

Each of the kids detained here had a separate room with en suite facilities. The website boasted of comfortable and cheerful rooms, 'carpeted', as if this was an indulgence beyond the imagination of most. Sommerville, the website enthused, encouraged its detainees to personalise their rooms with posters and photographs.

Stephen's room had no posters. Marnie had known it wouldn't have photos. The carpet was the colour and texture of porridge, hard-wearing *faux* wool that hid the dirt in its tightly knotted ply. The walls were papered in orange. Limp curtains at the window let in lymph-coloured light.

Stephen was lying on his back on the bed. One arm blocked the light from his eyes. He was wearing a white T-shirt and grey sweatpants. Dark marks above his elbows, where two sets of hands had held him down. Red scratches on his jaw and under his chin, scabbed indents where fingernails had broken the surface of his skin.

None of the worst damage was visible.

It was hard to look at him, knowing what'd been done.

159

Marnie rested her eyes on the window, then looked around the room. She hadn't been in here before.

A shallow desk held a handful of books, one of which was the short-story collection she'd brought at the weekend. The room had an astringent smell, like ointment for bruises. The hospital had prescribed tramadol. He looked as if the pills had knocked him out. She pulled a chair from under the desk and sat next to the bed. 'Bruton said you asked to see me.'

Stephen kept his arm across his eyes. 'I changed my mind.' He folded his hand into a fist. His elbow was sharp, bony. She had a flash of memory: reaching him down from a new climbing frame in her parents' garden when he was eight, his body lighter than she'd expected, with small, jutting bones.

'It took me three hours to get here,' she said. 'I'll stay for a bit if you don't mind.'

'I don't want to talk.' His voice was hollow, scooped out.

'Okay.' She reached for a book. 'Mind if I read?'

He didn't answer. She sat and turned the pages, unable to make out the words. She was still seeing the pictures Paul Bruton had put in her head of Saturday night, Stephen being held down, fingernails sinking into his face . . .

'Don't you have police stuff to do?' he demanded.

She waited a beat. 'Bruton says you won't speak with the police about what happened. You should at least tell him who did it. They deserve to be punished.'

Stephen said, 'You'd know all about that.'

'Less than you might think. I know that you have the right to feel safe here.'

He murmured something like, 'I waived that right.'

'What did you say?'

'Can't you piss off?' Her pity was the last thing he wanted.

'The hospital took swabs. We could find out who was responsible from those.'

'Good luck with that. They used a bottle.'

'What?'

He raised his voice. 'I said they used a bottle, not their dicks.'

The assault had lasted twenty minutes, maybe more, based on the schedule of checks by staff. They'd found Stephen in the bathroom, naked and bleeding, incoherent with shock. He'd needed stitches, fluids for the blood loss.

She put the book back on the desk. 'They took swabs from your face, where the skin was broken. We could match DNA from that.'

He didn't respond.

'Where's your guarantee they won't do it again?'

'Talking to you'd be begging for it.'

This was more than fear. It was shame. The way he kept his face covered; the beaten note in his voice – it reminded her of Leo Proctor.

'How many of them were involved? Bruton thinks at least three.'

'Bruton doesn't have the first fucking clue about anything,' he said savagely.

'So how many? Four, five? No one could have fought those odds.'

He clenched his fist. 'You don't have a *clue*, any more than he does.'

Marnie looked at the fingernail scratches on his jaw. Neat half-moons cut into his skin. Slowly, on a note of disbelief, she said, 'It was girls, wasn't it? Girls did this.'

His throat convulsed. 'Piss off . . .'

She could see the girl's hand-span at his jaw, too small for a boy's, and a boy wouldn't have nails that could gouge skin. They held him down and raped him, brutally, with a glass bottle. Teenage girls had done this. 'Stephen . . .'

He lifted his arm, tears scalding his eyes. 'I said piss off! I don't want you here. You're the last person I want here.'

She held his stare. 'Why? I'm the last person likely to feel sorry for you. Unless you *want* people to feel sorry for you.'

He pushed himself up on his elbows, pain stripping the colour from his face. She knew what he was going to say before he said it; read his need to pass the pain, like a baton, from him to her. 'I stabbed your fucking parents, bitch. I'll stab you.'

'No you won't.' She stood, staying beside the bed, looking down at him. 'You haven't got a knife, for one thing.'

'I can find one.' He lifted his chin, pointing at the scabbed wound on the underside of his jaw. 'How'd you think those cunts kept me still?'

'Which cunts? Give me names.'

He made a hard sound, like coughing. 'You think you're so brave, coming here every month . . . Finally paid off, hasn't it? That's why I asked to see you. So you'd get what you want and leave me the fuck alone.'

'What is it you think I want?'

'Me.' He spat the word. 'Like this.'

'That's why I've been coming here? In the hope of seeing you in pain, beaten up.'

'Yeah. *Yeah.* If you weren't such a hypocritical bitch, you'd own it.'

'You don't think it was enough, seeing my parents like that? I see that stuff every day. *Police stuff.* I don't need to come here to see a nineteen-year-old kid who's too ashamed to name his rapists. It's on my doorstep.'

'So piss off then!' His anger was like a wall. Every word she gave him was another brick to build it higher, deeper.

'One thing, before I go.' She held out her right hand. 'I'd like my dad's glasses.'

His shoulders shook, his eyes blown into a wild black stare.

Marnie waited with her hand out, her face schooled to

indifference. Stephen collapsed back on the bed, blocking her out with his arm, the lymph-coloured light lying up the side of his face. 'In the desk.' He hiccuped. 'In the drawer.'

She crossed the room to the desk. The drawer was hard to open, full of paper and card – and her father's glasses case. She took it out, laid it aside so she could search the rest of the drawer's contents. Under the glasses case, a wallet she'd made at school, as a present for her dad, two squares of brown leather stitched roughly together.

Her mother's seagull brooch.

Marnie had searched for it, back at her parents' house. A little enamel seagull with a white wing, a blunt chip of blue glass for its eye. The pin had been snapped from its back, by Bruton's team probably. She put the brooch next to her father's glasses.

Also in the drawer: a page torn from the *Guardian*, the Quick Crossword completed in her mother's handwriting, with her workings-out in the margin. Envelopes with Christmas stamps, addressed to Greg and Lisa Rome in Marnie's handwriting: the cards she'd sent them each year. The last three envelopes she'd addressed to 'Greg, Lisa and Stephen'. Family photographs, one of her when she was eight, in jeans and a green T-shirt, a band of shadow blanking her eyes. She was wearing the new charm bracelet with the silver horseshoe, for good luck . . .

She swept the rest of the drawer with the flat of her hand, searching for the charm bracelet, but it wasn't here. Just more photos, of her as a child, with her parents, on her own. In her school uniform, in her new police uniform, appallingly proud. She was afraid she'd find another photo, of the writing on her skin. The sort of photo you could probably trade for cigarettes in a place like Sommerville.

Stephen's chest wasn't moving. He was holding his breath. He'd wanted her to see inside the drawer, to know he still

163

had the power to hurt her. To show her that nothing had changed between them.

No naked photos. She resisted the urge to pull the drawer out and search for anything taped to the wooden back, but it was pointless; Bruton and his team probably stripped these rooms down at least once a week.

She touched the tips of her fingers to the seagull brooch, its enamel smooth and cool as glass. She could smell her mother's scent, green. The edges of the home-made wallet were rough, badly finished; she remembered her struggle with the school's thick needle, her fingers pricked red. Her father kept a key in the wallet's pocket, for the carriage clock in the sitting room. Those clocks . . . She remembered watching him wind each one in turn. She remembered the feel of her father's hand on her shoulder, the sense of safety it gave her, of weight and substance. At school, when they taught her about the laws of gravity, it was her father's face she saw.

Stephen made no sound, so still it was hard to believe he was in the same room.

Marnie stood by the open drawer, touching her hands to its contents, cautiously, tenderly. A cool, dim spot had cleared in her chest. Perhaps she should thank him, for keeping her loss alive. She'd spent so many hours – months, years – holding it at bay. Stephen had brought it close and it felt like a kindness even when she knew it was not. She'd crept around the memories, as a child creeps in a dark house, afraid of disturbing shadows. Stephen . . .

Stephen forced her to look, and touch, and smell her past. He made it real again.

She sucked a breath and held it in her mouth until it soured, wondering if the boy on the bed felt it too. The static charge between them. It pulled at her skin. Something more than silence, more than the secrets Stephen was keeping, about how he'd killed her parents, and why. It was deeper, more dangerous than that. Not a threat, not quite, but . . .

The rubble around them had shifted. The mess and pain of the past. If Marnie didn't take care, she'd bring the whole thing down, burying the pair of them a second time.

Very softly, she shut the drawer, leaving her father's spectacles inside. The seagull brooch she took, holding it in the cup of her hand.

Without looking at the bed, she walked out of the room and back down the long corridor to Paul Bruton's office.

'It was girls.'

'Excuse me?'

She shut the door and crossed the room to Bruton's desk. 'He wouldn't give me names, but it was girls.'

A flicker in Bruton's eyes gave him away. 'You know who it was.'

'No, no. I suspected boys, of course I did, but with Stephen so uncooperative . . .'

'He was raped. That's bad enough. The fact that it was girls . . .'

'He's humiliated. I do understand that. The psychiatrist—'

'Forget about the psychiatrist for a minute. I want to know how you're going to find out who was responsible.' She looked him in the eye. 'I'm sure I don't need to tell you that the police can start an investigation with or without Stephen's cooperation.'

Bruton sucked air between his teeth, tapping the desk with his thumb. 'One of the girls . . . Julie. She's nineteen. She's in here because she . . . lured a fifteen-year-old boy with the promise of sex, got him drunk and held him down while her sixteen-year-old boyfriend raped him. The boyfriend got five years. Julie was identified as the ringleader and sentenced to seven.'

'How long has she been here?'

'Eight months.'

Marnie looked at the happy family photos on Bruton's desk, the upbeat posters on his walls reminding inmates of their right to rehabilitation. He'd filled the room with false promises, as slickly smiling and wolfish as anything the Grimm brothers had dreamt up. The family photos were a cruel, teasing touch – rubbing the offenders' faces in what they'd lost, or never known.

'She's locked up with teenage boys.'

'Sommerville takes offenders of both sexes. We segregate where appropriate, but . . .' Bruton rearranged his hair with his hands. 'I'll question her, and the other girls. We'll follow the necessary procedures, you can be sure of that.'

'You were following them before,' she said, 'weren't you? It didn't stop this happening.'

# 39

*Six months ago*

The second time, it's different. Not like the nightclub, the cheap hotel. She's a mess, but she's not bleeding, not to begin with, anyway.

It's different because he's expecting it, knows exactly what he's getting into, and *fuck*, he thinks, *this isn't what I wanted*. It's out of his control. Another thing out of his control. When what he wanted was a chance to even the odds. Leave Freya and the twins behind for a couple of hours and be someone else, someone they wouldn't recognise. A stranger.

He wanted to hide from the three of them, Freya and the twins, inside someone else's skin. Deep, deep down. Except the second time, it's different. The second time, she really hurts him. Uses her teeth and nails, and her fists.

*This wasn't what I wanted*, he thinks. *I wanted to be the one in control.*

Then he thinks, *I'll have to explain the bruises to Freya.*

That – the thought of Freya's shock, and her questions – turns him on. The thought of something on his skin that isn't dried formula milk, or baby puke, or stinking sweat from sleepless nights . . . It turns him on, and so he lets her do it. Hurt him. And when it's his turn, he knows exactly what she wants.

She wants him to mark her, make her different. A stranger – a shock – to whoever she goes home to, when he goes home to Freya and the twins. If there is anyone.

Perhaps – and this is what he really thinks – there's no one.

She goes home to an empty house. Mirrors in the house, but no people.

That's where she looks.

In the mirrors.

That's where she wants to be unrecognisable.

A stranger, to herself.

## 40

*Now*

'The prick in the Prius,' Noah Jake said. 'Where're we up to with that?'

Ron Carling looked up from his mug of tea, sporting a Danish pastry moustache. 'Got a name and address. No criminal record. Just a couple of points on his licence.' He looked disgusted. 'Might turn out to be nothing.'

'Might not.' Noah walked to his desk, asking over his shoulder, 'What's the name?'

'Henry Stuke.' Carling stood up, handed Noah a sheet of paper. 'Current MOT. Full service history. The points were for speeding, but something pathetic like thirty-two in a thirty-mile zone. Hardly Jenson effing Button.'

Noah switched on his computer, calling up the man's address.

Henry Charles Stuke lived in West Brompton. His insurance said he was married, with two dependants. Noah requested a print-off of the DVLA paperwork, before logging on to the missing persons database.

Carling watched over his shoulder. 'Welland's after the

DI,' he warned. 'CPS's shitting its shorts over the scimitar. That's your case, right?'

'Right.'

'So where's the DI?'

'Working the case.' Noah made a careful study of the screen, not wanting to give the impression that he hadn't the foggiest where Marnie was.

'Getting her hands dirty?' Carling folded his arms, perching his large arse on the edge of Noah's desk, as if he was testing Noah's powers of resistance. 'That's what she's got *you* for, isn't it?'

'We're working two cases. The scimitar and a separate stabbing.'

Carling peered at the screen. 'Missing persons. Who's that, then?'

'Simone Bissell and Hope Proctor.'

'Which one got stabbed?'

'Neither. Hope Proctor stabbed her husband at the refuge in Finchley.'

'Right, that one. Been knocking her about, had he?'

'It looks that way.'

'Scum.' Carling leaned back. 'Your lot don't get much of that, unless it's mutual.' He tapped his nose. 'You into the old leather dog-collar scene?'

Noah continued to scroll through the online database. 'I prefer sounding.'

'What the shit's *sounding*?'

Noah shut down the database and got to his feet, clapping a hand to Carling's shoulder. 'Look it up on Wikipedia.'

It had rained, but now the sun was out, lifting steam from the pavements and crazing the windows of parked cars. Noah unpocketed his phone and dialled Marnie's mobile, getting voicemail. 'Carling says Commander Welland's looking for you. I thought I'd better pass it on. The CPS is getting nervous about Nasif Mirza. I'm heading to the refuge with Ed, to ask Ayana some questions. I'll probably be there a while.'

The refuge looked less inviting than ever after the rain, its roof wrapped in black plastic sheeting. No sign of a workforce up there, or elsewhere. Noah found the main entrance locked and pressed the intercom, showing his badge to the security camera. After a delay of maybe half a minute, the door buzzed open. He walked to the office, where Jeanette was sitting with a mug of Horlicks. She gave him a sour look but said, 'Hiya.'

'Hi. Is Ayana in the dayroom?'

'Yes.' The emphatic way she said it made Noah suspect that she had no idea where any of the women were.

In the dayroom, Shelley Coates was painting her toenails neon pink. Tessa Stebbins sat next to her on the sofa, vacant eyes on the TV, chewing gum. Mab Thule was in an armchair, asleep by the look of it, gloved hands folded in her lap.

'Hi,' Noah said. 'Has anyone seen Ayana?'

'At lunch.' Shelley adjusted the foam that was wedging her toes apart. 'Not since.'

'Thanks. I'll try her room.'

He walked back to the office and asked Jeanette to direct him to Ayana's room.

'In trouble, is she?' Her eyes grubbed at Noah's face.

'No. I just need her help.'

Ayana's door was shut. He knocked with two knuckles. 'Ayana? It's DS Jake. Noah. I need your help with something.' He waited, but there was no answer from inside the room. 'Ayana?'

After hesitating, he tried the handle. She'd locked the door.

171

SARAH HILARY

'It's about Hope, and Simone. If we could talk, just for a few minutes?'

No answer. No sound of any kind from inside the room.

Noah was on his way back to the office when he met Ed Belloc coming the other way. Ed read his face and looked alarmed. 'What's happened?'

'Possibly nothing. Ayana's locked in her room. She isn't answering the door.'

Ed turned on his heel and jogged back to the office, returning with a set of keys. He searched for the right key, knocking on the door. 'Ayana? It's Ed. Are you okay?'

Nothing.

'I've got a key. I'm coming in. Is that okay?' He waited another couple of seconds, then unlocked the door and pushed it open.

The room was empty, the bed flatly made.

Ayana was gone.

# 41

'Lee Hurran.' Commander Tim Welland sounded as if he'd swallowed a wasp, his voice an angry buzz in Marnie's ear as she sat in traffic on her way back into London.

Scimitar. Severed hand. Ayana Mirza's brother, Nasif.

'Lee Hurran,' she repeated. 'What about him?'

'He's dead.'

'*Dead?*'

'MRSA infection, a couple of hours ago. So I say we go after manslaughter. Maybe even attempted murder. Have we got enough to charge this maniac Mirza, or not?'

'We're working on it, sir.'

'Really? I thought you and the boy wonder were fannying about in Finchley trying to figure out why some battered wife took a knife to her husband. Hardly the zenith of investigative police work. Meanwhile, the CPS is showering six shades of shit on me because our suspect hasn't any form and we haven't any evidence to put him in the relevant dark alley, let alone armed with a scimitar.'

'Nasif Mirza looks good for it, sir. We're talking with his sister, just as you suggested. I think we can persuade her to give evidence against him, maybe even press charges for the bleach attack.'

'You can't cut off someone's hand with a bottle of Domestos. We need to link him to the scimitar.'

'He's already linked to it, sir. His fingerprints . . .'

'We need more, and you know it.' Welland retracted some of the barbs from his voice. 'Where're you anyway?'

'Just getting on the A4, sir. I'll be back in London any time now.'

She should've been vaguer.

'What's happened?' Welland demanded.

'An assault.'

'Stephen Keele? How bad is it?'

'He's . . . out of hospital. Recovering. But it was as nasty as it could be.'

'I'm sorry to hear it. Under other circumstances, I'd recommend time off, but we both know that's not going to happen. I need you back on the scimitar case.'

'Understood, sir.'

'Good.' Welland rang off.

Marnie took the turning for Finchley. Welland was right about the scimitar assault. If racially motivated, maybe even gang-related, it'd have worse repercussions than Leo Proctor's stabbing. They needed Ayana's evidence against Nasif. According to his voicemail message, Noah Jake was already at the refuge. With luck, he was persuading Ayana to help put her brother where he belonged: behind bars.

Noah was standing with Ed outside the office where Jeanette Conway sat, watching the two men across the rim of a mug. The mug, dressed in a red woollen glove, looked aggressively festive. Jeanette had new earrings, Swarovski crystal, not cheap. Marnie wondered if the men had noticed the bling.

'What's up?' she said, seeing their faces.

174

'Ayana's gone,' Noah said.

'When?'

'Sometime after lunch.'

Marnie pulled shut the door, leaving Jeanette inside. She turned her back on the office, facing the two men. 'Why?' She looked at Ed. 'I thought she said she couldn't leave here under any circumstances.'

'I don't think she chose to go.' He looked shattered. 'I think she was tricked, or taken.'

'We tried her phone,' Noah said. 'It's switched off. I put a call through to the station, asked a uniform to go to her parents' house. No one's home.'

Marnie let that hang for a second. 'Any news of Hope or Simone?'

Noah chewed at the inside of his cheek. 'No sightings yet, but Ron Carling spotted something, on the CCTV. The same car, parked outside the refuge on Friday then again at the hospital earlier today.' He handed her the DVLA print-off.

'Coincidence? The hospital's local. And if the Prius was parked . . .'

'It wasn't just parked. CCTV shows the windscreen wipers going for more than ten minutes during that downpour on Friday. What if he was sitting in the car, watching the refuge, or trying to watch it?'

'Henry Stuke.' Marnie showed the print-off to Ed. 'Does he look familiar?'

Ed studied the mug shot and shook his head. 'No.'

Marnie pocketed the sheet. 'What does Jeanette have to say about Ayana?'

'Jeanette was in the kitchen,' Noah said, 'helping with the washing-up. Ayana ate with the others, seemed her usual self. Jeanette didn't see her leave, swears blind no one came into the refuge until I got here, just before five.' He paused. 'The entrance was locked this time.'

'What about the men working on the roof?'

'Good point.' He put his head around the office door. 'Were they working on the roof today?'

Jeanette shrugged. 'As much as they ever are.'

'Did they come into the refuge?'

She widened her eyes, as if the idea was incredible. 'No.'

'Do you have a phone number for the contractor?'

'I can get it.' Ed took out his phone, dialled a number, walked away.

Noah asked Marnie, 'Everything all right?'

'Apart from missing witnesses in every direction? Peachy.'

He took his cue from her tone, returning to the business in hand. 'Something from the hospital: Hope had a phone call late last night. The ward sister says she was talking for twenty minutes. Abby confirmed it, said she came back from a comfort break to find Hope on the phone. I'm guessing the caller was Simone.'

'So they were making plans. How did Hope seem after the call?'

'Very quiet. The ward sister put it down to the length of the call, thought maybe the caller was one of those pushy friends who mean well but don't understand that the best thing for a patient is rest.'

'Do you think Hope was reluctant to leave?'

'Possibly. From what Ed says, Simone can be forceful, and Hope's been conditioned to do as she's told.' Noah paused. 'I checked Simone's room. She took most of her clothes, just a few things left behind. Hope's room looks like Simone stripped it down. Not that she had much to start with. I don't think they're planning to come back.'

Ed rejoined them. 'Calvin Roofers.' He handed Marnie a scrap of paper with the number on it. 'I thought you'd probably want to make the call.'

'Thanks.' She handed the number to Noah. 'And the

CCTV'll need checking again, in case she left that way. Show me the other exits?'

Ed nodded, leading the way.

The fire exit at the end of the corridor was barred, but not alarmed. 'All the windows have locks,' Ed told them, 'but most of them aren't big enough to climb through.'

'It wouldn't need to be very big, for Ayana.'

'She didn't leave,' Ed said again. 'She was tricked, or she was taken.'

'Who would take her?'

'Her brothers. Her family.'

'I should tell you . . . Lee Hurran – the man Nasif attacked? Died two hours ago. We're going after attempted murder.'

'You think Nasif Mirza knows it's a murder inquiry now?' Noah asked.

'The timing's a bit too much of a coincidence. What bothers me is how her family knew she was here. She held out this long without calling home. Why snap now?'

Ed shook his head.

'The office,' Marnie said. 'Do they hold contact details in there? Could someone have lifted her records, found next-of-kin that way?'

'Not from this office,' Ed said. 'I checked as soon as I saw how . . . diligently Jeanette was doing her job. There's nothing here. We use central records, very secure.'

'So she must have called them herself.'

'She wouldn't do that,' Ed insisted. 'Why would she?'

Noah said slowly, 'She wouldn't need to call anyone.' He put a hand across his mouth before taking it away again. 'They could have followed us. The brothers. They know we're investigating Nasif. They know we need evidence against him. They could've guessed where that would lead us. Maybe they even hoped it *would* lead us. Here. To Ayana.'

'You think you were followed,' Marnie said, nauseated. 'Or I was.'

'We've been here more than once since the scimitar attack.' Noah looked from Marnie to Ed. 'It could've been us who gave her away.'

'If her brothers came here, someone would've seen them. If not Jeanette, then one of the others. She wouldn't have gone quietly. Ed?'

'I'd like to think not. But if they turned up here . . . she'll have been in shock.'

'Where are the others?' Marnie asked. 'It's time we asked some tough questions.'

On the dayroom television, an axe-faced woman was gesticulating at a spotty boy, listing his failings in graphic detail.

'You go, girl.' Shelley snapped her fingers at the screen.

Tessa was sitting on the floor at Shelley's feet. Mab was sleeping in a chair, her head nodding on her chest. Marnie crossed the room to switch off the TV, standing with her back to it, fixing the three women with a firm smile. 'We need your help.'

The sudden silence woke Mab. She lifted her head and looked at Marnie. Shelley crossed her arms at her chest, rolling her eyes. On the floor, Tessa hugged her knees.

'Ayana's missing. I think you all saw her at lunch, is that right?' A trio of nods. 'Did anyone see her after that?'

Shelley said, 'She was in her room. That's what we thought, right, Tess?'

Tessa nodded. She angled her shoulders away from Shelley. Her eyes flickered from Ed to Noah, and back to Marnie.

Mab said, 'The roof.'

Ed crouched at the side of her armchair. 'The roof?' he repeated.

Mab groped for his hand and held it between hers. 'She went up.' She pointed his hand at the ceiling. 'Through the roof.'

Shelley made a scoffing sound. 'Don't be daft.'

Mab faltered, gripping at Ed's hand. 'She did . . .'

'Ayana went up on the roof. When? After lunch?'

'He pulled her up.' Mab tugged on Ed's hand, demonstrating the action.

Marnie's throat fisted in fear. 'Who pulled her up? Was it someone she knew?'

'Someone new,' she nodded, misunderstanding the question. 'Not a face I've seen.'

'Where?' Ed asked. 'Can you show us?' He helped Mab to her feet.

Shelley was scowling from the sofa. 'This is mental. She's seeing stuff.'

On the floor, Tessa squirmed.

Marnie followed Ed and Mab from the room, nodding for Noah to stay with the other two. Mab headed for the fire exit at the end of the corridor. Ed didn't rush her, letting Mab lead the way. At the exit, she lifted his hand, still held between hers, and pointed at the ceiling tiles. 'Through here . . .'

Marnie fetched a chair from the nearest bedroom and climbed up to push at the ceiling tiles. They gave, easily. Cold air came in a rush from the hole in the roof, where the repair was half-done. The hole was large enough for a man to get through.

She climbed back down. 'Can you remember when this happened?'

Mab nodded. 'The afternoon play. Radio Four. I wanted to listen, so I used the loo before it started.'

'Two fifteen,' Ed said.

'Yes.' Mab beamed at him. '*The Archers* was over. I don't

179

like *The Archers*, always a fuss about who's to blame for what's gone wrong.'

'You popped to the loo,' Ed said, 'and that's when you saw Ayana being pulled up through here.'

'Yes.' Her smile dissolved into a look of distress. 'I told Jeanette. I told the other girls, but they said I was making it up. Then I must've nodded off.' She began to weep, silently.

'It's all right,' Ed said. 'Did the man come down into the refuge? Through here?' He pointed at the ceiling tiles. 'Can you describe him?'

'Dark, like her.' She fussed at the front of her cardigan. 'Another Indian.'

Marnie eyed the distance from the floor to the ceiling. It wasn't possible for one man to lift a struggling girl through the gap in the tiles, not without help. Assuming she *was* struggling. 'Just one man?' she asked Mab.

'Hands. More hands, through there.' She pointed upwards. 'Pulling her up.' She looked at Ed, her bottom lip turning out. 'Fireman's lift. She was over his shoulder. Her hair was hanging down . . .'

'Didn't any of them see you?' Marnie asked.

She shook her head. 'I stayed out of sight. I didn't want any trouble.'

'Did you hear them speaking?'

'I don't speak Indian.'

'What about Ayana? Didn't she call for help?'

'She was being rescued. Firefighter's lift. To safety.' Mab looked up and down the corridor, her face creasing in confusion. 'There must've been a fire. It's out now. They put it out. She'll come back, now it's out.' She turned to Ed. 'Won't she?'

## 42

'Mab told you what she saw. Why didn't you report it?'

Jeanette Conway crossed her arms defensively. 'For real? It didn't make any sense. I figured she was imagining it.'

Marnie turned to the other two women. Shelley Coates shrugged. 'She's loopy, like my gran.' She admired the polish on her toenails. 'This one time, right? My gran tried to get the bus in the middle of the night, to go dancing. The police had to bring her back.'

'So you didn't believe her.' Marnie turned to the other girl. 'How about you, Tessa? I think you *did* believe her, didn't you?'

'Dunno.' Tessa threw a look at Shelley, scared. 'Maybe.'

'You didn't.' Shelley kicked at a cushion on the sofa. 'You're not mental.'

Ed had taken Mab to her room. Of the women remaining in the dayroom, Noah didn't trust Shelley or Tessa. He trusted Jeanette least of all. Marnie was right: these were the worst witnesses imaginable.

'What about Hope and Simone?' Marnie asked.

'What about them?' Shelley slid her eyes to Noah. 'This is getting on my tits. We come here for a bit of peace. I want the third fucking degree, I'll go home to my Clark.'

181

'Hope Proctor went missing from the hospital earlier today. With Simone.'

Tessa looked miserable. Jeanette consulted her watch. A good watch, not cheap. Noah hadn't noticed it before.

Shelley rubbed a knuckle under her nose. 'No way. For real?'

'Yes.' Marnie didn't elaborate, waiting to see what the women would say.

'So you reckon . . . what? They're a couple of dykes?' Shelley challenged Marnie with a stare. 'No offence.'

'Tessa?' Marnie prompted.

'What?' Tessa sounded on the verge of tears.

'Did you know Simone was planning to leave?'

In a small voice, crushed by Shelley's presence at her back, Tessa said, 'She was in a weird mood last night.'

Shelley opened her mouth to speak. Marnie shut her up with a look. 'Simone was in a weird mood. In what way?'

'Like she was excited about something. She was in Hope's room. I heard her. It sounded like she was moving things around, and she cleared her stuff from the bathroom. I was waiting to have a shower. She was putting her shampoo in a carrier bag. I thought that was weird.'

'Did you ask her what she was doing?'

'No. I didn't like to be nosy.'

Shelley hefted her legs into a sitting position on the sofa. 'I'm not being funny, but this is meant to be a place of safety, right? Only you're saying like three of them are missing. Are you going to move us, or what?'

'Not my decision.'

'Ayana,' Shelley said. 'How'd her scumbag brothers know she was here?'

'We don't know.'

The girl gave Marnie a shrewd look. 'We were okay until you lot turned up. Then it all kicked off. Can't blame us for not trusting you.'

182

'Maybe not, but I can blame you for failing to report what Mab told you. And for giving this address to your boyfriend.'

Shelley's face turned fiery. 'For real? No fucking way.'

'You gave this address to your boyfriend, Clark. Are you denying that?'

Jeanette made a scoffing sound, triumphant. She fingered her new, expensive earrings. Marnie turned to her. 'You knew Clark was visiting the refuge, but you didn't report it. I'm guessing you saw him in Shelley's room, more than once. Why wasn't that reported?'

Jeanette glared at Shelley, who glared back.

'You were paid,' Marnie said, 'to turn a blind eye. Paid quite a bit if the new jewellery's anything to go by. How many times has that happened? With how many people?'

Ed had come back into the room, quietly. He was standing by the door, looking dismayed at what he was hearing.

Jeanette said, 'I told you, they can't help themselves. *She*,' pointing a finger at Shelley, 'can't help herself. She's like a bitch on heat.'

Shelley surged up from the sofa, fingernails aiming for Jeanette's face. Noah stepped between the two women, blocking Shelley's attack with a raised forearm.

'Sit down!' Marnie snapped at Shelley.

Shelley flung herself down on the sofa, her face knuckled with aggression. Tessa moved away, putting distance between herself and Shelley.

Jeanette stood with her arms folded, trying to hang on to a look of triumph.

'I'm guessing Mr Belloc has the paperwork relating to gross misconduct,' Marnie told her. 'I'm going to want a list of everyone you've allowed into this building, or out of it, during the time you've been *doing your job*. After that, I'll decide whether or not to charge you with obstructing a police investigation.'

183

She nodded at Tessa, more kindly. 'You and I need to talk. In your room, please. DS Jake, if you could take a statement from Ms Coates regarding her movements in the last three weeks, that would be helpful.'

Shelley started to speak, but Marnie cut her off with a stare that made her earlier one look like a smile. 'For real.'

# 43

It was after 8 p.m. by the time they were ready to leave the refuge. Ed had called in a favour: a bright-eyed woman called Britt with big shoulders, colourful clothes and a no-nonsense smile. Mab was pleased to see her; she knew Britt from another refuge.

'She'll keep Shelley in line,' Ed told Marnie and Noah. 'And keep things ticking over until we can find someone to take Jeanette's place.' He stuck his hands in his pockets, the boyish gesture at odds with the terse set of his mouth. 'We'll need to get the roof covered over, make sure everything's secure in that respect.'

'I can help with that,' Noah offered. 'We've got a list of emergency repairers, back at the station.'

'Thanks.' Ed looked at Marnie. 'Could I cadge a lift home?'

She nodded, guessing that he asked not for his sake, but hers. She'd given up trying to disguise the fatigue in her face. 'No problem. Noah, do you need me to drop you at the station?'

Noah shook his head. 'I'll walk. Thanks.'

They'd put out all the calls they could about Ayana's disappearance. The rest would have to wait until the morning.

'She has a phone,' Noah said. 'I gave her a top-up card for it. Maybe she'll get the chance to use it.'

'Maybe,' Marnie said. She hated going home under circumstances like this, knowing a young woman was in danger. She knew she wouldn't sleep.

Ed's living room was a controlled explosion of clothes, books and CDs. The mess made her feel better, insulated. Safe. Ed shoved a space clear on the sofa and she sat, putting her head back into the cushions. Her clothes smelt of Sommerville. When she shut her eyes, she saw Stephen lying on the bed, with his arm across his scratched face. Ed went into the small kitchen behind her, clicking on the kettle.

She was going to tell him, she realised. About her visit this afternoon, about what had happened to Stephen. She'd thought she'd go home to her empty bed, but she wanted to talk about it. To Ed.

He brought the coffee from the kitchen, setting two mugs on the low table between precarious towers of magazines and newsprint. One mug was yellow, with a smiley face motif. The other was a heat-reactive novelty mug: James Bond materialising from a black background, gun in fist.

'Biscuits?' he offered. 'Or I could make toast.'

'No. Thanks. This is good.'

He sat next to her, leaving a gap between them, respecting her personal space.

She cradled the mug in her hands, watching Bond emerge from the heat-sensitive ceramic. 'I saw Stephen this afternoon. He'd asked for me. That's what they said. Only when I turned up, he'd changed his mind.' Not the most articulate statement she'd ever made. It didn't come close to saying what she needed to say, about what'd happened at Sommerville. She blinked, and sipped scalding coffee from the mug in her hands.

Ed waited a while, then said, 'Have you considered that he needs you? Your visits. You're the only one showing an interest in him.'

'Maybe.'

'If you stopped going . . . It'd be interesting to see how he responds to that. Whether he'd stop playing games, start engaging with you.'

'Maybe.' Did she want that? She didn't know. 'Something happened,' she told Ed finally. 'On Saturday, after we'd left. He was raped.' The words dried up, her tongue parched and clumsy.

Ed sucked a breath, then let it go, a slow puncture of regret. 'Damn. I'm sorry.'

She nodded. 'Me too.' She set down the mug. Studied her hands. 'Except . . . when they told me – before I knew it was rape, when I thought it was just a thumping – I was glad. Just for a second. As if . . . it was proper punishment, at last. Instead of that private room, those books, an *en suite* bathroom . . . and I *know* it's not like that. I know what prison is, of course I do, but he always looks so . . . *well*.'

She shoved her hair from her forehead, impatiently. 'Christ, Ed. What's wrong with me? I'm a DI. I'm supposed to believe in rehabilitation. I *do* believe in it. With Stephen, though . . . I don't know, maybe it's all about punishment. I really think – it's about punishment. Why else would I be glad, to get news like that?'

'It was a knee-jerk reaction. You said you only felt it for a second. For most people it would've lasted longer than that.'

She felt the hot stab of tears in her eyes. 'I disgust myself. I've no business doing this job if I can be glad when a kid gets a kicking. Any kid. They wanted . . . He's my kid brother. That's how I ought to be thinking of him. They loved him.' She shut her eyes, shaken by a new surge of anger and self-pity. 'They loved him.'

Ed said her name softly, moving close as if to hold her. She held him off with a stare. 'I said this was about trying to forgive him, but it's *them*. They took him in, made space for him in the family. *My* family. They made me a victim. That's what I can't forgive. Not him. *Them*.'

She let him hold her, finally.

Wept, finally.

For her parents, for herself and for Stephen. The whole mess. The unfinished scarf and book. The eight-year-old girl with the silver charm bracelet, and the eight-year-old boy in the bedroom he wouldn't change.

'It was girls,' she said, when she was done. 'They held him down, raped him with a bottle, so badly he needed stitches. The ringleader was nineteen. The others could've been younger.' She dried her tears with the backs of her hands, easing away from Ed's embrace. She was supposed to be the strong one, in control. Another thing Stephen had stolen from her. 'The psychiatrist said he'd been neglected before he was fostered, but not abused, or not that they knew of. I couldn't believe how he'd gone that long in the system without anyone realising how deep the damage went.'

She stood and walked away, going to the kitchen to fill a glass with water, bringing it back to the room where Ed was sitting, waiting for her.

'He had emotional difficulties. That was the official line. His parents were addicts. The middle-class sort, who serve up a line of coke at the end of Sunday lunch. God knows what he saw when he was a little kid. Social services warned us that he didn't talk much, but they made a point of saying what a good boy he was, well-behaved, nice manners. No problems with previous foster-carers.'

She sat next to Ed on the sofa, rubbing her thumb at the lip of the glass, raising a bat's squeak of sound. 'I met him maybe six times. When I was home for birthdays, or Christmas. He was quiet. Watchful. He didn't seem unhappy, or dangerous. There were no clues, I swear . . . No clues. The only creepy thing was my room, the way he hadn't changed it.' She frowned, sipping at the water. 'The whole house felt that way, as if he'd left no trace of himself until the violence, the killings.'

'Has the psychiatrist at Sommerville been able to talk to him?'

'She talks. He doesn't. Today . . . it's the first time I've seen him show any emotion. The first time he let me see what he really thinks of me.' An idea was knocking about in the back of her head, like a moth at a dimly lit window. She couldn't pin it down. Something to do with Stephen, the girls, what Ed had said about shame and silence –

'He has this drawer in his room, full of Mum and Dad's stuff. Not just Dad's glasses. Cards, photos . . .' Stephen had wanted her to see inside, to know what he'd taken. Not just their lives, Greg and Lisa's, but their *lives*. Her childhood.

'I was inside a house once.' She hadn't told Ed this before. 'After a really bad fire. Everywhere was . . . dripping. Black. It smelt . . . bitter, like a fired gun.'

She could see that house as clearly as if it was yesterday. The front door was in the back garden. All that was left of the staircase was six steps, leading nowhere. From the hall, she could see straight through to the garden at the back, piled high with blackened masonry. Part of the ceiling was still coming down, plaster shrapnel exploding in the puddles left by the fire hoses. 'There was nothing left. Part of the bed was buried in this . . . pit where the floor used to be. No upstairs rooms. No roof. Just this pit.' She wet her lips with the glass. 'Two bodies in the bed. The fire didn't kill them. It was the smoke. They were . . . lying back to back in the bed. It didn't look like they woke up. We thought it was one body, at first. Until forensics separated it into two.'

She shut her eyes tight for a second, then opened them.

'I keep thinking . . . did they do something to provoke him? Stephen. I can't believe it, but then I remember the way I felt, before I left. Dad could be so . . . impatient. Mum wanted to help, with everything. I used to think maybe they started fostering to have someone they could shape, the way I wouldn't let them shape me.' She looked into the glass, wishing she'd filled it with wine not water.

When she spoke again, Ed had to lean in to listen. 'There were defence wounds on her hands. The pattern of the bodies . . . probably meant Dad was trying to protect her.'

She shut her eyes, holding the glass to her chest. 'I coped, at the time. That's the thing. I coped with everything. The funeral, the wills. I rented the house, because I wasn't ready to sell it, but I didn't let it slow me down.'

She heard her voice harden, defensively. 'I didn't lose a day more than I had to. Welland was waiting for me to come apart at the seams. I put up with his positive-discrimination bullshit, bit my tongue – I've been biting it ever since. Just lately, it's been like . . . trying to cram one of those toy snakes back into the tin after it's out. I didn't even know I'd let anything out. I thought I had it all tied down.'

'You started to relax,' Ed said. 'Maybe. That gave the emotional adrenalin the chance it needed, to tank.'

'I guess you're right.' She finished the water and put the glass down on the floor. 'So what d'you recommend? Please don't say therapy.'

'You don't need therapy.' He sat forward, so they were shoulder to shoulder. 'You just need to cut yourself some slack. And to talk, when you can.'

'Sounds easy, the way you say it. You make it easy. Thank you.'

'No need,' he said lightly.

'Yes.' She moved close enough to kiss his cheek. 'Thanks.'

Her phone buzzed between their bodies. She leaned away from Ed to answer it.

'Yes. Noah. What've you got?'

'Calvin Roofers took on cheap labour for the job in Finchley. Two of the men were Asian. The names they gave turned out to be Bollywood actors, and the addresses don't exist. According to Calvin Johns, both men were desperate to work at the refuge and agreed to be paid less than the others for the privilege. He was surprised, because his usual workforce is Polish. These two called up after the work started, but he took them on because of the cost saving.'

'They hustled the job,' Marnie said, 'in other words.'

'That's how it sounds. They asked Johns for the job on Friday, after we'd been to the refuge.' Noah sounded sick to the stomach. 'They were Ayana's brothers, I'm sure of it. And they followed us there . . .'

'The uniform who tried their house earlier . . .'

'They tried twice. The second time they got Mrs Mirza. Ayana's mother. She said the family hasn't seen or heard from Ayana since she left home. We'd need a warrant to be sure Ayana was inside the house. If she is . . . Can't Ed get her out of there?'

'Not unless she's prepared to inform on them. Then she could go into Witness Protection and we could change her National Insurance number, her name . . .'

'What did Tessa have to say?' Noah asked.

'Not much. Just that she believed Mab's story about the men taking Ayana through the roof. She's scared stiff of Shelley. Ed had to promise to find a new place for her before she'd admit to having seen Clark on the premises. Which he was, whenever he could afford to buy Jeanette Conway's silence.' Jeanette had said: *And that's not all I seen.* Marnie had expected her to spell it out. When she didn't, she'd guessed the woman was taking backhanders to keep quiet.

191

'What I don't understand,' Noah said, 'is why Shelley didn't just leave the refuge, if she wanted to be back with him.'

'Tessa says Shelley prefers it this way. At the refuge, Clark knows the parameters, Shelley feels in control . . . Apparently, it's a turn-on sleeping together there. The way Jeanette described the place . . . you'd think it was a bunny farm for bullies and predators. She denies taking money from anyone other than Clark, but I wouldn't be surprised if she let others into the refuge. It'd explain how the roofers got inside, all the way to Ayana's room without an alarm being raised.'

'Ed's sacked her, right?'

'He's seeing to it. Not his job, but yes. She's going to have scorch marks by the time he's through with her.' She stood up from Ed's sofa. 'We need to talk Tim Welland out of wringing our necks when he hears we've temporarily lost our witness.'

'What about Hope and Simone? That car that was outside the refuge, and the hospital.'

'Henry Stuke.' Marnie hadn't forgotten the man's name. 'Speak with Ron Carling about Stuke, and the rest of the CCTV. I can't believe one Prius is all we've got to show for those hours of footage.' She dusted her lapels briskly. 'Too bad Leo Proctor isn't dead, then this would be a murder investigation and we'd get proper resources . . .'

## 44

'Detectives . . .' Commander Tim Welland's voice was like gravel in treacle. In *hot* treacle, thanks to the temperature in his office. 'As I understand it, you started out with seven women and now you're down to four. I thought this was a refuge, not a sinkhole. Can someone talk me through the maths?'

'Simone Bissell and Hope Proctor went missing from the North Middlesex Hospital,' Marnie said. 'Ayana Mirza was taken from the refuge, we believe by people acting on behalf of her brothers.'

'Nasif Mirza.'

'And the others. We have a witness who saw two Asian men abducting her. I think kidnap's reasonable grounds for a warrant.'

Welland leaned forward, with the effect of an approaching avalanche. 'Good to see you're capable of thinking. I wouldn't have known it, from this shitstorm.' He shoved back his chair and folded his arms, eyeing Noah unkindly. 'What's this about invisible monkeys?'

Noah hid his surprise; he'd expected Marnie to keep that theory from Welland, whose tolerance for what he called psychobabble was sub-zero. 'It's a problem we have with the witnesses to the stabbing. It's not connected to Ayana's kidnap.'

'You keep using that word, *kidnap*, but where's the evidence she resisted?'

'We think she was in shock . . .'

'Your witness saw two men *helping her* through a hole in the roof – a hole in the roof, for Pete's sake – but she didn't hear any shouting, or screaming. Nor did she raise the alarm, which she surely would've done had she witnessed a *kidnapping*.'

'Conditioned behaviour,' Marnie said. 'All these women have learnt to be afraid of men, to keep quiet. Their witness statements reflect their own experiences. It's about what they *expected* to see.'

'What about what *you* expected? Seems to me you've been hoping to conjure evidence out of thin air. Not to mention persuading one of these petrified women to stand up to her psycho of a brother.'

'It's what the CPS wanted.' Marnie tried an encouraging smile. 'Ayana Mirza helped DS Jake to save Leo Proctor's life. She's tougher than the rest.'

'I see your boy wonder,' Welland nodded at Noah, 'and I raise you hard evidence.'

'We're trying to trace the men who signed on with Calvin Roofers, and to connect them to Nasif. We have grounds for a warrant to search the Mirzas' house and to bring Nasif back in for questioning.'

'You do, do you? Let me put you straight on that score. The CPS is warning of probable complaints arising from our harassment of the Muslim community. *Our* harassment of *them*. We have to respect their honour system right up until it kills someone.'

'It's already half blinded Ayana Mirza. And it cost Lee Hurran his life.'

'Not proven. Not enough for us to go knocking on Nasif's door again. Unless it's to ask, politely, if he's seen his sister.'

Welland sank back in the chair. He lifted a hand and rubbed absently at the taut skin over his eye. 'Tell me why Hope Proctor wasn't under police guard. Better than that, tell me why she wasn't under arrest.'

'It wasn't clear what'd happened. We were waiting to re-examine the witnesses, and to speak with her husband. She didn't look like a flight risk, sir.'

'So we've got two missing witnesses, and an absconded murder suspect. And it's only Tuesday morning.'

'Hope isn't a murder suspect,' Noah said quietly. 'It was self-defence, sir.'

Welland managed a smile; it looked like someone was mugging the lower half of his face. 'I refer you to my earlier statement, DS Jake. Hard. Evidence.'

'Her medical exam showed evidence of long-term abuse—'

'She didn't look like a flight risk,' Marnie repeated. There was a warning to Noah in her tone, to be quiet. It stung. He sat back, biting his lip.

'But she managed to take off,' Welland said, 'all the same. What about this Simone Bissell? What's her story?'

Marnie recounted the worst parts of the history Ed had told them.

'Ugandan,' Welland repeated when she'd finished, as if this was the only part of the story that mattered. 'So I can expect more hand-wringing from the CPS.' He gave Noah a hard look, as if estimating the mileage in having a black detective in his unit. 'This Bissell girl, why d'you think she ran off with Hope Proctor?'

'We don't know,' Marnie said. 'Perhaps because she thought we'd arrest Hope, once Leo Proctor was awake. Or because she feared Leo's reprisals.'

'Is she dangerous?'

'Simone? I wouldn't have thought so, but if she's as damaged as Ed Belloc says . . .'

'She could crack.' Welland looked at the paperwork Marnie had submitted so far. 'You'd better check out this Lowell Paton – the boy who abused her – see what he has to say, and ask her adoptive parents. Damage limitation.' He pinched his long lower lip between his thumb and forefinger. 'Back with Ayana . . . Assuming it was her brothers who took her from Finchley, how did they know where to find her?'

'We're not sure,' Marnie said steadily. She didn't look at Noah.

'You don't think she made a phone call? A lot of them do.'

'That's what Ed Belloc says. I don't think Ayana would've risked it, and neither does Ed. She's too smart. She knew what was waiting for her back home.'

Noah sat very still, conscious of a caustic burn in his gut. Ayana's brothers had followed him from the police station to the refuge. He was sure of it. He'd led them right to her. Now she was gone, back to that place where they'd half blinded her. God knows what punishment they'd devise for her this time.

Welland said, 'You'd better get on with it.' He nodded at Noah. 'DI Rome, I need a further word with you.'

'Coffee,' Marnie told Noah when she came out of Welland's office. 'I'm buying.'

Her expression gave away nothing of what had happened after Noah left the meeting. Not that he needed many clues; Welland had made his mood clear enough. Noah wished Marnie had let him tell Welland a few more facts about their investigation, instead of cutting him off at the knees.

In the local coffee shop, she ordered two flat whites, both with an extra shot. 'I've got an address for Lowell Paton. It's not far. Let's walk.'

196

A three-mile run would've been better for both of them, but this way they could keep working. Noah sipped at the coffee, keeping pace with Marnie.

'Welland's pissed off about Hope. He's insisting she should've been under police guard at the hospital. "Attempted murder", I'm quoting here, "is still a crime in our neck of the woods, whatever hymn sheet you're singing from, DI Rome." That clears us for putting resources behind finding her.'

'Why didn't you tell him about the cupboard under the stairs? Or the medical exam.'

She heard the edge in his voice and raised her eyebrows. 'We didn't have a warrant. Hard evidence needs to be iron-clad, remember?'

*You're the one who forgot it,* Noah thought, *when you questioned Leo at the hospital.*

'What about Ayana?' he demanded. 'Is Welland going to let us get a warrant?'

'I've called Ed, to see what he can do. Welland thinks Victim Support might stand a better chance with the family than us right now.'

'Ed's not the police.'

'No,' she agreed, 'he's not.'

'So we're delegating to him just because the CPS is neurotic.'

'We're not delegating anything, Detective.' Her tone was a slap on the wrist. 'We're making proper use of the resources available to us.'

Trying to pick a fight with Marnie Rome was like trying to dig your fingers into marble; you just ended up with an ache in your fists. 'It's idiotic.'

'It's politic, and it's pragmatic. Idiotic would be running in blind, because we didn't stop and think first.' Another slap, this one on the face. She didn't like him criticising Ed, that much was clear. They walked on, not speaking.

London was still waking up, although it was close to ten o'clock. The office workers were entrenched, the school run was over. It was a dead hour of the day, before the lunchtime rush. Two passenger jets cross-hatched the sky: white lines on a whiter background. Closer at hand, a couple of sparrows practised their spring flight patterns.

Birdsong was an eerie sound in central London. Like hearing the sea before you could see it – a reminder that Nature was behind or beneath everything, even those places where men had done their best to obliterate her.

Noah wondered if Ayana could hear birdsong, or the sea. He wanted to think she was near a phone, or a weapon. He realised he was wishing for a crime like the one Hope Proctor had committed at the refuge.

Marnie walked ahead of him, to drop her empty coffee cup into a litter bin. 'Guess where Lowell Paton is living.'

He read the distaste on her face. 'Not in the flat where he kept Simone prisoner?'

'Near enough. Home sweet home. At his dad's expense. Maybe Ed was right and Paton senior helped his son tidy up after Simone got away. If Daddy's home, we'd better be prepared to listen to the bullshit in stereo.' She tidied her hair. 'Families closing ranks . . . Makes a change from beating the crap out of each other, I suppose.'

'There're all kinds of ways you can abuse someone. It doesn't have to be physical.'

She shot him a look. 'True. Do you think Ron Carling had a happy childhood?'

Noah was on his guard against the question, wondering what she'd heard – or guessed – about the situation with him and Carling. 'Why him?'

'Because he's a bigot and a blag artist.' She adjusted the cuffs of her shirt. 'And because I suspect he's been giving you more grief than you choose to share with me.'

'It's nothing I can't handle.'

'Bully for you. I still need to know if there's a rotten apple on the team. Insofar as we are a team. He has a problem with you, doesn't he?' She kept her eyes ahead, making it marginally easier for him to answer.

'Apparently. He's getting over it, though.'

'Because you're good at deflecting or because he's learning tolerance?'

'A . . . bit of both.'

'Is it going to be a problem, in the team?'

'There's no problem. Nothing serious, just mucking about. Macho stuff. You know.'

'Not really,' Marnie said. She came to a standstill, nodding at the phallic apartment block ahead of them. 'Let's see what Lowell Paton's got to say for himself. Maybe it'll shed some light on where Simone's gone, or what's going on in her head.'

## 45

Lowell Paton was twenty-three, but with his skinny frame and show-off sportswear, he could have passed for eighteen. He rubbed sleep from his eyes, inviting Noah and Marnie into the penthouse apartment at the top of the block. No more underground living for Lowell.

Marnie had warned Noah that they weren't to push Paton. They didn't have a warrant, or even a formal complaint. The best they could hope for was an insight into Simone's state of mind. Lowell was unlikely to give the information freely, but a guilty conscience was a funny thing. Sometimes it provoked the party in question into sharing more than he intended. Monsters weren't very good at staying hidden, and Lowell Paton had been a monster to Simone Bissell. There was a flaw in this logic, however, as Noah realised after ten minutes in Paton's apartment, with its noisy decor: twin sofas in blood-red leather, red-and-black mosaic wall segregating the kitchen from the living space. Mirrors on all sides, one framed in light bulbs; not the room of someone who wanted to avoid his own reflection. White rugs, pretending to be bleached animal skins. An AV system that looked as if it could land a jet plane, Swarovski crystals stuck like shrapnel in the sleek black corners of the console.

Pimp my penthouse.

Lowell Paton moved around the apartment with the easy neglect of someone who didn't pay rent, or insurance. Noah guessed Paton senior had that covered; cosseting his son for whatever reason he'd found to excuse the indulgence. Perhaps he thought he was keeping him safe up here, away from the streets where Lowell had strayed, albeit briefly. Noah's heart sank when he saw the spoilt, satisfied boy this indulgence had bred. Lowell Paton didn't have a guilty conscience. The monsters in his past, with or without his father's help, had all been exorcised.

In the kitchen – black rubber peppermill, polished granite trivet under an Alessi kettle – Lowell opened a fridge the size of a space shuttle, studying its contents. 'I've got Coke or,' he grinned up at them, 'Bud.' His face had the forward slant of a fox's. Wide mouth, thin-lipped, drawn tight across the lower half of his jaw. Long eyes under longer brows, sandy-brown like his hair, like his eyes. His left earlobe was pierced, impaled by a broad Perspex talon. Street face, gangland, but too studied to be the real thing. And too smooth. There wasn't a mark on him.

'Nothing for us, thanks.' Marnie fed Lowell's smile straight back, not missing a beat. At the door, she'd shown her badge with a hint of apology, as if deferring to the privilege evidenced by the security here, the uniformed concierge, the glossy lift that delivered residents to carpeted corridors outside their front doors.

Lowell carried a bottle of cola to the sofas, inviting Noah and Marnie to sit one side of the coffee table while he sprawled on the other. In his shiny white tracksuit on the red sofa, he resembled a maggot in an open wound.

Noah, remembering what Ed Belloc had said about the

boy's blood kink, felt his gorge rise. Paton kicked his legs apart, angling his crotch in Marnie's direction. Where was Mrs Paton? What brand of motherly love had resulted in this self-assured machismo? Or had there been no love, was that Lowell's problem?

'So how can I help you guys?' Lowell Paton swung the bottle between the knuckles of his right hand. Rings on three of his fingers: gold sovereigns. Gangsta bling. The rings made good weapons, whenever Paton felt like punching someone. Not men or boys. He wouldn't last two minutes on the street. Paton punched girls. He'd broken Simone's nose with the hand he was using to swing the cola.

Marnie said, 'We'd like to ask some questions about Simone Bissell.'

Lowell passed his tongue over his skinny upper lip. Not nervous, just tasting whatever he'd eaten for lunch; the penthouse smelt of chorizo and cheese. 'Sure,' he said. 'Simone, yeah.' He put the bottle to his mouth. 'Cool.'

'You remember her.'

'Sure. We hung out together for a bit.'

'More than that.' Marnie smiled.

Lowell sprawled lower on the red leather, getting comfortable. 'Yeah.' A long swig from the cola bottle left his mouth wet, open. 'Lived together for a bit. Must've been about a year. Cool times.'

'You lived together for a year. When was this?'

'Two, three years ago.'

'Then what happened?'

'She did a ghost.' Lowell kissed the neck of the bottle, blowing a note from it. 'Vanished. But that was cool. Peace out, *vato*.' He splayed two fingers from the side of his head.

'She left, after a year. Why did she do that?' Marnie looked around. 'This is a great place you have here.'

'Yeah.' Lowell stroked his left thigh. He glanced at Noah, from under his lashes.

Someone else might've mistaken the glance for fear, or flirtation, but Noah knew it was Paton's prejudice for his skin colour; wanting to impress the black man he was aping. Paton would've loved Noah's little brother, Sol.

'Simone didn't like it here?'

'We didn't live here.' Another swig from the bottle. No sweat on his face or hands. No evidence of nerves. 'They hadn't finished the place back then.'

'Your dad owns the block, is that right?'

'Yeah.'

'So where did you and Simone live?'

'Down in the basement.' He laughed, nodding. 'Yeah, I know, bit of a shithole, but still . . .' He edited the laugh, turning down the corners of his mouth, caricaturing regret. 'They were some good times.'

'You were fond of Simone.'

'I loved that girl.' Lowell sat forward, his face changing. For a man with no lips, his pout was impressive. 'What's with all this?' He looked at Noah. 'What's up, man?'

'Simone's missing,' Marnie said. 'We're asking around anyone who knew her, seeing if they can suggest places she might've gone. You're the person who spent the most time with her. We thought you might have some ideas for us.'

'Missing.' Lowell sank back, sucking at the neck of the bottle. 'For real?'

Noah's dad would've slapped him, no hesitation: 'Learn some respect, boy,' believing women should be worshipped, not seeing this as sexism in another shape.

'So you loved Simone,' Marnie said. 'How did you two meet?'

'On the streets.' Lowell was desperate for Noah's approval, some sign that he was winning respect from that quarter.

Noah gave him a bland face, guessing this would elicit further attempts, maybe a boast, anything to give them an excuse to take Paton in for questioning, better still if they could charge him with false imprisonment and assault, although Noah didn't ask for miracles. It was clear that Lowell was insulated by his father's wealth, to the point of complacency. Noah was surprised he hadn't insisted on calling Paton senior before answering police questions. Did Lowell really believe he'd done nothing wrong in keeping Simone a prisoner for a year, beating and raping her? He was so relaxed on the sofa, he looked boneless.

'How did Simone feel about living in the basement?' Marnie asked.

'Anywhere's better than the streets, right?'

'Where did she go when she left?'

Lowell shrugged. The light slid off the shoulders of his tracksuit, pooling in his lap. He fidgeted with the cola bottle. 'No idea, sorry.'

'Why did she leave?'

'Dunno. Maybe she got a better offer.' He flashed his teeth, rotted by cola. Daddy needed to shell out for some dental implants.

'Better than this?' Marnie looked around again. 'Hard to imagine.'

'I told you, we weren't up here. We had the basement flat.'

'Still, anywhere's better than the streets. And you loved her. You'd have moved her up here, when it was ready.'

'I guess.'

Noah was watching Paton's hands on the bottle, his knuckles white above the yellow rings. 'What sort of better offer?' he asked. It was the first time he'd spoken. He used Sol's street accent. 'You said maybe she got a better offer.'

'Yeah.' Lowell wet his upper lip. 'She liked it hard, you

204

know?' He flicked his eyes at Marnie, then back to Noah. 'Stabbing.'

The silence in the penthouse was broken by Lowell insisting, 'Daggering, man, you know what I'm talking about.'

'She liked rough intercourse.'

'Yeah.' He bounced on the sofa, juggling the bottle from hand to hand. 'Oh yeah.'

'It got too much for you.'

Lowell grinned. 'Nearly broke my dick. *You* know what I'm talking about . . . Blacks fucking *own* this shit.' He stopped abruptly, as if he'd heard his dad's voice in his head, telling him to mind his manners, or watch his mouth.

'That's why she left, to find someone who could satisfy her appetite for rough sex.'

The flat note in Noah's voice penetrated Lowell's defences, finally. He squirmed upright on the sofa, looking towards the phone he'd dropped on a side table. Thinking of calling his dad? 'I loved her,' he whined. 'Tried to give her everything she wanted. Flowers, man. I brought her flowers, every week.' His eyes filled with self-pitying tears. 'Yellow roses. Her favourites.'

'But she left, without saying where she was going.'

'It was a long time ago, man. A long time.'

'You didn't try and find her?'

'She didn't want to be found. It was pretty obvious, the way she left. Just cleared off one night, when I was sleeping.' He rubbed his hand under his nose. 'Didn't even say goodbye. Didn't thank me for finding her this place. Nothing.'

'You think she should've thanked you,' Marnie said.

'She was living rough. I found us this place. Yeah, a thank-you would've been nice.' The pout crept back on to his fox's face. 'Guess I never really knew her. Never understood where she was coming from, you know? She was cool, but a bit of a freak. I mean, she looked like a street kid, right?' He stared at Noah. '*You* know what I mean, man. The streets. I thought she was well hench. But when she spoke . . . the things she said . . . that was different.'

Marnie reached into her bag. 'Would you mind making a note of your phone number for me, in case you think of anything else?' She held out a notebook and a pen.

Lowell shrugged, climbing to his feet. He scrawled the number, adding his signature underneath as if she'd asked for his autograph.

'Thanks.' Marnie took back the notebook and pen. 'By the way, did Simone tell you why she was living on the streets?'

'Yeah, her mum and dad giving her shit, usual story.' Lowell yawned, his lower jaw swinging as if it might come free from the rest of his face. 'I could dig that.'

'You have problems with your parents?'

Paton looked through slitted eyes at Marnie. 'I'm one of the lucky ones,' he said.

## 46

'I need a shower,' Marnie told Noah, when they reached the street outside Paton's apartment.

'I need a colonic.' Noah buttoned his coat, looking savage.

'What's daggering?' she asked him.

'You really want to know?'

'I can hazard a guess. Rough sex, you said. I'm thinking very hard and fast.'

Noah made a non-committal sound of disgust. He looked back up at the penthouse. 'Do you think Daddy's going to keep him up there forever?'

'Out of harm's way?' Marnie said. 'Why not?'

'He needs bringing back down to earth.'

She hadn't seen Noah like this before, his jaw clenched so hard she could hear it popping. She tried to lighten his mood. 'He was tight with you, man. Thought you well hench, whatever that means.'

'It means I could trash him in a fight.' He sent a last look up at the apartment. 'I wouldn't mind a go . . .' He'd used a different accent, inner city, when he was talking to Paton. Marnie wondered where it came from, whether it was the voice he'd used to get by in school. There was a lot about Noah Jake that she just didn't know.

'So did he write the threatening letter?' Noah nodded at the notebook she'd slipped into her bag.

'No. At least I doubt it. I'm beginning to think Hope got that wrong . . .' They walked in the direction of the police station. 'You know Lowell's problem?' she said.

'Where do you want to start?'

'Invisible ape.'

'*He's* the ape.'

'Precisely. He can't see what's under his nose. I think he really believes he gave Simone what she wanted: a warm place to stay; sex on tap . . .'

'He broke her nose.' Noah made fists of his hands, burying them in his coat pockets.

'He couldn't sit still. Do you think he's on something?'

'Drugs? It's the usual way kids like that pretend to rebel against their parents, and he can afford it.'

'You really didn't like him.'

Noah looked at her. 'Did you?'

'No, but after Leo Proctor . . .'

He glanced away. 'Leo showed remorse. Paton? Is a deluded freak.'

What was making him so angry? Paton? Or the set-up in the apartment, the way Lowell's dad had padded the place with money, security. The polar opposite, she knew, of Noah's upbringing. On the other hand, as far as she knew, Noah's childhood had been a happy one. Somehow, she doubted Lowell Paton had received a tenth of the natural affection Noah's parents had given their son. 'One thing's for certain. Simone didn't take Hope to the basement flat. She wouldn't go within five miles of that place.'

'Did you really think she might've done that?' Noah was incredulous. 'Gone back to the basement?'

'She doesn't know a lot of places in London, from what Ed says. People can make odd choices when they're feeling trapped.'

Like leaving home to live in the damp basement of a friend's house because you can't stand seeing the impatience on your father's face any longer. Or renting out the house where your parents were murdered, because you can't sell it until you've at least got close to understanding *why* . . .

'Do you think Simone's dangerous?' Noah asked. 'What was it Ed said, about the war zone under her skin?'

'I don't know whether she's dangerous or not. I thought I might get a clearer idea, after seeing Lowell.' She shook her head. 'He's got denial down to a fine art, and she lived an isolated life before she met him, narrow frame of reference . . .' She dug out her phone, pressing Ed's number on speed-dial, getting voicemail. 'It's me, hoping for an update on Ayana. Call me.' She returned the phone to her pocket.

'Maybe we should try the Bissells. See if they can give us anything to go on. Ed gave me an address in Putney Hill.' She named the street.

'Nice address,' Noah said shortly. 'It's on my run route. You can do five miles just going up and down the private driveways round there.'

'Lots of money,' Marnie deduced. 'Not that it did Simone much good. I doubt the Bissells can help us, but we should cross them off the list for Welland.'

They were clutching at straws, Noah's silence said as much, but they needed to keep moving, keep busy. If they couldn't find Ayana, they could at least find Hope.

'We'll need the car,' she told Noah, when they reached the station. 'You'd better check in with Carling, see if he tracked down the Prius driver. Stuke, was it?'

Noah nodded. 'I'll meet you in the car park.'

\*    \*    \*

209

Noah took the station steps two at a time, aware of the angry heat in the pit of his stomach. He knew he'd puzzled Marnie with his reaction to Lowell Paton, but how was he supposed to explain that Paton's patronage was worse than Ron Carling's prejudice? Noah didn't understand it himself. He found Carling at his desk, with a message for Marnie: 'Phone call from a Felix Gill. For the DI. You want it?'

Noah took the piece of paper. 'Thanks.'

Felix Gill, the Proctors' neighbour. He'd phoned to say he'd seen Hope with a 'coloured lass' at the Proctors' house 'just now'.

Noah called the number written on the note. 'Mr Gill? It's DS Jake. Thank you for the message you left. Is Hope still at the house?'

'She wasn't here more than ten minutes. I phoned as soon as they left. Four hours ago, give or take.'

Four hours. *Shit.* Why hadn't Carling, or someone, passed on the message sooner?

'Did they leave together, Hope and the other woman?'

'A coloured lass, yellow beads in her hair. Thick as thieves they looked.' Gill freighted his voice with suspicion. 'Took a suitcase. Brown. I made a note and called you right away. Couldn't get through, mind you, but I kept trying.'

'You didn't speak with them?'

'I didn't like to, knowing you people were on the case.'

'Were they on foot,' Noah asked, 'or in a cab?'

'On foot, far as I could see. Could've been a cab waiting on the corner, I suppose.'

'And this was about eight o'clock this morning?'

'More like seven thirty,' Gill said. 'As I said, I'd trouble getting through to you lot, but I kept at it.'

'Thanks.'

'Useful to you, is it?'

'We appreciate the call. Thanks.' Noah rang off. He walked

to Carling's desk. 'That call came through four hours ago. Who sat on it so long?'

'Search me. I handed it across as soon as I saw you.' Carling looked pleased with himself for having managed this much. 'Sorted. Like a chav in a filing cabinet . . .'

'I was here at nine this morning. Gill called at eight. The note should've been on my desk when I got in.'

'Don't look at me.' Carling put his hands up. 'I just passed it along. Front desk took the call. You've got a problem, take it up with them.'

Noah moved his mouth into a smile that made Carling flinch with its ferocity. 'I've just spent two hours inter- viewing a deranged shit in a shiny tracksuit because we're trying to find one of the women this phone call was about. If I'd got that message when I was supposed to get it, we could've picked her up and I wouldn't now have a taste in my mouth that makes me want to throw up – and nut someone.'

'Don't look at me,' Carling repeated, but he was nervous now. He sucked at his teeth. 'I'll talk to the desk. Tell them to be quicker off the mark next time. Okay?'

Noah held hard to what was left of his temper. 'How'd you get on with Henry Stuke?'

'No one's answering the phone. I could go round, but I figured you'd want a piece of that action . . .'

'So where're we up to with the CCTV?'

'Nothing from around the North Middlesex.'

'How about Finchley, the refuge?'

'Still waiting on it.' Carling reached for the phone. 'I'll hurry them up.' He looked straight-mouthed, serious.

'Thanks.' Noah nodded. 'We need to expand the search area from the hospital to include the house where the women were seen this morning.' He wrote down the address and handed it across. 'And keep trying Stuke.'

211

'Where'll you be?' Carling asked.

'Wherever the DI wants me.'

Marnie was waiting in the car. She started the engine as Noah got into the passenger seat. He said, 'Felix Gill called. He saw Hope and Simone, at the Proctors' place. Four hours ago. I rang back. He's at home.'

Marnie rested her hands on the steering wheel. 'Four hours ago,' she repeated.

'I know. I gave Carling a hard time about it. He says the front desk took the message and only just passed it on.'

'What exactly is Gill saying he saw?'

'Hope and Simone going into the house, around seven thirty. Leaving with a suitcase, on foot. I've asked Carling to check the CCTV from near the house as well as the hospital.'

'Good. We should get over to Leo's place.'

'It's a better lead than the Bissells,' Noah agreed.

Marnie released the handbrake, frowning. 'They went to her house? That was a bit risky. If Simone wanted the pair of them to go into hiding . . . I'm surprised she let Hope talk her into collecting a bag of clothes from a house we could've been watching.' She glanced at Noah. 'Gill was sure it was Simone, with Hope?'

'From his description, yes. A "coloured lass with beads in her hair". He said they were as thick as thieves.'

'What do we think of Gill?' Marnie asked. 'Is he just a nosy neighbour?'

'I'd say so. There's one just like him across from me and Dan. It's one of the reasons we got curtains instead of blinds . . . Lonely, I suppose.'

'Neighbourhood watch . . . I'll bet Hope hated being under his surveillance. Too bad she wasn't under ours.'

'No one was watching the house.' Noah felt a fresh flare of anger under his ribs. 'What the *fuck* is wrong with us?'

Marnie flicked him a glance. Noah read regret in her eyes, and hard necessity in the line of her jaw. 'Ask the accountants . . .'

'I'd have done it myself if you'd asked me to.'

'Not how it works.' Marnie retracted the flippancy from her voice. 'All right, let's beat ourselves up later. Right now, we need to get on. How well do you remember the house?'

'The Proctors' house? Pretty well.'

'Good. Let's see if we can figure out what they took that was worth the risk of returning there.'

## 47

Felix Gill answered his front door promptly. He must have been waiting in the hall. 'You'll want to find out what they took away,' he said, 'in the suitcase.'

'Do you know?' Marnie asked.

'It was heavy. The coloured lass,' he stole a glance at Noah, 'took it off Mrs Proctor, when they came out of the house. She looked surprised by how heavy it was. I said to myself, "That's not just clothes, is that." Off they went, down there.' He pointed to the corner of the street, where it joined the main road.

Marnie had brought a torch from the car. 'You didn't speak to Mrs Proctor?'

'They didn't see me.' Gill looked proud of his powers of subterfuge.

Noah asked, 'How did they seem to you?'

'In a hurry. *She* had her head down, as per usual. It was the other lass in charge.'

'How do you mean?' Marnie asked.

'She took the suitcase for one thing, and she was holding Mrs Proctor's elbow, steering her along. She had the whip-hand, all right.' He glanced at the torch in Marnie's hand. 'You'll want to look inside, see what's missing.'

214

'Yes, we'll do that.'

'Mind you, it's her house,' Felix Gill said. 'She's entitled to take what she likes. That's right, isn't it?'

The Proctors' house had the same chill as before, with no immediate clue that Hope and Simone had been inside four hours earlier. Noah and Marnie went upstairs, searching the bedroom for missing clothes. It wasn't easy to see what Hope had taken. No gaps in the wardrobe, or the drawers. Beds smooth, shutters closed. Dust line-danced through the white slats. From the look of it, no one had been in either bedroom since Noah and Marnie's last visit. Someone had opened the bathroom cabinet: a smudge of fingerprints on the mirrored glass. The bottle of antidepressants was missing, together with the Vaseline, antiseptic cream, plasters. The makings of a first-aid kit. Nothing to account for a heavy suitcase, assuming Felix Gill had read the situation right.

They searched the rooms downstairs, finding everywhere the same as before. Noah wondered if his memory was letting him down, but Marnie said, 'I can't see that anything's gone, can you?' He shook his head. 'So what was in the suitcase?'

They stood in the kitchen, looking at the knife rack. Nothing new was missing, just the knife that was bagged in the evidence locker back at the station. 'We should've conducted a proper search. Then we'd know for sure what they'd taken.'

'We didn't have a warrant,' Noah reminded her. 'And the show-house furniture, new beds . . . It didn't look like the place was hiding anything.'

'No,' she said slowly. 'It looked like it was hiding everything.'

In the hall, they stopped outside the cupboard with the latched door.

Noah's skin crawled. This was where the Proctors had kept

215

at least one of their secrets, in the torturously small space under the stairs. Marnie slid the latch. It came easily, without a sound, as if Leo oiled it regularly. She shone the torch inside, the light moving muddily over the stone floor and walls. 'Are those scratch marks?'

Noah peered. 'Hard to tell.'

'Check it out, would you?'

Noah glanced at her. 'You mean . . .'

She handed him the torch. 'Get a proper look at what's in there. Tell me what you think.'

Noah stripped off his jacket and hung it over the banister. He crouched and drew in his head, moving sideways to fit his body into the small space. The slant of the stairs forced him to keep his chin drawn in against his chest. His shoulders blocked the light from the hallway. Not enough room to move his elbows properly. He ended up holding the torch under his chin as he searched the floor and walls, painstakingly, every cold, gritty inch.

Raw stone grazed the ends of his fingers. He kept his nose closed against the ammonia stink of Hope Proctor's fear. How long had she been in here, each time Leo locked her up? Minutes? Hours? Days? Noah didn't think he could've lasted minutes, never mind any longer.

The weight of the house was crushing. He was acutely aware of Marnie standing behind him in the hallway. Near enough to reach out and shut the door, slide the oiled latch and lock him in. He set his teeth and completed the search. Not just the floor, the walls too. Hope could've banged on the wall that joined this house to the neighbours. They'd have heard it, surely. These new-builds had hollow walls. She hadn't banged on the wall, Noah was certain of it. Sitting instead with her knees hugged to her chest, and her head drawn in, making herself as small as possible so the space would feel less like a box, or a coffin.

216

He ran the torch's light over the place where Marnie had spotted scratches, touching his hand there. Scarred patches snagged at his fingers, thin grooves in the stone and plaster. Maybe Hope hadn't sat still the whole time . . .

'Anything?' Marnie asked when he climbed out.

His shirt was sticking to his skin. 'You're right. Scratches on the walls and the floor. Could've been made by fingernails, or boxes being moved in and out. Most people would use a cupboard like this to store boxes.' He glanced back at the space. 'But these were made by fingernails. I'd put money on it.'

'Fingernails,' Marnie repeated.

'Yes. She's scratched right around the walls, must've broken most of her nails.'

Marnie was silent, the expression on her face hard to read. She looked serious, severe even, but it was more than just that. 'What?' he asked quickly.

'I'm not sure yet.' She took the torch from him. 'You'll want to wash your hands.' Her tone was clipped, and distant, as if she was speaking to him down a phone line.

He waited a second or two, puzzled. Did he look that freaked out? That she regretted delegating the dirty work his way? 'I'm okay,' he said.

She nodded. 'Good. Wash your hands.'

In the kitchen, he used the sink, drying his hands on a sheet of paper towel.

Marnie held out his jacket. 'You said Hope was on the phone the night before she went missing. We assumed the caller was Simone. Are we sure she called Hope, not the other way around?' A crisp edge to her voice now, as if she was checking off the facts.

Noah pulled on his jacket. 'You think Hope might've called Simone?'

'Hope had a motive to leave the hospital, knowing Leo was going to wake up. I'm not so sure of Simone's motive.'

217

'Welland thinks she's crazy . . .'

'Let's hope he's wrong.'

'The hospital would know if the call was incoming or outgoing.' Noah searched his phone for the number for the North Middlesex, dialling it and asking to speak with the duty nurse.

The signal was poor inside the house, so they went out into the street. Marnie locked the front door and pocketed the keys she'd taken from Leo at the hospital, waiting while Noah spoke with the ward sister.

'Thanks.' He ended the call, looking at her. 'The phone call was outgoing. Hope rang Simone, not the other way around.'

'She called *someone*,' Marnie corrected. 'We don't know it was Simone.'

'Who else does Hope have?'

'Good point.' She looked up at the sky. After a beat, she turned away. Tension redrew her profile, making it forbidding.

What was she thinking? Noah's wrists itched.

'It's still possible Simone instigated the escape,' Marnie said. 'She must've given Hope her number, told her to call if she wanted anything.' She frowned. 'We should've had someone watching the house. If resources weren't so tight . . .'

'I wish I'd been here.'

'You have to sleep sometime, and so do I.' She glanced up the street. 'We need to speak with Leo again.' She shot Noah a look. 'Not like last time. We need to find out where Hope might've gone. Assuming the escape plan was hers and not Simone's.'

She looked at the shuttered windows of the Proctors' house. 'She risked coming back here, for the suitcase. She knows her neighbour keeps watch. Why didn't she and Simone come at night, when there was less chance of being seen?'

'Or more.' Noah pointed out the street lighting, positioned like a searchlight directly opposite the house. 'Where d'you think they've gone?'

'Ed said Simone doesn't know many people in London. That should make it easier.' She didn't sound as if she believed this, eyeing the Proctors' house unkindly.

'Maybe Simone insisted they come here,' Noah suggested. 'Gill said she had the whip-hand, held Hope's arm, took charge of the suitcase . . .'

'Why? What was in it?'

'I don't know. Maybe Leo does. You're right. We need to get back to the hospital.'

'You need to get back to the station. See where Ron Carling's up to with Henry Stuke. You'll have to trust me to ask the questions at the hospital.' She saw him hesitating. 'Don't worry. I won't give Leo a hard time. About the suitcase or anything else. For one thing, we need his help.'

'I suppose so.' Noah was frustrated, and didn't bother to hide it. 'What about Ayana? We can't just—'

'Ed will call as soon as there's news. Stop beating yourself up about being followed. We don't know for sure how they found her. Let's concentrate on how we're going to get her back. I'll be in touch as soon as I hear anything.'

She nodded at him. 'Go. Let me know how you get on with Stuke.'

# 48

*Six months ago*

It's the first time he's seen her in the street, and it's a shock. She looks so . . . *clean*, and she's done her hair like a doll's, straight to her shoulders. She's wearing black, a neat little knee-length dress under a coat. Sensible shoes, expensive, like a solicitor would wear. At the nightclub, at the hotel, she always wears the same tight clothes. Cheap, stretchy stuff that tears if he pulls at it too hard, and spiked heels, ripped-up fishnets. Her hair's full of this gel with sharp bits in it; he has to scrub it off with a loofah in case Freya spots the glitter on his skin.

The bruises are different. Freya actually *looks* at him, makes the little noise of sympathy she usually reserves for the twins, smears on a dab of the ointment she saves for their sore arses. He's grateful, pathetically grateful, to be touched at all. She thinks he's helping a workmate during his lunch hour, that the cuts and bruises are from hefting boxes, screwing shelves. He attempts a joke – *the only thing I am screwing* – but it falls flat. It takes a miracle to make her laugh these days.

As for *her*, she laughed when she was giving him the bruises. Told him he'd need better excuses when she really got to work on him. He still doesn't know her name. A dozen ways to make her squirm – he knows that. But not her name.

In the street, without the heels, she's four inches shorter. Doesn't look like she could hurt a fly, let alone a man. Nothing about her is the same. He wouldn't know it *was* her, except his skin contracts and heats everywhere, recognising something – her slim wrist maybe, even though it's empty of the cheap bangles she usually wears, the rattle of them like a baby's toy. His body knows it's her.

Now he knows where she lives. By accident, because he's on his way across town, on an errand for the boss. He hasn't seen her in daylight before, let alone in the driveway to a house, looking like every other house in the street.

She locks her front door, slips the key into a posh bag at her shoulder. The kind of bag Freya calls an investment buy. She's coming his way. He fumbles for his phone, ducking his head and pretending to check his messages.

She's dressed for a funeral, or a law court. Her face is small, her mouth set. She looks like a little girl, someone neat and spoiled, well cared for. She doesn't look like she knows what the inside of a nightclub smells like, let alone the rest of it.

Anger makes his stomach ache.

She's been lying to him. Every time they screwed, every time she let him twist her wrists, pin her down . . . Until it was his turn and she was back on top, sweat sticking the glitter to her face, blood at the edge of her mouth . . .

She's been lying to him. The whole time. Pretending to be someone who doesn't fit, someone who's hiding, like him. *Better* than him, because she didn't wear a disguise during the day, didn't have a home to go back to. He realises he's made up a whole life for her – dirty, different, *brave* – and none of it is true. It's all lies.

She's coming up the street towards him, but she isn't looking his way. Busy concentrating on her lies, on being a neat little black-clad doll on her way to work in her expensive suit.

'Hey,' he says when she's close enough for it to be a whisper.

Her head jerks up. No make-up, soap-and-water skin, but he smells her, underneath the disguise she's put on. She can't hide from him.

'Hey,' he repeats. 'You want to go somewhere?'

She shakes her head, like a kid refusing a gobstopper from a pervert. 'I'm sorry,' she says, and even her voice is a lie, but he hears the sing-song in it, and something else – a warning? 'I'm in a hurry.'

Like he's selling insurance, or he's a street beggar and she's stepping past him with her skirts held up in one dainty hand.

He knows every inch of her. The bruises behind her knees, the blue under her right breast. 'Come on,' he says, and it's his dick talking, of course, but that's her fault, that's how she's trained him to be, 'I've got an hour before I need to be anywhere.'

She looks right at him, cold-eyed. 'I haven't.'

'Later, then.' She won't want a scene, he thinks. Not right here on her doorstep. You don't shit where you sleep.

To get rid of him, she says, 'Maybe. Yes. Later.' She smells expensive, of scent, but he knows that underneath, she's coppery, rusted.

The way she's looking at him . . .

She could freeze a lit firework with that stare.

The ache's at the base of his balls.

He thinks, *this is going to be the best yet.*

## 49

*Now*

Leo Proctor cringed in the hospital bed when he saw Marnie.

'Mr Proctor.' She pulled up a chair and sat at his side. 'Hello.'

He wore hospital pyjamas, a shade of blue washed so many times it resembled water. He clutched at the Aertex blanket, the way his wife had clutched, the night that Marnie questioned her about the stabbing, the abuse.

Leo's room smelt of sickness. A fretful, sour smell. 'Tell me about your broken hand,' she said.

Leo looked wary, not trusting the gentle tone of her voice. A contrast to the last time she was here, asking awkward questions. Accusing him. 'What . . . what d'you mean?'

'The hospital said they treated you for two broken bones in your right hand, eight months ago.'

He looked at the hand in question. With an effort, he relaxed its grip on the blanket. 'An accident, at work.' His voice was dried-up, small for such a big man. The pads of his fingers were raw, his nails ragged and split.

Marnie poured a glass of water from the plastic jug on the

bedside cabinet, holding it out. He took the glass. 'Thanks.' He sipped at it, avoiding her eyes.

'I know it didn't happen at work. There would be a record. It's a legal requirement.'

His face twitched. 'They kept it quiet, didn't want their safety record looking bad. There'd been other things, accidents on site . . .'

'Mr Proctor. Leo . . . I know it didn't happen at work.'

'You don't. How could you?'

'A marriage is private.'

His mouth worked, sweat on his upper lip.

'That's what Hope told me. A marriage is private. What goes on behind closed doors is nobody else's business. Is that what you believe, too?'

His hands moved. She heard the rasp of his split nails on the blanket, and saw Hope's pearly fingernails, that first night at the hospital. She saw the scratches on Stephen's face, the wound where a girl held a knife to his throat.

That was it, she realised, the moment when she glimpsed the truth of what had happened in Finchley. It'd taken her too long to get from there to here. Much too long.

'Do you believe a marriage is private?'

He didn't speak, clenching his jaw. Marnie glanced at the monitor, checking his vital stats. He'd had time, since her last visit, to dream up a whole raft of excuses for the broken bones, and the rest of it. Time, too, to get defensive. Angry.

Hope had resented Marnie's questions, a fugitive coldness in her stare. Marnie had put it down to intrusion, loss of dignity. She hadn't known she needed to look deeper.

Leo Proctor wasn't angry. His body language was defeated. Shoulders slumped. Head down. Like a beaten bull.

'The space under the stairs,' Marnie said gently. 'What happened there?'

He shrank in the bed, muscles shortening all over his body.

She needed to be careful, alert for signs of his blood pressure increasing, or his heart rate. Too many ways this could end badly, the way it nearly did at the refuge when Hope stuck a knife in his lung. 'Leo?'

'I don't know what you mean.'

'I was at your house.' She folded her hands in her lap. 'It's very nice. Very smart. Did you decorate it together? You and Hope.'

He shook his head, then nodded. 'Yes.' He risked a look at her, sideways. He thought she was baiting him, getting ready for another attack.

She smiled at him. 'It's okay. I'm sorry.'

'For . . . what?'

'Last time. I was out of order. It's not like that now.'

'What's happened?' He looked fearful. 'Has Hope . . .?'

'She's gone. With a woman from the refuge. They left the hospital yesterday. We don't know where they are, but we're looking. I could really use your help.'

He pulled himself up against the pillows, wincing. 'What woman?'

'Take it easy,' Marnie warned. 'I'll be sent out of here if the doctors decide you're distressed. Then we'll never get to the bottom of this.'

'What woman?' he repeated.

'Simone Bissell.'

The name meant nothing to him. He looked blank. 'I don't understand.'

'Hope didn't tell you about Simone, when she called you from the refuge?'

He shook his head.

'Are you sure?'

'Yes.'

'What *did* she tell you?' Marnie asked.

'Where . . . where she was.'

'What else, Leo?'

He ducked his head away from the question, still unsure of her.

She couldn't blame him, after the verbal pasting she'd given him last time. 'Did she tell you to bring the knife?'

He was white-faced, his lips cracked open. His hands fisted in the blanket.

Marnie looked down at her own hands for a moment, before returning her gaze to his face. 'The moment I smelt the space under the stairs, I knew someone had been kept there. I thought it was Hope. But it wasn't, was it?'

He didn't speak, didn't take his eyes from hers.

'I went back there, earlier today. With DS Jake. You probably don't remember, but DS Jake saved your life at the refuge. He's not as big as you are, but he's tall. Six foot. I asked him to get inside the space under the stairs. I wanted to see if he'd fit. He said he found scratches, on the walls and floor. Made by fingernails.'

She spoke very softly. 'I saw Hope's fingers at the hospital. Very pretty. She didn't make those scratches, but someone did. That was obvious from the smell. DS Jake couldn't get out of there fast enough. I can't imagine what it's like, being kept in a confined space for – what? Hours?'

She took a moment. 'How long did she keep you there?'

Leo shook his head, sucking a shattered breath into his chest. His eyes were hot with unshed tears.

'Hope,' Marnie said. 'How long did she keep you locked under the stairs, and how often? Because it was you, wasn't it? Leo? You were the one kept in there. Not her.'

# PART 2

PART 2

# 1

*Then*

Lowell's redecorating the bathroom. He has a hammer to break up the tiles, working to a rhythm, swinging, bringing it down.

Simone likes the pattern, the pulse. A noise like living.

When he goes away, she's frantic. Pacing, snapping her fingers, counting the bricks from one end of the room to the other. The new line of tiles isn't even. She gets into the habit of placing the level everywhere, along the door jamb, on the floor, across the tops of shelves. She stands on tiptoe and holds it on the ends of her fingers, flush to the ceiling, seeing the green spirit seesaw. Nothing in the basement flat is straight.

She worries the food won't last until he returns. She sets the spirit level on the lid of the chest freezer, then places it inside, where ice has formed a scummy shelf. The green eye runs away, blinking, winking from a polythene glacier of pork chops. She thinks, *What if the floor isn't the floor but the ceiling? What if I'm living on my side?*

She pushes her ear to the wall, filling her head with the hot thwapping of her blood.

The spirit is strange, a beautiful bubble shaped like a heart being squeezed, bursting back and forth. Boiling. Smoothing flat and low in the level.

She could watch it for hours.

The idea of smashing it comes and goes, exciting her.

At night she sleeps with the spirit level against her sternum, feeling her lungs inflate, deflate, chasing the spirit to and fro. She dreams she cracks the glass but the spirit keeps its shape, filling the cup of her hand: a green globe.

In the morning – another morning; how many more – she thinks of falling on the spirit level, like a samurai. Of driving it up inside her body. She would walk stiffly, but always find her balance.

He comes back. Always. This time, bringing the sharp stink of outside, bitumen and burning leaves. Autumn already? He's brown and there's sand between his toes.

He's been on holiday. He's brought her a big bunch of roses, yellow.

'Hey, babe,' he says.

She hates him for a long time, fears him for longer, but when he comes back smelling of outside, bringing the familiar beat of his feet on the basement floor, Simone reaches for him with something like love.

# 2

*Now*

'I'll put the suitcase here, okay?' Simone turned to Hope, rubbing her hands on her skirt. She was sweating, her scalp crawling with the sensation of eyes watching, back at Hope's house. 'Are you all right?'

Hope nodded, not looking at her. She'd been like this since the hospital. Simone was afraid she'd changed her mind, but here they were: safe. Away from Leo, and the police. Away from everyone. She looked around the familiar room, and shivered. She'd never thought she'd be back. The key had been in its old place, under the bedding for a tomato plant, wrapped in silver foil like treasure. She rubbed at her forearms where the scar tissue itched whenever she was tired, or anxious.

'Show me,' Hope said.

Simone turned to look at her. 'What?'

'Your arms.' Hope's stare was glazed, hot.

'Are you okay?' Anxiety prodded under Simone's ribs. Had she done the wrong thing, coming back, bringing Hope here?

'Show me,' Hope repeated.

Obedient, Simone rolled back the sleeves of her jumper. The right arm first, where the scars were less impressive. She was right-handed, making a mess of the first few attempts before she learned to bind the ends of her fingers with Elastoplast so that the razor blade wouldn't slip. Vaseline on the outer edges of the area to be scarred, keeping them clean. At the refuge, she'd seen Ayana Mirza use the same trick to apply nail varnish. Varnish chipped, but Simone's scars were forever. The ones on her left arm were wonderful, like tribal markings. She'd copied the patterns from a library book. Scrolls and dots, each one symmetrical, across the inside of her elbow. Whenever she was anxious, she would read the scars on her arms, finding peace there, or anger, if what she needed was anger.

Hope stared at the scars, coming close. She reached a finger, tracing the scrolls and dots. Her touch was precise, reverential. 'You did this yourself?'

'Yes.' Simone stood very still, afraid to break the spell that was binding Hope to her. Her whole chest ached with love, with longing.

Hope's touch was the only warm thing in the room.

Sunlight shrank from the pair of them, across the tiled floor of the kitchen, red in retreat. Simone shivered again, but she didn't try to draw down her sleeves, standing with both arms out, like a child waiting to be dressed, or hugged.

'The other scars,' Hope said then.

Her voice was so low that Simone doubted what she'd heard. 'Other?'

Hope raised her gaze at last, finding Simone's face. 'The other scars. The ones you didn't do yourself.' She waited a beat. 'The ones your mother made.'

Simone flinched, fear slipping up her spine as sudden as a snake.

Hope's blue eyes were a doll's, fixed and intent. Fierce.

'Show me,' she said. 'I want to see.'

## 3

Leo Proctor sobbed. A terrible, betrayed sound. His head went up and down, as if on a pulley; Marnie realised he was nodding. 'Hope locked you under the stairs. Did she break your hand, too?' Another nod, like an automaton. 'What else?'

'Every . . . everything. Beatings. Kick . . . kickings.' Each word wrenched up, sounding bloody in his mouth. 'Rope. She beat me with rope. Burnt me.' He started to gasp. 'Hit me with bricks, weights. Anything she could lay her hands on.'

Marnie waited for him to start breathing more easily. 'What about the damage on her? I saw the medical exam. She had bruises, scarring.'

'She – made me. It was the only way she liked . . . sex. Contact. Anything. It was what she wanted. I didn't like it. I just wanted . . . I hated to hurt her. *Hated* it. She said it was what men did. What we were like. That I should be a man. It was what she wanted, the only thing she wanted. We both had to be hurting, all the time.' He was shaking, the bed creaking under him. 'Not . . . not her fault. Not really. Her dad . . . her mum and dad . . . she told me . . .'

'She had an excuse? There's no excuse, Leo. Not for what she did.'

'She *needs* me,' he sobbed. 'She does!'

'Leo.' Marnie reached out and took his hand. 'Okay. It's okay. Take a minute.'

His palm was patchy with sweat. She could smell the stress leeching from his skin, along with the fluids and painkillers. After a minute or two, he was calmer.

'Why did she leave? For the refuge.'

'I asked her to stop. Begged. It got so bad. I was drinking . . .' He hid his face in his shoulder, rubbing tears on to his pyjamas. 'I was sick all the time, from the drink mostly. I was afraid of what would happen if I wasn't around. I didn't know how she'd cope.'

He freed his hand from her grip and drove his thumbs into his eye sockets, making Marnie wince. 'She never went out, not really. She spent her whole time in that place, the house, but not – not happily. She wouldn't let me make it comfortable. Just clean. I was always cleaning, or she was. She had to have the rooms kept nice. For best, she said. She wouldn't let me make her happy, or even just comfortable. I'd have made her a bed, any kind she wanted. She knows I'm good with my hands. But all she wanted . . . The only time I could touch her was to . . .' He edited each sentence, as if he'd already said too much. 'Four months ago, it got worse. I was scared of what would happen.'

'You begged her to stop.' Marnie repeated the words he'd used.

'She *did*.' He raised his head and wiped at his eyes, looking lost. 'She stopped hurting me, but she wouldn't stop the rest of it. Me hurting her.'

'How long ago was this?'

'Four, five months. After her mum's funeral.'

Five months for the damage on Leo to heal. Hope needed her bruises, as an alibi. From what Leo said, it went deeper than that. Satisfying some urge to be punished?

234

'How could she force you to hurt her? I don't understand.'

'When I refused, she . . . she went out and picked up men. In bars. She let them . . . they hurt her. She came back covered in bites and bruises. I asked how she could be sure they wouldn't kill her. She just . . . laughed. "I'll do it again," she said, "worse. You won't recognise me." That's when I agreed to do it. To try and keep her safe.'

'Do you know the names of any of these men?'

'No. I didn't want to know their names.'

'Why did she need to be hurt? Did she explain that to you?'

He shook his head. 'I asked her. *Kept* asking, but she only got angry. When she gets angry . . . I learnt to shut up.'

'What happened after she stopped hurting you?'

'It was worse, much worse. It got – I wanted to make it stop. It was her, hurting *her*. That's what I couldn't stand. I said . . . the police. I'd go to the police.'

'You were going to the police,' Marnie said. 'That's when she went to the refuge?'

'Yes . . .'

'And she called you, to let you know where she was.'

'Yes.'

'She told you to bring a knife to the refuge.'

Leo nodded, his nose and eyes streaming. 'And roses. Yellow roses.'

'Why the roses?'

He flung out his hands. 'I don't know! She hated flowers, said they made a mess. Just made a mess and then died. She *hated* flowers, even roses.'

'Why do you think she wanted the knife?'

'I don't know. I didn't think. She just said she wanted it, and I didn't think.' His face worked, wrung by emotions, painful to watch.

'Did you know what she was going to do?' Marnie said. 'With the knife?'

'No. No . . .'

'But you took it anyway.'

He nodded, weakly. She wondered what else he would have done on Hope's say-so. Murder? Suicide? Not suicide, or Hope wouldn't have had to kill him, or attempt to kill him. 'Didn't you worry about the other women, at the refuge? Knowing what she was capable of?'

He didn't speak. She doubted he was able to consider the safety of others, after years of living with Hope. 'How did you get inside the refuge?'

'She . . . unlocked the door. She told me when it would be safe to come, when the woman in charge would be on a cigarette break.'

Jeanette Conway's slack attitude had been a gift to Hope. She couldn't have guessed it would be so easy to breach security. 'Hope took a suitcase from your house this morning. Do you know what might've been in it?'

Leo pushed his hands at his face, messily. 'What?'

'A brown suitcase. According to your neighbour, it was heavy.'

'Heavy.' His eyes glazed over. He looked exhausted, grey-faced and ill.

Marnie bit the inside of her cheek. The doctor had been strict about how long she could question Leo. Her common sense, and her compassion, said he'd been through enough for one session. If Hope had been alone when she ran, it would be different. As it was, Marnie had to consider Simone's safety.

'Leo. I have more questions. Because Hope is missing, and so is Simone Bissell. But if you need to rest, or if you'd like me to get a doctor in here . . .'

'No.' He looked scared. 'No one else. No men.'

She understood. It was bad enough that she knew his secrets. 'I'm okay,' he said, swallowing. 'If it's just you . . . I'm okay.'

She refilled his glass of water, putting it into his hands,

keeping her hands around his for a second. 'You said Hope didn't mention Simone Bissell.'

'No.' He gulped at the water. 'Who is she?'

'A woman living at the refuge. She made friends with Hope.'

'No,' Leo said mechanically. 'Hope doesn't make friends. Not with women. Especially not women in places like that. Weak. Victims.'

'She got close to Simone. Everyone at the refuge remarked on it.'

Leo just shook his head, looking foggy.

'Is she dangerous? To someone like Simone? To other people. Obviously she was dangerous to you.'

'I don't know. I've never seen her with anyone else.'

'What about her parents? She told me they were dead.'

He shook his head. 'Her mum died. In October. But her dad's still alive.'

Another lie Hope had told Marnie. 'You said she had trouble with her mum and dad. What happened to her?'

Leo drew a breath, holding it in his chest before letting it out, slowly. 'Nothing happened to Hope. It was her mum. It was what she saw happen to her mum, Gayle. Her dad beat Gayle, but he never touched Hope. I thought she'd hate him, but it was her mum – she hated *Gayle*, for not standing up to him. For losing control, that's how Hope put it. It was her mum who lost control, not her dad.'

'What's her dad's name?'

'Kenneth Reece.' Leo took another gulp of water, washing it around his mouth before swallowing, as if the name had left a nasty taste.

'He never touched Hope?'

'Never. She learnt how to manage him, that's what she said. From when she was tiny. He loved his little girl, so that's what she was, for him. A good little girl. She couldn't understand why her mum didn't manage him the same way.

Take control of the situation. He wasn't clever, her dad. She was always saying that. He was a typical man, an animal. *She* was clever. She told me she knew she was clever by the time she was six, but she learned not to show it, because it wasn't what he wanted. He didn't think girls should be clever. He just wanted a pretty, well-behaved kid. A doll. So that's what she gave him.' His face twisted as he said it.

'When she first told me about him, I called him a monster, rotten. It made her – angry. I was no different, she said. No man was any different and he was her dad. I wanted her to have nothing to do with him. I said I was glad I got her away from all that, but she said she didn't need rescuing, that I needn't think I was a hero. I was the same as him, the same as all men. *She* was the one who was different, because she knew how to handle us. Men, she meant.'

'But she married you. She must have wanted to get married. What did she expect?'

'Maybe she didn't know how else to get away from that place, from her dad . . .'

Or maybe she wanted to prove she could succeed where her mother had failed. Was her marriage an exercise in control – power? Plenty of marriages were.

'What about her mum? Wasn't she worried what would happen to her if she left?'

'She thought her mum let it happen. She couldn't understand why she allowed herself to be hurt. "I was just a kid and I could manage him," that's what she said. She blamed her mum for being clumsy. Gayle broke a mirror once. Seven years' bad luck. "She brings it on herself"; Hope learned to say that. I suppose her dad used to say it.'

It wasn't Hope who broke a mirror. It was her mother, Gayle. How much more of the act from the hospital had Hope borrowed from her mother, for Marnie's benefit? Perhaps it was more than an act. Perhaps it was an involuntary impulse. Empathy, however twisted or repressed, for what her mother suffered.

'She thought Gayle could've stopped it,' Leo said, 'if she'd wanted to. "Maybe she liked it." That's what Hope always said.'

'You said *Hope* liked it. Being hurt.'

'It's what she wanted. Needed.' He gulped again at the glass she'd put into his hands. 'The tattoos . . . She made us get tattoos.'

'Hearts, with arrows through them.'

Leo searched her face. 'Yes. I . . . thought it was a love thing, but it wasn't. Her dad had the exact same tattoo.' He held the glass to his chest. 'It hurts, getting inked over your ribcage.'

'It really does,' Marnie agreed.

He didn't notice. 'She needed that. The hurt. It's what she wanted.'

'But she preferred hurting you.'

'I was an animal.' He dropped his voice into the pit of his throat. 'She wanted me to behave like what I was. An animal. Then she punished me for it.' His face contorted, as if this was too much truth for him to stand. 'But she could be sweet, gentle, and I understood, after what she went through at home, what she saw happening to her mum. She thought it hadn't affected her, but it must've done. It *must*.'

'Yes.'

Empowering Leo, then emasculating him, making him complicit in the abuse. Demanding he behave like her father, then beating him for it. Making him beat her. That was more than a split personality, a combination of her mother's submission and her father's aggression. Marnie didn't know exactly what it was. It would take a professional to figure Hope out, but it made sense of her resentment during the interview at the hospital, the way she swung between tears and toughness. 'She was prescribed antidepressants. Didn't her GP realise something serious was going on?'

'She was good at hiding it.' Leo propped his head to the pillows, wearily. 'She hid it from you.'

True. Marnie had fallen for the little lost girl. Hope had perfected the act at an early age, her defence against her father. She looked the part, frail and blonde, with those china-doll eyes and hands. Hard to imagine, even now, that she'd terrorised Leo Proctor, a man more than twice her size and weight. Marnie wanted to ask how Hope had made Leo climb into the space under the stairs, what words she'd used to make that happen. Conditioned behaviour was complex, a tangled mess of love and lies, threats and promises. How many times had he crawled in, sat scrabbling at the floor and walls? How many times had he forgiven her, only for her to beat him again, worse than before? He'd held down a job, which meant he left the house five days out of seven, always returning for more of the same. What was he holding out for – a proper explanation for her cruelty? Reconciliation? The chance of redemption, for the pair of them?

'Do you think she intends to hurt Simone Bissell?'

'I don't know,' Leo said.

'But she despises weak women. Victims. If she sees Simone in that light . . .'

'Maybe. I don't know.' He looked up at her, exhaustion lining his face.

'Leo . . . What about the suitcase? Are you sure you don't know what was inside the suitcase she took from the house?'

The answer was in his eyes.

It was nothing good.

# 4

Two men – one white, the other black – stood on the doorstep, waiting for Henry Stuke to answer the bell. His first thought was Jehovah's, but these two were empty-handed, and the white one had grubby skin, tired-looking, like an elephant's hide.

Police. They were police. Plain-clothes detectives.

A rush of panic brought bile to the back of his mouth. He swallowed it, hearing the doorbell shrill a second time. If they kept that up, the twins would wake.

He went into the hall, past the mirror that Freya had insisted he put up so she could check her face on the way out, back in the days when she cared how she looked to strangers. In Freya's mirror, he looked pasty, guilty. He smoothed his hair and buried his left fist in his pocket, before answering the door.

'Henry Stuke?' The detective with the grubby skin showed his ID, holding it up the way a preacher would hold a bible, fingers splayed.

Henry couldn't really read the ID, with the sun squirming on the plastic wallet, but he nodded. 'What's this about?'

'I'm DS Carling, this is DS Jake. You own a Prius.' He read off the registration number. 'Is that right?'

'Yes. Yep, that's right.'

'Where were you on Friday afternoon, Mr Stuke?'

'I was . . . Let's see. Friday? Working. Yeah, most of the day I was working.'

'Where do you work? Actually,' DS Carling looked up and down the street, 'tell you what, can we come inside to chat?'

That meant they didn't have a warrant. Maybe this wasn't as bad as he'd feared.

'Okay, but can you keep it down?' He pulled a look of apology. 'I've got babies sleeping upstairs.'

'Babies?' DS Carling mirrored Henry's look of apology, adding a touch of sympathy. 'They sleep much?'

'Not as much as I'd like.' They shared a grin. It wasn't as bad as he'd feared.

The young one – DS Jake – hadn't spoken yet. He was good-looking enough for TV. Henry had seen him before, in the unmarked Mondeo at the refuge, and at the hospital where they'd taken *her*.

'Sit down. I mean, if you'd like.' He kept his left hand in his pocket.

'How old are they?' Carling cast his eyes at the ceiling.

'Nine months next week.' Henry tried to sound happy, the way he was supposed to feel. He was praying they wouldn't wake. If they started their grizzling, he didn't know if he could keep up the proud dad act. 'Twins.'

'Nine months. That's a nice age,' Carling said. 'Are they walking yet?'

'No. No, not yet. Crawling a lot, you know. Getting about.'

Carling nodded. He sat on the sofa, picking up a plastic toy: a red truck with beads inside that rattled when you rolled it across the floor. Henry couldn't remember if he'd wiped the puke off it. The sitting room smelt dirty, of nappies and dust. God knows the last time they cleaned in here, he and Freya. The twins' stuff was everywhere. Baby wipes in green boxes, tippy mugs, board books with soggy chewed corners.

Henry lowered himself on to the sofa next to DS Carling, keeping his hand in his pocket, his fingers wet with sweat. DS Jake stayed standing, looking around the room.

'So . . . what's this about? Friday, you said.'

'You were working.' Carling held the red truck in his hands, fondly. How many years since he was wiping up sick and shit? So long, he'd forgotten, smiling like all the memories were good ones, like fatherhood was one long laugh.

Henry clenched his fist in his pocket. 'I'm a plumber, do a bit of carpentry sometimes, put in new kitchens.' He laughed. 'Mind you, you should see the state of ours. I'll have to get it sorted before they're walking.'

'Nah, you just fix up a safety gate, you'll be fine.' Carling put the truck to one side. 'You weren't in Finchley on Friday, then?'

'Finchley . . . Actually, yeah, I think I was. Shit.' He looked from Carling to DS Jake and back. 'This isn't a parking thing, is it? Only I was on an emergency call. All that bastard rain brought down a ton of guttering . . .'

'It's not about parking,' DS Jake said.

Henry stared at him. He didn't like DS Jake. Didn't like the way he stood there looking like nothing could put a crease in his suit, or a line on his forehead. Speaking softly, as if he understood about sleeping babies when what the fuck could he know, at his age, about anything?

DS Carling must've been thinking the same thing, because he said, 'Don't mind DS Jake. He's counting his lucky stars none of this is in store for him.' He winked at Henry, rolling his eyes in a matey gesture that Henry only half understood.

'So what's it about?' Henry asked. 'Something about the car, you said.'

'You were in Finchley on Friday, then at the North

Middlesex yesterday.' Carling sat forward, elbows on the saggy knees of his suit. 'We're investigating something that happened at those two places, on those two days.'

'What happened?'

'We can't go into details right now.' An apologetic grin. 'We just need to know why you were at the hospital yesterday. Friday, you say you were working.'

'That's right.' He wet his upper lip. It tasted stale. 'And I took the twins to the hospital yesterday. They were coughing and I panicked. You know how it is.'

Carling nodded. He looked at the family photos along the bookcase. 'Your wife's not home?'

'She's at her sister's, just became an auntie.' His smile felt sickly on his face. 'More new babies. I said I'd look after our two, but you know how it is. First-time nerves. I'd not heard them cough like that before.'

'But they were okay. I mean, you didn't go into the hospital.' Carling looked a bit embarrassed. 'CCTV showed you sitting outside, in the Prius. You didn't go in.'

'They calmed down. Fell asleep.' Henry managed a laugh. 'I felt a right wally.'

Carling nodded. He'd started looking bored, like this was a waste of his time. That should have made Henry happy, but it pissed him off. As if the fact of the twins meant he couldn't be a suspect, or a threat. Carling should've seen Henry with that bitch. Not the last time, the night of the funeral, but the time before. If he'd seen the stuff Henry had done to that bitch, he wouldn't be looking bored, like he couldn't wait to get out of here and back to some proper police work. *This* was proper police work, Henry thought savagely. *You should've seen what I had planned for her.*

Carling shifted on the sofa and the red plastic truck rolled to the edge of the cushions and fell, nearly hitting the floor except Henry caught it in time. His reflexes took him by surprise; he'd been scared of the noise the truck would make; a noise the twins knew, and loved. Scared they'd wake and start up.

DS Jake said, 'What happened to your hand, Mr Stuke?'

'It's . . . Henry. I'm Henry.' He held on to the truck.

'What happened to your hand, Henry?'

He turned the hand so they could both see it, clawed like an old man's, fingers pulled into a fist, skin scarred and puckered up the heel, like someone had cut it open and stitched it, badly, shut again. 'Six months ago . . . I was fixing a sink,' he lied. 'Old pipes collapsed, trapped me.'

He'd been trapped, that much was true. Bitch had pinned him down, sat on his chest, for what felt like hours. He thought he'd die on that hotel floor, under her.

'They had to cut me free.' He turned the hand to the light, ashamed of the sight of it. He had to hide it from everyone, on buses, in the street. People stared otherwise. If he'd gone straight to casualty, maybe they could've fixed it better, but he'd stayed hidden in the hotel, afraid to leave in case she was waiting for him.

He should've guessed what was in store for him when he'd seen her dressed like that. Like she'd come from a funeral. He should've guessed when he saw that rage in her eyes. He'd thought it'd be great – the best time yet – but he was stupid, clumsy.

He turned his back when she told him to, thinking – what? That she was going to surprise him with sexy underwear, maybe a new tattoo. Never saw it coming, until she hit him with that fucking thing, his ribs cracking like rusted pipe.

'Looks like you were lucky to keep it,' DS Carling said. He meant Henry's hand.

'Yes. Yes, I was.'

A low warning noise from overhead, like an engine starting up: the twins waking.

All three of them looked in that direction.

'I'm sorry,' Henry said. 'I'll have to go up to them.'

'That's okay.' Carling stood. 'I think we're done here.'

# 5

'My father had a driver,' Simone said. 'I never knew his name. If I needed his attention, I had to – press the intercom in the back of the car. I was only to press it in an emergency, if I needed him to pull over, because I was unwell. I wasn't to press it just because I wanted to talk about my day, or because it was lonely in the back of the car.'

Hope was peeling an apple, with a knife. The apple's skin was a thin red bracelet around her wrist. When Simone stopped speaking, Hope glanced up, her stare like the knife, sharp. Simone swallowed the dryness in her mouth. 'My father's driver wore a peaked cap. I'd sometimes catch his eye in the mirror. He always looked away first. His – his uniform suited him, better than my leotard suited me. Pink and black do not go together, whatever my father said. The man who called himself my father.' She dropped her voice to a whisper. 'Charles Bissell.'

Hope licked apple juice from the back of her hand.

'He had a tattoo on his neck. The driver. A hawk, blue. I remember thinking it wouldn't show against my skin.' Simone spread her palms, pink and empty.

'What did he do?' Hope said.

Simone dipped her head away, chasing after the memory. 'The ballet teacher was always tapping me on the shoulder with her stick. "You are rolling. We are not waves. We do not roll." Everywhere on me was flat, then, even my feet. I didn't understand what she meant. When I looked into the mirror, if I concentrated, I saw my mother.' She covered her eyes with her hands. 'Mine was the only black face in the room. All that pink. Leotards and – and tights and satin shoes. And me.'

She'd stuck to the leather seat in her father's car. The car was black, but the inside was the colour of whipped cream. Simone had to peel her bare shoulders away from the buttoned seat, her skin making a kissing sound. Sometimes she kicked her feet at the back of the passenger seat and her father's driver looked at her, in the mirror. He wasn't angry. He wasn't allowed to be. When he looked away, she stuck her tongue out at him. Not all the memories were painful, but Hope only wanted the ones that were.

'Tell me about the soldiers,' Hope said. 'In the village. Before the Bissells.'

'They – they came at dusk, and dawn. The most dangerous times of day. I remember . . . their arms.' Simone stretched out her own arms, no longer expecting a hug from Hope. 'The muscle wound like – like ropes.'

A sound outside made her stop, her heart drumming in her chest. Hope glanced in the direction of the noise, then back at Simone. It was a car passing, that was all. A car.

'Your father,' Hope said next. Her voice was the same as it had always been. Soft, sweet, drawing confidences from Simone as a soap plaster draws splinters from a thumb.

It hadn't been like this between them at the refuge. Then, it was silence that brought them together. Silence and some-thing like peace. Perhaps all the time Hope was holding in these questions, her need to know everything about Simone's past. She didn't understand why Hope needed to know; she only knew that the telling made her *less* – and Hope *more*, as if the other woman drew power from Simone's words. More than words – pain. Hope wanted to hear about Simone's pain, the things from her past that had hurt her the most.

As long as she kept talking – as long as she did exactly as Hope said, no more and no less – it would be all right.

'When – when he asked about the ballet classes, I said I hated them. He would look sad, then he'd smile, as if it was a joke we shared. He would put his hands on my head.'

She remembered the thinness of his fingers between her cornrows, this stranger who'd stolen her. Charles Bissell, his wife's face lined like a riverbed after a long drought.

'He was only my father on paper. He said it was the same, but I knew it was not. He took me from the village. My brothers and sisters . . . The soldiers took them, for the Lord's Army. All the children in the village were stolen, one way or another.'

The ache in her head was awful, but it was nothing, she knew that. 'Each morning before class, he would pin an orchid to my leotard. For luck. In the car, I would peel its petals on to the carpet. The car smelt . . . like decay. They – the Bissells – were afraid of how I was growing up, the questions I was asking. They were afraid I'd find out that they'd stolen me. The only good thing was that I was one less recruit for the LRA.'

She could see her old anger, remote as a bird circling in a full sky. 'I used to think – even that would have been better than them. Their rules. Their silence. Lies.'

Hope ate a slice of apple, passing her tongue across her lips.

'In my village, I remember, one night, hiding from the rebels. I was so scared, trying to keep still, not to scream.' She put her hand up to guard against the memory.

Bats. She remembered bats flying down from the trees, warm and squirming, like the sky splitting into bits. Her anger was nothing, a cold firecracker after a night of crazy celebration. Speaking like this, she was back in the village. Eight years old, watching for death from every corner, heat pressed like a blank face to the windows. The red stench of dying. Men with their guts held like infants in their arms.

'Some of the soldiers were children, taken from other villages. Kids in camouflage, cut down to fit. The rebels' flag stitched to their chests. Red, black and blue. My hands . . .' She spread them again, searching the pink of her palms. 'My hands stained . . . wet with fear.'

'You were afraid,' Hope said.

'Yes.'

'Of what?'

'Of being taken by the soldiers. Of being killed. Dying there, in the dirt.'

Her mother had spread a blanket over the dirt, when Simone was eight. The blanket was green and gold. Dark patches lay on it, like shadows. There was no sun inside the house. The patches were stains. Her sister's blood, and her mother's. Her mother's mother's. Her aunt's blood and her aunt's aunt's. They held her down, all these women, on the stains they'd spilled on the green and the gold. Her blood was a new shadow, red. It soaked through the blanket, into the dirt. 'I was afraid of dying in the dirt.'

Tears wet her skirt, like rain falling. She didn't know how to make it stop. She only knew she had to keep doing whatever Hope said.

'Now,' Hope said. 'Tell me about Lowell.'

# 6

'Rome?' It was Ed Belloc. 'You wanted me to call you.'

'Is there news of Ayana?'

'Nothing. Where are you?'

'Just leaving the North Middlesex. I have to call in at the station, then we can meet, if you're free.'

Ed, hearing the sharpness in her voice, said, 'What's happened?'

'Nothing good.'

The station stank of coffee and whiteboard markers. Someone had switched on a fan, churning the air to soup. Marnie went to Noah's desk. 'Where's DS Jake?'

From the adjacent desk, Abby Pike looked up. 'He went with Ron Carling, to West Brompton. Ron called in, said it was a waste of time. They're on their way back.'

'A waste of time,' Marnie repeated. 'They were seeing Henry Stuke, the man who was watching the refuge?'

'Except he wasn't.' Abby made a face. 'Ron says he's in a right state, trying to look after new twins, doesn't know whether he's coming or going. He was driving around, trying to get the kids to settle. Ron says he's on the level.'

'What does Noah say?'

'I didn't speak with him. Ron said Noah was going to walk back. He seemed to think it'd freaked him out, being in a house full of baby stuff, but I should think Noah just fancied some fresh air.' Abby looked up at Marnie, her full face smooth and trusting. 'Any news about Hope and the others?'

'You need to change the missing person status,' Marnie told her. 'Hope Proctor is now a suspect. Assault, kidnap and attempted murder.'

'Hope?' Abby's eyes were saucers.

'I need a list of sheltered housing in Dulwich. Can you get that for me?'

The Millennium Bridge hung improbably over the Thames, like a rope bridge across a jungle pass. The river was busy with boats, its saline stink ripe with rust. Impossible not to look at the London Eye; it had eaten the skyline alive, a giant span of steel and glass, hollow moon in orbit above the city. The bridge's structure had been reinforced after pedestrians detected swaying. Even now, when the wind got above a stiff breeze, Marnie could feel it moving. It didn't stop people using the bridge. They expected it to sway. These expectations were everywhere in London, shaping the city.

Ed was standing on the bridge, his face fractured with worry.

'Tell me about Ayana,' she said first.

'I called at her parents' house. Strictly in the role of Victim Support. One of her brothers answered. Turhan. What did Ayana tell Noah his name meant? *Of mercy.*' Ed's mouth wrenched at one corner. 'He denied knowing where she is. I asked to speak to his parents, but he said no one else was home.'

'Do you think she's there? At her parents' house?'

'No. Turhan was too relaxed for that, but he knows where

she is. He knew she wasn't in the refuge, before I told him why I was calling.' Ed turned and gripped the steel lip of the bridge, looking down at the water. 'He was smiling. I could hear it in his voice.' A patrol boat was making its way upstream, tannoy stuttering, driving a thin margin of litter to the edges of the shore. From where they stood, they could smell the silt of the river's bed. 'He knows where she is.' Ed rubbed the crook of his elbow at his face. He was wearing yesterday's clothes, slept in. If he had slept. 'I'm sure of it.'

'What about her mother? Did you believe Turhan when he said she wasn't home?'

'Hard to tell.'

'Ayana warned us,' Marnie said, 'about women and violence. Look what those girls did to Stephen, at Sommerville. Look at Simone, what *her* mother did. All the way down the line, I've been staring at evidence of what women are capable of, but still I chose their side. Instinctively. Male aggression's part of the job. I see it all the time. Not just sexism or strutting. Boys like Lowell Paton . . . It blindsided me. Too many gorillas on the court.'

Ed turned to face her, propping his back to the steel bar. 'What's happened?'

She didn't know where to begin. She needed to test the soundness of what she was going to say, to see if it stood up. Not that she thought Leo Proctor had lied, but she could hear the CPS picking holes in the evidence already. 'At the hospital, the night of the stabbing? I spoke with Hope, and with the doctor who'd examined her. It looked . . . black and white, but it wasn't just that. It was the way she spoke, the things she *knew*. About all the worst ways people can hurt one another. How you can buy silence not only with threats or violence, but with promises. Secrets. I thought it proved what she'd been through. She knew everything there was to know, about abuse.' The river's traffic pulled lines from the current. Silver scars on the water's brown skin. 'The other person who'd know that much about it is the abuser.' She paused, the woman's name sticking in her throat. 'Hope Proctor.'

Ed said slowly, disbelievingly, 'Hope?'

Marnie nodded. 'Hope. She was the abuser, not Leo. He was the victim.'

'You're wrong.' There was a lick of anger in Ed's voice. 'You must be wrong.'

She looked at him, steadily. 'I'm not.'

'Where's this coming from? Leo? It's bollocks. Every abusive husband on the planet denies it at some point or other. He's not the first who's tried twisting the facts to make it look like he's the victim.'

'Ed . . . It was Hope. I know it was. She broke his hand, and his ribs.'

'What about *her* injuries?' Ed demanded. 'How's he explaining those?'

'She made him hurt her. It was a condition of their marriage.'

Ed made a sound of exasperation. 'Jesus, Rome . . . I can't believe you fell for that.'

She'd slipped in his estimation. She was surprised how much it meant, how much it hurt. She hid her hands in her pockets, driving her fingernails into her palms. 'Leo refused to do it at first, so she went to bars and picked up strangers, before going home to show him their bruises on her.' Connection. Was that what Hope was chasing? The need not to feel like a stranger inside her own skin. 'Leo was terrified she'd end up dead. She wouldn't tell him why she needed it. Punishment of some kind, I imagine.'

Ed had turned away, his jaw tense, a muscle wrenching in his cheek. She studied his profile, looking for something she'd lost. 'I know how it sounds. I didn't want to believe it either. A woman asking for those sorts of injuries, inflicting them on her husband? I was happy to think she fought back, at the refuge. That the stabbing wasn't panic, that maybe she meant to kill him because he'd been raping and abusing her, for years. Because it fitted with my personal preference. What was it you said, at Sommerville? I thought she was *my kind of victim*, the kind that fights back. I didn't stop to think that she might be the abuser, but that's exactly what she is. Do you think I'd be telling you otherwise? Ed . . . I need you to listen to this. Then tell me I'm wrong.'

He straightened to face her. Nodded. 'How did you find out?'

'Leo admitted it, after I asked some awkward questions. I think he'd have kept it secret if he could. I began to suspect after what happened to Stephen at Sommerville. It was the way he defended himself . . . It reminded me of Leo, that first time I questioned him.' She wanted to reach for Ed's hand, but couldn't. 'I didn't really get a fix on it until I heard that Hope had been to the house, with Simone. For a suit-case. I couldn't imagine Simone risking a trip like that. It got me wondering who was behind the escape from the hospital. I'm not saying Simone wasn't up for it, but I couldn't see her motive for running. Hope was the one with a motive, especially after Leo woke up.'

Ed drew a short breath. She watched his face change, making room for this new, appalling truth. She regretted the shadows she'd put in his eyes, the lines around his mouth.

'Then . . . it was attempted murder,' he said. 'The stabbing. Can you prove it?'

'I don't know. I don't even know if I can persuade Leo to make a formal statement. He's not in great shape.' The breeze had untied her hair. She reknotted it. 'If Hope gets away with it, it'll be because she blindsided Simone and Shelley – all of them. Took their fear, and their suffering, and twisted

255

it into the perfect alibi. Talk about witness protection. We have to prove what really happened, not what she wanted them to see. If we can't . . .'

Ed said nothing.

'Yes,' Marnie murmured sadly. 'I was afraid you'd say that.'

She looked out across the water to where the sun was setting behind the Houses of Parliament, making a tourist postcard of the view, London's outline gilded in rose and orange. The Eye was a cool ring of steel, lit with white light.

'I swear this bridge still moves,' Ed said. 'Like standing on a snake.' He shook his head at her. 'I should've heard you out before jumping in. I'm sorry.'

She smiled at him. 'Hope . . . The last thing out of Pandora's box. After all the evils, plagues, whatever. I know the legend, but I never knew if hope was meant to be the consolation prize, or the worst evil of the lot.'

'I think Pandora's hope was intended to give us something to cling to.' Ed stood with his shoulder at hers. 'The medical evidence . . .' he began.

'The doctor said she presented like a sex worker. In other words, it could've been consensual. I was the one who decided it wasn't. Just as I decided Leo's nervousness at the hospital meant he was guilty.' She bit at the inside of her cheek, tasting iron. 'The cupboard under the stairs was big enough for a man. His broken hand and ribs . . . We added it all up – *I* added it up – and made eight from four, because it fitted what I thought I knew about men and women. What I *expected*.

'At the refuge, Hope made sure Shelley saw her bruises. She told the women about Leo, let them see how afraid she was, how desperate. She abused their trust, made them witness a stabbing, knowing how vulnerable they were. Maybe she enjoyed it. The power trip. Making them provide an abuser with an alibi . . . Can you imagine how Simone's going to feel when she finds out she's been protecting an abuser?'

'You're assuming Hope will let her go,' Ed said shortly.

'I'm not assuming anything. I'm *hoping*.'

He walked away from her, watching the water. Marnie moved to join him. The bridge breathed under their feet.

'Simone will have told Hope what happened to her, with Lowell.' Ed held his neck in his hand. 'If she told *me* . . . she'll have told Hope. She'll have made a gift of her worst nightmare, to a woman who thrives on manipulation, torture . . .'

'If Hope's got any sense, she won't hurt Simone. She could still make a case for self-defence with Leo. The evidence . . .'

'Why try to kill him?' Ed asked. 'Just for the power rush?'

'He was working up his courage to come to us. She knew she'd pushed him as far as she could, and she needed an alibi if he went to the police. There was too much evidence of abuse, if he chose to expose it. She couldn't cover it all up.'

They looked upstream, at the sprawl and soar of the city. 'She meant to kill him. I'm sure of that. When she realised he wasn't dead, she was terrified. That was probably the only honest emotion she's shown us.'

Perhaps there was another motive, too. The need to kill the one person who knew everything about her. The only witness to the real Hope. Had Stephen killed Marnie's parents for the same reason? To expunge that truth?

'Back at the refuge,' Ed said, 'when you were talking about the invisible gorilla . . . You said Ayana didn't think it was self-defence. She thought Hope meant to kill Leo, even if she didn't suspect her of the abuse.'

'None of us suspected Hope of that. She resented my questions at the hospital, but I put it down to the fact that I'd taken what was left of her dignity. She was weeping, for God's sake. That's supposed to be the hardest emotion to fake. Tears blur your vision, bad for survival, isn't that what they say?'

She'd made more mistakes than she could count. She turned to face Ed. 'You saw her, at the hospital. Did you pick up any threatening vibes?'

He shook his head. 'Nothing.'

'She likes to play the little girl lost. I bet men fall for that all the time.' She studied his face. 'Control turns her on, but she despises men. Sees them as lower primates. I bet she saw you as a challenge, someone higher up the food chain . . . She wanted witnesses. *Needed* them. Not just as an alibi. As . . . vindication. Witnesses mean justice. In some way, even if it's twisted. Witnesses make it real.'

'You really think she won't hurt Simone?'

'I can't be certain,' Marnie admitted. She was thinking about the flowers. The roses that Hope insisted Leo bring to the refuge, even though she hated flowers.

*They make a mess and then they die.*

The roses were a trigger, had to be. Hope's way of binding at least one of the women to her, so tightly she could be sure of an ally if things went wrong, or if she needed a passionate advocate.

'It's possible that Hope stage-managed more than the stabbing. She told Leo to bring a big bunch of yellow roses to the refuge, but Leo swears Hope hated flowers.'

'I thought they were to hide the knife,' Ed said.

'Maybe, but why yellow roses especially? That's what Hope insisted he bring. So I'm thinking, what if the roses weren't for Hope?'

Ed repeated, 'The roses weren't for Hope?'

'You told me Lowell Paton took Simone flowers, every week.'

'Yes . . .'

'Lowell said the same thing. He said he took her yellow roses. What if Hope knew the roses would be a trigger, knew *what* they'd trigger? That way she'd be certain of at least one person's reaction to Leo's arrival at the refuge. Complete shock. Fear. Simone wouldn't have had any trouble seeing Leo as a rapist, a potential killer. She'd see the roses and she'd remember Lowell.'

'Hope told Leo to bring yellow roses?'

'Yes. She insisted on yellow roses, and a knife. I fixed on the knife, we all did, but the roses were a weapon too. A way to make Simone remember – and react. A way to prime her as a witness and as a backup plan in case the stabbing went wrong.'

Ed half turned away, linking his hands behind his head. 'Jesus . . .'

Marnie moved so the breeze was at her back, thinking of the suitcase Hope took from the house. Leo had been reluctant to tell her what was inside the case, but in the end he'd confessed, the way he'd confessed the rest of it. No – not the *rest* of it, not everything. She doubted that she'd seen more than the tip of the iceberg. All couples hid their private lives to one extent or another, and the Proctors had more to hide than most.

'How can I help?' Ed asked.

'By keeping things calm at the refuge. We'll have to re-interview everyone, about Hope. How's Britt getting on? Is she keeping Shelley in line?'

'I hope so.' Ed grimaced. 'Not sure *hope* is the right word, under the circumstances. Makes you wonder what was going through her parents' minds, when they named her.'

Marnie sketched a quick picture of Hope's childhood. He listened in silence, then sighed. 'What does it say about me, that I'm not surprised? I've heard much worse . . .'

'Parents don't breed psychopaths. They don't always help, that's for sure, but look at Ayana, and Simone. They didn't let their early experiences turn them into monsters.'

'Where're Hope's parents now?'

'Her mum died six months ago. Cancer. I'm wondering if that was the tipping point, for what happened in Finchley. The timing fits. Her dad's in sheltered housing, in Dulwich. Leo didn't go into details. He didn't think her mum's death was significant, but from the way he described what happened? I think it must have been a catalyst. After her mum's death, Hope started getting a lot worse.'

'You don't think there's a chance she'll go after her dad?'

'Kenneth Reece. I'm tracing him, but from what Leo said, Hope never had a problem with her dad. She blamed her mum, for being a victim.'

'That doesn't sound good for Simone.'

'Simone's a survivor,' Marnie said.

Ed nodded, but he didn't look happy. 'Let's hope she gets the chance to prove it.'

# 7

Abby Pike was working late. 'Here's that list of sheltered housing in Dulwich. Do you want me to start ringing round?'

'Thanks.' Marnie scanned the list and handed it back. 'We're looking for Kenneth Reece, late fifties, widower. His wife was Gayle Reece. She died in October. I don't have the exact date.'

Abby wrote it down. Her desk was chaotic, but it was an organised chaos. Marnie bet she could lay her hands on everything she needed, when she needed it. 'Tell me about the CCTV.'

'Nothing from the hospital yesterday. I got the Finchley footage, but it doesn't show the roof and that's where they took her, isn't it? Ayana.'

'How about footage from the Proctors' house?'

'The nearest camera's two streets away, by the tube station.' Abby nodded at the monitor on her desk. 'Here.'

Marnie crouched to see the screen better. It was the usual poor quality. Muddy imagery, stilted delivery. Nothing like the crystalline data secured in television dramas, where every courtroom in the land presented jurors with infallible evidence captured by cameras in the well-lit locations chosen

261

SARAH HILARY

by criminals for the purposes of recording their misdemeanours. The CCTV outside Woodside Park tube station relied on yellow sodium street lighting, the worst kind. Of course it did. What was it Marnie had said to Noah, right at the start of this? *No one loves us that much.*

She peered at Abby's monitor. Hope Proctor and Simone Bissell had gone into the underground station at 8.11 a.m. Nearly twelve hours ago. Simone was carrying a suitcase. Hope had her head down.

'Woodside Park,' Abby said. 'The Northern Line runs all the way to Elephant and Castle. After that, if you want Dulwich, it's buses. I've asked for CCTV from the British Transport Police. So far, I can't find them coming out of the tube at Elephant and Castle, so maybe they weren't headed for Dulwich, but I thought it made sense to start there, if that's where her dad's based.'

Marnie straightened up. 'Good thinking. Keep looking.'

'Are we going public with the missing persons? The new status, I mean.'

'Not yet. I need to be sure Hope won't panic and do something stupid . . . Can I have the footage on disk? I want Ed Belloc to take a look at it.'

'Of course.' Abby took the CD from the computer drive and slipped it into a plastic case. 'Here you go.'

'Thanks,' Marnie said. 'And you'd better call in Noah, and DS Carling. It's going to be a late night.'

Ed was waiting in her office. He'd made coffee. 'I've got the footage,' she said.

'Great.' Ed pulled up a chair next to hers.

Marnie was tired of studying the CCTV's tide of people going in and out, London's streets rendered in lurid video-game Technicolor that made everyone look like a suspect. She was going blind, searching through the pictures. Except for the images of Hope and Simone at the tube station. She couldn't stop looking at those. She and Ed watched the footage three times.

'It looks like Simone's in charge,' Marnie said. 'Doesn't it?'

'Yes, it does.'

Marnie touched her thumb to the picture. 'Simone doesn't know. Yet. She thinks she's helping Hope. She thinks she's in control of the situation.' Her neck prickled at the thought of Hope shattering that illusion, once the women reached whichever hiding place Hope had chosen for them. She picked up her coffee, holding the hot mug against her face, hoping the flare of pain in her cheek didn't signal the onset of a migraine.

'Woodside Park . . .' Ed was still studying the image. 'You said Hope's dad's in sheltered housing, in Dulwich, was it? Woodside Park's in the right direction.' He'd drawn the same conclusion as Abby Pike.

'Yes. I should have an address for her dad very soon. Kenneth Reece.' She checked her watch. 'Can I ask a favour?'

Ed said, 'Sure. If I can ask one.'

She knew what he wanted. 'We're looking for Ayana. I promise you that.'

'The Mirzas' house is on the way to Dulwich,' he pointed out.

'Okay. Let's do things in that order.'

Ayana's parents lived in a terraced house that opened directly on to the pavement. The street was a mess of roadworks, abandoned for the night. A deep trench ran up one side, exposing pipework so corroded it looked like the trunk of a tree growing horizontally under the tarmac.

The Mirzas' house had thick net curtains at the windows and a pane of frosted glass in the front door, impossible to see through. Marnie rang the bell and stood back so that Ed would be the first person the Mirzas saw when they came to the door.

No one answered until the third ring, and only then with the chain on. A young man in a newly ironed shirt peered through the gap. He looked like an office intern, very smart and groomed. 'Yes?'

'Hatim?' Ed smiled. 'Can we come in?'

'Sir,' he wrinkled his brow, 'I don't know you.'

'I'm Ed Belloc, from the Victim Support Unit. This is Detective Inspector Rome.'

Hatim's eyes scared to Marnie. He couldn't have been more than seventeen. Ayana's little brother. What part did he play in the bleach attack that blinded his sister? Marnie could smell garam masala; saw in her mind's eye the cloth purse Noah said Ayana wore at her waist, memory and warning in one.

'Sir,' Hatim deferred to Ed, keeping the door chained, 'what is this, please?'

'I spoke with Turhan earlier. Didn't he mention it?'

'Sir, no, he didn't.'

'Are your mum and dad in?'

'No, sir.'

'Nasif, maybe? Turhan? He was here earlier.'

Hatim shook his head at each name. It was Marnie's guess that his brothers had briefed him for this task, leaving him home in case of a visit by the police.

'Can we come in, please, Hatim?' she asked.

He paused, then nodded, sliding the chain free and opening the door, standing like a sentry as they stepped into the square sitting room. Everywhere was tidy, a whiff of room spray under the cold scent of cooking. School textbooks on the table, patterned throws pulled neat on the sofa. Photos on the walls, all boys. None of Ayana. Marnie knew straight away that they wouldn't find Ayana here.

'We're wondering where we can find your sister.'

Hatim stayed by the door, his shoulders pulled back. 'I haven't seen my sister in a long time,' he said.

It was what they'd told him to say, she guessed, but it sounded like the truth. Hatim was slight, with an adolescent's awkward, outsized hands and feet. She had the sudden, horrible suspicion that he'd poured the bleach into his sister's eyes. He didn't have the weight to hold anyone down. The older brothers would have done that, delegating what they saw as the easy task to Hatim.

She picked up one of the textbooks from the table. 'We're worried about Ayana. We think she might be in danger.'

Hatim looked possessively at the book in her hands. 'She should have stayed here. We would have kept her safe.'

'I don't think she knew that.' Marnie opened the book, riffling the pages. 'I think she was scared to be here.'

He bit his lips together. 'She wasn't scared. She found it difficult, that's all.'

'What did she find difficult?'

'School. Home.' He pulled a face. 'Boys. It isn't pleasant to be a girl here.'

'Here?' Marnie gestured around the tidied room.

He lifted his chin. 'In England,' he corrected her. 'London.'

'Hatim . . . where do you think Ayana is?' Ed asked the question, drawing the boy's gaze away from Marnie and the book she was holding.

'In a hostel,' he said quickly. Too quickly. 'A shelter.' He tidied his hair with one hand. 'You know, sir, what I mean.'

'A women's shelter.'

'Yes.'

'Where, do you know?'

Hatim shrugged, glancing towards the table. A good student, eager to learn. He didn't like Marnie handling his books. He wanted to get back to work. It was nearly nine o'clock at night. He was studying late, especially for a teenager home alone.

'Finchley,' Marnie said.

'Yes. No. I don't know.' He was angry at the way it had slipped out, his stare accusing her of tricking him.

'You knew she was in Finchley.' Marnie closed the book and put it down on the table. 'How did you know that?'

'I didn't. I told you, sir,' appealing to Ed, 'I don't know where she is.'

Ed nodded. 'Where's your mum, Hatim? Isn't she usually at home?'

'She's gone to my auntie's. My auntie is ill.' He was back on-script. 'My mum's looking after her.'

'That's nice of her. Where does your aunt live?'

'Auntie Nada is in Leicester.'

'Could you write down her address and phone number?'

Hatim hesitated, then came to the table where Marnie was standing. 'Pardon me.' He reached past her for a pen and pad, writing in a rounded hand before tearing off the page and passing it to Ed.

'Thank you.' Ed read the page, then folded it and put it into his pocket.

'May I see Ayana's room?' Marnie asked.

Hatim nodded; this was in the script. 'Upstairs. The room next to the bathroom.' His eyes filled with ghosts.

Marnie's stomach flipped over. The bathroom where the bleach attack happened. It was right there, in Hatim's face. Not just the appalling injury done to Ayana. The damage done to Hatim, to the whole family.

Ayana's bedroom was as tidy as the room downstairs. Books on a shelf, a table with a jewellery box. School books, nothing too challenging, intellectually or politically. Pretty, modest clothes in the wardrobe. Half a dozen scarves, some in brilliant silks sewn with sequins and stars.

'Follow the left-hand wall.' She remembered her training officer telling her this, about crime scenes. 'Follow the left-hand wall of a room. Like you're going through a maze, to find the middle.'

She stooped and picked a gold sequin from the carpet, holding it on the tip of her finger. She wanted to believe that if she searched the room, if she followed the left-hand wall, she'd find a clue to Ayana's whereabouts. A secret compartment in the jewellery box, say, which her clever detective's fingers would unlock.

Ayana hadn't hidden any secrets here. This room had never been hers, not in any real sense. You had to feel safe in a place before you could start trusting your secrets to it. This had never been a place of safety for Ayana.

Marnie found empty hangers in the wardrobe, a handful of underwear dug from the neat piles in the chest of drawers. Someone had taken a week's worth of Ayana's clothes, and recently, judging by the dust dislodged from the empty hangers. Wherever she was, they'd dressed her again as their daughter. No more red dresses for Ayana.

Hatim hung back as she searched his sister's room, guarding the bathroom the way he'd guarded the front door.

'Excuse me.' Marnie sidestepped past him, into the bathroom.

A bath, sink, toilet. Bath mat, striped jute, spread on the slice of floor by the side of the bath. Just enough space for three people to hold down a fourth, assuming the fourth was slim and prevented from struggling. On a low shelf by the toilet: a bottle of bleach.

Black plastic as thick as a forearm. Red cap, childproof.

Marnie shut her eyes, seeing Ayana's feet, kicking. Hearing her screams echoing round the cramped space. The men passing the black bottle from hand to hand. Two of them kneeling, panting, on her chest and knees. The boy, Hatim, fumbling with the childproof cap. Was he screaming too? She was sure she could hear it, a chorus of shrieks. The family flaying itself apart. It came close to numbing her. Too much outrage, too much agony to process. She didn't have the frame of reference to make sense of what had taken place here.

She refused to be numb. She *refused*. Anger was the only proper response. She dug her nails into her palms, making them sting.

She should *make* Hatim tell the truth. Give up his brothers' hiding place, the address where they'd taken Ayana. She could do it. If she dragged Hatim in here, the way Ayana was dragged, and pushed him down, called to Ed for his help . . .

A flash – too fast for her to censor it – of Hatim on the floor, her knees pinning his shoulders, Ed's capable hands working the bleach bottle's cap, the threat of it sufficient to get what they needed, an address for Ayana's rescue. It would be easy. Hatim was already afraid. If he felt that thick plastic against his cheek . . .

The image was so vivid she could feel his sweat branding her skin.

She couldn't have done it. And Ed . . .

Never in a lifetime would he let himself cross that line. Just asking him to do it would ruin everything between them. They weren't those people, Ed and Marnie.

Ed wasn't that person.

Hatim was waiting outside the bathroom, his eyes full of the ghosts she'd just seen.

'Why did you do it?' she asked him.

He knew what she was asking. There was no misunderstanding. 'She looked . . .' He stopped and tried again. 'She *looked* . . .' He couldn't finish the sentence. He didn't understand why they'd done it.

Marnie turned away from him. Hatim followed her back down the stairs to where Ed was waiting. As they were leaving, she stopped and looked straight into the boy's eyes.

'If you know where she is, Hatim, you can pay your debt by telling us. We won't use your name. You would know that you'd done the right thing, this time.'

He shook his head blindly, speaking across her, to Ed. 'Goodbye, sir.'

'It's true, Hatim.' Ed touched a hand to the boy's elbow. 'This is your chance to put things right. You're the one with the power to do that. And the courage.'

Hatim's eyes clouded with tears. He drew back from Ed's touch. 'Goodbye, sir.'

Ed took a card from his wallet and put it with the books on the table. 'Take care, Hatim.'

'Well, we know she's not in Leicester.' It was dark outside, the street lighting buzzing on and off, a faulty connection somewhere.

'Maybe Hatim will call.' Ed didn't sound hopeful. 'You should contact the airports. Put an alert on Ayana's passport. If they take her out of the country . . .'

'Abby Pike's doing that. I asked her as soon as we knew Ayana was missing.'

Marnie pulled out her phone, checking for messages from Abby, or Tim Welland.

A missed call from Noah an hour ago, when he was home, so it couldn't be news from the station. 'They took a week's worth of clothes,' she told Ed. 'That's something.'

Her pulse was racing from the images she'd summoned inside the house. How close had she been, really, to threatening violence against Hatim Mirza? Her palms were clammy. She was sure she could smell bleach in her clothes. Could she have asked Ed to do that, to help her hold down a schoolboy and terrify him into speaking? Ed would have stopped it – stopped her – but he'd never have looked at her the same way again. Not if she'd let him see the species of anger that lived under her skin.

'I wish I could go and look for her. Ayana. But without any real leads . . .'

Ed nodded. 'I understand. You need to get back to looking for Hope.'

'That, too.' She dug out the list Abby had given her. 'Time to try her dad, in Dulwich.' She sidestepped the potholed trench in the road. 'Don't say I never take you anywhere nice.'

# 8

From the outside, it was just a house in a nice white middle-class part of town, miles from the nearest council estate. Detached, walled in by a well-tended garden, flowers flanking the driveway to the front door. Light from the storm porch planted pale roses in the beds. Inside the porch, wellington boots and gardening gloves conjured the ghosts of the householders.

Noah Jake knocked at the porch door, wondering if he was wasting his time here.

After the house call with Ron Carling, he'd gone home, changed into sweats and taken his foul mood for a five-mile run. He hated doing nothing, couldn't shake the idea that he might've led Ayana's brothers to her hiding place. He wanted to be working, following up the leads he and Marnie had abandoned earlier when she returned to the hospital to quiz Leo Proctor. The trip to West Brompton with Carling had sealed Noah's bad mood; Carling winking at Henry Stuke, joking about Noah's sexuality, all blokes together. He'd taken his usual route but failed to outrun either his temper or his guilt, which burned like battery acid in his bloodstream.

Tomato plants inside the storm porch. Exotic-looking seed

pods stood along a narrow shelf. The pods weren't from any plant that grew in this part of London's leafy suburbs. He tried the handle, and discovered the storm porch was unlocked. Going inside, he knocked again, this time on the door leading into the house.

'Hello? It's DS Jake. If I could have a moment of your time . . .'

Footfall in the house. He stepped away from the door, embarrassed to be in the porch, among the flowerpots and boots. He wiped perspiration from his face, regretting the marathon. More sweat, in a deep V, stained the front of his shirt and the thighs of his sweatpants. He hoped he didn't stink.

Hope Proctor answered the door, wild-eyed with terror.

Noah stared. It hadn't even crossed his mind that she might be here. 'Hope? Is Simone with you?'

She stared back at him. Then put out a hand and pulled at his sleeve. 'Help. Please.'

'What's happened?'

She didn't answer, just pulled at him.

He went with her, inside the house.

The house felt empty. Lived in, unlike the Proctors' show home, but empty.

Hope led him through a sitting room – tapestry sofas, rugs on the stone floor, a round mahogany table with a clock that showed the late hour, after ten now – to a big kitchen at the back of the house.

Simone Bissell was standing behind a central island topped with polished stone, under a hanging rack of kitchen utensils. Like Hope, she had blank terror in her eyes.

Was someone else here, with them? Not in the kitchen, but this was a big house, and it didn't belong to Hope, or Simone. Noah looked from one woman to the other, wondering what was scaring the pair of them so badly.

'Hope?' he asked, feeling his way.

She shook her head at him, mutely. He looked at Simone. She stared back, her eyes glossy, reflecting the bright surface of the island, the steel overhang of saucepans and pots. She looked drugged. Behind her, a door led into a glass-roofed conservatory, its windows packed with night. Was someone in there, hiding from the police?

'What's going on?' Noah asked. 'Are you okay?'

Hope kept hold of his sleeve, watching Simone. 'She's crazy.' It was a whisper, fierce. She clutched at his arm.

Simone held her head high, her shoulders back, standing to attention as if she was in ballet class. The island hid her body below the waist.

Noah couldn't see her hands. Something in those shining eyes went beyond fear, to a place he didn't know.

He looked down at Hope's hand, small on his sleeve, its fingernails varnished pink and perfectly shaped.

Perfectly shaped.

It wasn't her, he realised with a shock. It wasn't Hope who'd scratched at the floor and walls under the stairs in the Proctors' house, trying to get free.

If it wasn't Hope, there was only one other person it could have been. He couldn't keep the knowledge from his face. Hope saw it, her pupils contracting, free hand reaching to the island for a weapon.

If it'd been just Hope, he might have been able to stop her.

But it wasn't just Hope.

It was Simone.

It was Simone, coming at him fast, with a hammer.

She swung at his left leg, low down.

Knocked him from his feet, pain punching the breath from his lungs. Knocked him to the floor.

273

## 9

Excalibur House in East Dulwich was a Victorian villa dressed in so much concrete it was hard to see the once-grand facade under the brutal add-ons: pigmented cement render, storm windows and a crop of satellite dishes. Floodlighting illuminated the entrance, motion-activated, clicking on when Ed and Marnie approached the main door.

Southwark Council had divided the villa into a dozen self-contained flats for people over sixty, or those with special needs. Hope Proctor's father was fifty-seven, below the age threshold. Marnie wondered what argument he'd used to secure a flat here. She stopped wondering when he opened the door.

Kenneth Reece stooped, as if his body had caved in on itself. Skeletal physique. Jaundiced whites to his eyes, nose marred by ruptured veins, mouth shrunken to the self-pitying moue of an aged starlet.

'Yes?' His voice was high-pitched, but hoarse. He fussed at the chain on the door with one hand, the other holding a grubby green bathrobe shut at his sunken chest.

'Kenneth Reece?' Marnie showed her badge. 'Detective Inspector Rome. This is Ed Belloc. We'd like to come in for a moment.'

'It's very late,' he objected.

'Even so, we'd like to come in.'

'For what?' His eyes slid past her shoulder to Ed, his brows arching.

'We'd like to talk to you about Hope.'

He sniggered through his nose. 'You sound like God-botherers . . .'

'Your daughter, Hope.'

His eyes were instantly wet with tears. He clawed at the door. 'What's happened?'

'Can we come in?'

'My girl,' his voice cracked, 'she's my girl. I've a right to know what's happened.'

'Let's discuss your rights,' Marnie said, 'inside.'

Kenneth Reece stepped back from the door, flapping his hand at the narrow hallway. 'Go through, go through.'

# 10

Noah got lucky. If Hope had used the hammer, she'd have smashed his ankle. Simone hadn't hit him as hard as she could've done, but it was hard enough. He was on his back, on the kitchen floor. Hope dropped down and sat on his legs, her fist full of sharp white light. A knife. She put its tip to his chest. 'Careful,' she warned, 'that bitch with the phone card isn't here to help you this time.'

He saw her properly then. For the first time. Everything fell into place, crystallised in the threat of steel through his shirt. Who she was, and what she'd done.

What she meant to do.

Hope was angry, but he had to look hard to see it, under the tight layers of self-assurance. This was what she did, what she excelled at; Hope was in her happy place.

'Too many weapons in here,' she decided, looking around the kitchen. 'We'll have to move him. Get the rope.'

Simone flinched into action, dropping the hammer and going in the direction of the conservatory. 'Simone . . .' Noah wanted her to stop, think about what she was doing, stand up to Hope's bullying, whatever tactics the other woman had deployed to turn her into an automaton, obeying Hope even when a person's life was at risk. He'd never seen anyone so blankly terrified; there was no room in Simone's eyes for anything other than whatever threat Hope had made, to make her follow orders.

'Shut up.' Hope moved the knife meaningfully. 'She doesn't have to listen to you or anyone else any more.'

Noah fought to control his breathing so that his words would come out without shaking. 'Except you . . .'

She smiled, freezing his blood. 'Except me.'

Simone brought rope from the conservatory. Blue plastic-coated rope.

'Where're your foster-parents? Simone—'

Hope hit him with the rubber handle of the knife, in the throat.

Everything went red, and black. He choked, kicking under the impact.

Hope sat on his legs, hard. 'You. Don't get to talk to her.' A beat. 'Tie his hands, over his head.' She set the tip of the knife to the bruise she'd planted in Noah's windpipe. 'Be helpful.'

He forced his eyes to focus on her face. She'd do it. Cut his throat. Then there'd be no one to get Simone out of here. He surrendered his hands, putting them on the floor above his head. Simone looped rope around his wrists, tying it off.

Hope checked the tightness of the knots. 'Good, that's perfect. You see?' She shone a smile at Simone. 'You can do this. Now his feet. Take off his trainers.'

Noah set his teeth against the distress signals from his injured ankle. Hope watched his face with a clinical interest that made his skin crawl. She was a sadist, he'd worked that much out as soon as he'd realised it was Leo's fingernails that had scratched under the stairs. What else – worse – was she? He didn't know anything about Hope Proctor, not really. Not even the name on her birth certificate. He knew enough

277

about Simone to understand her quick, reflexive obedience to Hope's commands. Doing as she was told, from fear or for survival, came naturally to Simone.

Simone had spent a year at the mercy of Lowell Paton. For years before that, she'd been trying to please her foster-parents, to fit into their life here in England. Gardening, wellington boots, roses.

How had Hope spent her childhood? Not happily, if these were the consequences: Leo Proctor's near-murder; Noah with a knife at his throat, waiting to see what form her revenge was going to take; and whatever damage she'd done already to the Bissells in their safe middle-class home.

# 11

Kenneth Reece's sitting room was fitted with a dark carpet that sucked up the light and coughed it back in miserly patches. An oversized sofa and armchair filled most of the space, upholstered in fraying corduroy. Brown dust shrouded the light fitting and the curtains. The wall nearest the window was freckled with mould; the thick green smell of damp was everywhere in the room. An upright fan heater, doubling as a humidifier, stood to the left of the sofa, its plug separated from the socket in the wall.

Marnie had been in dozens of rooms like this. Temporary shelters for those who'd opted out of mainstream society, or been elbowed out of it. She'd learnt to look for personal details, the clutter that marked out an individual's ownership. The living space loaned by the local housing authority was featureless, replicated all over the city.

The council had screwed handrails to three of the four walls in Kenneth Reece's sitting room. Either the previous resident was elderly and needed the rails, or this was Kenneth Reece on a good day, when he was managing to be upright without assistance.

On a table next to the sofa was a lamp with a cellophane-wrapped shade, a glass tumbler cloudy with fingerprints and four corner-shop-sized bottles of gin, three of them empty, one with a pink plastic rose stem in its neck. Marnie wondered if she needed any further clue to Reece's life here. She looked at the sofa – stained, low-slung – and opted to stand. Ed perched unobtrusively on the arm of the chair.

Reece walked carefully, with the exaggerated dignity of a drunk, to the sofa. He sat and crossed his legs, holding the bathrobe shut with both hands. The robe was a good match for the mould on the wall, the same colour and with the same patchy texture, falling apart in places. Reece tidied himself, eyeing Marnie and Ed.

There she was.

Hope Proctor.

In his false modesty. The prim, resentful shape he made of his mouth.

Marnie registered an odd pain in the pit of her stomach. Stephen Keele had spared her this much: the image of her old age in her parents' faces. Not all loss was about grief. Sometimes it was the loss of fear, or consequence. Loss could be liberating.

Had her mother's death liberated Hope Proctor? If so, what were the consequences of that liberty?

'What's all this about?' Reece asked.

'Hope. We're here about Hope.'

She didn't know what she'd expected, but it wasn't this arch, effete man. His shins were hairless, white. He had hairless toes with yellow nails so long neglected they'd toughened nearly to bone. This detail, more than any other, made her certain that every bad thing she'd heard about the man was true. No logic to her judgement. Just instinct.

She lifted her eyes to the wall behind the sofa, where,

framed in shiny orange wood, he'd hung a floral tribute of the kind found on coffins. Purple flowers in the shape of a crucifix, sprayed with plastic to preserve it. From his wife's coffin? Marnie dropped her gaze to the gin bottles on the side table.

'What's this about my little girl?' A whine rode the pitch of his voice, like a surfer on a high wave. Kenneth Reece was a drunk, with all the self-pitying conviction that entailed. He probably considered himself a victim, just like Lowell Paton. When he looked in the mirror – if he looked in the mirror; there were none in this room – the last thing he saw was a wife-beater.

'We were wondering,' Marnie said, 'if she's been in touch recently. Hope.'

'Not in over an age. That husband of hers . . .' Reece smoothed a hand at his thinning hair. The backs of his hands were marked with muscle, wasted now, but it reminded Marnie of his daughter's hands, the muscle definition she'd imagined came from housework. She'd been wrong. It came from lifting bricks and whatever else Hope had used to break her husband's bones.

'We're concerned for Hope's safety. She went missing from hospital yesterday.'

'Hospital?' Reece wet his lips, looking towards the gin bottles.

'We hoped you might have some idea where we could find her. We think she's in central London. Do you know of anywhere she might've gone?'

'What's wrong with her home?'

'We know she's not there.'

'That husband of hers doesn't know where she is?'

'Leo Proctor is in hospital.'

Same reaction. His eyes going to the gin, voice vague. 'Why's that then?'

'Hope stabbed him.'

That got his attention. 'With a knife, stabbed?'

'With a knife. That doesn't surprise you?'

'She's my tough nut.' His smile was thirsty. 'My girl.'

# 12

In the bathroom, Hope searched Noah's pockets, taking his wallet and ID, his phone. Simone had gone back into the kitchen, after helping Hope drag Noah here, tying his ankles, roping his hands to the pipework under the sink. He couldn't stop Hope taking what she wanted from his pockets.

She'd left the knife in the kitchen, but she'd brought the hammer in here, together with a brown suitcase, the one Felix Gill had described to Noah and Marnie. Noah remembered the fruitless search in the Proctors' house for whatever Hope had taken away. Now, he didn't much want to know what was inside the brown case.

Hope thumbed through the contents of his phone. Noah willed her to use it. Even if she didn't, as long as she left it switched on, the Met could get a trace. 'Where's Simone?' he asked. 'And Pauline?'

Hope looked over at him.

'That's her mum's name, isn't it? And her dad, Charles, is he here?'

Pauline and Charles Bissell. He hoped he had that right, struggling to remember the detail of the conversation with Ed Belloc at the North Middlesex.

Hope held up his phone. 'You're a funny sort of policeman.'

Noah lifted his head from the tiles to see what she'd found on the phone. An old text from Dan, smiley face in the sign-off. Noah only kept the texts that made him laugh, or the filthy ones, which reminded him that there was more to life than his work.

*A funny sort of policeman . . .*

'Because there're people who care about me? There are people who care about you, Hope. And about Simone, and her mum and dad.'

'Pauline and Charles.' She sat on the floor, five feet from him. 'I suppose they teach you that. To use first names. Make the hostages more human. Or is it the hostage-taker who's supposed to become more human?' She crossed her legs under her, the grey sweats swamping her slight body. She'd pulled her blonde hair into a ponytail. Her face was heart-shaped, free from make-up, its skin translucent.

'You're human,' he said.

She pointed the phone at him. 'You're gay.'

What was that – an insult? An accusation? An excuse for whatever she intended to do next? It didn't really matter what it was; his answer was the same: 'Yes. I am.'

'What if I happen to hate gays?'

'What if you hate Jamaicans? Am I supposed to lie about that, too?'

*What about men?* he thought. *What if you hate men?*

She toyed with the phone, wrinkling her nose at Dan's text. 'Don't they teach you to keep quiet about your personal life?'

'You didn't ask about my life. You asked if I was gay, and I told you the truth.' He waited a second before adding, 'You'd have known if I was lying.'

That pleased her. She cocked her head at him. 'Why?'

'Because you're so good at it. Hiding. Pretending to be what you're not.'

'You pretend. You're pretending to be a detective, but you don't look much like one, lying here.'

True. Most detectives didn't spend their evenings roped to the plumbing in a stranger's bathroom. None of the ones Noah had met, anyway. Maybe he should ask Commander Welland to introduce him to some senior-ranking officers . . .

He blinked, to focus. The ache in his arms was inching towards pain, and his ankle alternated between blazing and throbbing. But she hadn't done anything to hurt him, not really, not yet. 'Where's Simone?' he asked again.

'She's cooking supper.' Hope kicked a foot at the bathroom door. It swung open, letting in the smell of frying fish. 'Are you hungry?'

'I'm thirsty,' Noah admitted. 'And I need to use the lavatory.'

She uncrossed her legs and stood. 'It's a tiled floor. We can rinse it down.'

For the first time, Noah felt despair flare under his ribcage. 'Hope . . .'

She held up his phone again. 'Can they trace this?' She saw him debating how to answer. 'You'd better tell the truth. I'll know.'

'They'll have traced it already.'

'In that case,' she said, 'we'd better lay some extra places at the table.'

She was insane. Was she?

'Hope, don't go. We need to talk. You need someone to listen to you.'

She curled her mouth. 'They teach you that, too. Hostage-takers want to be heard. I guess I can't be a hostage-taker, in that case. Because I don't have anything to say, to you or anyone else.'

She shut his phone in her fist. 'And now? Neither do you.'

# 13

In Excalibur House, a neighbour of Kenneth Reece's was running taps. Filling a sink, or a bath. The sound travelled through the pipes, gulping and belching. 'It doesn't worry you that Hope is missing?' Marnie said. 'On a charge of attempted murder?'

Reece didn't need to know she hadn't had the chance to charge his daughter, yet.

'I'm sure she had her reasons.' Reece swept his stare around the room, idly.

'For trying to kill her husband.'

'For whatever. She's a tough nut, like I said.' He leaned forward. The bathrobe hung open on wasted thighs, mottled violet, like the floral tribute on the wall. He managed a smile, cracked with disuse. 'Would you nice people like a drink?'

'No thank you. It wasn't the first time she'd hurt Leo. There was an established pattern of domestic abuse.'

'Was there?' He didn't care about anything she was saying. Unless he had a drink soon, she'd get nothing.

'It doesn't concern you that your daughter abused and nearly killed her husband. That she's wanted by the police for the kidnap of a disturbed woman.'

'You didn't say anything about that.'

'I'm saying it now. Mr Reece, we need to find your daughter.'

'I'd love to help.' He used the pretence of enthusiasm to lean across and fill the tumbler with the dregs from a bottle. 'But as I say, I've not heard from her in an age. Not since her mother.' He had just enough self-control to stop himself sucking at the glass, waiting a beat before lifting it to his lips.

'Her mother died in October, is that right?'

He nodded, wet-eyed again. She realised that he was waiting for her condolences. He'd wait a long time for that.

'Hope came to see you, when her mother died?'

'She did.' Another sip at the dirty glass.

The bathrobe was forgotten, hanging open to his waist, showing a whittled ribcage above a paunch the size and shape of a rugby ball. There, below his left nipple. A tattoo of a heart pierced by an arrow. The same tattoo Hope had insisted she and Leo get. On Kenneth Reece, it looked like a festering red wound. 'Was she very upset?'

'Hope? Not her.' He thinned his lips at the rim of the glass. 'Hope's my sweet little tough nut. My survivor.'

'What did she survive, Mr Reece? The sort of thing her mother couldn't?'

'I object to that.' He nodded towards Ed. 'You might like to make a note of my objection. I assume you're here to take notes, since you're not opening your mouth.'

Ed smiled at him, neutrally. His presence irked Reece, which was exactly why Marnie had wanted him here. 'What's your objection?' she asked Reece.

'Your insinuations about my wife.' He pointed at her with the glass, then returned it jealously to his mouth.

'What is it you think I'm insinuating?'

He shook his head, making the gin last. Gin, the weeper's drink. His tears were probably eighty per cent proof.

287

Marnie said, 'Let's remove any confusion, shall we? I'm referring to the fact that you routinely beat your wife, Hope's mother, in front of your daughter. That Hope grew up in a house ruled by violence and abuse. Her frame of reference was whatever you did with your fists on any given day.'

Kenneth Reece shook back the frayed cuff of his bathrobe. 'Excuse me, Detective Inspector, but what would you know about my family life? If you've been listening to that builder my girl married, well . . . I warned her about him as soon as she brought him home. "You'll have to take charge of *that*," I told her. What sort of man,' he looked at Ed, 'sits around with his lips sealed while the women run their mouths? If you've been listening to *him*—'

'I've been reading your wife's medical reports,' Marnie said. An exaggeration; she'd requested a copy of the report after seeing Leo at the hospital but she'd spoken, briefly, with staff at the hospice where Gayle Reece died. 'The ones that pre-date her cancer. But yes, since you mention it, Leo Proctor did share with us what Hope had told him, about your treatment of her mother.'

Kenneth Reece batted this away with the back of his hand. 'Hope never had a problem,' he said, 'with anything I did.'

# 14

Light bulleted off the tiles and chrome in the bathroom. Hope had gone back to the kitchen, leaving Noah alone in here. He worked his hands mechanically, trying to get the blood back into his fingers.

Where was Marnie Rome? Why hadn't she warned him, given him a clue to Hope's psychosis, when she first started to suspect it? She'd known something when she asked him to crawl into that space under the stairs at the Proctors' house. The questions she'd asked, about the phone call Hope made from the hospital . . . She'd suspected Hope, he realised that now. She'd suspected Hope, and she'd said nothing.

Noah had no weapons, no words, to use here. All he could do was hope for a rescue.

Wrong choice of word. *Hope'll kill you*. Wasn't that the saying?

Hope will kill you. Not a lot of doubt about that. She'd stuck a knife in Leo Proctor, puncturing his lung. What had she done with the Bissells? This was their house, but Noah hadn't seen or heard any proof that they were alive.

He yelled, because it helped with the fear. Yelled for Simone, for Hope. Kicked his bound feet on the floor and against the side of the bath.

The sound bounced like a ball in the tiled room.

He curled his fingers round the steel pipe where she'd tied off the rope. Hauled, willing the sink unit to come away from the wall. Hauled until his shoulders screamed at him to stop, by which time he was panting.

*All right, calm down.*

*Stop it. Stop.*

He could see little balls of dust under the sink, and dark hairs, white at the root. Pauline Bissell's hair? He looked up at the cabinets on the wall, imagining all manner of weaponry, out of reach. Razor blades and improvised Mace in the form of aerosol sprays. All too far away. He needed something nearby.

The brown suitcase, but it was at the foot of the bath and he still wasn't keen to discover what was inside. He squinted at it, seeing a dull red dot on the front of his T-shirt, like a sniper's spot.

Blood. She'd nicked him with the knife. It was nothing, in the scheme of things, but he wished she had a steadier hand.

How long did it take to eat fried fucking fish?

He kicked at the bath again, raising the same hollow ball of sound.

'Hey! Hope. Simone!'

Anything was better than waiting. That's what he was thinking. Anything was better than waiting.

Wrong.

Waiting was a killer, but Hope was worse.

She pushed open the bathroom door with the head of the hammer. She didn't look at him. She swung the hammer in her hand, its shadow stretching and shrinking under the light. Fear shut the back of Noah's throat. 'Hope . . .'

She went to the brown suitcase. He couldn't see her except in profile, the childish curve of her cheek. She propped the hammer at the end of the bath – away from his feet – and reached into the suitcase. Got hold of something and lifted it out.

Solid. Black. She set it on the floor.

A Russian kettlebell, pot-bellied.

A rock with a handle.

# 15

The smell of gin was overpowering, oily, as if Kenneth Reece had bathed in it. It was his sweat, Marnie realised, coming out through his pores.

'You used to lift weights,' she said. 'Is that right?'

Hope's father smiled, a mouthful of fake modesty marked by rotting teeth. 'You're not in bad shape yourself, Detective Inspector.'

'What sort of weights? Dumbbells?'

'Kettlebells.' Kenneth Reece held his drink at arm's length, so that the light fell into the glass and swam, whitely. 'Russian.'

'How much could you lift?'

'Forty, fifty pounds.' He shot Ed an idle look, laced with contempt.

'That's more than a hobby,' Marnie said.

'Hobbies are for children.' Reece adjusted his robe. It was hard to imagine him with body mass, proper muscles. Hard, but not impossible.

'Did Hope have any hobbies, as a child?'

'She liked to watch me work.' He shaped his mouth to the glass again. 'But she wasn't a frivolous child, if that's what you're asking.'

'I was wondering if she was any kind of child. If she had anything I'd recognise as a childhood.'

Reece gave an elaborate shrug, as if physically dislodging her objection. 'Just because she wasn't spoiled, or indulged . . .'

'She liked to watch you work. Do you mean *work out*, with the kettlebells?'

'Yes.' He sipped at the drink.

*Sipped.* Such self-restraint.

Marnie remembered the reluctance with which Leo Proctor had divulged the contents of the suitcase his wife had taken from their house. No such reluctance on the part of Kenneth Reece, who named his weapon of choice with candour, even conceit.

'You let Hope keep one of the bells, when she left home. That's what her husband told me. Is it true?'

'She asked for it,' Reece said. 'So, yes. I let her have it.'

'Why do you think she wanted it?'

He curled his lip to the glass. 'They make good doorstops.'

'Is that what you used them for? As doorstops?'

'I lifted them. As I said.' Reece put his arm out again, finding something to admire, apparently, in its etiolated wrist, bony elbow. 'Sixty, seventy pounds. That's professional standard.'

Too bad wife-beating wasn't an Olympic sport; this psychopath would've won enough medals to put Lowell Paton's gold chains in the shade. She wondered, briefly, if she could have Reece arrested for inciting violence, providing Hope with a weapon, and intent. 'Is that all you did with the kettlebells? Lift them?'

'What else would I have done with them?'

*Gee, Mr Reece, I don't know. Broken your wife's bones? Pinned her to the ground, cracked her ribs or her skull. Whatever took your sick, twisted fancy.*

'Do you know what Hope did with the kettlebell you gave her?'

Kenneth Reece reached to refresh his drink. The snapping sound of the metal cap set Marnie's teeth on edge. 'Specifically, what she did to her husband, Leo. The man you warned her would need knocking into shape.'

'I stopped being responsible for my child,' Reece said piously, 'when she turned eighteen.'

'Still, you'd like to know, I'm sure. I'm guessing it would make you proud. Like father, like daughter.'

'I'm flattered by your concern for my paternal instinct, Detective Inspector, but—'

'Paternal instinct?' Marnie echoed. 'You mean the way you showed your child what damage could be done with twenty kilograms of Russian cast iron?'

# 16

Noah tried to guess at the weight of the kettlebell Hope had taken from the brown suitcase and placed on the bathroom tiles. From the effort she put into lifting it, the bell was twenty kilograms. He hadn't lifted anything heavier than eight.

Simone had carried the suitcase from the Proctors' house. She was stronger than she looked. So was Hope, if she was about to do what Noah feared she was.

'Hope. You don't need to do this. I just – I was worried about you and Simone . . .'

She bent, both hands gripping the kettlebell's stout handle. It was an old-fashioned bell. Not the glossy kind you saw in modern gyms. This one belonged to her dad's generation of weight-trainers. The bell was important; she'd risked returning to the house for it. Why? What did it represent?

Symbol of machismo. Strength. Or something more . . .

Look at the way it was anchoring her to the ground.

*Okay, enough thinking. Try talking.*

'Hope. Please think about this. Please. Stop, and think. You don't want to do this.'

'You,' she said, 'have no idea what I want.'

True, but he could hazard a guess. Leo Proctor had broken

ribs, and a broken hand. Like someone else he'd seen recently
. . . His mind veered at an angle, chasing after the memory,
smelling soiled nappies, soured milk. Like . . .

Henry Stuke.

Oh, fuck. *Stuke*. Stuke was watching the refuge. The
smashed hand he'd explained away as a work accident – was
that Hope?

Noah curled his own hands into fists, shielding his face
with his forearms, aware of the vulnerable bones in his
elbows, and his wrists. Over two hundred bones in the
human body. She could break him in over two hundred
places. He drew his knees to his chest and twisted on to
his hip. The foetal position made him feel even more
exposed to her attack. From under the shelter of his arm,
he saw her lift the bell, muscles roping the backs of her
hands. She swung her arms and straddled his waist with
her feet.

'On your back,' she warned. 'I don't want to call Simone
in here to help.'

Noah cursed in his head. He didn't want Simone in here
either, not like this, made to play helpmate in Hope's sick
game. He had to force down his defences, one by one. Knees
first, straightening his legs before he gathered a breath and
rolled on to his back, his chest exposed to the kettlebell. He
couldn't uncover his face, or unfist his hands. He tried, but
he couldn't, his body in lockdown.

It didn't matter to Hope. She had what she wanted. His
chest, exposed. She positioned the squat base of the bell over
his heart and lowered it.

Let go.

The sudden impact was horrific, solid weight crushing him
into the tiles. Pain bolted up his ribs to stuff his throat with
a scream. He fought for air, trying to dislodge the weight by
twisting back on to his side, wanting it off him. Needing to

breathe. Animal instinct, no real thought involved. *Get it . . . off me . . .*

The kettlebell swayed and toppled. Fell. Rolled three feet and thundered into the side of the bath. Hope bent. Heaved it back over him. Screamed, 'Simone!'

Noah couldn't make Simone part of this. He couldn't. 'Don't . . .'

Hope's eyes slitted. She hissed, 'On your fucking back.'

He did as she said, and she dropped the kettlebell again, over his heart.

His teeth shredded the scream, but not by much.

He was still screaming when her shadow lengthened, reaching away from him, then back, a bigger shadow now, knuckled at its end.

That was when she used the hammer, for the first time.

# 17

Someone was pacing in the flat above Kenneth Reece's. Across the floor and back again. Across and back. Like a caged animal. Marnie blocked it out, focusing her attention on Hope's father. 'Hope never had a problem with you beating her mother in front of her.'

'I never laid a finger on Hope, if that's where this is headed.' Reece eyed the armchair where Ed was perched. 'Not even to discipline her. I didn't need to.'

'You were torturing her mother. It's hardly surprising Hope didn't put a foot wrong. Let's be clear, however. What you did – to Hope as well as her mother – was abuse.'

'You don't know what you're talking about.' He patronised her with a smile. 'A marriage is a private affair. You'd never hear my wife complain. As for Hope, she didn't have a problem with anything I did.' He raised the glass as if in a toast. 'She refused to let her mother ruin her with weakness, although God knows Gayle tried. She suffered all her life with emotions. Anything and everything made her cry. The television, kiddies in the street, books . . . She had no control over it, more's the pity.'

*Pity.* Nice choice of word for a serial torturer.

'But *you* did,' Marnie said. 'You had control. Hope told her husband all about it.'

Reece reached for a fresh bottle, pouring a precise measure into the glass. Only the very tips of his fingers trembled, and his top lip as it waited for the drink.

'What did you and Hope talk about, when she was last here?'

'Heaven knows. Her mother, I imagine, since Gayle had just died.'

'You hadn't been living together, during the last year of her life.'

'She was in a hospice, so no.'

'She was in a hospice for the last four months of her life. Before that, she was in a women's refuge. Isn't that the case?'

'If you say so.' Reece closed his eyes as he drank. She noticed for the first time that he had no eyelashes. 'We'd lost touch.'

'Had Hope been in contact with her mother, after her diagnosis?'

'You'd have to ask Hope. Personally I can't see her setting foot in a place like that, a breeding ground for neurosis.'

'This is the women's refuge where Gayle went, to get away from you.'

Reece ignored her. 'Hope never mentioned seeing her, when we met.'

'At Gayle's funeral. Is that the meeting we're talking about?'

'I thought that was clear. I last saw my daughter at her mother's funeral. Very nice she looked too, in her black suit. The builder hadn't bothered. He wore boots. Can you believe that? Workman's boots. I never knew what Hope saw in him.'

'You don't think she loved him?'

Reece snorted. 'Of course not.'

'Then why marry him?'

'I suppose she thought she could make something of him.'

Marnie waited for more, but Reece was silent. 'You said she wasn't upset, at the funeral. Her mother had died. How could she not be upset?'

'She didn't show it, if she was. The opposite of her mother's amateur dramatics.' Reece looked up at Ed and Marnie, pride shining in his eyes. 'I never once saw Hope cry. Never once.'

'You don't think she should've cried at her mother's funeral?'

*You* didn't, Marnie's conscience pricked her. She'd been in a state of shock at her parents' funeral, numb in her extremities and everywhere else. Was that how Hope felt, at her mother's funeral? Numb. Too much violence could do that, like too much wine. Take the edge off everything, even the things that mattered. Sometimes pain was a blessing. It woke you up, helped you to *feel*.

'Did you know that your daughter seeks out violent men? Men who hurt her, physically.'

Hope's father self-administered another mouthful of anaesthetic in silence.

'A doctor said Hope had the sort of injuries seen on working girls. Prostitutes who service sadistic clients.'

And another mouthful. Hollow legs. To go with his hollow heart.

'Leo wouldn't hurt her,' Marnie said. 'He hated it. When he refused, she picked up strangers in bars and went back with them, to be beaten. It's lucky she's still alive.'

Unlucky for Simone Bissell.

Reece cradled his glass like an infant to his chest.

'Your daughter needs to be beaten. Do you think that makes her a survivor?' Marnie wanted to see his hand shake, even if it was just tremors from the gin. She wanted to see some sign that he understood what he'd done. 'I think it makes her a sad, damaged woman. And dangerous. To herself and others.'

'I stopped being responsible,' Reece repeated, 'when she reached eighteen.'

'You're responsible. You'll always be responsible. If you can't see that, I pity you. It's pathetic. Leo Proctor's five times the man you'll ever be.'

Kenneth Reece looked across the rim of his glass at her, his eyes dulled by drink.

He was too far away for her to touch him. Right out of reach.

Just like his daughter.

**18**

In the Bissells' kitchen, the dishes sat in the sink, unwashed. Simone had scraped her portion of fish into the pedal bin. The mouthful she'd eaten was full of bones, spines sticking in the tender roof of her mouth.

It was quiet in the house, no noise from the bathroom. Simone was afraid to look in that direction, in case it prompted Hope to go back there. She'd left the policeman screaming. Brought the hammer and kettlebell into the kitchen and propped them at the side of her chair as she sat and ate. He was quiet now, DS Jake. Simone had no proof that he was still alive. She was afraid to ask, in case the answer was bad.

After they'd eaten, Hope sat on the floor by the bell and hammer, nodding for Simone to join her. She did what Hope wanted. It was cold on the floor. Simone's legs felt stiff, like an old woman's.

'Daddy's kettlebell was warm,' Hope said. She touched the black iron bell, as if it was a crucifix, or a pet. 'The handle smelt of his skin. I'd watch him with it. Bending and stretching, lifting it from the floor to his waist then up – high – over his head.'

Simone wanted to cover her ears, but she didn't. She sat and listened, and tried hard not to weep. Hope had stopped asking questions about her childhood, and for that, Simone was grateful. Hope wanted her to listen now. It was hard to listen when Simone was so scared, so cold. It was almost worse than talking. She didn't know what Hope was going to say. She only knew something terrible must have happened, to make her like this. Simone was afraid to hear the terrible thing, afraid of the pictures it would put in her head.

'He lifted the weight over his head, too high for me to reach,' Hope's eyes misted as she remembered, 'even though I stood on tiptoe and stretched the ends of my fingers. Trying to reach, trying to touch.' She caught Simone's hand and held it. She didn't seem to notice how cold Simone's fingers were, or how badly they shook. 'He screwed his eyes shut as he worked.' Hope mimicked the expression, and Simone swallowed a gasp, from the relief of being free just for a second from the woman's searing stare. 'His muscles . . . looked like mice moving under his skin.'

Hope opened her eyes again. 'He didn't look at me. I wished he would. I wished and wished he'd lift me like that, to his waist and then up. High, high over his head.'

She twisted her fingers through Simone's, guiding their twinned hands to the kettlebell. It was so solid and hard.

Simone flinched.

'Hush,' Hope said. 'Hush. Look at me.'

Simone did, seeing the woman through a flush of tears.

Hope said, 'I've never told anyone this before.' She looked angry, just for a second.

Simone cringed, wanting to free her hand, but knowing she could not. *She*'d done this. Brought this woman here. She had to listen to what Hope wanted to say. She had to stop Hope taking the hammer and bell back into the bathroom.

Hope stroked the kettlebell with their linked hands. 'I'd put my face to it, when he was finished. You could hear it ringing, feel it *humming* against your lips, but it got cold too quickly. And heavy. I couldn't move it, not even when I put all my strength into it. It was as if he'd glued it to the ground.' She laughed.

It was the first time Simone had heard her laugh.

'I wanted to be strong enough to move it,' Hope said, 'so I could hand it to him when he asked. It was always so heavy. Cold, like taps, except when he'd finished exercising. Then the handle was hot. Slippery.' She bent her head and laid her cheek to the bell's handle.

It was obscene. Simone did not know why, or how. Just that it was. Obscene.

'I slept curled round it. Sometimes,' she laughed, 'I'd slip my fingers inside the handle and hold on, begging him to lift me too, when he was working out.'

Her eyes glittered against the black iron. 'It was like *flying*, all the blood racing to my heels and toes, my head so light. *Empty* . . . I loved it. Sometimes he'd kiss me, before he swung me back down to the ground.'

Then she did something terrible. Worse than the pictures Simone had feared putting in her head, much worse, because it made so little sense.

She lay down on the ground and kissed her lips to the fat black bell.

Because she was holding Simone's hand, Simone had to lie down too. Beside Hope. Curled around the belly of iron, fingers fastened through its handle.

'Nothing else could move me,' Hope whispered. 'Only him. *She* didn't have the strength, even when she wasn't ill.' Disgust in her voice; Simone recognised its bitter flavour. 'Only *he* could lift me up. No one else.'

A sound slipped out of Simone, a sob she couldn't keep inside any longer.

'Hush,' Hope warned. 'Hush.'

She raised her head, her eyes as madly blue as a summer sky. 'I've never told this before,' she said. 'Not to anyone. You're the first.'

# 19

Outside Excalibur House, the moon was shining, fitfully. Marnie looked up at the curtained window of Kenneth Reece's room. 'He has no concept, does he? No concept of the monster he made Hope.'

'She was his alibi.' Ed rested his arms on the open door of the car. Fatigue frayed his voice. 'The person telling him he was a good father, even a good husband.'

'She can't have believed it, can she?'

'Hard to say. She needed to believe *something*, to make sense of what was going on in the house. In effect, he made her complicit, a part of the violence – and the silence. That's a huge burden to put on any child. You were right about her mum's death. It must've been a wake-up call about what he did when she was a kid. What *she* was doing to Leo. That must've been a tipping point.'

Marnie waited a moment longer, to see if the curtains would twitch at Kenneth Reece's window, but Reece's interest was elsewhere. At the bottom of a bottle. She unlocked the car and climbed in, waiting for Ed to join her.

'He's not what I expected,' she admitted. 'Kenneth.'

'Bullies come in all shapes and sizes.' Ed rubbed the heels

of his hands at his eyes. 'Christ, I'm tired. You'll have to excuse the clichés.'

'D'you think she chose Leo because he's physically so unlike her dad? Someone without Kenneth's slyness, his excuses . . .'

'Maybe. From what you've told me, everything's about control with Hope. She saw what happened when her dad lost control, and she never believed her mum had any. The manipulative behaviour's one thing – a trick she learned early on – but control's different. It's needy. Addictive.'

Marnie said nothing straight away. He was right, of course; control could become an addiction. From an early age Hope had witnessed violence – the destruction of her family; it was a natural reaction to want to toughen up, take charge. Vow never to be a victim. That much Marnie could empathise with, but not the rest. 'The abuse isn't all one way,' she reminded Ed. 'Hope likes to be hurt too, which means punishment is in the mix. I really thought he'd react to that. But he doesn't care about any of it.'

'That's his protection. If he starts caring, he'll go to pieces.'

'If he's *capable* of caring. D'you think he is? I don't.'

'It depends when he started drinking,' Ed said, 'and why. That degree of jaundice . . . I'd be surprised if his liver lasts much longer.'

'Is that how he got a place here? I'm assuming they don't make a habit of housing wife-beaters.'

'Without a conviction . . . with no record of what he did to Gayle, and Hope . . .'

'We're screwed.' Marnie joined the queue of traffic back into the centre of town. 'We still don't know where she is, or where she might've gone.' She checked her watch. 'Do you know what they teach us about missing persons? "If in doubt, think murder." I was hoping for something from Kenneth Reece to give me a good reason not to think his

daughter might resort to murdering Simone Bissell. Now?
I don't know.'

Ed was silent, his head propped to the passenger window.
Eventually he said, 'We're assuming Hope ran from the
hospital because she knew Leo was awake, or likely to be
awake, in which case he might've told the truth about her
abuse, and her self-defence alibi would be out the window.
That doesn't explain why she took Simone. Surely she'd be
better off on her own. From what we've heard, she doesn't
need backup, or sympathy. I can understand Simone's value
as a witness, back at the refuge, someone who'd swear blind
that Hope was a victim, but Simone as a travelling companion
doesn't make any sense.'

He was right. This was more complicated than hostage-
taking, or revenge. There was a connection between Hope
and Simone.

'Maybe she wanted a different kind of witness,' Marnie said.
'What d'you mean?'

'I don't know, exactly. I'm still trying to figure it out.'

Traffic lights brought them to a halt again.

A hen party crossed the street, holding one another
upright. Pink bunny ears and tails, a pink veil for the
bride-to-be. Not one of the women was sober.

'She must know now.' Marnie took her hands from the
wheel, flexing her fingers. 'Simone. She must know the truth
about Hope by now. How Hope used her, what she wanted.'

Ed was silent, watching the women staggering up the
street. 'What did Tim Welland have to say? You said you
spoke with him, when I was at the refuge.'

'He lectured me about hostage negotiation,' Marnie said
drily. 'Quoted Aristotle.'

'Ethos, pathos, logos.' Ed made a sound of sympathy. 'Did
he mention Polybius?'

'No, but I might've blanked that bit out. Who was Polybius?'

'Son of a Greek governor, held hostage in Rome for years and years. Went on to kill most of his captors in the sacking of Carthage. I got the same lecture once, from someone who wanted to prove that Stockholm syndrome doesn't affect every hostage.'

'It didn't affect Simone Bissell.'

'Not in the obvious way,' Ed agreed, 'but Paton kept her prisoner for a year. That must have left a mark, emotionally.'

'She's a survivor.' Marnie realised she was repeating the phrase, like a mantra. They both were.

'She might need to be more than that,' Ed said. 'There are a lot of dangerous ways to survive. Look at Hope. She survived her childhood, managed to avoid her mother's fate, if we can believe that. It left more than a mark – twisted her entire personality.'

'All right. So Simone's more than a survivor. She's a fighter.'

The hen party had vanished from sight, but the noise of their heels snagged back, flinting from flagstones.

Marnie drove in the direction of Ed's flat. It took fifteen minutes, bringing them close to midnight by the time Ed was climbing from the car.

'Doesn't Leo have any idea where Hope might've gone?' he asked.

'He says not, but maybe I need to ask better questions. I'd take you along for that, but . . .'

'I don't have anything else to do.' Ed kept his hand on the open door of the car. 'As long as I'm being helpful.'

'You are, but I need to do this bit alone. Leo's not happy around men right now.'

'Makes sense.' He nodded. 'Well, you know where I am if you need me.'

'*When* I need you. Thanks, Ed. Get some sleep, if you can.'

## 20

The moon pitted its hard light on the kitchen floor, where Simone Bissell sat shivering.

In over half an hour, there had been no sound from the bathroom. She didn't dare look in that direction, afraid of drawing Hope's attention. With Lowell, she'd kept her head down and done as he said, the way she did with the Bissells to begin with. Her whole life had been about keeping her head down, except in ballet class, where she had to hold it high, higher, the back of her neck burning with worry that the teacher would single her out for disciplining. It became its own discipline, the fear of failing to do as they said; a voice in her head berating her before anyone else could.

Keep off the grass, stick to the path. Pick up your feet. Don't dawdle. No lights in the house after ten o'clock. Keep yourself to yourself. Quiet. Be quiet. None of your business. Say nothing.

Not now. Keep out. Go away. Your father's sleeping. Mother needs her rest. Stand up straight.

Don't give me that face.

Knock before entering, wait to be asked, this is not your room. Stay away.

*Not now! Get out!*

Don't touch. That is not a toy. Don't give me that face.

Clean up this mess. Those hands are filthy. Look at your clothes! Wash dark colours separately. Use a nailbrush. Leave things the way you found them. Go to your room.

*Good girl.*

Hope called her a good girl.

Simone didn't know what Hope wanted. If she knew, she could do it. But she didn't; she didn't know anything about the other woman.

The silence she'd mistaken for strength between them was only silence. She had dropped a pebble of trust into that well – and she would never, *never* hear it land.

Hope had made her strip. She'd made her show the scars from her mother's knives. Simone had trembled, waiting for her touch, expecting – what?

Benediction – that was the word the women used at the church in Apac. Simone did not think that Hope wanted benediction. Not after she had seen the way Hope held the kettlebell, the way she *kissed* the kettlebell.

Hope wanted her pain. Somehow . . . it fed her.

When they had sat together in the dark, at the refuge, it wasn't Simone's hands that Hope was holding. It was her scars. Her past. All the things that had ever hurt her. All the ways she had ever mended.

Hope had taken it, crept under her skin and stolen it. Now she was strong, and Simone was nothing.

Hope hadn't hurt her, not yet, but she'd hurt *him*; Simone knew that smell. She scratched at her forearms, fretfully.

Kicking, from the bathroom.

He was trying to get out again. Simone froze, holding her breath, keeping still. If she could, she would have stopped her heart beating.

Hope didn't shout, or sigh. She got to her feet and turned

in the direction of the bathroom. The clothes Simone had given her were too big, grey sleeves hiding her hands as she stooped to pick up the kettlebell, and the lump hammer.

That is not a toy. A hammer is not a toy . . .

Hope reached the door to the downstairs bathroom, pausing there to look back across her shoulder at Simone. 'I'll only be a minute,' she smiled. As if she was going to wash her face, or brush her hair.

Simone wanted to pray, but she couldn't think of the words to any prayers except those taught to her by the Bissells, and even those she couldn't remember past the opening lines: *All you big things, bless the Lord. All you little things, bless the Lord.*

But what were the little things? Ants and . . . fleas. What else?

Tadpoles and mosquito larvae. Pollen dust and tsetse flies. Locusts and water drops.

Nasiche. She was Nasiche Auma. *Born in the locust season.*

Hope pushed at the bathroom door with the head of the lump hammer.

Went inside.

The kicking stopped.

Iron ringing. Iron on iron.

Screaming.

Simone put her hands over her ears, rocking back and forth. 'All you little things,' she recited, to drown out the sounds from the bathroom, 'all you little, little things . . .'

# 21

Leo Proctor wasn't sleeping, despite the late hour. 'He's awake,' the on-duty doctor told Marnie. 'Otherwise I'd be sending you away, badge or no badge.'

'I'll leave,' Marnie promised, 'as soon as he's tired.'

Leo looked relieved to see her, once he was sure she was alone.

'I saw Kenneth Reece,' she told him. 'He wasn't very helpful.'

Leo searched her face. 'You still haven't found her.'

'I'm afraid not.' She drew up a chair next to his bed. 'We're worried about Simone. And Hope.'

'Simone is the woman she made friends with, at the refuge?' Leo heaved himself upright, wincing.

'Yes.' She helped him with the blanket. 'Take it easy.'

'I'm okay.'

'Good, but take it easy anyway.' She smiled. 'I don't want to get kicked out of here for harassing the patient.' He returned the smile, then blinked and looked away. It was a long time, she guessed, since he'd used the smile.

'Hope doesn't drive, is that right?'

He nodded.

'How about a mobile phone – does she use one?'

'No. She's never used one.'

'All right . . .' The next question was the tricky one. 'You said she sometimes picked up men, in bars. Is there any chance she might've gone to one of them?'

He recoiled from the question.

'I'm sorry,' Marnie said, 'but we need to rule it out.'

'I don't know any names. I don't think *she* knew their names.' He looked at his hands, turning them over slowly. 'I can't imagine them taking her in. They weren't interested in her *safety*, that's for sure.' He raised his eyes. For the first time, Marnie saw anger – defiance – in his stare. A glimpse of the man he was going to be now this was over. Out in the open. 'Your DS . . . I can't remember his name.'

'DS Noah Jake.'

'You said he saved my life. At the refuge.'

'He did. With the help of one of the women.'

'Was it Simone?' Leo demanded.

'No, another woman.' Marnie paused. 'She's missing from the refuge too.'

Leo's eyes scanned the hospital room, as if he was searching for something to make sense of the mess they were in. 'If Hope wanted me dead and he saved my life . . . *he'd* be the one she'd go for. For getting in her way. She'd hate that.'

A shock of pain gripped Marnie's right side. 'You think she's bearing a grudge against DS Jake?'

'Against anyone who was in her way. She has to have control, because of what she saw happening to her mum, what happened when *she* lost control.'

Leo looked at her. 'You should warn him. Your DS. If he doesn't already know what she's like . . . You should warn him.'

\* \* \*

314

It was chilly outside the hospital, clouds lying like camouflage across the night sky. Marnie called Noah, but the call went straight to voicemail, so she rang the station.

'Abby? Is Noah there?'

'Not yet, boss. I left a message. He'll be on his way.'

'Is DS Carling there?'

'Yes.'

'Put him on, will you?' She waited, aware of the hospital buzzing with light at her back. 'You were with Noah,' she said, when Carling came on the phone. 'This afternoon. That's right, isn't it? Any reason you didn't come back together?'

'I took the tube, boss. He said he'd walk. Is something up?'

'Let's hope not.' She rang off, trying Noah's number again.

'I hope you're home,' she said into his voicemail. 'I'm coming over.'

# 22

It was one o'clock when she reached Westbourne Grove.

'Hello?' Dan Noys answered the buzzer, sounding wide awake.

'It's Marnie Rome. Sorry it's so late. Can I come up?'

She'd counted to three before he buzzed her into the building.

The flat was up a flight of stairs. Dan Noys was waiting at the top, in jeans and a red T-shirt, propping the door open with his bare feet. As soon as she saw his face, Marnie knew Noah wasn't home. Her stomach clenched, coldly.

'What's happened?' Dan's voice was harsh, blank terror in his eyes. 'Is he all right?'

She needed to be honest. 'I can't get hold of him. Can you?'

'No.'

'Can I come in?'

Dan stood back to let her into the flat. Worry had aged him by ten years, robbing his face of its boyishness. He was as good-looking as Noah, in a blond-blue-eyed mould. The sort of looks that let you coast through life, assuming you had charm as an accessory. Marnie hadn't seen much of

Dan's charm, yet. Fear was making black ice of his eyes. She stayed standing, deliberately not looking at the room, keeping her eyes on Dan. 'When was the last time you heard from him?'

'This afternoon.' Dan put his hands into his pockets, bringing up his shoulders. Then he took them out again, moved his fingers to circle his right wrist, holding it in a hard grip.

'What time was this?' she asked.

'Close to five o'clock. He said he'd be working late.'

'Have you tried calling him since then?'

'No.' His voice was chilly. 'I thought he was at work.'

'Did he say what he was working on?'

Dan shook his head. 'Of course not.' He dropped the wrist he'd been holding. There were ugly marks around it, white. 'But you're a murder investigation team. So I'm guessing it's a murder.' His eyes blazed with unshed tears.

She wanted to say something to reassure him. She also wanted to leave, now, so she could get on with the job of finding Noah.

'What do you think's happened to him?' His voice hitched on the last syllable. 'You must have some idea.'

'It's possible . . . he responded to a phone call from a missing person.'

'Without letting you know?'

'Possibly. He was anxious about the person in question. He may have responded without thinking.'

'Without letting *anyone* know,' Dan insisted. He was frantic. Doing his best not to betray it, but frantic.

'I agree it's unlikely. We'll trace his phone . . .' She stopped, spreading her hands in apology. 'I'm sorry. I know you don't want to hear platitudes, but I promise we'll do everything we can to find him.'

His eyes emptied, his face flinching. She'd said the wrong

thing. It wasn't a platitude, but it wasn't much better. It threatened a fruitless search, and the worst possible news at the end of it. A muscle tensed at the side of Dan's mouth.

'Go ahead and say it,' she invited.

'Say what?' he demanded.

She kept her voice light, impersonal. She could give him that much, the chance to let off steam in her direction. 'That you can't believe this has happened. Where was the backup? Don't we have procedures in place to prevent this sort of thing happening? And anything else you want to add.'

'You seem to have it all covered.' His eyes thawed a little.

'I'll keep you informed of anything that happens.'

He looked directly at her. 'Thanks. For keeping the bullshit to a minimum.'

She nodded. After that, it was impossible to end the conversation in any of the traditional ways: a firm handshake, an unqualified promise: *we'll find him*. She didn't offer a promise, or her hand.

Lowell Paton had kept Simone Bissell hidden for a year. Marnie doubted Hope would take that long to exact whatever revenge she deemed appropriate for the man who'd got in the way of her husband's murder.

Ed called as she was heading back into the station.

'I told you to get some sleep,' she said.

'I'm working on it. How'd it go with Leo?'

'He thinks Hope's bearing a grudge against Noah, for saving his life.'

She heard Ed wince. 'You said Ayana helped with that.'

'Yes, but Ayana's gone.'

A fear nipped at her: that it was Hope who'd called Ayana's brothers. She shook the fear away. Hope couldn't have got hold of the phone number. How could she?

Ed said, 'So you think . . . Hope's going after Noah.'

'I don't know. I'd be happier if I knew where he was right now.'

'You don't know where he is?' Ed asked in alarm.

'He's not answering his phone. No one's seen him since five o'clock yesterday afternoon.'

Five o'clock yesterday afternoon, Noah had been with Ron Carling, in West Brompton. That was the last anyone had seen of him.

'Does he know about Hope?' Ed asked.

'No,' she admitted. 'I should've warned him at the Proctors' house, when I was testing my theory about the space under the stairs, but I'd made such a mess of it with Leo the first time round. I wanted to be sure . . .'

'Noah's smart enough to pick up on any vibes you were giving out. In any case, he wouldn't be that reckless, would he? Going off without checking with you first?'

Noah had wanted to be shot of Ron Carling, she was sure of it. God knows what mood he'd been in. 'Not usually, but he's beating himself up over Ayana. If he saw a chance to put part of that right . . .' She should have taken the time to talk to Noah about guilt. She'd seen him struggle with it, but she'd shelved the lecture for a later date. A mistake. She should've talked it through, told him why guilt wasn't a bad thing, wasn't about regret. Guilt kept you focused, alert. Alive. 'I'd better ring off,' she told Ed. 'I'm going into the station. I'll let you know if there's news.'

'Okay. Take care.' Ed ended the call.

London had never felt so large, impenetrable. What was it she'd said to Noah, at the start of all this, in Finchley? *Imagine living without trace. I don't think I could do it. Could you?* and Noah had said, *If I was desperate, maybe. If there was no other choice.*

Her eyes were hot. She blinked, concentrating on the traffic. No hen parties this time. The only people she saw were alone. Solitary shoppers in all-night stores, or bouncers outside clubs.

Two streets on, her phone buzzed again.

'Boss?' It was DS Carling. 'CCTV footage of Proctor and Simone. They didn't get off at Elephant and Castle. It was Kentish Town. Seven stops after they got on.'

Marnie checked the car's mirrors, looking for a place to turn.

*Kentish Town.* Lowell Paton's penthouse was in Kentish Town. Was that Hope's plan? To show Simone how she should've dealt with Paton?

'I need you to do something,' she told Carling. 'Get a trace on Noah's phone.'

A beat passed before Carling asked, 'Why?'

'I can't get hold of him. There's a chance he's at risk.'

'From Hope Proctor?'

'Yes. Speak with Welland, would you? See if he can shake some skirts at Tandem.'

Tandem supplied the Met with its covert surveillance software. Software that hacked off all the civil liberty groups, but sometimes found the Met what they needed, before it was too late for anyone but Forensics. 'I'm on it,' Carling promised.

'Kentish Town. Do we have any carriers in the area?'

'Should be someone patrolling . . . Want me to put in the call?'

Did she? Want a police support unit smashing into Lowell Paton's apartment, on the off-chance Hope and Simone were there? She could see Commander Welland cocking an eyebrow in inquisition. 'Give me a chance to get over there and speak with the concierge. But check who's in the vicinity, in case we need backup.'

'You want me over there?' Carling asked.

'No. I want you looking for Noah. Stay where you are.'

\*　　\*　　\*

She tried Noah's number again, as she cut through traffic between Notting Hill and Kentish Town. His phone was still off. She left another message: 'Where are you?' She didn't bother editing the panic from her voice. 'Call me back as soon as you get this.'

Hope Proctor had taken her dad's kettlebell when she ran. Was it wrong that Marnie was hoping to find Lowell Paton pinned underneath it? Noah, if he was there, attempting to negotiate? He'd switched off his phone in concession to Hope's demands, but otherwise he was okay. Hope was punishing Lowell Paton. There was justice in the world, and peace between nations, and free French toast with every cup of coffee from Marnie's favourite café.

'No one,' she reminded herself, 'loves me that much.'


Pearly light shrouded Paton's apartment block, as if the building was wearing a giant prophylactic. The front desk was fiercely lit, the front door securely locked. Marnie showed her badge to the concierge through the reinforced glass. Not the same man she and Noah had seen yesterday morning. This man was younger, less concerned about the police presence. He buzzed Marnie inside without much more than a glance. 'When did you come on duty?' she asked him.

'Six. I start at six.' He was eastern European.

The foyer smelt of new carpeting, rubber underlay and whatever polish they used to shine the mirrored doors of the lift. The lift was purring, on its way down or up.

'Lowell Paton, on the top floor. Do you know if he's had any visitors?' The man's eyes glazed over. She could tell he was trying to recall the appropriate passage from the manual. 'I'm sure it's not your policy to give out information about residents, but this is a police emergency. Has Mr Paton had any visitors since you came on duty?'

The man shrugged. He smiled. 'Two women.'

'Two women.' She wished she'd brought photos of Hope and Simone. 'Can you describe them?'

'Black. African.' He mimed long hair with his hands. 'One . . . blonde.' He repeated the same mime.

The lift pinged, its doors sighing open to release a weary-looking woman with a vacuum cleaner. 'Did they have anything with them?' Marnie asked.

The concierge shook his head. 'I don't remember.'

'And Mr Paton let them in?'

'Sure.' He smiled again. He'd assumed the women were prostitutes.

Marnie wondered if Lowell made a habit of using call girls. 'Are they still up there?'

'Sure, they stay.'

'No one else. Visitors, I mean. No men.'

He shook his head emphatically. 'No men.'

'Thanks.' Marnie walked a short distance from the desk, calling Carling's number. 'All right, I've got enough to justify the police support unit. Call it in.'

## 23

The PSU pulled up outside Paton's apartment just before 3 a.m.

Marnie was glad to see Rex Carter heading up the unit. Carter was phlegmatic, with a tight rein on his team. No happy-bashing accidents happened on his watch, although she knew better than to be complacent where shields and batons were involved.

'What're we looking at?' Carter had recently swapped Marlboros for nicotine gum, which he snapped between his teeth with the expression of someone short-changed at the corner shop.

'No firearms, as far as I know.' How to sum up what she thought was happening in Lowell Paton's apartment? 'It's a hostage situation, but I doubt it's negotiable. Two, possibly three hostages. Hope Proctor absconded from the North Middlesex, where they were treating her for shock after the attempted murder of her husband.'

'They were treating her for shock? What were they giving him?'

'A couple of pints of blood. She stabbed him.'

Carter snapped gum. His eyes were all over the building. 'Knife?'

'Yes.'

'No firearms. You're sure about that?'

Marnie thought about Lowell Paton's gangster pretensions, his swagger; his father's money. 'I can't be sure,' she admitted.

Through the reinforced glass, they watched the concierge leaning on the polished reception desk, looking at the woman vacuuming the new carpet.

'Why's it non-negotiable?' Carter wanted to know.

'I don't think there's anything she wants.' Other than to punish Lowell Paton, and Noah Jake if he was in there.

'Everyone wants something,' Carter said. 'Right now, I'd kill for a Four Seasons pizza and some seriously high-tar cigarettes.' He showed his teeth, in a humourless smile. 'She knows you? Hope Proctor.'

'She knows me. Not sure she likes me. No way she trusts me.'

'Mad, bad or sad?' Carter asked. The standard question for a hostage situation.

Marnie wished she could answer it to her satisfaction, never mind Carter's. 'A bit of everything,' she hedged. 'But if I had to come down one way or the other? Mad.' She only half believed it, but she needed to give Carter something to work with.

'Mad,' Carter repeated. 'Terrific. My favourite.'

'We could wait for Welland,' Marnie offered.

Carter schooled his face to an expression that said red tape was his very favourite thing. '*Should* wait for Welland.' He hated red tape as much as she did, especially at moments like these.

'Noah Jake might be one of the hostages.' It was the first time she'd said the words aloud. They'd been shouting in her head for the past two hours, since Leo Proctor had warned her of what his wife might do.

Carter gave a nod, empathy in his eyes. 'Your DS, your

call.' He touched a hand to the police baton at his side. 'I'm not an SFO yet. No need to wake anyone in Marsham Street. Not that I'm suggesting the Home Office ever sleeps.' They stood side by side on the pavement, eyeing the apartment block.

'How's the firearms training working out for you?' Marnie asked. 'Abseiled down any tall buildings recently?'

Carter looked at the pearly light sheathing the block. 'This one looks like it's ribbed and lubed . . .'

'They're on the top floor, penthouse.'

'High-rise window-licker . . .' Carter turned to brief his team. 'And they wonder why I want a gun.'

They took the lift to the floor below Paton's, and then the stairs. Lozenge-shaped windows showed the moon and stars above London's skyline. Music pounded from behind Paton's door: the mindless beat of electronic pop. In the breaks between the beats, a different percussion, unmistakably that of fists on flesh. Pain. Sobbing. Electro-pop. A rhythm to the different sounds, as if the damage was synchronised to the music in an attempt to drown it out, or possibly because whoever had started couldn't stop.

Rex Carter moved the gum to his cheek. 'You want to try knocking?'

Marnie pointed at the battering ram. 'With that, maybe.'

Adrenalin was making her fingers dance. Her mouth was dry. Carter had insisted she put on a stab vest, or stay in the carrier. She'd opted for the vest. It was heavy, dragging at her chest. The carpet throbbed underfoot with the volume of the music in Paton's flat. The neighbours downstairs must've been used to his sound system; no one had reported a noise nuisance. The music was camouflage for whatever was going on inside the flat.

Rex Carter nodded at the officers with the battering ram.

To Marnie he repeated what he'd said in the carrier, 'Stay wide until I give the all-clear.'

His team swung the steel nose of the ram at the door.

It splintered cleanly at the point of impact, delivering the PSU officers into the apartment to loud warnings rapped by Carter.

When Marnie heard Rex curse in surprise, she stepped over the fractured wood of the door, into the open-plan apartment.

One of the red leather sofas was messy with flesh.

Three bodies. Two women. One man. All naked.

Lowell Paton was wearing his gangster chains, and nothing else. He'd wrapped one chain around his right fist and was using it to hit the two girls on the sofas. Marnie could see the indented pattern of the gold links on the girls' thighs and breasts.

Not Simone Bissell or Hope Proctor. Marnie had never seen these girls before. Both were dark-skinned, with dreadlocks. One girl had bleached her dreads blonde. Daggered heels and fake-fur jackets lay on the spare sofa. A large weekend bag in cracked black plastic pretending to be patent leather was open on the floor. Filled with cheap S&M novelties, including a whip and handcuffs. Lowell had opted for the gold chain instead.

Rex Carter stooped and picked up a remote control, using it to switch off the music.

In the silence that followed, the girls' sobbing was a lament, rising to a wail when they saw their audience.

Carter and his team checked the flat routinely, but there was no one else here. Certainly not Noah Jake.

Marnie took out her badge. 'Lowell Paton? You're under arrest for two counts of wounding with intent.'

'No fucking way!' Lowell balled his fists at his crotch, glaring at Carter, at the other officers, at Marnie. 'This junge and she? They beg me to bang them!'

The two girls had curled up on the sofa, wiping blood and mucus from their faces. They weren't much older than the girls at Sommerville who'd attacked Stephen Keele.

'Wounding with intent,' Marnie repeated to Paton. 'That's a possible life sentence. I hope your dad's feeling rich, because you're going to need an expensive lawyer.'

# 24

Eyes in the white tiles next to his head. Eyes and a mouth, unsmiling, chipped at the edges. Noah Jake lay and looked at the chips, the way they formed a face. It helped with the pain. Of breathing. Being alive. Not that he expected to be that for much longer. His left leg spasmed involuntarily. He prayed for it to stop. If she thought he was kicking again . . .

*Focus.*

On the face at floor level next to his head. A friendly face. Not smiling, but not shouting either, not whispering threats and promises. Just a face. Made up of a short crack and twin chips: a mouth and two eyes.

This was the way sight worked. How seeing happened. The eyes supplied an image and the brain found the nearest fit. It wasn't perfect, or trustworthy, but it was close enough most of the time. We're wired to recognise foe or friend. The brain sees faces in brick walls and clouds, ink spots and plug sockets, chipped tiles.

Psychology 101. The women in the refuge all saw a violent husband, an abused wife. Noah had seen the same thing. He knew Marnie had.

*God, it hurts . . .*

Breathe. Focus. Ignore the crushing agony in your lungs and the fear that the broken rib will cause an internal bleed or, worse, a puncture . . .

Slow death by suffocation.

Leo Proctor had kept quiet. He'd been through what Noah was going through, and worse, but he'd kept quiet. He'd let Marnie accuse him of rape and torture, when he was the one who'd suffered, not Hope. At the hands of Hope.

Noah understood the weight of machismo. He understood how Leo Proctor had struggled to keep his abuse secret, for the sake of friendships, work relationships. Pride.

Still, there came a point, didn't there, when the secrets had to stop.

His chest heaved, panicked by the lack of air getting into his lungs. He sobbed, pleading with his body to stay calm. Panic only made it worse.

Each time he'd twisted free of the kettlebell, she'd replaced it. Each time, she'd hit the bell with the hammer until he thought his chest would explode.

Crash course in conditioning.

She'd taken the kettlebell away, for twenty minutes, maybe more. While she was eating her supper. By the time Noah was ready to trust the relief, she was back – and so was the kettlebell. The hammer.

He'd learned to lie still. To put up with the crushing weight of the bell on his chest. It was the hardest thing he'd ever done in his life. He didn't know how much longer he could keep doing it.

He could tip the bell off him. He just about had the strength left to do that. But it would make a noise, falling. Hope would hear and come back, with the hammer. He couldn't face the hammer again. Better to lie still and let the kettlebell crush his chest than to move and have her do it, harder.

He blinked up at the ceiling. Faces there too, unfriendly.

A ghoul in a patch of damp above the bath. Tears crept from his eyes, into his ears. He couldn't feel his hands any longer, tied over his head to the pipework that ran under the sink. He couldn't feel his hands, or his fingers.

*Focus.*

What'd they taught him, on that trauma course, or at college? Coping mechanisms. He stifled a laugh in his throat, afraid to let it out. He'd like to see one of his college lecturers lying here next to him on the bathroom floor, with a kettlebell on his chest. Asking questions about his childhood, seeing what good it did either one of them, since Noah was about to be dead.

*Dan*, he thought. *Shit, Dan, I'm sorry.*

No good thinking like that. Only made it all worse, like the hammer. He apportioned a smile instead, to keep those muscles working. He needed the smile, for work. For when he was out of here and reliving it, with jokes, for the boys back at the station, Ron Carling and the rest: 'Weights, on my ribs. Didn't even have to pay a gym membership . . .'

The bones at the back of his head found out the hard places on the floor. A pulse of warmth suggested under-floor heating. Someone should tell his spine that the floor was heated. According to his spine, he was lying on a block of ice.

He should've fought when he had the chance, when she'd dragged him from the kitchen, but she'd made Simone stand over him with the hammer. Simone would have used it, too. The hammer. One look at her face was enough to tell him that. God knows what Hope had threatened to make her look like that.

*Simone*, he thought, *I'm sorry.*

He was in a stranger's house, at the mercy of a madwoman who thought all men were apes and who'd tried to kill one, if only he'd paid attention, to give him the measure of her madness.

*Dan. Dan, I love you.*
*God, it hurts.*

Marnie Rome would work out where he was. She'd suspected Hope, that was why she'd asked him to crawl under the stairs at the Proctors' house. She'd needed to know if a man could fit under there. They'd been so close, Noah and Marnie. So close to solving it. If it hadn't been for Felix Gill's phone call stopping them heading to the Bissells . . .

Marnie would work it out, even so. She was good, all smooth, cool surface, like a sheet. But underneath, she was red hot. If you listened hard, you could hear her ticking.

Marnie Rome would get an ARV – shields, firearms – and ride to his rescue. She had to. To believe in any other outcome was to give up all hope.

## 25

'What do we know about this woman, Hope Proctor?'

Toby Graves had an unfortunate name for a hostage nego-tiator, but Marnie liked his manner: quiet, attentive to the detail of what she and Ed Belloc had to say. She'd called Ed into the station when she got back from taking Lowell Paton to a cell. There hadn't been time, yet, to tell Ed the news of Paton's arrest. Graves was the on-call hostage negotiator, here at Tim Welland's request as a matter of urgency.

It was the early hours of the morning, but no one was going to sleep. Not until they'd found Noah Jake.

The station was on red alert, Ron Carling and Abby Pike on standby for news of the GPS trace on Noah's phone. Toby Graves, in a dark jumper and jeans, was drinking coffee with Marnie and Ed.

'Hope stabbed her husband in front of a hand-picked audience of abused women, knowing they'd say it was self-defence.' Marnie put the medical report on the table, along with Leo's statement. 'This is what she did to him prior to the stabbing, and what she persuaded him to do to her.'

Toby Graves read the pages in silence. 'She's not been seen

since she came out of Kentish Town tube station yesterday afternoon,' he said. 'Is that correct?'

'Yes. We thought she might've taken a cab, but so far no reports of sightings.'

'Why Kentish Town?'

'We thought she might be thinking of putting on a show for Simone, a demonstration of her control.'

Graves put his thumb on the printout of Hope and Simone in Kentish Town. 'Maybe *this* is the show. Maybe the show's for you, not Simone.'

Marnie studied the image of the two women, wishing her brain would move faster. She was missing something, she knew it, just couldn't figure out what. 'You think she wanted us to believe she was headed to Lowell's place?'

'Maybe.' Graves turned to Ed. 'You know more about this than me, but these women know how to stay off-radar, yes? I'm talking about women like Simone Bissell.'

Ed nodded. 'Not just Simone. Hope, too.'

'You'd put her in the same category?'

'For the purposes of the question you asked, yes, I would. I don't think any of us would argue that she wasn't the victim of abuse, growing up.'

Graves took this on board, nodding. 'Tell me about the suitcase.'

'According to Leo, it's where she kept her dad's kettlebell, and a hammer. Her "kit", Leo called it.' The thought of it made Marnie sick with worry for Noah.

'So she's armed. The kettlebell's her weapon of choice . . .' Graves touched his thumb to the photo again. 'She's running. Why slow herself down with luggage, with Simone?'

Ed said, 'She wants a witness.'

'That's what the refuge was about,' Marnie agreed. 'An audience. Witnesses. People to approve of what she's doing. To vindicate her.'

'Okay.' Graves nodded. 'I can see why you think she might've gone after Lowell Paton. To show Simone how it's done, how you deal with abusive men. Let's assume she went to Kentish Town because she knew the police were looking for her. She lets the CCTV catch her a couple of times, looking like she's Simone's hostage rather than the other way around. Then what? She vanishes. With Simone.' He took a moment, in respect for the situation. Then he asked, 'Where does Noah Jake fit in?'

'He saved Leo's life, at the refuge. Leo thinks she wants revenge for that.'

'Leo also thinks,' Graves referred to the statement, 'that Hope loves him. Even when she's smashing his ribs with house bricks.'

'Noah's missing. I don't see where else he could be right now, unless he went to help, thinking Hope was the one in danger, from Simone.'

'How'd he know where to go?'

'Hope must've called him. Maybe she tried the station first.'

'Must've, maybe . . .' Graves didn't like it. 'What do we know? Her dad lives in sheltered housing. She didn't go there. Who else does she have, who might help her hide out?'

'No one. We don't know of anyone.'

Hope had no other family or friends. Perhaps Marnie should pity her for that. She didn't. She pitied Simone Bissell, and Noah Jake. Noah had plenty of people, loved ones who'd suffer – grieve – if Marnie couldn't find him in time. His parents. A kid brother. Daniel Noys.

Graves heard the frustration – and the fatigue – in her voice. He looked from Marnie to Ed. 'If she isn't after her dad, is it all about revenge on Noah? For saving Leo's life?'

'It can't be,' Ed said. 'She took Simone. Simone was her friend, at the refuge. She'd have done anything for Hope,

334

from what the others say. Hope took her, when she left the hospital. That has to mean something.'

'Maybe Simone took charge, for a while anyway.' Graves folded his arms, frowning as he thought it through. 'Hope let her do that, keeping up the pretence that she was the weak one, letting Simone take the risks. Making it look like Simone was the one who suggested they run. That's an alibi, if Hope needs one. She'd have to be very sure she could handle Simone if things got nasty. Say when the police started putting out statements about Hope, who she is, what she's done.'

'She convinced Leo that she was a victim,' Ed said, 'even with everything she was putting him through. Classic abuser's technique, sharing the blame about, to secure silence. Making the other party complicit. It's what Hope's father did with her.'

'This is about families,' Marnie was thinking out loud, 'the shapes they make . . . Triangles . . . Hope's family and Simone's.'

*My family*, she thought.

She knew what it was like to grow up an only child. Three in a family was a triangle, all angles and pointy corners. She'd sometimes wished for siblings, to soften the shape to a circle. When she left, her parents fostered Stephen Keele to restore that spiky, familiar shape.

'Hope was Kenneth Reece's alibi.' She repeated Ed's words from earlier. 'She told him he was a good father, which meant he could lie to himself about the sort of man he was. She was the only witness to their marriage. Her dad's violence, her mum's suffering. The war that went on behind closed doors . . .' Marnie hadn't been aware of any unhappiness at home, between her parents, but she'd understood from an early age that she was the shock-absorber. They'd had to replace her when she went.

Hope was an only child.

Nasiche Auma had brothers and sisters, but Simone Bissell was an only child, the prize Charles and Pauline brought home from Uganda, the ultimate tourist souvenir. Dressing her in pink, pretending her past never happened.

'This is about families,' Graves repeated, prompting her with a look.

'We were going to the Bissells,' Marnie said. 'Before we got the phone message from Felix Gill. That's where Noah will have gone, to pick up where we left off.'

She was on her feet. She couldn't believe it'd taken her so long to get here. If she wasn't so intent on keeping her mind away from her past, her family . . .

'Noah's gone to the Bissells, to ask them about Simone. It was his run route, that's what he said. And it's where we'd have gone if Gill hadn't sidetracked us. I bet it's where Hope's taken Simone. To show her how it's done, how you manage a family that's trying to destroy you.'

'These are Simone's parents?' Graves asked.

'Her foster-parents,' Ed said. 'Charles and Pauline Bissell.'

A noise at the door made them all turn their heads.

'Boss?' It was Ron Carling, bright-eyed with news. 'GPS came through.'

'You've got a fix on Noah's phone.' Marnie looked at Ed. 'Can you remember the Bissells' address?'

'Putney Hill?' Ed hazarded. 'SW15, I think.'

'Is that what you've got?' Marnie asked Carling.

'No. I mean, yes, that's the location. But it's better than that.' Carling held up a handset. 'He sent us a text. Noah. There's a text.'

'He texted the station's mobile?' Marnie demanded. Why hadn't he texted her? She took the phone, holding it where Graves and Ed could see the text message.

Noah – or someone – had typed *Nasicheauma*.

Graves frowned, peering at the screen. 'Nonsense, isn't it?'

'It's Simone's real name.' Ed's eyes met Marnie's. 'Nasiche Auma.'

## 26

It was pitch dark in the bathroom. Hope had switched off the lights. At first, Noah was grateful; the dark swallowed some of the pain, made it easier to think. He listened for noises in the house, some clue to what Hope was doing, but could only hear the echo of his own pulse throbbing back at him from the blackness.

Where was she? Where was Simone?

He knew Simone was scared. He'd seen it in her face, when she swung at him with the hammer. She was back in that place where Paton had put her, trying to survive. Noah didn't blame her for the hammer, or anything else.

Perhaps he shouldn't blame Hope, either. Chances were there'd been a Lowell Paton in Hope's life. Someone who'd made her afraid to live any way but this. Hurting those around her, enforcing her will . . .

Marnie Rome had told him about Hope's medical exam, the evidence of abuse. Hope was a victim, damaged. Noah should hold on to that. It might make a difference.

The bathroom door crept open.

He held his breath, blinking his eyes wide open in the dark. No light spilled from the other side of the door. The house was in darkness, and dead quiet. A breath of air skimmed his feet, moving up his body to his face. He set his teeth as a precaution against begging. He couldn't be sure that begging hadn't made it worse, last time.

Ticking, like a clock, but at head height.

Beads, tapping together?

'Simone?' He whispered the name. His voice was in bits at the back of his throat, crushed by the weight on his ribs.

The door eased shut. Silence. She was in here with him; he could feel the shape she made in the darkness.

'Simone . . .' Words hurt, but he might not get another chance to talk with her. 'Are you okay?'

For a long moment, she didn't move. He was beginning to think he was hallucinating, *wanting* her to be here when she wasn't.

The air stirred above him. Beads ticking, her braids swaying. He searched the dark for her face, the whites of her eyes.

'Simone?'

She knelt at his side. The smell of fried fish was in her clothes, and the damp scent of fear. He could see her now. Not with his eyes. With his nerve endings, the way wounded soldiers learnt to see again.

She reached out and touched the handle of the kettlebell. The tremor in her hand passed like a shock of electricity through the cast iron, into his chest. His teeth tore the air left in his lungs.

Where was Hope? Had she sent Simone in here, to hurt him? No, Hope would want the lights on for that. She'd want to watch.

'Simone . . .'

She leaned forward. He felt the tap of her braids against his cheek and he flinched because, God help him, he no longer believed in a rescue.

Both of Simone's hands were on the weight. The shock

338

turned to a dull ringing, like the tongue of a bell rolling inside his ribcage. She straightened, her skirt brushing his side, the air lifting back into his lungs as she stood, gripping the kettlebell, taking it away from his chest, away from the broken rib that stabbed at his heart, away from the hot spread of bruises that hurt more than he'd have believed possible.

He sobbed; a hard, fractured sound.

Simone knelt and put the damp palm of her hand on his cheek. He realised she could see perfectly in the darkness. He felt exposed, but it no longer mattered because the weight – the *fucking* weight – was gone. He didn't care about anything else. Not the rope tying him to the pipework. Not the cold fact of Hope, somewhere in the house, with a hammer, knives . . .

'Thank you . . . *God* . . . Thank you.'

'She wants me to cut her.'

Too many endorphins dancing in his head. Dancing and doing tequila shots . . . What did she say?

'She wants . . . what?'

Simone lay down next to him on the floor. Reached over his head to his bound hands. Found his fingers and brushed their ends across her skin. The bump of a bone in her wrist. Her pulse, jumping. Above it, her forearm. The glassy feel of scar tissue in spots and swirls, like Braille.

Noah couldn't read Braille. He didn't need to. Her story was there, in the deep damage she'd done to her skin.

'She wants me to cut her,' Simone breathed. 'Like this. And – and worse.'

'Where . . . where is she?'

'Sleeping.' Simone's whisper was bewildered. 'On the floor. She sleeps on the floor.'

Noah got a flash of the show house, the Proctors' bed with its pillows starched and its mattress stiff, not slept on. 'Simone. You need . . . to untie me.' He had to pause between words, to gather his breath. 'We need . . . to help her. Hope. She needs . . . help.'

'I'm scared.'

'Me too.' He gripped her hand. 'Me too.' He waited for the shaking in his chest to subside. 'Where're your mum and dad?'

'Nowhere.'

'I don't understand.'

'Away, they went away.'

He could sense her attention slipping, stress and exhaustion taking its toll. 'Who else is in the house?'

'No one. Only her.' She sighed against his cheek, her breath sour.

'Get a knife from the kitchen and cut me free.'

She didn't respond.

'Simone? Get a knife. Quickly. Before she wakes up.'

Nothing.

He had to try something else. 'Nasiche.'

Her whole body stiffened, reflexively.

'Nasiche. Get a knife. Now.'

# 27

Daniel Noys was waiting at the front desk when Marnie left the station with Toby Graves and Ed Belloc.

'I got a text from Noah.' Stress bleached the skin under his eyes. 'What's going on?'

'What did the text say?' Marnie pulled on her jacket, nodding at Ed and Graves to go ahead, to the car park where a police carrier was waiting.

'Nothing.' Dan held up a phone. 'This.'

A smiley face. No greeting, no signature.

She winced when she saw it. 'What time was it sent?'

'Forty minutes ago. I tried to call him, but there was no answer. I tried to call you, but they wouldn't put me through, so I came down here.' Dan clenched the phone so hard she heard his knuckles crack. 'I need . . . to know what's going on.'

She nodded. 'I know you do, but right now, I have to go. We know where he is.'

His eyes jumped to her face. 'Did you speak with him?'

'Not yet.'

They'd been trying Noah's phone since the text came through, but without luck. Graves had hoped to negotiate that way, but unless someone answered the phone, it wasn't going to happen.

'Stay by a phone,' she told Dan. 'I have your numbers. I'll call you as soon as there's news.'

Dan dropped his head, looking at the phone in his hand. 'He didn't send this.' He looked back up at her, a blaze of tears in his eyes. 'Did he?'

Toby Graves was waiting in the Mercedes Sprinter, with Ed and a team of four PSU officers. Marnie nodded a greeting as she got in next to Ed, buckling up. 'Someone alerted the ambulance service, yes?'

Graves nodded. 'It's taken care of.'

'Good.' She was juggling two phones, one of which she was keeping clear in case of more texts from Noah, or whoever had his phone. Dan Noys was almost certainly right. Noah didn't send the smiley face.

'Nasiche Auma' read like a warning.

The smiley face was cruel, personal. Marnie suspected Hope of sending it, but why would Hope warn them about Simone? Unless she was setting her up . . .

Her other phone buzzed, the one she wasn't keeping clear for texts. She answered it as the Sprinter cut through traffic, headed for Putney Hill.

'Ms Rome? It's Paul Bruton, at Sommerville.'

Her mouth, already parched, dried up completely. It was the middle of the night. Why was Bruton calling so late?

'Is it an emergency?' She didn't want to hear what he had to say. There wasn't room in her head – or her chest – for any more anxiety. 'I'm dealing with an emergency here.'

A tiny pause, then Bruton said, 'In that case, of course it can wait.'

'Is he all right?'

'Yes.' It sounded like the truth.

'Good. I'll call you when I can.' She ended the call, rubbing her thumb at her fingerprints on the phone's display.

Ed touched a hand to her elbow. 'Okay?'

She nodded. 'Stephen, but from the sound of it he's fine. Maybe it was an update on their investigation into the assault.' She wanted to close her eyes. Hide for a second from the crowd of faces in the Sprinter. She was glad of Ed's nearness, his unspoken support. He was here at the behest of Toby Graves, because of his connection to Simone, but Marnie was glad of his nearness for her own sake. She wasn't sure she could do this – face whatever was waiting for them in SW15 – without Ed.

*One day*, she thought – *and soon – I'll give something back.*

Graves had been speaking into his phone. He ended the call, nodding at Marnie. 'That was Welland. The Home Office has cleared an ARV, if we need it.'

'I'd rather wait and see what we find when we get there.' She didn't want guns in the mix, if they could avoid it.

The roads were nearly empty, but they still weren't moving as fast as she'd have liked. Every second counted, she knew that. They could be late by as little as a second, and it would mean life or death for Noah Jake.

Ron Carling was the next caller, with news of the Bissells. 'They're in Marrakesh. They flew out a week ago, not due back until next Tuesday.'

'So the house is empty.'

'No reports from the neighbours. It's alarmed, according to police records, but there's been nothing to suggest a break-in.'

Marnie turned to Ed. 'Simone wouldn't still have a key, would she?'

'I doubt it.'

'But she knows the house . . .' Marnie spoke into the phone. 'Are we going to have to clear lots of bodies?'

Carling knew she meant the neighbours. 'Shouldn't think so,' he said. 'The house is detached. I'm sending street views, so you can see the set-up.'

SARAH HILARY

'Thanks.' She ended the call, telling Ed, 'The Bissells are in Marrakesh. I'm guessing they gave up aid working.'

'They gave it up after they adopted Simone.' Ed watched the street lights through the Sprinter's window. 'They never thought she'd go back home to them. Now she's there, but they're not.' He met her eyes, smiling slightly, an attempt at optimism.

Neither one of them asked the question of what they were about to find at the house in Putney in the Bissells' absence.

## 28

The bathroom floor was no longer warm. Noah was beginning to think it never had been warm, that he'd imagined the pulse of heat under him. If the Bissells had gone away, they wouldn't have left the heating on. It made him wonder what else he was imagining.

Where was Simone? Nasiche. He hadn't seen her since he'd sent her to the kitchen for a knife. How long ago was that? Seconds, surely. A minute at most. In the dark, it was easy to forget what this room looked like, to imagine he was in another bathroom, not tied to anything except by his curiosity and fear.

Rosa, his mum, is cleaning. He's hiding in the airing cupboard, watching through a crack in the door. Her elbow swings in circles as she scrubs and wipes. Dirt is everywhere. Germs. She'd clean all day, if she could. The airing cupboard smells of fresh laundry, towels and bedding. The hot-water tank mutters when she runs the taps to rinse the sink, and the bath. He's afraid to come out, in case she starts on him. Scrubbing and wiping. He's six years old. An only child. Sol won't be born for another year. Noah knows he should help his mum. Not just with the cleaning; with whatever drives her to do it, the way she sees danger everywhere and how her eyes fix on him, fearfully. Later, she'll take him to the hospital, tell them about night terrors or bedwetting, or a strange rash on his skin that's not there now but it was, it was. He's seen police at the hospital bringing in partygoers, drunks. He should ask for help; maybe someone can find out what's scaring her so badly. He doesn't ask. He doesn't help. He hides like a coward in the clean towels, until she's finished.

Screaming from the Bissells' sitting room snapped him back to the present.

'Simone!' He hauled at the rope tying his hands. Pain tore at his chest. 'Simone!'

It wasn't Simone, or not just Simone.

Hope was screaming too. Both women, shrieking in terror, and rage.

The house shook with the sound, the air warping as if it was on fire.

Screaming. Raging.

He couldn't get to them, couldn't see what was making the house shake.

The sound rose, no longer human, like foxes fighting or mating, out in a night he didn't know had fallen.

## 29

The house was thirties, detached. Reached by a private driveway. A security light lit the last six feet of the drive. Roses, again. Ranks of thorned bushes, black. Marnie registered the rose bushes dimly, her eyes on the windows. A storm porch at the front, two doors instead of the usual one. No lights at any of the windows.

'Method of entry's going to be easier at the back,' Graves said. 'How many rooms downstairs, d'you reckon?'

'Four,' Marnie said. She knew this type of house. 'Big kitchen, at the back. Sitting room and reception, and a bathroom.'

'Bathroom on the ground floor?'

'Yes.' She pointed out the way the drainpipes ran down the side of the house, and the wire cage covering a ventilation outlet on the ground floor. It was the same as her parents' house. Four up, four down.

Memories jostled for her attention – rusty handprints on the kitchen wall, something thick sticking her shoes to the floor – but she pushed it all aside.

She needed to focus. Here. Now.

The PSU officers went in for a closer look, staying below

window level. Graves wanted to go in through the back door. Dawn sat on their shoulders, lifting yellow light from black flak jackets. Marnie looked at the satellite views supplied by Ron Carling.

'Conservatory at the back,' one of the officers reported. 'Kitchen's clear. Curtains drawn in the other two rooms, but someone's in there. We heard movement.'

'What do you think?' Graves wanted to know. 'Do we wait for the SFOs?'

'There's no reason to think firearms are involved.' The PSU team looked to Marnie to confirm this. She nodded. They shrugged at Graves. 'It's your call.'

'We could try talking to Hope,' Grave said, 'on Noah's phone.'

'We've been trying that for the past half-hour. She's not picking up.' Marnie crossed her arms across the stab vest, the second time she'd worn one today.

Ed Belloc had kitted up too, even though Graves wanted him to stay in the Sprinter. To be on hand if they needed him, for Simone's sake, but otherwise to stay wide of whatever was happening in the house.

Marnie didn't want to talk to Hope Proctor. She wanted to get inside the house, to Simone and Noah. 'Let's go,' she said to Graves. 'It's been too long already.'

# 30

She knew this house. The shape of the windows, where the rooms fell. Only the extension at the back was different. The Bissells had filled the conservatory with travel books and photographs, souvenirs. An Aztec rug, hand-thrown pots, what looked like a baby's cradle woven from reeds. Marnie was hyper-alert, noticing every detail shown up by the team's torchlight. The burnt ends of the reeds, grains of sand and soil on the stone floor, creases in the spines of the books. The peppered patch below Toby Graves' left ear, where he hadn't shaved high enough.

The PSU team picked their way through the clutter in the conservatory, to the kitchen. The ghost of the other house was all around her. The house Stephen Keele had destroyed, as surely as if he'd set a fire, or planted a bomb.

In the big kitchen at the back of the Bissells' house, the light from recessed bulbs in the ceiling was a hard constellation of white. Police torches snagged at the bulbs, showing each in turn. The dimensions were familiar, despite the extravagance of a central island and a showy hang of utensils, spice racks climbing two walls. The kitchen stank of breadcrumbed fish. The torches swept the space for signs of life.

Marnie stayed behind the PSU officers, behind Toby Graves. Blanking her eyes at the familiar space around her, putting her stare on the door to the sitting room. Afraid of ghosts, the retinal shadows of her parents. Defence wounds in her mother's palms. Her father's blood pooled on the blond-wood floor. She couldn't keep the memories at bay, so instead she marshalled them: the blunt feel of brightness in her eyes on the night of the funeral, waiting for the last of the mourners to depart. The next morning, she's the first at work, still drunk, wired, wanting Welland to throw her back in the deep end, because it's preferable to grieving and it keeps her moving; no chance to stop and think about the hole ripped in her life by their deaths.

A knife was missing from the Bissells' kitchen block. Another missing knife. The stab vest was heavy on her shoulders, as if a child was clinging to her front. It wasn't like last time, in Kentish Town. There was no battering ram or warnings yelled over loud music. In this house, silence was stiff as two fingers.

*You're too late.*

The thought was too swift and sly for her to stop it.

Too late. Again.

The hairs on the back of her neck lifted. She drove her memory hard after something to see her through the next few minutes. Found her mother with her arms out, folding sheets in proficient semaphore. Marnie could sneak under the sweet-smelling cotton and steal a hug from her mum's arms. She doesn't, but she could.

The whole time, she's praying.

Agnostic's prayer, for Noah Jake.

For this familiar house to have a different ending.

Ahead of her, lights went on, sending shadows running for the walls.

They'd found the women. Toby Graves was talking in the sitting room. A low, professional patois. Appeasing.

Marnie moved to the doorway, looking into the room.

Hope Proctor and Simone Bissell were huddled together on the floor, so close it was hard to tell where one woman ended and the other began. There was blood, but not as much as Marnie had feared. She stayed long enough to be sure both of them were alive, then followed the PSU team to the front of the house.

'Simone . . .' The echo of a shout, ragged, from the ground-floor bathroom.

Marnie beat the PSU to it, punching her fist at the light switch outside the door, tripping over the suitcase by the bath, ending on her knees at Noah's side.

'Noah . . .' She didn't know what to do with her hands.

His hands were over his head, tied to the steel underside of the sink with blue rope. He'd flayed the skin at his wrists, trying to get free. More rope tied his ankles. His feet were bare. Sweat glazed his face, and his breathing was tortured. She turned her head and shouted into the hall: 'I need help in here!'

Noah shuddered, blinking wet from his eyes, trying to get a fix on her face. She was near enough to feel the wave of relief that went through him.

'Where're you hurt, and how badly?'

'Simone . . .' He spoke in gasps. 'Where's . . . Simone?'

'She's safe.' His pulse was thready, fretful under her fingers. His skin was clammy, cold. 'Tell me how bad it is.'

'Ribs . . . broken.'

She glanced down his front, her eye catching the dull gleam of a kettlebell placed two feet from him on the tiled floor. She stripped off her jacket and laid it over his chest, grabbing a handful of towels from a rail and covering him before curling a careful hand to the side of his face.

351

'Okay, it's going to be okay. Ambulance's here. You're okay now.'

'Hope . . .'

She waited to see what he'd say, but the words died in his throat. 'Noah, I need you to stay awake. *Noah.*'

'Yes . . .' He unstuck his eyes obediently. Blinked at the ceiling.

A fuss of noise in the hall. Marnie moved aside for a female paramedic. 'Broken ribs and he's dehydrated.'

The woman nodded at her, crouching by Noah's side, checking his vital signs.

Marnie sat on the edge of the bath, feeling like a fifth wheel. What was happening in the next room, with Hope and Simone? She didn't move from the bath; she wanted to be able to tell Dan Noys that she'd stayed with Noah, the whole time.

'How were these ribs broken?' the paramedic asked.

'Kettlebell—' Noah jumped under her touch, the word bitten short.

'Sorry.' The medic moved her hands more cautiously over his chest.

He gave a vague nod, his eyes stuttering shut until he remembered to open them again, moving his gaze feverishly across the ceiling.

A second paramedic was in the doorway. There wasn't enough room for three bodies in the bathroom. Marnie stood up, light-headed for a second. She moved aside to make way for the people who could help Noah.

Standing in the doorway, keeping watch, she heard voices again, from the sitting room. Toby Graves, asking questions.

Paramedics had separated Simone and Hope; she could hear the overlap of the medics' voices as they treated the damage she'd yet to see. Even at this distance, Ed's silence was a comfort. Marnie leaned into it instinctively, wondering which – if either – of the women in the other room was doing the same.

Outside, on the gravelled drive of the house, she called the number in Westbourne Grove. 'It's Marnie Rome. He's here. We think he's going to be okay. We're taking him to St George's Hospital, in Tooting.'

'I'll be there.' The relief in Dan Noys' voice was sharp, staggering. 'Thanks.'

An ambulance took Noah Jake to St George's. Paramedics would follow with Hope and Simone in separate cars. Ed had elected to go with Simone. Marnie and Toby Graves intended to go with Hope.

A paramedic held Hope's left arm elevated, for a defensive stab wound. There was a matching wound on her right arm, not as deep but still serious. She would need stitches, and possibly a blood transfusion.

The Bissells would need a new sitting room carpet.

The paramedics were still washing the blood from Simone, but so far they'd found no cuts on her. One of the PSU team had bagged a kitchen knife at the scene. After taking it from Simone's hand.

Hope kept saying, 'It wasn't her fault. It wasn't her fault.' She was crying as she said it.

Simone wasn't saying anything, dry-eyed, her gaze going beyond Hope. Beyond everyone. Whatever she'd witnessed, whatever happened here, she wasn't capable of telling.

*Too late*, Marnie thought again.

In front of Graves and the others, Marnie spoke the words she should've spoken days ago, at the women's refuge in Finchley: 'Hope Proctor, I'm arresting you for the assault and attempted murder of Leo Proctor.' She paused, looking

353

straight into the woman's wet blue eyes. 'And for causing grievous bodily harm with intent to Noah Jake.'

Hope wept until her shoulders shook. To Simone, Marnie said gently, 'I have to caution you, until we know what happened.'

The PSU officers were watching her. She could hear Welland's voice in her ear, speaking of past mistakes. 'Do you understand?' she asked Simone.

Simone looked straight through her, to the wall behind.

Marnie recited the caution, then turned to Ed. 'Stay with her, will you?'

He nodded. 'Yes.'

DC Abby Pike joined them at St George's. Marnie briefed her on the charges against Hope. 'Make sure you stay with her. And handcuff her, as soon as the doctors say it's acceptable to do so.'

Abby nodded. 'How's Noah?'

'They took him into surgery. Unless they find internal bleeding, his chances are good. Great, even.'

Marnie left Abby with Hope, going through the hospital's reception to the main entrance to wait for Daniel Noys.

The sun was struggling up, shining from the roofs and windscreens of cars. It had rained at some point in the night; the tarmac held skinny pockets of shimmering water. Too early for the sun to offer any warmth, but she turned her face towards it anyway, towards the pale orange push at the horizon.

She knotted her hair blindly, wondering if the night's excitement had written itself all over her face, the way the stab vest had left welts in the front of her shirt.

She listened to the sound of the hospital at her back, the buzz of bodies moving, the sound-confetti of doors shoving open, swinging shut.

After a minute, she took out her phone and rang Paul Bruton, at Sommerville, listening to what he had to say, holding his words at a distance from her new mood.

# 31

A flat slant of light lay over Noah Jake. He was conscious of its angle and heat on his face, but he couldn't open his eyes to identify its source. There was a pressure on his eyelids, like a blindfold. Drugs? Drugs.

Every inch of his chest felt raw. Surgical stitches, each one a separate and distinct pain, pulled at the skin over his ribs. His temples burned. He stayed still, breathing through his nose, wary of deep breaths, knowing his ribs were broken. He'd better be awake, for DI Rome. She needed a statement.

'Hey.'

Dan? Dan.

Noah hoped his smile made it past the drugs, on to his mouth. 'Hey . . .'

Dan leaned his forehead to Noah's, staying that way until Noah could feel the beat of Dan's heart against his shoulder. He missed the next words. Felt them as breath against the bridge of his nose, the brush of lips. 'What? Dan. I can't . . .'

Dan's kiss was bitter black coffee, tasting of sleepless nights and stress.

'Sorry . . . Ruined . . . your plans. For Friday night.'

'For a whole month of Fridays,' Dan said. 'Unless the doctor can recommend a good position for broken ribs.'

'Not . . . on the NHS.'

Dan pressed the ball of his thumb to Noah's brow bone. 'Damn . . . You do know you nearly killed me.'

'Said . . . sorry.' He wanted to reach up and thread his fingers through Dan's fringe, pull him close. He settled for turning his head to kiss the inside of Dan's wrist. They stayed like that, a long time.

'Time's up,' Dan said, at last.

'What?'

'They gave me five minutes. Time's up. You need a lot of bed rest.'

'Rather do . . . tequila body-shots.'

'Hold that thought.'

'You too . . .'

Noah moved his hand for Dan's, then realised he was already holding it, weightless, the same body temperature as his own.

# 32

Hope Proctor sat behind one-way glass, her mouth lush with silence. An alibi of bruises on her body, and now these cuts, deep, on her arms.

Victim, written right through her.

She'd lied to Toby Graves, and to Ed Belloc. In a minute, she would begin lying to Marnie Rome. She lied fluently, with her whole body. Her heart-shaped face lied, and her blue eyes. The bloody, bandaged mess of her arms and the thin stoop of her shoulders lied. The tears she could turn on at will, as if grief was a faucet.

Kenneth Reece would have been proud of his tough nut.

His survivor.

Ed was waiting up for Marnie, wearing the clothes he'd worn to the hospital, his shirt cuffs rusty with the blood from Simone's hands. Marnie wondered if she looked as bone tired as he did. They went through to Ed's living room, with its welcome chaos of books and CDs, the place she'd come to associate with peace and quiet.

'Coffee?' Ed offered. 'Or I've got Peroni.'

'Peroni sounds good.'

Ed brought two bottles and a bottle-opener, snapping the caps and handing a beer to Marnie. She tapped its neck to his bottle. 'Cheers.'

'Cheers.' Ed perched on the arm of the sofa, five feet from her.

'Seriously?' she said, gesturing at the distance between them. 'Only I could use a shoulder. Not to cry on, just . . . to mark my place.'

Ed scooched over.

'Better.' She leaned into him, gratefully.

They drank in silence. Until she said, 'So, the girl who raped Stephen? Slit her wrists. She's okay, they found her in time, but she's on suicide watch. Bruton says Stephen hadn't been near her since the assault.' She drank another mouthful, the lager crisp on her tongue. 'Bruton didn't sound convinced.'

'How about you?' Ed asked.

'Am I convinced? I don't have enough relevant information to make an informed judgement.' She tipped her bottle to his. 'Spoken like a proper detective, see? I can still do it, when I have to.'

'Will you go and see him?'

'In a few days, perhaps.' She'd lost the nagging edge of urgency about Stephen. 'There's no rush. He's not going anywhere, and neither am I.'

Ed propped his head on his hand. 'Can I ask what's going to happen to Simone?'

'I don't know, not yet. She isn't talking, and neither is Hope.' Marnie thumbed the neck of the Peroni. 'We were too late, Ed. *I* was too late. Again.'

'Not too late for Noah.'

'Too late to know what happened in there. With Hope and Simone.'

'Simone will get better,' Ed said. 'It might take a while,

359

but she'll get better. She'll tell you what happened. You weren't too late. Noah's alive. And Simone.'

Marnie rested her head on his shoulder. Maybe it wasn't too late, for Stephen. Her parents had wanted to rescue him. Maybe that was what she should be trying to do – honour their memory by honouring that hope. Optimism.

'Rome . . .'

'Mmm?'

'You can stay, you know. I have a bed.'

'I thought we were on the bed.'

'Another one,' Ed said. 'Cleaner. And bigger.'

'In that case, yes please.'

In the half-dark of his bedroom, she stripped and stood under the light.

Ed's eyes moved down her body, reading.

'Wow. Rome.'

'You can touch,' she said, keeping still.

He took her face in his hands, carefully, and kissed the skin under her eyes, then the skin at the edges of her mouth, and finally, warmly, her mouth.

## 33

'It was my fault,' Noah said. 'I told Simone to get the knife. I called her Nasiche.'

Marnie sat by his hospital bed, knotting her hair. 'I was going to talk to you about guilt. But I got a really good night's sleep, so I'm shelving the lecture for another time.'

Not just sleep, Noah guessed. She was lit up inside.

'Simone was bringing the knife to cut me free,' he said. 'I don't know what Hope did, to end up like that. Simone said Hope wanted her to cut her.'

'Hope wanted Simone to cut her?' Marnie frowned. 'Are you sure?'

'That's what she said. I told her Hope needed help. I told her to get the knife, to cut me free. I don't know what Hope did . . . I couldn't see what was happening.'

'You didn't hear anything?'

'I heard . . . screaming . . .'

Marnie watched his face. 'What kind of screaming? Fear, or anger?'

'Both. They were . . . both screaming. Scared and angry.' He shifted against the pillows, wincing. 'I couldn't see what was happening.'

The pain was worse this morning. He knew it meant he was mending, but it got in the way of understanding what Marnie had said. She'd told him about Leo, the yellow roses brought to the refuge because Hope knew what they'd trigger in Simone. Kenneth Reece's careless attitude to his daughter's psychosis, his drinking, his contempt . . .

From the adjoining room, the low chatter of the hospital radio ratted at Noah's concentration. He tried to block it out, so that he could focus on what mattered. 'Simone attacked Hope. That's what happened?'

'That's how it looks. Simone won't speak to anyone, not even Ed. I don't trust a word coming out of Hope. No independent witnesses, but Hope's the one with the defensive wounds. Simone doesn't have any physical injuries.'

'She said . . . Hope wanted to be cut, that she wanted Simone to cut her.' Noah fingered the bandaging at his wrists. 'Have you seen her scars?'

'Simone's or Hope's?'

'Simone's. I didn't see them, but I felt them. She . . . was petrified.'

'Hope terrorised her.'

A sudden harsh weeping from the adjoining room. It didn't last, seguing into stagey laughter, embarrassed.

'Is she here?' Noah asked. 'In the hospital? Simone. Is she here?'

'Yes, but not on this floor.' Marnie looked at him. 'The surgeon said you were lucky. No serious internal bleeds.'

'Is Hope here?'

'No. Do you think she meant to kill you?'

Noah didn't need to think about that. 'Yes.'

'You know how this goes.' She smiled in apology. 'Did she *tell* you that she intended to kill you?'

'No, but she demonstrated total disregard for my

362

well-being.' Too many words; he had to stop to get his breath back. 'Kettlebell. Ditto hammer.'

Marnie glanced down the bed, at his damaged leg. 'That's how she hurt your ankle? With the hammer.'

Noah blinked at the ceiling, then back at her. 'That was Simone. Hope would have . . . broken my leg.'

Marnie was quiet. At last she said, 'Simone hit you with the hammer.'

'She was . . . terrorised. Doing as Hope told her.'

Another beat of silence.

'Hope told her to hit you with a hammer,' Marnie said. 'You heard her do that.'

Noah chewed at a raw spot inside his cheek. 'No. But it was . . . obvious that's what was going on.'

'Hope denies it.'

'Denies what? Forcing Simone to do as she said?'

'All of it. She denies all of it.'

Noah's mind turned like a broken dynamo, bringing up nothing. 'She . . .'

'Denies everything. It was all Simone. Simone forced her to leave the hospital. Simone took her home, to get the kettlebell. Simone broke into the Bissells' house. When you showed up, Simone attacked you. Simone tied you up, and proceeded to torture you.'

Noah swallowed a spike of nausea. 'The kettlebell. She says that was Simone?'

'Yes.' Marnie's voice was steady, taking no prisoners. She'd had her fingers burned, he knew, with the mistakes they'd made first time around, at the refuge. 'I'm going to need a list from you of exactly what Hope said and did.'

'She . . . put a knife to my chest. Punched me. In the throat. Put . . . the kettlebell on my chest and . . . hit it. With the hammer.' He was sobbing for breath by the time he'd finished even just that much.

Marnie touched the back of his hand. 'Not now. When you're well enough.'

He shook his head. 'I want . . . to do it now. She needs locking away.'

'She's locked away.' Marnie kept her hand on his. 'Get better, then we'll talk properly.'

'Ayana . . .' he began.

'No news, but we're looking.'

'Simone's mum and dad . . .'

'In Marrakesh. We've contacted them.'

They'd never know. Charles and Pauline Bissell. They'd never know what went on in their house while they were away. No one would, unless Simone could find a way to tell the truth. Simone was in shock, otherwise why wasn't she telling the police what really happened in the house?

Marnie stood. 'Dan's waiting. I'm going to get back to the station.'

Noah didn't want her to go, not yet. He had too many questions. 'Hope said I was . . . pretending. Not . . . a proper detective.'

She paused in the doorway to look back at him. 'She lied. About Leo. About Simone. About You. It's what she does.'

'I told Simone to get a knife,' Noah said despairingly. 'I called her Nasiche. I wanted her . . . to be Nasiche.'

She nodded, accepting this without surprise or censure. 'It's what we were all wishing. Me and Ed, and Toby Graves. Nasiche knew how to stay alive.'

Noah didn't have the strength to put into words what he was feeling. He was one more person who'd manipulated Simone Bissell. No wonder she'd shut down. He tried to imagine how it had happened. The knife in Simone's hands. Hope woken from her sleep on the floor, putting up her arms in self-defence . . .

Was it that simple? Hope defending herself against Simone's

364

attack? Because Noah had triggered a different set of memories to the ones Hope had triggered with the yellow roses. It'd saved his life, maybe even saved Simone's, but at what cost, if Hope was denying it and she was the one with the defensive wounds?

'One thing,' Marnie said from the doorway. 'We got Lowell Paton. The CPS is bringing a case of wounding with intent.'

'Simone . . .?'

'Not Simone, not yet. Two other girls. Dream catch: red-handed.'

Like Simone. Red-handed, with a knife, sitting in a pool of Hope Proctor's blood.

'Henry Stuke,' Noah remembered. He tried to pull himself upright. 'He had a broken hand. He blamed it on his work, but he was watching the refuge – and the hospital. We couldn't connect him to the other women, Simone or Ayana. Ron thought he was a waste of time, but he had a broken hand. Like Leo.'

Marnie closed the door and came back to the bed. 'Tell me.'

Noah shook his head, wishing it didn't feel stuffed with wire wool. 'He'll never admit to it. If it was Hope . . . he's worse than Leo, much worse. A real man's man. He'll never admit that a woman beat him up.'

'Maybe,' Marnie said. She sat at his side. 'Tell me anyway.'

## 34

Two floors up, the sun was sneaking in through reinforced windows, finding bronze highlights in Ed's hair. 'Rome . . .' He grinned at her through his fringe. She resisted the urge to tidy his bedhead, since she was responsible for it.

'How's Simone?' She nodded in the direction of the private room. A window in the closed door showed a glimpse of the girl lying in the bed, her profile a dark woodcut against white pillows.

'Sleeping,' Ed said.

'Drugs?'

'No, just sleeping.'

'That's something . . . We arrested Lowell Paton last night.'

Ed looked at her quickly. 'Where?'

'At his penthouse apartment. He was beating up a couple of call girls. The CPS is debating whether it's ABH or wounding with intent. Lowell's lawyer is trying to pass it off as common assault with consent, but with five witnesses and two split lips, there's no way that will wash. He can't plead consent to wounding.' She sketched a smile at Ed, glad of the chance to give some good news. 'He's going to prison.'

'For how long?'

'At least five years, longer if we get lucky.'

Ed looked into the hospital room, at the sleeping girl. 'Lucky,' he repeated.

'It shouldn't come down to luck, I know. And he deserves worse, for what he did to Simone.' Her eyes stung. She closed them for a short moment, thinking about the arrest in Paton's apartment. The cheap bag of bondage gimmicks, the girls' wails. They hadn't known what they were getting into. Probably imagined there was safety in numbers, that it was just a game. A rich white boy's game. They hadn't known the kind of animal Paton was, or the things that turned him on.

'Were they badly hurt?' Ed asked. 'You said wounding . . .'

'He'd knocked them about a bit, but we got there before the real fun started. Lowell's idea of fun . . .' Marnie glanced at her watch. 'He's due in court at one. I should go to Talgarth Road, as the arresting officer.'

He nodded. 'Have you got time for breakfast first?'

She smiled at him. 'My treat.'

Her favourite café, for French toast and coffee. Too early for the lunch crowd, too late for breakfast. The proprietor led them to a table at the back, bringing a pot of coffee, another of hot milk, laying their places with care before withdrawing to the kitchen.

Marnie watched Ed take a cup in his hands, a slow curl of steam softening the angle of his cheek. Her eyes followed his fingers, to his square wrist, lightly freckled where the bone rose to the warm surface of his skin.

'I'm in trouble,' she said. 'At work.'

Ed put the cup down. 'Tell me?'

'Hope . . .' She traced a pattern on the tablecloth with the pad of her thumb. 'She's blaming everything on Simone. The escape from the hospital, what was done to Noah, every-thing. She has a lawyer. I haven't met him yet. He's threatening a case of police negligence. I failed to provide her with adequate protection against Simone.'

'She . . . You're kidding.'

'Nope. It's neat, you must admit. She should never have been left alone at the hospital, after what happened to Leo. Her lawyer wants to know why she wasn't under arrest, or at least under proper police guard. He has a point.'

Commander Welland had described Hope's lawyer as 'a whoring tic, put on the face of the earth to annoy me', which didn't do much for Marnie's confidence, as the target of the tic's wrath.

'What about Noah's evidence?' Ed asked.

'Her lawyer says he's biased. It's a race thing. Noah Jake doesn't want to admit that the black girl was the aggressor.'

Ed looked so serious she had to smile, reaching to thumb the frown from above his nose. 'Cheer up. I'm not done yet.'

He took her hand and held it. 'If she gets in front of a jury . . .'

'I know. What'll they see? We're right back where we started, with another audience for her victim act. Another set of expectations to be played with.'

Ed shook his head. 'I wish we could count on someone from the refuge to tell the truth about what happened with Leo . . . Ayana came closest to seeing it.'

'But she's still missing.' Marnie nodded, resting her fingers on the pulse in his wrist. 'At least we know she hasn't left the country, not yet. I'm guessing Hatim hasn't been in touch.'

'Sorry.' Ed shook his head. 'One thing, though. Kenneth Reece. I made some calls, about his place at Excalibur House. He's in an advanced stage of cirrhosis. The liver's too scarred for a transplant and he's being treated for a hepatitis C infection. In other words . . . he's dying.'

'Natural justice. Do you think Hope guessed as much, the last time she saw him?'

'Possibly. She's sharp enough. And she knew him when he was well.'

The French toast arrived, smelling so good Marnie's mouth watered. The cutlery was warm, wrapped in heavy linen. Soft brown sugar dusted the lips of the plates, dissolving to gold in the hot heart of the toast. The café's owner brought freshly frothed milk, a refill of coffee.

'Thanks.' Marnie smiled at the man. This place was her secret, jealously guarded. She wondered if Ed knew what a big deal it was that she'd brought him here. 'Have you got time to go over there, after this?'

'To Finchley? Sure.' Ed ate a mouthful of toast. 'Oh wow. Rome? This is the best thing I've eaten since—'

'Careful.'

He grinned, attacking more of the toast. 'Okay. I may need to come here every day.'

'As long as you pick me up en route.'

Sugar at the corners of his mouth made his smile sparkle. 'All roads lead to you, Rome.' His phone yelped. He wiped his hands and checked it, frowning abruptly. 'Text from Tessa. She says she's got something she needs to show us.'

He handed Marnie the phone. Tessa's text was enigmatic, not urgent or anxious, just a request for Ed to come to the refuge, when he could. *Bring DIR.*

'That's you,' Ed said.

In Finchley, the scaffolding was empty, the roof's plastic sheeting shifting with the breeze. The door was secure. Britt let them in, before returning to the dayroom. She sat down beside Mab, filling her lap with a purple scarf she was knitting. Mab was helping, a heap of heather wool held between her gloved hands. She beamed at Marnie and Ed, looking alert and content. 'Hello! Look who's here.'

Britt asked, 'How're things with you two? Any news for us?'

'A little,' Marnie said. 'We found Simone, and Hope.'

'Aw, that's good! Isn't that good, Mab?'

Mab nodded, still beaming. Britt's arrival had transformed the refuge, and the women. Everywhere looked clean and comfortable. Fresh flowers on the table, a new shelf of books, cushions brightening the sofas, a rug doing the same on the floor.

Tessa was sitting next to Shelley. The TV was on, but Tessa wasn't watching. She was filling in a book of crossword puzzles with a pen. When she saw Marnie and Ed, she nudged Shelley. 'They're here.'

'I can see, can't I? I ain't blind.' Shelley turned the gold hoop in her left ear, hunching her shoulder at Marnie, her eyes on the TV, her fists in the stretched pockets of her tracksuit. Some of the rhinestones had fallen off the black velour, leaving behind hard little glue stains.

Tessa rolled her eyes. 'We were talking with Mab, after you left. We thought you should hear what she's got to say.'

'Okay.' Marnie took a seat at Mab's side, waiting until Ed was sitting also. 'What was it you wanted to tell us?'

Mab beamed approval at Ed. 'Teddy. You're a nice boy.'

'Thanks, lovely. Did you want to tell us something?'

'We're making a scarf.'

'Yes, I can see.'

'Tell them about the phone,' Tessa said. 'Go on, Mab. It's important, remember?' When Mab didn't speak, Tessa said, 'She thinks she's in trouble, but we told her it's not like the rings and stuff.'

'Yeah,' Shelley put in, 'no one gave a shit about my rings.'

'Shut up,' Tessa told her. 'Tell them about the nice phone, Mab.' She glanced at Marnie. 'There was a phone ad on the telly and, well, we felt bad about not listening to her before. About Ayana. So when she started up about the phone . . . We thought you'd want to know.'

Ed dug his own phone from a pocket and held it out for Mab. She smiled. 'That's a nice phone.'

'It *is* nice.' Britt hadn't stopped knitting, the tick of her needles like a clock.

'Not as pretty as the other one.'

Tessa nudged Shelley in the ribs, nodding at Marnie.

'Which one's that?' Ed asked.

Mab said, 'The one with the diamonds. She left it in her room.'

Ed kept his tone light, inconsequential. 'Ayana left it?'

'Not Ayana, she only thought I had hers. The other one. The new one. Hope.'

A fresh flood of adrenalin heated Marnie's skin.

'Mab.' Ed crouched at the woman's side, reaching for one of her gloved hands. 'Where's the pretty phone now?'

Mab looked flustered. She gripped at Ed's fingers. 'I have it safe,' she said. 'I'm keeping it safe for her.'

Ed nodded. 'I know you are. You're very careful. You take good care of everything. Will you show me the phone, please? Just so I can see how pretty it is?'

## 35

'Mab had Hope's phone?' Noah Jake, banked by pillows in the hospital bed, looked better for a morning's rest.

'Hidden in the cushion of her chair.' Marnie sat next to him. 'Ed told me she was a magpie, collecting things the others left lying around.'

A frown pinched at Noah's face. 'Hope never mentioned a missing phone . . .'

'Cover story. Leo swore blind she didn't use one. Implied she wouldn't know how. I've no doubt he believed that. It was part of her alibi; he isolated her, wouldn't let her use a phone. Mab found it right after the stabbing. Hope must've intended Simone to bring it to the hospital. She thought she'd be safe, having Simone to mop up after her. She didn't know that Mab had already found the phone and stashed it in her chair.' She poured a glass of water. 'Nice phone. Snazzy cover, a bit like Ayana's, but more expensive. We're lucky Mab wears gloves. Hope's are the only prints on it.'

Noah's frown was lifting. 'Go on. There's more, I can tell.'

Marnie measured a pause before telling the next part. 'Ayana's phone went missing overnight, a day before the stabbing. She reported it to Jeanette, who told her to sort it out with Mab. They all knew Mab took things from time to time. Ayana asked about the phone, but Mab denied taking it. She got upset, so Ayana left it alone. The phone turned up again, and she assumed Mab had put it back. The day after the stabbing, Mab found another phone, Hope's phone, hidden in her room. Mab took it. I'm guessing Hope was counting on Simone bringing the phone to the hospital. Hope couldn't risk taking the phone there herself, because it didn't fit with her alibi.' She watched Noah add this together. 'We have the log, from Hope's phone. She made a call right before the stabbing. To Ayana's home number.'

'Ayana . . . had her *home number* on her phone?'

'Like Ed said, it's hard to let go. The number was stored in her contacts. She never called it herself, but Hope did. Right before she stabbed Leo.'

Noah shut his eyes, opening them again as suddenly. 'Hope called the number in Ayana's phone?'

'And got through to Ayana's brothers. Yes.'

'Then . . .'

'No one followed you to the refuge. You didn't give Ayana away. It was Hope.'

'Why?' Noah looked lost, despite the evidence implanted in his ribs of the sort of woman Hope Proctor was.

'Most likely because Ayana saw through Hope's act. Maybe not the whole way through, but enough for Hope to know she had a hostile witness on her hands. Someone she could get rid of with a phone call. It was the last thing she did before stabbing Leo. Clearing her way.'

Noah shifted against the pillows, wincing. 'Have you found her? Ayana.'

'Not yet, but we will.'

'And Hope?' Noah asked.

Marnie crooked her mouth. 'I'm dealing with Hope. She

doesn't know yet that we found the phone. I'm looking forward to telling her. And her lawyer.'

'Have you spoken with Henry Stuke?'

'Not yet. But I will.'

'What about Simone?'

'She needs time. The same as you. Time to mend.' She stood, staying by his side a moment. 'How's Dan?'

'Good, thanks. How's Ed?' Noah asked, innocently. He was smiling.

'Not a proper detective?' Marnie clicked her tongue. 'Told you she lied.'

# 36

'So Simone Bissell isn't talking.' Commander Tim Welland was behind his desk, polishing a photograph of his favourite car, with his favourite tie.

It was close to 3 p.m. Marnie was back from Talgarth Road, where the on-duty magistrate had refused bail to Lowell Paton. She was nursing a new optimism, cautiously. Ed had good news for Simone, when she was well enough to hear it; Paton was going to prison for a long time.

'She's not even talking to Belloc?' Welland asked. 'He's usually the charm with these women.'

'Simone's in shock. I'm sure she will talk to Ed, but she needs time.'

'Meanwhile Patrick Rolfe is gearing up to a charge of police negligence. You're in his sights, Detective Inspector. How're you going to head that off?'

'I've got a pretty good idea.' She paused. 'It involves hard evidence.'

'Glad to hear it . . . Hope Proctor looks the part.' Welland restored the photo to its proper place on his desk. 'Especially with those bandages. Rolfe's wheeling her out like a ribbon-wrapped prize.'

Marnie nodded, accepting this. 'Her entire defence rests on her credibility as a victim. We put cracks in that – and it all breaks down.'

Welland began rearranging pens in an empty Stilton jar. The jar gave off the faint, offensive tang of its original contents. 'Rolfe wants to know why we're not gunning for Simone Bissell. Seems to think the CPS would lap her up. He has a point, especially after the business with Nasif Mirza. This one's got a weapon, fingerprints, the lot – but we're asking them to prosecute the victim.'

'It's a long time since Hope Proctor was a victim. If Rolfe had any sense, he'd go for that angle. The things that happened to her as a kid.'

'Plead insanity, when he can get her off scot-free and win compensation into the bargain? Not Rolfe's way.'

'You know him better than I do. Isn't he expensive? I'm wondering how that sits with Hope's isolation alibi. The world is such a big scary place, but she knows exactly where to lay her hands on a great lawyer? It doesn't hang together.'

Welland quashed this with a shake of his head. 'Rolfe's an opportunist. He can sniff public sympathy at a thousand paces. More, when it comes with compensation thrown in. *He* approached *her*, not the other way around.'

He stood, reaching for his jacket. 'I'm going to sit in on this one.'

Marnie blinked. 'You don't trust me?'

'I'm counting on you,' he corrected. 'To run Rolfe and his client off the road. DI Rome,' he put a large paw on her shoulder, 'slayer of dragons.'

She blinked again, absurdly grateful for the heavy hand holding her in place. 'Patrick Rolfe isn't a dragon. He's a tic.'

'A lizard,' Welland temporised. 'One of the dragon family.

Thrives in arid terrain, adept climber . . .' His smile was lethargic, warm. 'You could handle him in your sleep.'

'Rolfe, maybe. It's Hope I'm worried about.'

## 37

Hope, in her baggy grey sweats, looked about sixteen. She'd pulled her hair into a ponytail that emphasised her scrubbed-clean soap-and-water skin. Worry in her eyes, but it wasn't real. Not yet. Manufactured, like everything else about her. Marnie needed to make it real. Strip away the layers of Hope's disguise, and show Tim Welland and Patrick Rolfe the real Hope Proctor née Reece. She sat, putting a box file of paperwork on the metal table. 'I met your dad, in Dulwich.'

Hope's mouth moved. When she spoke, her voice was very small. 'How – how is he?'

'How is he?' Marnie folded her hands on the table. 'He's proud of you.'

Hope opened her blue eyes wide, wordless. Rolfe made a whistling shape with his mouth. Welland folded his arms, an entrenched expression on his face.

'Proud of you,' Marnie said. 'For surviving. For being, and I quote, his *tough nut*.'

Hope shook her head, looking to Rolfe.

'Don't you get tired of this?' Marnie really wanted to know. 'Don't you get tired of playing what you're not – his good little girl? His nicely behaved *dim* little doll. I would. I'd get sick and tired. Especially after I'd stuck a knife in someone.'

All those years switching between golden girl and survivor. The balancing act, always having to get it right, fearing what would happen if she got it wrong. She couldn't ever have been happy, not truly. And never secure.

'Is this headed anywhere? Preferably in the direction of evidence.' Rolfe wore a red tie and a white shirt, cufflinks with a club crest. The cufflinks were a mistake, embellishing his ego every time he moved his hands.

Marnie ignored him, addressing Hope. 'Your dad said you never had a problem with anything he did. We know what he did. To Gayle, your mum. Did you really not have a problem with that?'

Hope shrank. She fretted with her fingers at her hair. She'd been biting her nails since her arrest, destroying the pearly pink evidence.

'He said you'd not been in touch since your mum's funeral. Why's that?'

'Leo wouldn't let me,' she whispered. 'He . . . didn't like my dad.'

'And your dad didn't like him. Why? Because Leo wasn't enough like a real man? Pumping iron, beating women, or whatever real men do.'

'Is this going to be at all relevant, at any point?' Rolfe sat forward in the chair, the red of his tie like an autopsy wound opening his chest. He wasn't in a hurry, patience lacquered like an extra layer to the smooth surface of his face.

Marnie served up a careful smile. 'The iron is relevant. A forty-four-pound cast-iron kettlebell, with your client's fingerprints on it. She used it to break her husband's ribs. And Detective Sergeant Noah Jake's.'

'We've been through this. My client was under duress, in fear for her life.'

'That's not what DS Jake says. He's pretty clear about how much your client enjoyed what she did. What's more, it was his definite impression that she meant to kill him. We have a deliberate choice of weapon. The kettlebell belongs to your client. It was taken from her house. She used it to break DS Jake's ribs, after threatening him with a knife.'

'The knife found in Simone Bissell's hands,' Rolfe specified. 'The knife used to inflict life-threatening injuries on my client.'

'Explain to me again DS Jake's reason for lying about the way in which he nearly died.' Marnie nodded at Hope.

'By all means.' Rolfe settled his shoulders inside his bespoke suit; Marnie swore she could hear Tim Welland growling. 'No one's denying that DS Jake suffered trauma at the hands of a disturbed young woman. Given Simone Bissell's past, I'm sure we can all sympathise with his chivalrous instinct to protect her. But not at the cost of justice for my client.'

'She sat on my legs,' Marnie read from Noah's statement, 'and held a knife to my chest. She warned me to be careful because "that bitch with her phone card isn't here to help you". When I spoke, she punched me in the throat with the handle of the knife.'

'Chivalrous and politically expedient,' Rolfe said.

'Politically what?' Welland demanded.

'Correct, if you prefer. Politically correct.' Rolfe shot his cuffs. 'I doubt it's a coincidence that DS Jake and Simone Bissell share the same skin colour . . .'

Marnie said, 'He's Jamaican. She's Ugandan. And you're a bigot.'

'. . . and the same sexual preference,' Rolfe finished.

'I take it back. You give bigots a bad name.'

Rolfe gave a slow nod, like applause without the noise.

'She's right.' Welland pointed his thumb at Rolfe. 'You

play those cards with the CPS and you're going to get your head handed back to you on a big plate. Noah Jake makes a terrific witness. We all know it.'

'He'd better.' Rolfe's face was a lengthy study in smugness. 'Since he's all you've got. Your PSU team took the knife from the Bissell girl. DI Graves was a witness to my client's trauma immediately after the attack. Your witness was in another room when that attack happened.'

Welland's brows climbed. 'Tied to a sink pipe by your client.' He nodded at Hope. 'You tie great knots for someone who's never done it before.'

Hope did her shrinking trick; any minute now she'd be invisible. Just for a second, Marnie felt sorry for her – was this how she'd survived as a kid? By taking up as little room as possible in that godforsaken house? They weren't seeing Hope Reece, or even Hope Proctor. Not really. They were seeing what little was left of her after Kenneth Reece had worked his paternal magic.

Noah Jake had seen the real Hope, in the bathroom at the Bissells' house. Marnie summoned the image of his bleeding wrists, the skin he'd torn trying to get free so that he could save Simone. 'DI Graves was a witness to your client's acting ability. She puts on quite a show. Noah got a private performance, off-script. And Commander Welland's right, he's a hell of a witness. First-class degree in psychology. You should've taken advantage of that,' she told Hope, 'instead of amusing yourself with his torture. Still, I expect old habits are hard to break.'

'I seriously doubt,' Rolfe said, 'that Leo Proctor has the guts to perjure himself for the sake of hurting his wife more than he's hurt her already. Bullies are like that . . . all cowards under the skin.'

'Is he right, Hope?' Marnie looked at the woman sitting next to Rolfe. 'Are you a coward under the skin? Like your dad?'

Hope scratched at her elbows. The gesture lifted her sleeves, showcasing the bandaging on her arms. 'Show him your tattoo.' Marnie smiled across the metal table at her. 'The one that matches your dad's. He's talking about skin. Show him what you did to your skin. We already know what you did to Leo's.'

'My client has suffered enough as a result of your prejudice against her, Detective Inspector. If it wasn't for your incompetence, she'd be in a hospital bed right now, where she belongs.'

'She was *in* a hospital bed. She left it as soon as she realised there was a chance her husband might tell the truth about what she'd been doing to him.'

'What she'd been doing to him,' Rolfe repeated. 'You've seen the medical evidence of my client's injuries at the hands of her husband. Are you really expecting the CPS, or anyone, to close their eyes to that?'

'Your client picked up strangers in bars, with the express purpose of being beaten by them. Did she tell you that? I'm sure we can find one or two of those men. In fact, we already have. It's going to be hard to pretend she was a victim when it's proved she sought out sadomasochistic sex.'

'As I said, your prejudice against her.'

'Detective Inspector,' Welland said, 'can we move this along? Only I'm getting a distinct pain in my arse sitting on this metal chair.'

Marnie reached for the box file and drew it towards her. 'You said you weren't in touch with your dad after October, because Leo didn't like it. You could've called him, though, couldn't you? When Leo was out at work.'

Hope held her ponytail in both hands, stretching the skin taut at her forehead. 'He . . . checked the phone records. To see who I'd called.'

'You didn't think of getting a mobile phone? Hiding it from Leo? Lots of abused women do that, as a precaution.'

That landed. A fugitive spark, cold, in those blue eyes.

Hope didn't look at the box file, but she was afraid of what was inside it. 'I didn't have any money of my own. He didn't let me have any.'

'You could have saved money, from the shopping. Couldn't you?'

'He checks everything. The house is like – it's like a list he can tick things off against. He needs to see where I've made mistakes so he can punish me for them.'

'Oh, we saw the house. Nice. Leo had his own room, right under the stairs.'

'That . . . that was *mine*. He put *me* in there.' Hope cast about the room, avoiding Welland's sceptical gaze. 'I tried to keep quiet. I did. But it was so hard. I couldn't breathe in there, couldn't get out . . .'

'Funny that he's the one with the split nails and you had a perfect manicure. Until you realised it was giving you away.' Marnie rested her hand on the file, letting Hope look a moment longer, trying to guess what was coming out of the box. 'So you never had a mobile phone?'

'Not . . . not one of my own.' She was hedging her bets.

'But you know how to use one. You sent texts from Noah's phone. To the police and to Daniel Noys.'

'That wasn't me – it was *her*. Simone.'

'Really? They read like warnings. Why would Simone warn us about Nasiche Auma? She *is* Nasiche Auma.'

'I don't know why. She's insane. It's not her fault. What happened to her was horrible. I *understand*.' She appealed to Rolfe, using the fierce tone Marnie had admired, back at the refuge. 'It's not her fault.'

'You're all heart,' Marnie said. 'Just to be clear: you do not own a mobile phone.'

'I told you – not of my own. He won't let me . . .'

Marnie lifted the evidence bag and put it on the table. The phone's rhinestone casing winked under the lights. 'Let's try that again, shall we?'

Hope snapped her eyes away. 'That's not my phone.'

Rolfe didn't like the look of the evidence bag. Any second now he was going to warn his client to stop talking, shut up.

'It's your phone. It has your fingerprints on it. And only yours.' Marnie took a sheet of paper from the box. 'This is the call log from this phone. You called Leo, at home. Who else would do that?' She took a second sheet from the box. 'This is the call log from your house. It confirms the call from this mobile phone.'

A third log joined the other two. 'And you called Ayana Mirza's house. The morning you tried to murder your husband. Because you saw straight away that she was a threat to you. The only one of those women who didn't buy your act wholesale. Because Ayana knows that women are as capable of violence as men.'

'No.' Hope shook her head savagely. '*No.*'

Marnie arranged the damning evidence, for Rolfe's benefit. The phone and the logs. No margin for error. 'Can you see what it is yet?' she asked.

A smile mugged the bottom half of Welland's face. '*Can you see what it is yet?* That's very good. Right, Rolfe?'

'That isn't my phone.' Hope turned to her lawyer, using the doll eyes to full effect. 'It's a trick. I told you, she hates me.' She shot Marnie a look, full of loathing. 'Right from the start she's treated me as a suspect. She's crazy. I don't know what her problem is. Why did she visit my dad, unless she was stirring up trouble? There was nothing for her there – nothing for anyone. I should know. I grew up with him.' She shuddered.

'You're accusing my client of owning a mobile phone?'

Rolfe took out a sleek BlackBerry, laying it on the table. 'You'd better arrest me, in that case.'

'Put it away,' Welland said wearily, as if Rolfe had exposed himself.

'Ayana Mirza,' Marnie said, 'is a young woman blinded by her brothers. They poured bleach into her eyes. She was living in the refuge in genuine fear for her life. Not putting on a show. Not manipulating traumatised women. *In fear*. Of being found by her family and taken home to be tortured again, or killed.' She put a hand on the evidence bag. 'Your client told Ayana's family where to find her. As a result, her family abducted Ayana from Finchley. She's missing. Probably tortured. Very possibly dead.'

'It's not true,' Hope whispered. 'It's not.'

'You asked why we were there that morning. The morning you tried to kill Leo. I told you we were there to see Ayana. If you hadn't hated her before, you must've hated her then. She ruined your plan, but you know what I think? I think she'd have saved Leo's life even without our help. She's tough and she's smart and she's got a *heart*. Compassion and strength. She's the real survivor. Not you. Ayana.'

Hope shivered, looking away.

'Your mother went into a women's refuge in the year before she was diagnosed with terminal cancer. It was a place of safety, the first place like that she'd known. She made friends there, people who understood what she'd been through and who supported one another. The first real friends she'd ever known.'

Hope was weeping. She hunched away from Rolfe, away from them all.

'Do you think she'd have been proud of you? Of what you did to those women in Finchley? To Ayana Mirza? Or is it enough that your dad's proud?'

Hope's face was wiped blank by tears. Marnie wanted to

believe the tears were real. She really did. Everyone, even Hope Proctor, deserved the chance of remorse. Nothing else – justice, prison, rehabilitation – made a blind bit of difference without it.

'You can't do anything for Ayana,' she told Hope, 'but you can help Simone. By telling the truth about what happened. She believed in you. She was ready to fight for you.'

'Detective Inspector . . .' Rolfe was composing an objection.

Marnie ignored him, holding Hope to her stare. 'We have Lowell Paton. He's going to jail for a long time. I think you'll agree that's a good thing. With Simone's evidence, he could get what he deserves. A life sentence. You could do that. Help Simone to put him away, get her life back. That's the power you have over her. I wish I had that kind of power.'

She watched for a change in Hope's face, wondering if she was wasting her time.

It was possible she'd just given this woman another kind of alibi, a different disguise to wear, but without the hope that people could change, where was she?

Where was anyone?

Welland was waiting for Marnie in the corridor, after Hope had been taken back to the cells. 'Bit of a long shot at the end,' he said. 'Asking her to help Simone Bissell.'

'I wanted to see if she was capable of real remorse.'

'That's Rolfe's job. We're building a case *against* her. Let him concentrate on her defence.'

Marnie nodded, feeling tired enough to weep.

'You think her husband's going to make a convincing witness?' Welland asked.

'Perhaps, with the right support.' She knotted her hair away from her face. 'And there's Henry Stuke. I'm going to see if I can't persuade him to make a statement about whatever it was the two of them did after he picked her up in that nightclub.'

'A man's man,' Welland grumbled. 'Isn't that how Noah described him? In which case, good luck. I imagine blood from a brick would be easier.'

'We need his evidence. Without it . . . I just don't see us getting a conviction. I've spent a lot of time with Hope, but I couldn't swear to what's going on inside her head. All I know is that she's dangerous. She can't be out on the streets. Stuke knows that. If we're right about what she did to him . . . he's a key witness.'

'All right. But take Ron Carling, since he failed to put two and two together first time around.'

Marnie shook her head. 'I don't want to spook Stuke. More chance of him talking to me if I'm on my own.'

## 38

In West Brompton, the street lights were coming on, putting fist-sized shadows in the stucco facade of Henry Stuke's house.

Marnie knocked on the door and stood back to wait, nursing a sweet spot in her neck where Ed had kissed her. He'd kissed her in a dozen places and more. It wasn't pain any longer, straying around her body. This was a new kind of ache. She shut her eyes and smiled, just for a second, looking up quickly when she heard the door.

'Henry Stuke?' She opened the ID in her hand. 'I'm DI Rome, just following up on DS Carling and DS Jake's visit, if that's okay.'

Henry Stuke was as broad in the shoulder as Leo Proctor, but with the crabbed stance of a tall man trying to fit under a low doorway; if he straightened up, he'd be imposing. Sallow olive skin, pale hazel eyes and a crook in his nose that Marnie bet plenty of women found attractive.

He glanced over his shoulder, back into the house. 'I've put the babies to bed . . . It's not the best time.' Deep voice to match his chest. Put him in chinos and a blue shirt, dancing alone in a nightclub, and she could see why Hope had singled him out: alpha male with a whiff of domesticity, or was it a whiff of disappointment? Either way, Hope would've known how to work the angle.

'That's okay.' Marnie smiled in response to Stuke's objection. 'I can talk quietly.'

He stepped back, holding the door wide, shutting it when she was inside the house. She could smell the kids, an exhausted post-play smell of heated plastic and skin.

The house was just the way Noah had described it: a shambolic shrine to the twins sleeping overhead. Toys had spilled into the narrow hall, fighting for space with shoes, anoraks and a folded pushchair that hadn't folded properly.

Stuke looked at the mess, defeated. 'Why don't we go to the kitchen? I could put the kettle on.'

'That sounds good, thanks.'

The kitchen was marginally better than the hall, smelling of stewed fruit and scalded milk, and the perfumed bin liners used to disguise the smell of soiled nappies.

'Tea or coffee?' Stuke asked.

'Whichever you're having. Thanks. Can I help?'

'I've got it.' Stuke filled the kettle and clicked it on, taking a pair of mugs from the draining rack and setting them on the counter, shoving aside a baby monitor, bottle steriliser. He did everything with his right hand, keeping his left hidden in his pocket.

The back of his neck was stiff and hostile; he resented her suggestion that he needed help. She was going to have to tread carefully if she wanted his evidence against Hope. He wouldn't give up anything that might compromise his masculinity. Hope had done a thorough job of emasculating him. Was his hand the only thing she'd damaged?

Marnie listened for the sound of the twins upstairs. The house was strangely quiet, as if the walls and ceiling tiles were soundproofed. A sticky brown film coated the tiles above the cooker. 'DS Jake said you're an uncle now, as well as a dad.'

Stuke kept his back to her, busy with the mugs. 'Yep.'

'Is your wife still at her sister's?'

'Sugar?'

'No thanks. Mr Stuke . . .'

'Henry.'

'Henry. I wanted to talk with you about Hope Proctor.'

'Who?'

'Hope Proctor. She was living in a women's refuge, in Finchley.'

Stuke didn't turn to face her. He set his right hand on the counter, squaring his shoulders. The kettle spat, heating up. 'Never heard of her, sorry.' A warning in his voice: *back off*.

'It's possible you know her by another name, or that she didn't use a name when you met her, but she's Hope Proctor. She's in police custody.'

'I haven't met her.' If he got any more rigid, he'd snap. 'What'd she do, anyway?'

'She stabbed her husband.'

Stuke reached for the fridge. 'Glad I never met her, in that case.' He opened the door, removing a carton of milk, swinging the door shut again. The draught dislodged a shopping list from the counter. The list floated slowly sideways to the floor.

Marnie crouched to retrieve it, reading: *wipes, juice, no-tears shampoo* . . .

Blue biro on lined paper. The ink had clotted in places, thinned in others. Stuke had gone back over some of the words, when his pen had failed. She straightened, holding the list in her hand. Her body rang steadily from head to foot with alarm.

*Wipes, juice, no-tears shampoo* . . .

It was the same handwriting as the threatening note from Hope's handbag. Stuke had disguised it, for that note, but it was the same. No one had written a threatening letter to Simone Bissell. The note was intended for Hope Proctor, and it had been written by Henry Stuke.

*You fucking evil bitch your dead. You think your safe. Think again cunt.*

'Put that on the table, would you?' Stuke didn't turn; eyes in the back of his head.

He knew Marnie had the shopping list. In all likelihood he could hear her heart bumping in her chest. He wasn't just Hope's victim. He was the man who'd threatened to pay her back.

The kettle boiled.

It kept boiling when Stuke picked it up, pouring angry water into the two mugs.

Marnie glanced about the kitchen for a defensive weapon, anything.

Everything sharp and heavy . . . Stuke had put it all out of reach of the babies. They were crawling now, Stuke had told Ron Carling. Everything was out of reach, on a high shelf.

Stuke set the kettle back on its base. He took his left hand from his pocket and stretched it to the shelf where the tea bags sat, next to a butcher's block of knives.

Cold seized at Marnie's stomach. 'Mr Stuke,' she said. 'Henry.'

He was letting her see his hand. His claw. He wouldn't do that unless he knew that *she* knew. 'You were there,' he said blandly, 'at the refuge, in the Mondeo.' His hand grappled for the box of tea bags, brought it down to the counter.

Marnie said, 'Yes. Yes, I was there.'

He turned finally, and faced her. Straightened to his full height.

She tried to smile. It wasn't easy. The light pulled huge shadows from his head, throwing them down at his face in bruises. He made the fridge look small, even though it wasn't. A big man, whose eyes she couldn't see.

'Where's Freya?' she asked. 'Where's your wife?'

'Upstairs.' Stuke dropped a tea bag into each mug, poking it into the hot water with his damaged thumb. Hope had done that, with a kettlebell: smashed Stuke's hand. Turned it into a twisted claw, a thing he could put in hot water without flinching. Stuke was a man's man, a bloke, but Hope had laid him low, disfigured him. He wanted payback.

'With the twins?' Marnie said. 'Freya's with the twins?'

'No.' Stuke stirred a spoon in the mugs, one after the other, watching her. 'Not with the twins.'

The back of Marnie's throat was burning, and the backs of her eyes. She waited for Stuke to say what he'd done to his wife and babies.

'She hasn't been out of bed in three days.' Stuke shook the spoon and put it aside. He rubbed at his mouth with his hand. 'She's on pills. They gave her pills.'

'She's . . . sleeping?'

He jerked his head in a nod.

'The twins . . . are sleeping?' Another nod. 'You're on your own. Looking after the three of them.' *Please God, let it be true.*

Stuke tossed the spoon into the sink, the clatter of it like shrapnel. 'Always,' he said.

Always on his own. Always looking after them.

'There isn't anyone who can help?'

He held out a mug of tea. His mouth curled at her. 'I'm coping, aren't I?'

'Hope—'

'Don't speak that bitch's name.' He put the tea on the table, where Marnie could reach it if she took a step nearer to him, got within range of his fists.

'She's going to prison. For a long time. Two counts of attempted murder, grievous bodily harm . . .'

'Two?'

'Her husband and DS Jake. You met him. He came here.'

Stuke wet his lips. 'What'd she do?'

'She smashed his ribs with a kettlebell.'

He nodded, slowly, sucking on his tongue as if he was testing the flavour of his reaction to this news. He wasn't Leo Proctor. He wasn't ashamed, or not just ashamed, of whatever he and Hope had done. He was damaged, dangerous. He was standing within arm's reach of a block of knives.

'What're their names?' Marnie asked. 'The twins. Your babies.'

He blinked at her, shifting on his feet, away from the shadows for a second. The overhead light shed hot white powder on his head, making his gaze filmy and unfocused. He blinked again. Slowly. 'Gabriel and Lily. Gabe and Lil.'

She held a breath in her chest. If he'd harmed them . . . he couldn't have said their names so easily.

'Lovely names. Unusual.'

He rubbed at his eyes with his knuckled fist. 'Freya chose them.'

'She's not coping well. Not like you.'

'She's got *pills*,' he said, as if he was naming a disease. 'She sleeps most of the time. They say she's getting better.'

'You could use some help. With Gabe and Lily. With Freya.'

*Concentrate on his family, keep saying their names. Remind him of what he's got to lose.*

He shook his head. 'I'm coping. The only bloody one who is. With them, with her. I do what needs to be done.' He hadn't harmed them, not yet. He wouldn't have been so angry if he'd harmed them. Would he?

'Yes, you do, but you can ask for help. That's allowed.'

'Why're you here?' he demanded. 'Because of her? What's she saying? That bitch. What's she saying I did?'

393

The anger made him bigger, lifting off him like smoke before a fire.

'Nothing. She's not admitting to any of it. That's why I'm here. I need another witness, someone who'll tell us what she's really like. Her husband's too scared. The women at the refuge are scared. But you're not, Henry. You have Gabe and Lily to think of. They need their dad back.' Marnie drew a short breath. 'If you help us put her behind bars . . . you can have that. Your life back. A second chance. Not many people get that.'

Stuke's chest shook. 'You think that's what I want?' He spat laughter at her. 'My life. *This* life? You silly bitch. You silly *fucking* bitch.'

Marnie wrenched a smile from her mouth. 'All right. Okay. I get it, and you know what? I'm going to leave now.' She put her hand on her bag. 'I'm going to let you sleep on it, see how you feel in the morning.'

He didn't stop laughing, the sound of it like snarling now. 'Go ahead and try.'

The kitchen door was behind her. She couldn't remember how high the handle was, or whether he'd closed the door when they came in here. She couldn't afford to fumble; as it was, she'd have to turn her back on him.

'You can't leave them,' Stuke said, lifting his pale eyes to the room above them. 'You can't leave them alone with me. It's not safe.'

Marnie listened to the tick of the watch at her wrist, the seconds going by. How many more before he made his move? He was vibrating with rage and lust, or worse.

'What do you want?' She stood still, hoping he'd follow her lead. 'If you don't want a second chance. If you're sick of this life you're fortunate enough to have . . . A wife and kids. What do you want?'

'Fortunate. You thinking I'm fortunate?'

'Plenty of people have a lot less.'

'Yeah? Lucky fucking them.' His tongue across his lips again. 'Take your jacket off.'

'What?'

'It's hot in here. Take your jacket off.'

It was worse. Much worse.

'Mr Stuke . . . you must know I'm not going to do that.'

He ran his pale stare over her, like torchlight. His lip curled higher. 'Yes you are. I know what you want. I know what all you bitches want.'

He was crazy. Furious. His lips shone with spittle. How much of it was Hope's doing, and how much was just him – Henry?

'What is it you think I want?' Marnie asked. As long as he was talking, he wasn't moving. When he started moving . . . that was what scared her.

'Same as her,' he said. 'You came here, didn't you? Knowing what I did.'

Yes, she did. Tim Welland had told her to take DS Carling, but no, she had to do this alone. DI Marnie Rome, dragon-slayer. She had to come here alone. Except she wasn't; she wasn't ever alone when she was scared. Ghosts crowded in the kitchen with her. Her parents, and Stephen Keele.

Stuke was saying, 'You're all the same. The only difference is *she* pretended to be weak. Out in the open, when she wasn't being *real*, she pretended she was pretty, and clean. Just like you're pretending to be tough, but I got good at seeing underneath, with her. And underneath you're not tough. You're desperate, or you wouldn't be here, grubbing after what I've got. Knowing what I did.'

'I don't know what you did. Not really.' Her pulse had slowed. She didn't take her eyes off him, not even to look for weapons, or a way out. 'Tell me what you did to her.'

Stuke took a step forward, swinging his damaged fist like

a mace. 'I gave her what she wanted.'

'*Tell me.*' She was stalling for time. Seeing the pattern of defensive wounds on her father's hands, seeing Stephen's head bowed in the courtroom, hiding from everyone.

*Get over it.*

*Use it.*

Fear, pain, anger . . . Unless she could get her hands on a real weapon, the emotional arsenal was all she had.

'Tell me,' she insisted.

'It won't help you,' Stuke sneered. 'It was consensual. You can't make a case out of two adults getting what they both wanted.'

Marnie nodded at his wrecked hand. 'Like that? Did you want that?'

He lifted the hand and looked at it. There was a fly in the kitchen, buzzing, knocking against the window. If she ran – if she turned and ran – how far could she get? Into the hall? All the way to the front door? She saw herself tripping on one of the toys out there, breaking her nose on the floor, Stuke's weight landing on top of her, trapping her . . .

'You should've seen the state of her,' Stuke expanded his shoulders, filling more of the kitchen, 'when I was done.'

'I saw her,' Marnie said. 'She didn't look that bad.'

Not what she'd planned to say. Not a safe thing to say. But it brought Stuke to a standstill, staring at her.

'I don't think you did anything. I don't think she gave you the chance.'

He pulled his lips back from his teeth and flexed his fists, the good one and the one that had no feeling left in it. Which would he throw first? Or would he reach for a weapon, cut this dance short? Part of her wished he would.

*Get on with it.*

They couldn't stop him. Greg and Lisa Rome. They couldn't stop a fourteen-year-old kid. Why not? If she knew how it happened – how he was able to kill them – maybe she could stay alive. At the corner of her eye, on its high shelf, she saw the dull glint of steel from the butcher's block.

She saw Stephen Keele wearing her father's spectacles, daring her to stop hating him.

*Stay with me,* she demanded of the memory. *I need you.*

Two adults couldn't stop a skinny fourteen-year-old kid they'd tried to love. Because they couldn't see him, the real Stephen, not until he was up so close he was killing them.

'I don't think Hope gave you a chance,' she told Stuke. 'She waited until your back was turned and she smashed you with a kettlebell before you could do a thing to her.'

Now he was coming, mouth snapped shut, no more words.

*Good.* She was done with talking. She needed her breath for better things, like . . .

Dodging the first grab he made for her, ducking and reaching the door, the handle jumping through her fingers as he hauled her collar and tossed her at the table, where she bounced, hard, hitting the fridge door as she fell, rolling away from his weight as he followed her down.

His face thrust close, his eyes boiling over, teeth snapping, thinking he's got her, he's got her now.

*Fuck that.*

She twisted sideways.

Kicked the grin from his face.

Found her feet.

He surged up, grabbing again. Something ripped at her neck and she kicked out; those self-defence classes paying off at last, except she kicked the wrong fist and it didn't hurt him, not enough to make him stop. It was like kicking at wet cement.

He wrapped his fist in the torn lining of her jacket and hauled her towards the table, shoving her face-down until she could taste disinfectant and powdered baby milk and her blood leaking between her teeth.

He breathed into her neck, 'Bitch,' fumbling with his free hand, feeling her up, fingers all over the ink on her skin. 'You want to know what we did? We fucked. We bit and scratched and *shagged*. She loved it. She wanted to be hurt. Loved the stink of her own blood. Got off on it. And yeah, I made a mistake, turned my back for two seconds, but that's the way it was – we took turns. First her, then me. Only I didn't get my turn, that last time. She did me.' His left hand clawed at Marnie. 'I didn't get to do her. She left me in that stinking hotel room and fucked off back to her pretend life. But I know what's real. I know *her*. Give me three minutes in a room with her and I'll show you – I'll show everyone. I know how to make her squirm. She knows it. That's why she tried to stop me. Because she knows I *see* her. She might have the rest of the world fooled by her act, but I can name every last fucking one of her kinks. What makes her tick. What she needs.' His breath hitched on the last word.

His hands had stopped moving but his weight had Marnie pinned, held down.

A flash of memory, neon-bright: the pavement outside her parents' house, hot and gritty, Tim Welland's hand holding her down, the glare from Dad's car, everything like glass, breakable. Everything. She's in a thousand pieces and can't get up, can't ever get up . . .

A high-pitched noise scrabbled from her left: breathless squawking mixed with static.

Stuke jerked upright, choking.

Marnie went limp, letting gravity drag her free from under him, kicking properly this time, no holding back, hearing cartilage crunch in his knee, seeing him go down, sideways, and following him with her elbow between his shoulder blades and his face in the floor, no fumbling this time, plasticuffs ripped tight around his wrists.

When she could, she stood.

Stuke was squirming in synch with the persistent squawking from the baby monitor. The twins, awake upstairs.

Gabe and Lily. They needed their dad, God help them.

They'd stopped this, shocked Stuke back to reality. Gabriel and Lily. He was scared of them. Scared of the weight of responsibility, the power they had over him. Hope's power was nothing, by comparison.

Marnie's jacket was hanging in two pieces at the back. She smoothed her shirt back into her waistband, and knotted her hair away from her face. By the time she'd done this, she'd stopped shaking.

'You're going to give me what I need to convict Hope Proctor. That happens, and I won't press charges. I'll get you help to sort out this mess and be a dad to your kids. Your family. Because you're lucky enough to have one.'

Stuke wasn't snarling now. He was sobbing. Pushing his forehead at the floor and sobbing.

Marnie stepped away. She took out her phone and speed-dialled the station. 'I'm at Henry Stuke's place. I need a squad car and a Family Liaison Unit, as soon as you can get them here. Sooner, in fact. Treat it as an emergency.'

The baby monitor was silent. Either the twins had gone back to sleep or their mother had woken and gone to them.

The house was quiet again, and now she remembered how, from the outside, it had looked like every other house in the street.

## 39

Noah Jake had given up the fight against the hospital radio. Its soundtrack was a constant chirruping from the adjacent ward. Dan had left his smartphone, tuned to LBC. Noah put in earphones and listened half-heartedly, in a bid to distract himself from the whingeing in his ribs.

He'd fallen asleep after Marnie left, dreaming of Hope in the dock, extracting sympathy from the jury as easily as water from a sponge.

Simone wasn't in the dream, but Noah woke thinking about her. Where she was, who was taking care of her. Whether she was talking yet, to Ed Belloc maybe. He remembered the way she'd snapped to attention when he called her Nasiche, and felt again the pang of guilt, about which Marnie had promised him a lecture. He flexed his ankle, experimentally. He wanted to be up and out of here.

LBC Radio was hosting a phone-in. He'd tuned out when he was testing his ankle, tuning back in when the DJ introduced a caller from Whitechapel.

'We've got a young woman on the line who wants to tell us about her experiences of growing up in north London. Is it Anna?'

'Ayana.' Her voice was very clear, as if she was in the recording studio with the DJ.

*Ayana.*

Noah put his fingers over the earphones, pressing them in place. His ribs stabbed sharply, but he ignored them. He looked around for a piece of paper, or another phone. He didn't want to disconnect from the radio station.

'Ayana. You're calling from Whitechapel?'

'From Fieldgate Mansions in Myrdle Street. Block Ten, Flat G.'

*Yes! Good. Stay on the line.*

The DJ laughed. 'That's . . . very specific! Thanks, Ayana. What was the point you wanted to make?'

'I need the police. I'm being held against my will by my brothers, Nasif and Turhan Mirza.' Her voice was steady, urgent but not hysterical. She'd practised this speech before she called the phone-in. 'Nasif is wanted by the police for an assault in which a man lost his hand. He is very dangerous and I am very scared. My name is Ayana Mirza. I am in Flat G, Block Ten of Fieldgate Mansions in Myrdle Street.'

*Brave, brave Ayana.*

Noah was cheering, his finger poised to speed-dial Marnie Rome as soon as Ayana rang off.

The DJ was asking something about the police, why didn't she call the police?

'I couldn't be sure of getting through to the right person. Not everyone in the police is the right person.'

The DJ said, 'Well, you – you're certainly getting through to – to the right people now, Ayana.' From the stammer in his voice, it was clear that the average phone-in hadn't prepared him for this type of revelation. 'I'm sure plenty of our listeners are dialling the police, and I know my editor is doing the same. Sit tight and someone will be with you very soon.'

*Don't be an idiot – she needs to stay on the line. We need to know she's safe. We need to hear her voice . . . People need to hear this . . .*

The DJ's editor must've said the same thing, because he added, 'Keep talking, Ayana, please. Let us know what's happening there.'

'I'm in the bedroom at the back of the flat. They've locked the door. My brothers are in the front room. My mother has gone out, to the shops. That's how I am able to make this call. I hid – I hid the phone. They searched me, but they didn't find it. I'm good at hiding things, but I am scared of what happens when she returns.' Her voice wavered for the first time. 'Very scared.'

'Stay with us, Ayana. Stay on the line. London's listening. You have over two million supporters out there, lots of them very close to you. You're going to be safe very soon.'

He was right: too many people knew where she was now. Smart, smart Ayana.

She'd learned the power of the phone-in when she was at the refuge, watching TV for the first time in her life. She was a fast learner. Her brothers couldn't keep this quiet, not now. Not with over two million witnesses to her call. And she was ready to give evidence against her brothers; Noah could hear it in her voice.

'London, we're talking with Ayana Mirza, a young woman being held against her will in Whitechapel. The police have been informed, and are on their way . . .'

Noah pressed call, and the radio went quiet as the phone rang for Marnie Rome.

# Author's Note

*Someone Else's Skin* is a work of fiction, but some of the characters and their stories were inspired (or informed) by research. In particular, I found the following books and websites inspirational and/or informative:

- *Daughters of Shame* by Jasvinder Sanghera, published by Hodder & Stoughton, 2009
- *The Invisible Gorilla* by Christopher Chabris and Daniel Simons, published by Crown, 2010
- 'The Real CSI: What Happens at a Crime Scene?' by Craig Taylor, published in *Guardian Weekend*, 28 April 2012
- Women's Aid, domestic abuse support network: www.womensaid.org.uk
- Karma Nirvana, honour-based abuse support network: www.karmanirvana.org.uk

# Acknowledgements

More words? Yes, a few. Without these people, this book would have been less, or not at all.

My agent, Jane Gregory, and her team, especially Mary who refused to let the slush pile have me. My editor, Vicki Mellor, and the team at Headline who welcomed me so well.

My beta readers, Elaine in Texas, J in Australia, and Becca. The Max posse, in particular Anne-Elisabeth, Claudia, Lisa, Manisha and Philippa. Rhian Davies, who talked such sense when I didn't. Linda Wilson, whose promise of a free lunch helped square it away. Alison Bruce, who has the best theories about Red John. My favourite cheerleaders, Vanessa Gebbie and Tania Hershman, and Venetia and Alan Sarll. Pita, for a terrific first edit. River, for the tequila and the avocado. Raven, for the ink.

Anna Britten, whose friendship made all the difference at all the right moments.

My family, who never seemed to doubt I'd get here and who always make everything better. My mother, the best in the world. My sister, Penny, who was my first fan. My brilliant brothers, Mark and Nick. My husband, David, and our awesome daughter, Milly. One day I'll let you read this book.